Passion Undercover in Tehran

One Woman's True Story of Espionage,
Passion and Deception in the Heart of Iran

SHALVA HESSEL

Producer & International Distributor
eBookPro Publishing
www.ebook-pro.com

PASSION UNDERCOVER IN TEHRAN
Shalva Hessel

Translation: Yossie Bloch

Contact: shalva36@gmail.com

ISBN 9798396336308

This book is based on the author's true-life story. It is partly a product of her imagination but its contents are inspired by events she personally experienced, operations in which she took part, and the story of her life.

Dedication

I would like to express my gratitude to the following people:
To my mother and father, Yael and the late Hanan Schwartzman, for the education they gave me in faith, giving, love for all people, love for the Land of Israel and belief in the values of Judaism.

To my beloved husband, the late Yoram Hessel, who was responsible for my being drawn into the fascinating experience of working for the Mossad. Thank you for the support, encouragement and freedom you gave me.

To my children, Roy and Michael Hessel, who fuel my strength, my spirit and my courage. You have been my security detail. I am so proud of the men you have become.

To my dear and beloved grandchildren: Liam, Isaiah, Eliah, Isaac, Daniela and Talia. You enrich my life, day by day. I hope that you will continue to grow up in the spirit of Judaism and Zionism, following the path of our family, imbued with Jewish values and tradition.

To the directors and senior staff of the Mossad over the last half century, Yoram's friends, who have been by my side and watched over me at every stage — not only during operational activities in hostile countries, but also in the trying moments after Yoram's death.

To all my friends, married, divorced and widowed. From each of you I have learned something to inspire and encourage me to face every new chapter of my life.

To the late G. Yaffit Greenberg, my loyal friend, always by my side through the tough times and the good times and is also featured in the pages of this very work. You encouraged me to publish my first book. There isn't a day when I walk in the park that I don't miss you and our conversations.

Finally, to the fascinating and diverse men whom I met after Yoram's death. You gave me the feeling that my life had not ended with the death of the man who had been with me since age nineteen.

Contents

Part I:

Journey to the Dragon's Maw

1

23:00 hrs.
Aboard a Gulfstream, en route from a secret
location in Greece

There was nothing in the flight supervisor's smile to portend the drama about to take place in the tiny cabin of the Gulfstream IV twinjet. Nor did the indifferent look of the passenger across from me augur the bloodcurdling scream which would come out of his mouth a moment later.

Ten minutes had passed since we'd taken off from a small military airfield near the port of Piraeus. Anat, the flight supervisor assigned by the Mossad, was tall, her face glowing and tanned, her cheekbones delicate, her golden hair in a thick, elaborate braid. Perhaps it was to match her eyes, which shone like spotlights, fountains of bright and dark amber bands bursting through her irises from her black pupils.

Her Hebrew was excellent but she did not look Israeli. She extended a soothing hand to me and said: *Shalom, Sally, I hope you're enjoying your time with us. Please fasten your seatbelt, we're expecting some turbulence on our route today.* I was spent, perplexed and preoccupied but I still caught the faintest trace of a German accent. I responded with my own small smile and felt the subtle click as I buckled the belt that strapped me to the leather seat.

In the meantime, I continued to scrutinize the four passengers who had joined the secret flight from southern Greece to Tel Aviv.

One of them, Yiftach Sela, was devastatingly attractive with a penetrating emerald gaze; I had met him two days earlier in Greece. I'd struggled with what I felt when I recognized his imposing frame filling the entire space of the door of the G4. My heart skipped a beat. He then settled into an armchair by the heavy mahogany table, preoccupied with his cell phone as if he'd never seen me.

A thin stab of insult pierced me. I sent a laser glance in his direction. There's no way he didn't notice the pair of eyes staring at him, but he didn't raise his head even slightly.

I was jumpy. My mind drifted to when, about two hours from now, I would be giving hugs of love and contrition to my two sons, Roy and Michael, for disappearing without notice. And it was precisely then, as I was about to return to them and to my role as a mother, that I began feeling a twinge of disappointment in myself. It was my own fault; my inability to disregard the instruction to leave for a training mission with only ten minutes' notice and without notifying anyone. An unquestionably cruel order. At the same time, I imagined Jerry's endless embrace and began weaving my story in my mind. Jerry already held a very senior position in the Mossad. Whatever they were up to on Greek soil, he would know about every detail. But was he also updated on all the minutiae of its operational activity? Was he also aware of what happened in the complex next to the port of Piraeus?

I needed to contemplate what I thought too. Was I satisfied with the two harried and hectic days I'd just experienced? Over the course of forty-eight hours there had been some atypical operational excitement. Not to mention several incidents that were not supposed to have happened.

Yiftach Sela was one of them. 'All in all, you did great,' I flattered myself almost aloud, replaying the intense and stressful chain of events that took place on Vasilissis Sofias Avenue within spitting distance of the American Embassy in Athens. At least one of these events could have ended in a resounding failure, in great shame, even in disaster.

Over the next few minutes, I indulged in an old pastime of mine: crafting a backstory for each of the passengers who sat reticently, ignoring each other, each immersed in their own thoughts. *They've assembled quite the cast for me*, I thought.

The guessing game began with Anat's mesmerizing gaze which radiated bursting charisma. *That's no flight supervisor,* I mused to myself. She impressed me. Little did I know that I would meet her again in another place, under other circumstances, in a different language, with my future — my very life — hanging by a thread.

My next contestant was Yiftach. I knew nothing about him except for his conspicuous attractiveness, his guttural voice, his especially prominent Adam's apple, his James Bond-level driving ability, his command of six languages and the taste of his lips.

This made a trio of men who had boarded the flight, blank-faced and tight-lipped, all wearing Chopard sunglasses that might have come from the same factory production line. Some of them sported suspicious coiffures as well.

Beside Yiftach sat a handsome man who looked to be about similar age. His tailored polo shirt strained to contain his well-developed biceps and pecs. His hair was straight and fair if a bit too long. When he lifted his sunglasses for a moment, I was startled by how big and blue his eyes were. I scrutinized him and came to a decision: someone to rely on.

On the other side of the mahogany table, with his back to me, sat a massive man with the neck of a bull, a fleshy fold all the way across; his palms were large and his fingers plump. He insisted on sticking with his black baseball cap as well as his silence. From time to time, he interlaced his fingers and stretched his hands in front of him, making unusual popping sounds as he cracked his knuckles. I was curious to hear his voice, to see his face.

The fourth man on board the plane looked to me like the responsible adult on the scene. His straight but tousled brown hair was interwoven with silver strands. His smooth and fair skin was marked with a few wrinkles that only added to his impressive appearance. A sculpted nose protruded from the center of his face. His eyebrows seemed tightly knit, almost touching each other. *This man is troubled*, I decided for myself. He had quietly taken a seat across the aisle from me, near the tail of the plane. Our heads were three feet apart.

I attempted some amateur telepathy, trying to figure out his story. Who was he? What was his job? Why was he older than the others? Did he know Jerry? Why was he on this flight? Why was he so quiet? What was stressing him out?

Anat came over to the mahogany table and set down a tray with three white demitasses of coffee. She didn't do it like a waitress or flight attendant. She slid the tray to the center of the table and patted the fair-haired man's shoulder forcefully. *How are you, Giora?* she asked.

Giora and Anat know each other and they both have an accent that sounds German to me, I noted in my memory, even as I followed the movements of Yiftach's hands. His right reached for the small cup in front of him, grabbing the handle with two fingers. As he lifted the demitasse, he extended the index finger of his left hand to pin its bottom. He upended the cup to gulp down its contents summarily, then coordinated the vessel's descent with his index finger, until it rested on the table once more. Intriguing. Bizarre.

Two muscular hands to lift a cup of coffee? I remarked to myself, and my pulse quickened. Deep down, I was furious. I didn't understand how it was possible for him to act as if I wasn't looking at him from all of six feet away. I casually set my gaze on him for another moment and then turned it back to Mr. Baseball Cap's thick neck.

Satisfied I had gathered all the information I could, I closed my eyes as I tried to unravel the enigmas of my fellow passengers, reveling in the lush deerskin upholstery. In the past forty-eight hours I'd slept far too little. In two hours I would try to make it up to my loved ones. Nevertheless, I stuck to my preferred sleeping position: left eye tightly closed, right eye open a crack to observe the plane and the other passengers. I wanted, as usual, to be in full control. To know at every moment what was happening around me. Keeping one eye open was a cardinal rule in my life; often, it was an essential element of survival.

I had learned this from my father, the *moshavnik* from the agricultural community of Hibat Zion in the Hefer Valley, who was the source of my spiritual and physical strength. His mind was as fertile as the ground he worked, producing the finest *etrogim* in all of Israel, the fragrant yellow citrus fruits that were the centerpiece of the Sukkot harvest festival. He diligently studied the sacred texts and determinedly worked the sacred soil, raising me to be connected to the land and the community, to always take control of the events in my life so they wouldn't control me.

However, what happened next struck like lightning out of a clear blue sky, a thunderclap sure to follow.

Through the thin slit of my right eye I noticed the older man sitting across from me leap as if the bolt had electrocuted him, until his head almost hit the ceiling of the plane. He spread both his arms to his sides and opened his mouth to shout. A split second later I heard the broken, hysterical words that came tumbling out of his mouth. *I think something hit us. Maybe something hit the wi—* Then he screamed, as if caught in a nightmare. Before he could finish his sentence the plane slid wildly to the right, jolting me to the left side of the seat. I took a slight hit in the ribs, but the seatbelt kept me from anything worse.

I darted a look at Anat; she was double belted to a bucket seat, close enough to the flight deck to whisper to the pilot and copilot.

The men at the mahogany table gripped their armrests tightly and murmured among themselves.

The adult-in-charge stopped screaming and spoke to Anat in an authoritative tone. *Reuveni, talk to Alon. What's going on?* he demanded with the assertiveness of a boss, at a volume that was clearly audible in the cabin. His voice was steady now. One that I was able to recognize. I had heard him the day before, although I had not seen his face.

After an unbearably long pause, Anat reported: *They say there's some kind of malfunction in the yoke. The landing gear isn't responding either. We're flying in circles. They're trying to figure out what the problem is and awaiting instructions from the control tower in Lod.*

Thanks a lot, of course we're flying in circles. Soon I'll be flying out of the chair along with the seatbelt, I said to myself sarcastically, sotto voce, just loud enough for me and the older man.

The plane continued to bank sharply. I looked out of the round window to my left and saw the tip of the left wing pointing into space amid some whitish clouds and a lot of blue sky. Even without being an aeronautics expert I could determine that the plane was tilting on its side to execute small turns, all the while losing altitude. The cabin was full of flying paper napkins and the tension was getting thicker.

What are they saying? barked the older man again, staring at me.

The mahogany trio also began to clamor. Every few seconds a nervous shout came from one of them. I wondered if time was crawling or flying madly forward. The lightheadedness and pressure were constant, grinding the gears of my internal clock. Then came the voice of the pilot, Alon, over the PA system: *All passengers and crew, prepare for an emergency water landing. Be advised, the sea is quite rough. Clench your jaw, tuck your chin to your chest and hold tight.*

It was time for me to start bargaining silently with God. *If we land safely, I pledge to be a better person. I pledge to be a force for improving the world.* I struggled to remember which psalm my father would have said at such a moment. Out of a hundred and fifty of them, which one fit the occasion of a crashing plane? Well, I was sure I could recite the *Shema* from memory. I closed my eyes and declaimed with great sincerity the words drawn from the depths of my childhood on the *moshav.*

Hear, O Israel: The Lord our God, the Lord is one.
You shall love the Lord your God...
And these words that I command you...
You shall teach them diligently to your children...
You shall bind them...
You shall write them on the doorposts of your house and on your gates.

With the end of the prayer still on my lips, I began to see fleeting images of my adolescence before my eyes, of my youth, of the moments of love and passion with Jerry and of an ocean of sweet moments with my two sons.

Damn the cynicism, it's really happening. Isn't your whole life supposed to flash before you at a time like this, like a movie? I managed to formulate the thought in my mind.

Then a spontaneous, primal instinct made me address Anat, in a loud and authoritative tone: *What's going on, Anat? We're going to be in the ocean in another minute! What's happening?* My words hung in the air. My soul raged within me. A surge of anxiety shook me, but I made sure that my voice remained steady and my speech calm. I even accompanied the question with a smile.

Though I addressed Anat and the flight crew, my gaze was focused on the older man closest to me. I also offered a grin to the mahogany boys, with a longer, more direct smile to Yiftach.

Then I thought about the two-day operation in Greece. I tried, unsuccessfully, to stop a glint of disappointment from creeping into my thoughts amidst the drama. What would they say about me? That I was killed on an administrative flight after a training mission in a friendly country? Was it worth dying for some milk run?

What would become of my children? Will my husband remarry? I could not bear the unbidden thoughts. Along with these thoughts came unbearable, inconceivable pain. A practical thought slipped through as well. *How awful to die now. I still have so much to do.*

The cinematic version of my life was premiering in my mind, each reel depicting some significant memory — my roots, my parents, my family, my children, my loves and passions — garnished with the petty dramas of the last two days.

Yiftach had a bright and sparkling starring role in the film.

2

Evading surveillance near the American Embassy
in Athens

What could go wrong walking down Vasilissis Sofias Avenue? I asked
myself.

It's the safest street in Athens, running past the American Embassy. Still, I made sure not to become complacent, doing everything as I had practiced, making sure no one was following me.

Of course I knew that several pairs of eyes were watching my
every step, along with several security cameras, as I passed by the
pair of marines standing stock-still and on edge, flanking the embassy gate.

This was my second exercise of the day. In the morning, I'd been
directed to make contact with and glean as much data as possible
from a girl sitting on the balcony of a dilapidated building, the address given to me in advance. I passed the test with flying colors.

I had never been intimidated by a task that required meeting
strangers, gaining their trust and extracting information from
them; but now I was in the middle of a supposedly much more complex exercise.

I continued making my way along the boulevard beyond the
grounds of the American Embassy, developing a remarkable interest in the architectural design of the Megaron Conference Center.

I used the feigned survey the building to see if anyone was following me. A basic exercise that I carried out complacently but, to
my surprise, I easily recognized a suspicious man — skinny, of average height, wearing a light-colored thin jacket and standing about
fifty yards away from me. I continued to the far end of the conven-

tion center and once again found a strategic and natural angle allowing me to observe what was behind me. The slight man in the light jacket was maintaining the same distance.

What an amateur! I remarked to myself. The man looked directly at me, but glanced down the second I locked eyes with him. I returned my indifferent gaze to the giant columns of the edifice, turned left and continued walking calmly south, but all my senses were on high alert. *Something is happening, Sally,* I told myself.

A few minutes later, having walked another two hundred yards up the boulevard, the tiny transparent earpiece squawked to life. A sentence, terse and resolute, popped out in impeccable English: 'The party has been cancelled due to inclement weather'.

The voice that emanated from the earpiece was deep, gurgling like honey. It belonged to Yiftach Sela, who had greeted me last night upon my arrival in Athens.

He accompanied me to my room in the Electra Metropolis and placed a thin binder in front of me. He waited for me to peruse it and get an impression of it — and the new 'me.' There was a British passport bearing the name Amelia Burton, along with a biography. I also received maps of Athens and of southern Greece and aerial photographs of several parts of the city and the surrounding coast. I had a list of meeting spots, codewords and pedestrian routes, along with a brief Greek-English guide to conversation and some telephone numbers.

This is your homework. Memorize and then destroy whatever you don't need. You won't have much time left to sleep, Yiftach said a bit caustically, about to leave the room.

Yiftach's profile conformed, spectacularly so, to the superficial stereotypes attributed to field agents in covert organizations. *A veritable twin of James Bond,* I told myself. Handsome with a tan complexion, startling green eyes, and plump, pouty lips. He was in excellent shape, muscular, but moderately so. He also looked intelligent, charming, his beautiful face marred only by a deep and wide scar on the left side of the chin. I gazed at him with transparent curiosity, trying to guess a few details of his enigmatic character, but I failed to do so.

Yiftach saw right through me, anticipating my questions and volunteering some answers. He was forty-eight and had spent two decades in the Mossad. He was divorced. He read, wrote and spoke a half-dozen languages fluently. His role on this mission was to get me settled.

His tone surprised me: quiet, authoritative, eloquent. His voice was guttural and deep, with a kind of continuous gurgling that struck me as the way puffed-up American CEOs might speak. When he talked about himself, he was dry and clerical. A shopping list of personal details. However, when he talked about his mastery of six languages, I detected some subdued hubris in his voice. He was proud of himself, enjoying my surprise and the challenge his statement presented to me.

After he had left my room, the question did cross my mind: *Which five languages does he speak aside from Hebrew?*

By the next morning around nine o'clock, most of the binder's pages were consumed by yellow flames, transforming into a fine ash which I poured down the drain of the bathroom sink. The new passport went into an inner side pocket of the red jacket I was wearing. I walked out of the hotel at a brisk pace.

Once I'd made my way to the American Embassy, what had started as a routine exploration on a crowded street took a drastic turn, thanks to my amateur stalker in the light jacket; then the drama was ratcheted up on account of Yiftach's message in my earpiece.

The codewords were delivered in laconic English, devoid of emotion or excitement, but very meaningful. 'The party has been cancelled due to inclement weather' indicated a snafu. The team had been exposed, was under surveillance, and may even be arrested.

It all sounded strange to me. What could a drill in a friendly country have to do with an operational foul-up? Clearly it didn't seem credible. After all, being arrested on Greek soil while holding a fake passport from another friendly country was the worst possible outcome.

What a disaster! I felt as if a huge clock hovered above my head, ticking menacingly as its digits lit up. I began to consider my immediate surroundings and prepare my escape quickly and efficiently. My stalker might be a real schlemiel, but the dramatic message sounded utterly unrelated to the amateur in the light jacket. I ran through several scenarios in my head. *The message is another component of the test they cooked up for me... Something serious has occurred, unrelated to me... The schlemiel is, in fact, no schlemiel, but purposefully revealed himself... The guy is not a lone actor by the embassy, but part of a team...*

Four lanes of bumper-to-bumper traffic trundled alongside me. The vehicles only disentangled themselves briefly when the light at the intersection turned green. I continued walking leisurely up the sidewalk, edging my way gradually towards the curb and the swarm of cars. As I approached the intersection, I studied the rhythm of the traffic light, how many seconds it held on red, allowing pedestrians to cross. By the time I made it to the juncture, I knew very well how much time to give myself. I counted to myself: *21... 22... 23.... 24.... 25.* Then, I turned abruptly to step off the curb and briskly cross all four of the throughfare's lanes.

I had timed it perfectly. A second after I planted my feet on the sidewalk on the other side of the snarl of vehicles, the traffic light changed to green. Dozens of impatient cars, motorcycles and mopeds burst through the intersection. The teeming horde was dense, impatient and fast-moving. The guy in the light jacket was thoroughly befuddled. He had no chance of crossing the road to catch up to me. He brought the hem of his jacket sleeve to his mouth and whispered something.

I had memorized the map for my drill the night before. A huge Factory Outlet store loomed over the intersection. I quickly ducked into it, rushing through the automatic glass doors and straight to the women's department on the second floor. I slipped between two fully-stocked racks of clothing, tall enough to conceal me until I came out the other side. As I walked between the rows, I slid off my red jacket, holding the ends of the sleeves to reverse it smoothly and put it on again. Now it was pink. My next move was to pull a matching scarf out of my black leather back, along with a pair of oversized gold-framed sunglasses. Then I took out a thin fuchsia fabric bag that unfolded to swallow the black bag. This metamorphosis took place while walking continuously and lasted less than ten seconds. I came out from between the clothing racks looking somewhat older, with bulky, golden eyewear on my nose, wrapped in a cerise silk scarf that completely hid my hair and a cloth bag on my shoulders. I moved on to examine the clothing on a nearby hanger, glanced nonchalantly at the clock, and then began walking briskly toward the exit on the other side of the department store.

Now I had to get to the prearranged meeting point. I had memorized the location over and over and recalled I needed to get to the streetcorner in front of the Athens Tower. Ten minutes of walking at a decent pace, while taking all the required precautions, brought me to the rendezvous.

As I arrived, I spotted Yiftach walking towards me on the eastern sidewalk. He moved with urgency, confidence and style; even from a distance, he struck an impressive figure.

Until I noticed his fly was open, vermillion underwear poking out from the barn door. I tried to raise my hand to alert him to his awkward situation, but he continued to stride towards me with all his swagger. Peals of laughter threatened to break through my facade, and I struggled mightily to contain myself. Hoping he'd read my lips, I mouthed the information to him exaggeratedly. It took until the third time, but he finally got the drift, sidling up to the wall of a store to rectify the situation with a deft motion.

3

The day was so dazzling and sun-dappled, it was hard to imagine that it would end in heavy gloom and bewildering emotional upheaval.

I positioned myself in front of the display window of a jewelry store and submerged myself in the depths of the tableau.

Yiftach also approached the window, showing great interest in it, his head not far from mine. In a low voice, almost a whisper, he uttered: *Good. Very good.* Then he continued in an undertone, his eyes fixed on the tray of necklaces and bracelets in the shop window: *We've got to get out of here quickly. On the other side of the building there's a black Land Rover waiting for us. Silver roof, spare tire with an eagle screeching on it. Get in the passenger seat. I'll come from the other direction.*

He spoke excellent English; that was two down, four to go, among the half-dozen languages in his repertoire . As he spoke the last words to me, he turned to the right and began striding away at a rapid pace.

Five minutes later I was sitting in the front passenger seat of a late-model Range Rover Sport parked, as promised, behind the conference center. It looked shiny and new, a hybrid apparently. *Why not diesel?* I wondered.

Yiftach got in the driver's seat without a word or a glimpse and soon had us weaving adroitly through the teeming Athenian traffic.

Finally, he broke the silence, as if reading my thoughts: *Don't worry about the suitcase back at the hotel. It's being taken care of.*

Then he shot me a sliver of a glance, tilted his chin forward and announced: *We're driving to the port of Piraeus.*

You mean we're flying towards Piraeus at low altitude, I responded, unclear whether it was a joke or criticism of his insanely aggressive driving.

Sorry, we've got to fly. We're running very late, answered Yiftach, surprising me. *Your exercise is over for now; we're being called to something urgent.* His speech was efficient, terse, precise. There was no defiance or arrogance in his tone.

The route we took crossed the southern neighborhoods of Athens, Kallithea and Moschato. Yiftach's driving brought me back to the evasive driving exercises I'd practiced in Tel Aviv a month earlier. He never let up. I had no doubt that he was a consummate professional.

After about an hour of enigmatic slalom driving, I turned an inquisitive eye towards Yiftach and asked: *So, are you going to tell me what happened?*

My question hung there in the lavish but tense interior of the SUV. Yiftach looked straight ahead, running a moist tongue along his upper lip as he accelerated. My gaze remained steady, piercing and fixed on his eyes. I waited for the answers I deserved. Why cancel the exercise? Why kidnap me for a mission that he defined as operational and urgent?

Yiftach's look said he didn't want to discuss it with me, but then relented. *There is a package we need to pick up at the port. It's a particularly sensitive matter. I have to make some preparations on the way. You take the wheel now.* He signaled and pulled off to the right.

A package we *need to pick up?* I took offense even as I switched seats with him.

My head was bursting with questions as I got us back on the road, but there was no one to ask. Yiftach was on his cell phone, shooting a blistering text at someone. Then he pulled out a gun with a silencer from his inner pocket and placed it under his thigh. *Keep your foot on the gas,* he directed, without looking up from his phone.

As we reached the neighborhoods on the southeastern outskirts of Athens, the traffic thinned out, the late-afternoon sunlight fading. Waze led us through two interchanges to get on to the A1. The multi-lane highway runs north-south, terminating near the entrance to the eastern ports of Piraeus — Zea and Munychia — both military ports, located in a well-guarded complex loaded with security checks. The map on the navigation screen showed that the road to the port was cut off; the waypoint for the meeting marked by Yiftach seemed to be floating in the air.

They may have closed this road to civilian traffic, he pointed out.

If we don't check, we'll never know, I answered, pressing the gas pedal. I understood that we were in a hurry, but it was also important for me to impress Yiftach. To prove that a woman could exhibit driving skills no less impressive than his.

Initially he was silent. After about fifteen minutes, Yiftach casually said: *They told me you were practically a Formula 1 driver. I see it was no exaggeration.*

I listened in silence, but a blush colored my cheeks.

A few minutes later, we were off the paved road and onto a dirt path, passing an abandoned military checkpoint and some official warning signs in Greek and English. They were each adorned with a garish crimson skull-and-crossbones on the bottom.

Something is wrong, Yiftach mused. *Why set up a rendezvous in a restricted area?*

We'll manage, just give me directions, I replied. I accelerated, then snuck a glance at the rearview mirror, following procedure for maneuvers like these. Yiftach did likewise, simultaneously. Then we looked at each other. We didn't need to speak; it was obvious that the military jeep a few dozen yards behind us was in hot pursuit. Yiftach stifled a curse as I mashed my foot down on the accelerator, speeding past a row of abandoned barracks that seemed to stretch into infinity. Prefabricated huts in disrepair, covered in heavy layers of sandstone dust.

I was focused on driving, staring straight ahead into the depth of darkness. I didn't look at the dashboard, but we had to be doing at least a hundred miles per hour on a narrow dirt road. Then there were four gunshots, muffled explosions that cut through the silence, one after the other at a steady pace. *They're shooting at us,* I said to Yiftach while looking straight ahead. I remained laser-focused on accelerating and keeping us on the road.

No, not shooting, I heard the laconic reply. In a relatively calm and quiet voice, Yiftach explained: *Those were illumination flares.* He bent down to pull out a revolver from his left pant leg. *Take it, it's loaded. Put it under your thigh,* he told me.

Seconds later, four novae exploded in the sky and fell to earth in delicate rotations. The car was flooded with light. I felt almost naked at that moment, Yiftach and I and our vehicle in a spotlight in the heart of darkness.

After about a hundred yards the dirt road curved to the left, allowing us to disappear from the field of vision of the pursuing jeep. A few seconds later I randomly chose one of the dozens of narrow paths that separated the huts, cut to the right, switched the SUV to electric mode and started a frantic but quiet drive to the south. The sandstone dirt under us rustled softly. From time to time, we ran over an old board or a pile of fallen leaves, but the noise we made was minimal. The circle of light was no longer above us and we were driving again amid complete gloom. Suddenly I understood why our SUV was not equipped with a diesel engine, why having a hybrid was a good idea.

The Range Rover sped forward soundlessly. Suddenly, out of the corner of my eye, I caught sight of a hut whose entire lengthwise wall was missing. I pulled up alongside it, braked, shut off the headlights, shifted into reverse and pulled into the hut, half-turning. I smashed right through a rotten wooden beam which ran from the floor to the ceiling of the hut. I held my breath and waited a few seconds, but it didn't cave in on us.

Now we were facing forward, ready to break out quickly, positioned so the Greek soldiers in the jeep couldn't see us from the road. We heard their diesel engine going back and forth several times until they gave up and drove away.

Yiftach could not hide his astonishment or his admiration. *Psssh,* he emitted with an exhale through clenched teeth, the continuous stream of air accompanied by a sincere look of appreciation.

After a few minutes in the shell of the wrecked hut, Waze miraculously came back to life. To my surprise and delight, the resuscitated app somehow recognized the narrow paths between the huts, then set about recalculating the route and showing us an alternative blue line to connect back to our original path. I folded the side mirrors inward, pulled out of the shack, and headed south. I sped through the precariously narrow gaps between the shacks. While driving, I pulled out the gun that was warming up under my right thigh, picking it up with two fingers and held it out towards Yiftach. *Two guns are too many*, I stated soberly, though not without a hint of humor.

A few minutes later we were again on the wide road towards the port, without a jeep in sight.

I increased the speed as we neared the meeting point marked for us. Suddenly a stationary jeep appeared in front of us, further down the road, in the dark. Its headlights were off and its parking lights on. It was our vehicle's twin: a dark Range Rover Sport with a silver roof.

Yiftach told me: *Pull up on the left, slowly.*

A moment later our passenger door was next to the driver's door of the doppelganger. Windows were rolled down, arms extended, and Yiftach pulled something that looked like an external computer drive into the vehicle. It all took about a second; then our counterpart sped away and disappeared into the darkness.

From what little I could see, our courier had been dark-skinned with a bushy beard. *Iranian?* The thought flashed in my mind, but I didn't have time to delve into it.

I resumed moving forward, slowly, trying to find a place to turn around and make our own getaway. Yiftach lifted his right pant leg to slip the drive into a broad, gray elastic bandage wrapped around his ankle. *Let's get the hell out of here, we're done*, he said, but then it all went to shit.

On the sandstone dirt a few dozen yards ahead of us stood a Greek soldier. He approached the passenger side of our Range Rover, screaming, an assault rifle slung across his chest and a powerful flashlight in his hand. Yelling, louder and louder, the same phrase over and over: *Stamáta to aftokínito!*

Yiftach translated the Hellenic hysteria filling the air: *He's telling us to stop.* He reached across the dashboard to press the far-right button on the radio and pulsating Greek music immediately blasted from the speakers. *Our sister Haris Alexiou will save us,* said Yiftach with a half-smile, turning up the volume.

I hit the brakes and brought us to a complete stop. I left the engine running, the bouzoukis providing a solid background as I shifted into reverse and put myself at the ready. I thought I might have to suddenly tear out of there backwards.

The Greek soldier still looked angry. It might have been because of a report he'd received about a disappearing SUV, but it might have been for some reason that had nothing to do with me or Yiftach. Either way, it wasn't looking good for us.

As he advanced towards us, he moved the submachine gun that had been hanging carelessly across his chest into a firm and menacing grip; he flipped off the safety, attaching a flashlight to the barrel. He knew how to hold a rifle and aim while walking fast.

The right window was still open. The bed of dry leaves gave the soldier's approach a rhythmic, brittle, crunchy sound. I looked over Yiftach's shoulder and saw the silhouette of the raised barrel and the burly figure approaching and uttered a series of curses. I tensed up. We could be in real trouble. The soldier continued towards us when I suddenly felt a strong arm grab my left shoulder and pull me. It took me another split second to realize that it was Yiftach.

His hand was surprisingly strong and his palm rougher than expected. He persisted in pulling me towards him, then whispered in English: *From this moment forward, we are lost lovers,* he told me.

My body responded to him as I leaned into him. Out of nowhere, I felt the fullness of his lips as they pressed against mine. It was a robust, perfect kiss. He didn't move his mouth or head. No virtuo-so French movements, no changes of position, the typical romance novel-style kiss. He just covered my fleshy lips with his. I was shocked by the intensity and the electricity in it. Seamless contact, soft, deep, moist as it ought to be.

Every cell in Yiftach's lips found a congruent cell in mine.

4

1930 hrs.
Weapon drawn, lips like water

Things became more complicated from moment to moment. I saw the Greek soldier and his swift and determined march. My thoughts swung between the approaching danger and the magical touch that gripped me. All the blood in my face drained to my lips which filled out and became even more fleshy and soft. Then I closed my eyes and said goodbye to the laws of time. It was four seconds, or forty, or maybe four thousand, a scene in slow motion. The sound of the angry soldier's footsteps became a distant though still-present echo.

He was already about twenty yards from the SUV, but I was all about diving into Yiftach's mouth. I ignored everything else. More shards of eternity passed by, amazing me. I suddenly understood the brief romantic lines I'd read once, about lips that turned into water.

Then our kiss for show became deeper. There was a thin, invisible line between the hot, static lip contact and the next step. A small slit opened and tongue touched tongue. At first, it was just tip to tip. The taste was divine. My facial muscles relaxed, my jaw was no longer tight, and our tongues mingled like a pair of oiled eels.

Understanding lagged behind emotion. A moment and another moment would pass before I began to digest what was happening to me, what I felt, what I understood, what I thought.

A technical presentation for a pissed-off soldier turned into a tsunami that could not be predicted or pre-empted. My pulse accelerated to a speed of ten thousand miles per hour. A fine trickling, a delightful tickling ran down my spine.

The soldier was already just a yard away from the open window, still roaring and, at a certain point, I felt Yiftach's lips and tongue disengage from mine.

That's it, is it over? I thought. But before my train of thought reached the station, I felt his warm lips gently brushing the tip of my nose, then caressing my right eyelid with a warm touch. Several moments passed and then I felt the same on my left eyelid. It was a subtle but clear glimmer of magic. Then his lips returned to their natural place, in front of mine, drowning again in the depths.

Our little show turned into a whirlwind amalgamating excitement, fear and loss of consciousness all in one. Something beyond the physical. An unfamiliar heat rose in my face, rising higher and higher until it reached the roots of my hair. The pores on my forehead opened and small beads of sweat appeared in them.

The soldier reached the vehicle and leaned against the window, still screaming. I could see his nostrils quivering, I could smell the sweat rising from him. He saw Yiftach and me pressed up next to each other as one body, immersed in the world of hallucinations, as if we were transparent, as if he did not exist.

His tone was belligerent as he demanded: *Taftótites parakaló!*

The word *parakaló* was the only Greek word I remembered amid all this stress, and that calmed me down. Someone who's going to shoot you doesn't say please.

Yiftach continued to drown in my lips for many more moments. Our tongues continued to touch each other, to complement each other with a taste I had never known.

Our disregard elicited another shout from the young soldier — this time more threatening, accompanied by two nervous knocks on the roof of the car. Then Yiftach turned his head to him with a smile and responded to his yell: *Geia sou, Dioikití! Den prépei na eínai edó?*

My brain had resumed working enough to translate: *Hello, Sir! Is there a problem here?*

For a moment I thought it was a recording, maybe the radio.

Yiftach-the-Sabra's Greek was excellent; the sound flowing; the accent authentic, convincing, perfect. The soldier screamed a few more sentences, knocked again on the SUV's roof and indicated with his hands the direction we ought to go.

Let's go my love, Yiftach said to me and set his chin forward, signaling to me to go. I shifted into drive and drove off serenely, but there was nothing calm inside the vehicle. My eyes were glued to the road, my hands and feet did what was necessary for us to get away from there, but I felt that I was doing it robotically.

My mind was about to explode, my pulse refused to regulate itself, and I felt that my whole body was hotter than usual. I knew what it felt like when my cheeks were going up in flames, and this time they were. And how!

It was good that Waze was there, it was good that it chose then to make its voice heard. The didactic speech forced me to focus on another task besides driving. The destination was a small airstrip near the port. *Airport?* I asked quietly, trying to break the thick silence that lay between me and Yiftach, but he didn't hear me. He wasn't there. He was preoccupied with texting again, a ping-pong match with someone I couldn't see.

Yiftach seemed more stressed than usual, but about his own business. I was more stressed than usual, but about my own business. My thoughts turned into a cyclone. I drove quickly, skillfully, responsibly — and in the right direction — making sure to glance back from time to time to make sure that another military jeep hadn't suddenly decided to follow us. But my head and soul were in another universe, weaving zigzaggedly between shame, self-blame, questioning and infinite joy.

However, those were not my only thoughts at the time. The touch of lips on lips still flickered in me. I felt waves of exquisite pleasure that reverberated down the slope of my back and sent electric charges through my loins.

After about ten minutes of navigation, we arrived at a small and dark wooden structure. Yiftach broke his silence, saying in Hebrew and matter-of-factly: *Sally, pull up to that building.* A second later, a heavy motorcycle appeared behind him. Its rider gently motioned for him to follow and raised a cloud of white dust as he sped off into the darkness. Yiftach thrust his chin forward again and I, like a robot, pressed the gas and followed the growl of the motorcycle.

Further up the road, we came to an open checkpoint. An armed security guard in civilian clothes gave us a thumbs-up and let us through. I felt we were out of danger.

I parked next to one of the concrete buildings, opened the car door and hurriedly got out, escaping from the SUV's interior which had suddenly become overloaded, compressed, heavy. Too heavy.

I tried to inhale deeply in an effort to catch my breath, but I couldn't. My chest muscles were tight. My legs couldn't bear my weight. I sat down on the narrow sidewalk, placed my cell phone beside me, put my elbows on my knees and held my head with both hands.

A second before that, I noticed the figure of Yiftach walking away from the car. He hurried towards one of the farther buildings and was swallowed whole by it. From that moment on, it was as if he had evaporated. Vanished without a trace.

Welcome, Sally! Do you feel unwell? An older man was speaking to me in Hebrew.

I'm fine. I just need some air, I replied without raising my head. I was afraid that anyone who looked me in the face would discover everything that had happened to me in the last hour. A stupid thought, but I left my face buried in my palms.

I hear you really proved yourself today. You did a good job in Athens, on the way, and at the port. He was firing the compliments at me as if he were emptying his clip. He went right on to adjure me: *What happened here tonight did not happen. I need your cell phone. There is a shower here in the shack. You can freshen up, rest a little, but lock the door. Do not leave the room until you are called. In about two hours we take off for home. In the meantime, maintain radio silence.*

Flying home? I asked myself out of the sensory fog that surrounded me. I detached my cheeks from my palms and raised my head to ask the question, but the older man had already turned his back on me, my cell phone in his hand.

He rushed towards the same building into which Yiftach had evaporated.

5

21:00 hrs.
Saying goodbye to my British passport at the
secret Mossad base

A couple of hours in the spartan barracks made for an experience of
loneliness unlike anything I'd ever gone through. A tempest raged
in my mind, making my abdominal muscles contract. Within me,
disturbing but exciting thoughts swelled and fell rapidly, one re-
placing the other, each engulfing its predecessor with love or rage.

I tried to recreate the divine sensation which had been sliding
down my spine pinned against the backrest of the Range Rover, but
my diaphragm felt constricted by guilt. I responded to those spasms
defiantly: *Why not? Why don't I deserve it?* My conscience had a ready
rejoinder: *What are you going to tell Jerry?*

Above it all hovered a billion questions about what I'd do the
next time I saw Yiftach — if I ever saw him again.

I was also deeply frustrated that I had no one to share this ocean
of emotion with. Yiftach had disappeared without saying goodbye.
Jerry was abroad, and he might be beyond the bounds of my circle.
My good friends, the Pastel Parliament of Tel Aviv, were definitely
out of the picture, since my prime directive was to maintain radio
silence — and my cell phone had been abruptly confiscated.

What else could I do? I showered for fifteen minutes or maybe
two hours. I have no idea. I let the hot water flow over me until my
skin was steamed, almost scorched. Then I sat down in a white robe
on the austere fabric armchair that stood in the corner of the room.
I put my hands on the wooden armrests, leaned my head back and
closed my eyes.

I turned it all over in my mind: my whole world, my life's journey. Questions, questions, questions. I was barely on the fringes of the operational activity of the Mossad but, somehow, I had already found myself on the blurred borderline between carrying out an important mission and surrendering quickly and easily to the circumstances. Here, as in all the stories I'd heard countless times, mission mixed with passion and professionalism spilled over into sentiment.

Eventually — although I couldn't say how long it was — there came a light knock on the door. I checked through the peephole. In the garish yellow light stood a thin guy of average height whom I had never met.

Hi, I'm Yaron, he said. *We have another few things to see to.*

I opened the door and he walked in with my favorite purple piece of luggage which I had left at the hotel in Athens. Out of the small carry-on Yaron retrieved my Israeli passport, my wallet and some personal belongings that I had left in the room. *There you go, you're back to being Sally again,* he said with a half-smile and asked for the British passport that I had been using for the past two days. *They probably told you this already, but what happened here tonight never happened. Also, you ought to forget the name and passport you've been using here. You're flying back to Tel Aviv on your real passport and on our plane. We're leaving in ten minutes.*

Yaron spoke like a high-ranked officer of an elite commando unit. He might have a baby face, but his youth was an illusion. He wasn't young at all. He was no Mossad rookie.

When I left the barracks, I spotted a trio of white Crossovers. The black Range Rover was gone. Yaron drove one of them, and he motioned for me to sit next to him. The second I buckled up, he took off at breakneck speed. Greek music played in the background. *You get used to it,* he smiled and was silent the rest of the way.

The next ten minutes passed quickly, bringing us to a tarmac illuminated by spotlights, at the center of which stood a Gulfstream painted white and devoid of any identifying symbols, except for the serial number GS222 shining on its tail. Its pair of engines growled softly.

Here's your taxi, Yaron told me and stopped the Crossover right in front of the air stairs. I opened the door and my feet were already on the first step.

A second later Yaron arrived with my luggage and loaded it into the open cargo hold of the plane. *Have a good trip, Sally. You ought to be pleased with yourself,* he said. With that, he disappeared into his vehicle, leaving me wondering who he was and how he knew.

6

As I climbed up the airstairs, with each step I felt as if lead weights were being removed from my shoulders. I had no idea that the flight would bolster the tension all the way back up — and beyond.

I was the first to embark. I entered the cabin, sinking into one of two luxurious armchairs upholstered in light deerskin. *I wonder who lent them the plane this time*, I thought. Then the two pilots arrived, followed by the impressive woman and then the trio of men who preferred the seating area around a heavy mahogany table at the rear of the plane. Finally, the relatively older man who favored the seat parallel to mine, closer to the tail, came aboard.

When the aerial drama began, I managed to surprise even myself. I had always excelled in improvisation. I always kept my cool. I was never afraid, even when Jerry and I violated Mossad conventions and went on a joint espionage mission in a Muslim country, fully undercover.

That was the last time I had been in such a stressful situation. We were on the verge of being captured in the heart of an enemy country, in the city of Rawalpindi in Pakistan's Punjab province. Jerry and I were invited to a large party at the house of General Mahmoud al-Sharif. Diplomats and businessmen were there, along with the heads of the Pakistani government and military. Unfortunately, in the midst of the fête, I realized that at a table not far from us was sitting none other than Vivian Moyal, ex-wife of a British millionaire whom Jerry and I had met in London. She would know us by the names and biographies composed for our time in England. Meeting her there, alongside the Pakistani generals who were the targets of our espionage activity, would have constituted a catastrophe beyond what I could allow myself to articulate or imagine.

We had a few seconds to improvise a solution that would allow us to get out of there without alerting Vivian or her entourage, without arousing the suspicions of our Pakistani friends — and without, of course, offending Mahmoud al-Sharif.

I took advantage of the intimate bond the general and I had forged to explain to him that I was feeling unwell and that Jerry and I would appreciate if one of his men could lead us out of the party without our having to pass through the dense crowd.

Two minutes later we were already outside, walking hastily towards our car, understanding each other in the silence, realizing that we were seconds away from a disaster that would have burned Jerry and me, plunging us into the most horrific affair Israel had known since the capture of our man in Damascus, Eli Cohen.

Being adventurous, we carried out the mission in Pakistan with a small child — and later also with a newborn baby. Every few days we encountered near-entanglements — big and small — like almost running into Vivian. I always knew how to overcome any fear. I always improvised. I always came up with crazy solutions that Jerry balked at which, in retrospect, turned out to be real strokes of brilliance.

However, I had never called upon my improvisational abilities at five thousand feet — in a situation which could potentially end my life, in pathetic circumstances, without a whiff of operational activity, without a hint of protecting the homeland.

Nevertheless, I took command. I felt, in my own way, that I had to smile in the face of danger and make a modest contribution to my fellow agents, whom I had only met a quarter of an hour earlier. In a short time, I was back to being soothing Sally. The frigid silence in the cabin was shattered by my suggestion that everyone write a few sentences to their loved ones. The words came out of me in sequence — in a steady, caressing, non-hysterical voice. I simply uttered them; and, as always, I didn't concern myself with questions about whether it made sense or what they might think of me. Even before I finished, I reached into my handbag, pulled out a stylish Kohinoor pad, removed the cap of the pen attached to it and started to write quickly.

I started with names — Jerry, Roy, Michael — declaring my undying love for them. I wrote that I trusted them to know how to be strong, to go on living, to maintain the values that were part of us as a family and as individuals. I was careful with my penmanship, my syntax clear and colorful, expressing ideas combining love of husband and children with love of homeland and the Jewish people.

Then I turned the page and wrote a short message to my parents. I offered gratitude for everything they had given me. I spared no expressions of love from a daughter to her parents. But I kept it short. Laconic, almost.

I looked around. I saw that only some of the occupants of the plane had accepted my proposal and were scribbling something on notepaper or on napkins. The rest sat with folded hands, in thunderous silence.

The adult in charge stared at me pointedly, but my gaze was directed elsewhere, trying to lock eyes with Yiftach. It was a momentary meeting of glances, charged with special intensity. *This may be the last meaningful look I exchange in my life*, I thought, and I had a hard time breaking eye contact as our gazes crossed and clashed.

A few more fragmented sentences, devoid of any real meaning, came out of the PA system. The responsible adult tried to talk to me and get some details out of me about the activity near Piraeus. I broke my visual connection with Yiftach, then glared at the adult and pursed my lips, making it clear to him that I had no intention of saying anything.

The plane continued to glide in circles, tilting on its side. When I could see out the window, I observed the wing stabbing the sky at a disquieting angle. More and more pale paper napkins were detached from their place, flying through the cabin like a flock of drugged seagulls. I started to feel a sharp pain in the ribs on the right side. All my body weight rested there as I was pinned to my seat. I grasped the left armrest and tried to pull my body up, to relieve my squeezed ribs.

Then it happened, abruptly. No PA address, no announcement from Anat, no word from the flight deck. The pressure on my ribs slowly eased, the floor of the plane balancing before my eyes. Our decaying orbit suddenly became a straight line, flying directly ahead. The silence in the plane was maintained. No applause, no shouts of happiness, no sighs of relief. Everyone present tried to demonstrate composure and a kind of indifference. It seemed strange to me, but I kept silent. After a minute or two, the pilot came on the PA system, announcing an imminent landing. The message was short, concise, devoid of ceremony.

Our landing was smooth as silk. I didn't even feel when our landing gear hit the runway, only catching Ben-Gurion Airport's terminals speeding past us out of the corner of my eye through the tiny window frame. We rolled down the runway towards a huge hangar in a corner of the complex unfamiliar to me. As the plane edged forward, I noticed big smiles and bursts of laughter among all the passengers, including the responsible adult who had gone from being a sourpuss to carefree and jovial. Anat's amber eyes were the only ones that looked at me with empathy. Yiftach, Giora, and the thick-necked man got off the plane a second after the hangar doors had closed behind us, casting the entire interior into deep shadows. After them, the older man descended the airstairs. I got the impression that he was in good shape. Then Alon and his copilot disembarked.

Anat and I were the last ones left on the plane. As soon as we were alone, she approached me. *I hope you are OK,* she told me in a quiet voice. *I had the same crash drill last week. It took me two days to recover,* running a delicate hand through my hair. I listened to Anat and was grateful for her information and her thoughtfulness.

Even so, I was still in a denial of sort. I clung to the last sliver of the idea that the plane had indeed suffered a malfunction. That shard might have been what helped me overcome my anger and shame. In a corner of the hangar, under a cluster of fluorescent lamps, there was a folding table with a disposable tablecloth, a hot-water urn, two trays with sandwiches covered in cling wrap, and several cans of Coke. The chef had prepared a large selection that day. *Egg or cheese*, said a young man who put down the trays and disappeared.

Around the table stood Alon and his copilot, Anat, the older man, the beautiful fair-haired man — as well as the thick-necked hulk who, even in the darkness of the hangar, kept his hat on his head and sunglasses over his eyes. There were also two strangers.

Everyone is here except for Yiftach, I noted to myself and took an egg sandwich. The bread had long gone stale and the omelet was bland, but I felt that I could devour the entire tray by myself.

The responsible adult approached me, offering a tiny, almost invisible smile. He extended his hand and quietly introduced himself as Shimon. I reciprocated and discovered he had a firm handshake. His palm was surprisingly large, engulfing mine with thoughtful strength. *Farmer's hands*, I thought. His eyes were soft. Something fatherly was in his gaze, so different from the figure I'd loathed during the flight.

After two rounds of applause from the crowd, Shimon quieted them down by announcing: *Yiftach had to run off with the package, they're waiting for him in Tel Aviv. I would like to thank each and every one of you for your part in the operation in Greece which, of course, never happened. This is also a double and triple opportunity to congratulate Sally. First, let's welcome her to our team. Second, congratulations on her performance and the execution of her mission in Greece. Yiftach gave her a grade higher than he had ever given anyone. Thirdly, a big thumbs-up for her resourcefulness when the plane malfunctioned.*

He spoke seriously, without a hint of a smile. But the audience grinned and chuckled when he mentioned the alleged aviation accident. Anat and two or three others around the table clapped their hands faintly and went back to sinking their teeth into the stale, soggy sandwiches. While we were chewing, the fair-haired man opened a door and disappeared. The thick-necked man continued to down one sandwich after another but didn't say a word, his ball-cap and his aviators in place.

While I listened to the short speech, I realized two things. Shimon, just as I thought, was the adult in charge and the commander responsible for everything that had happened to me, Yiftach and the rest of the team. I also realized that Shimon was the one who had spoken to me near the barracks in Greece. He was the one who had taken my cell phone from me. He was the one who had flattered me, while my face was buried in both hands, avoiding any light or look.

I stared at him, took a breath, counted to twelve and buried deep in my throat what I'd been thinking of saying. There was no point in protesting after the team members had applauded me for an excellent performance. I understood that, for Shimon, this was an extremely important test. So, I kept silent. I looked at him for a long time, realizing that he was actually Jerry's age, a senior agent.

Little did I know that my life would soon depend on him: his experience, his composure and the extreme professionalism of the entire team under his command.

7

9:00 hrs.
The Amir household, waltz on the kitchen floor

We sat in the kitchen, silently sipping our morning coffee. The children had already left for school. The house was hushed, the silence absolute.

Then Jerry began to speak. His tone was soft, as usual; but he went on at uncharacteristic length. As a senior agent in the Mossad, nothing had been kept from him. Not even the contents of the drive we'd received in the Range Rover near the port of Piraeus. He knew what had happened there. He knew Yiftach and I had proceeded to the rendezvous point, with me behind the wheel. He knew in detail about the virtuosic evasive maneuvers I'd executed to escape the Greek Army jeep chasing us.

All the while, he showered me with compliments. He used every superlative available; he knew precisely the right words to say. Having been together for so many years, we had experienced every possible scenario. Still, I found Jerry's words that morning especially moving. He praised me wholeheartedly, as a professional. As the best of the best in the game.

Nevertheless, there was a question hanging in the air, unspoken. If Jerry knew in detail everything about my mission, did he also know what was going on inside the SUV as that Greek soldier ran towards Yiftach and me? Had he ascertained what had been happening inside me at that time? Was that in my performance evaluation as well, in the report he received? I looked at him, but I couldn't penetrate his facade. If it was a facade at all.

A dense gray cloud enveiled me. All I could see were his lips moving, all I heard were snatches of the acclaim he bestowed. Finally, I couldn't take anymore and approached him, embracing him tightly and kissing him on the forehead. It was an unusual kiss. Long, hot, slightly wet, unstopping, unflinching. Jerry was surprised — by the intensity of the gesture, by the warmth of my lips touching his brow, by the duration of both.

Still, he responded in kind. He wrapped me in both arms, matching my ardor. I felt the heat rise in my own body to match his. I had so desperately missed this, the clever hands that knew how to hold me firmly but tenderly, pouring love into me, injecting into my body the security I needed, the old cocktail of emotions that we'd enjoyed since I was nineteen.

Jerry was and remains my man.

A while later, as I was still reeling from the passionate waltz on the kitchen floor, my cell phone began to vibrate. It was an unknown number. I didn't feel like responding to anyone or anything, but the anonymous caller wouldn't let up.

It was Shimon. He was brief and to the point. He asked me to come to his office.

I was silent for a moment, until he insisted: *Sally, it's important! This is urgent!* Then he hung up.

Jerry was no longer in the house and I soon realized I couldn't reach him on his cell phone either. He had probably sunk once again into the secrecy of his globetrotting missions. The decision was mine alone, to go or not to go to the meeting with Shimon. I had no one to consult with regarding the meaning of this summons.

Ultimately, it wasn't much of a choice.

The meeting was scheduled for three hours later, somewhere in the heart of Mossad headquarters. The responsible adult from the Gulf-stream flight was waiting for me beyond a mountain of documents and twin monitors filling his large desk. He introduced himself as Shimon Eitan, head of the Collections Department, reaching across the messy surface to offer me his hand.

My pleasure, Shimon, but we already know each other, I observed dryly, extending my hand for a polite shake.

The Collections Department oversees all of our agents' foreign operations, he said.

Of course, Shimon, I know the organization, I told him with obvious impatience. I couldn't help but wonder if he had synchronized all this with Jerry. As a senior agent, did Jerry know I was standing at the heart of the Mossad's headquarters right now? Had he known, during our amorous entanglement that morning, that Shimon would soon be calling me?

The stale, stilted conversation with Shimon abruptly turned dramatic and life-altering. His expression went from cold formality to something warmer, more personal. *Due to circumstances I will not specify now, you must depart for an assignment abroad earlier than planned,* his tone softening the harshness of the message.

My voice went up an octave in a swift retort: *I have two children at home!* Maybe I was yelling at Shimon, maybe I was yelling at myself.

Don't complain, Sally. Please, don't complain, Shimon replied in a relaxed manner that only annoyed me more. *Your actions are, in part, what compelled us to move up the deadline.*

My actions?! I replied.

Sally, there are no easy answers when it comes to these issues. The event which never happened in the Piraeus region greatly contributed to our ongoing o in Iran. That's why it has to be you, and that's why it has to be now.

Explain, I said with obvious impatience.

That night we received information that was pure gold — a windfall we didn't anticipate. To be precise, we got a treasure trove, a once-in-a-lifetime thing, but we need the full haul. Sally, something is happening — right now. Unfortunately, we failed to access some cell phones, as well as a number of computers situated in private homes. All our technological methods have failed. We are usually very good at electronic collection, but the other side has developed countermeasures. I don't like to exaggerate or get carried away with superlatives, but we are in quite a bind, missing details that are critical to the security of the State of Israel. We need human operations urgently. Very urgently, Sally. You could be immensely helpful in this case, as it is one to which your skills are uniquely suited...

You're not implying that I'm going to Iran, are you? I shot at him.

I'm not implying anything, but we are focused on the Iran-Qatar intelligence axis right now, replied Shimon, his gaze riveted to his computer, looking at something I couldn't see.

And why me? I answered before he finished. *Why are you betting on a rookie like me?*

Shimon replied without hesitation. *We put a lot of thought into this, Sally. You have the rare combination of all the qualities we need. What do you want me to start with? A compliment on your appearance because you look Scandinavian and not Jewish? Laurels for playing tennis as well as any man? I'm taking into account the confidence and experience you gained in a hostile Muslim country. We don't have anyone like that anymore. Even if we did, none of them have the expertise you do in programming, computers, applications. Your proficiency in information systems management is essential at this time. Listen to me carefully, Sally. This is critical knowledge. Beyond that, I cannot ignore your efficacy in making excellent connections in no time, nor the courage and resourcefulness you displayed in Greece. I'm also considering how you conducted yourself in the airplane exercise.*

Shimon, you can't be serious. You're exaggerating, I protested. *I'm no superwoman.*

I'm quite serious, Sally. It is crucial that you enlist in the fight. We have many troops in the field, so many; but you have your own part to contribute. Your abilities are a rare cocktail, concocted to suit the precise needs of the mission. This role fits you like a glove, trust me. Permit me to say something else, something less cynical and less scientific. This is about fate and luck. And you, Sally, bring more luck than a rabbit's foot. Jerry told me about your escapade in Islamabad, and I've come to the conclusion that there's something about you that cannot be quantified.

That's not luck, that's destiny, Shimon. These superstitions don't suit you, I responded sarcastically. *We are Jews; if there's anything I take* with me as I enter the dragon's maw, it is my absolute faith in who I am and that God will be with me and protect me. You know, you're reminding me of my mother's words: *When you do something you believe in, the Creator will be with you and you will succeed in your task.* That's what has helped me get to where I am today, and it's what I will always rely on. *Can you grasp these concepts, Shimon, or are they beyond you?* I demanded venomously.

Shimon muttered his concession and began to float in his own thoughts.

I relented. *OK, Shimon, OK… Qatar, I get it; Iran, I get it — but what exactly would a blonde with prominent cheekbones be looking for there?*

Shimon had anticipated the question and replied emotionlessly: *When the time is ripe, I will tell you.*

As soon as he told me this, it hit me for the first time that this was not child's play. I suddenly felt the full weight of the responsibility placed on me and began to realize what a challenge I was taking upon myself. Once again, I wondered what Jerry knew. Was he in on the secret mission which was being planned for me? Was he one of those who had decided to send me alone into the heart of hell?

With all due respect to the Mossad, to the State of Israel, and to the duty to defend the homeland, I cannot make any decision without consulting Jerry and receiving his blessing because, in the end, I trust only him. He has supreme authority on this issue. My inflexion with Shimon was loud, assertive, articulating every syllable. I emphasized each and every word. More than trying to convince him, I had to convince myself. *You understand that, right?* I asked and fell silent.

Shimon was quiet as well. The room itself was hushed. My breathing was audible. Maybe our heartbeats were as well. I took a long sip from the glass of water in front of me to gear up for what came next. *Remember, Shimon, always remember, that Jerry and I are connected with every cell in our bodies, even if we are very different people. We've been together since I was nineteen. We share a cosmic connection. I'm not even sure I can appropriately put into words what our bond means.*

Once again, there was that same prolonged, oppressive silence in the room.

I closed my eyes for a moment and it became clear that I had to meet with Ohr Barkan, my astrologer and spiritual guide. The figure that had become an essential component of my support system, imbuing me with self-confidence as I faced the array of decisions that life was forcing me to make.

Ever since my childhood I had believed in God, my youth shaped by the foundational values taught to me at home by my mother and father; but Ohr built on that foundation. He explained to me that there is discernible order in the universe. Things happen in patterns that can be deciphered. The conversations with him amazed me each time anew and put my mind in order. He spoke from inexhaustible wellsprings of knowledge, as he was well-versed in Western astrology as well as Chinese astrology.

As our relationship deepened, I learned that the essence of what he said was proven right, time and time again. Though I'd always embraced a practical and realistic approach to life, I came to know that it is possible to anticipate future processes... truths that Chinese, Indian and Jewish mystics wrote about thousands of years ago.

At first glance, Ohr had nothing new to tell me about this mission. However, I knew that I was embarking on a challenging and frightening adventure, one that would require all the powers of my mind. I needed to hear his insights about me once again; reinforcing his analysis of my abilities and the sources of my strength, adding his determinations regarding karma and fate, which he defined as a contract the soul made with God.

I got to him in short order. Ohr sensed what I was experiencing. He felt the stress I was under, smelled the anxiety that surrounded me. I said nothing, but his keen intuition did not need my explanations. It revealed to him that I was about to go forth on some kind of adventure.

Sally, you remember that each of has a map. Yours is strong and unique, he said after a few minutes of silence. *You are very balanced. There is a strong element of water in your birth date. And like water, you can flow, penetrate all kinds of places, adapt yourself to the route in front of you, change and transform yourself to infiltrate any point you wish.*

I listened to his words and, for a moment, I asked myself if his hydrological analogies implied that he knew something he was not supposed to. It was not the first time that the words Ohr had chosen perfectly suited the matter in question that tormented me, but I did not reveal that to him.

Your force of nature is wind, he continued. *You can be a hurricane, or you can be a soft and caressing zephyr. You know how to reevaluate a route when you reach a problematic crossroads. Your great advantage is the ability to control complex crises that you find yourself in.*

8

Five days after my conversations with Shimon and Ohr — after sleepless nights, rambling discussions with Jerry until dawn, rivers of tears until I was short of breath and my heart was beating a mile a minute — I was already in a training program that amazed me.

It was nothing like the abridged version I'd undergone before leaving for Pakistan. Haggai, the operational driving instructor, said he heard about my exploits in Greece, so we jumped right into advanced techniques in crowded urban areas. After long hours of driving at insane speeds in a battered Lexus, performing countless maneuvers to avoid being tracked and bouncing down dirt roads that brutally shook the car, Haggai directed me to drive towards the Holon intersection where we went down Levi Eshkol Boulevard. I flew down the two-lane highway, surprised at how routine and mundane that leg seemed to be. Just a straight road.

What's the point of such a boring drive? I asked myself, and it was precisely then that Haggai broke the distracted silence he'd been absorbed in.

Sally, do you see the big tree on the left? he asked and pointed towards a huge eucalyptus, unusual for the landscape, which rose from the edge of the opposite shoulder of the road. He didn't wait for my answer. *As soon as you reach the tree line, cut hard to the left and go up into the field across from us.*

Are you sure? I asked, not hiding the bewilderment and skepticism in my words. Cutting left meant crossing a double white line, weaving between speeding vehicles in the opposite lane and roaring up the shoulder of the road, which looked like anything but a reasonable driving surface.

There is no time for questions, Sally, answered Haggai with a raised voice and unusual stiffness, and immediately began counting backwards loudly. *Six, five, four, three, two, one... Now!*

I didn't have time to think. The trunk of the eucalyptus loomed on my left. The car behind me kept its distance but sped up to match my acceleration. In the opposite lane a silver tractor trailer was coming towards us at full speed. In the split second after Haggai screamed *Now!* I had two choices. To make an insanely sharp turn, cutting in front of the truck before it passed the eucalyptus and smashed us to pieces; or to continue straight and tell Haggai that I didn't feel like killing myself today.

Without another thought, I cranked the steering wheel as far it would go. A split second later the Lexus veered wildly, crossing the double line just before the eucalyptus. I went shooting across to the opposite lane — without looking to the right at the terrifying silver silhouette that raced towards me, without listening to the blare of terror that tore through the air — climbing over the mound of the dirt that bounded the road and flying down into the field beyond it. It took a long time for the sound of the truck's horn to fade.

My pulse pounded in my temples and neck as my cheeks burned. The thought came to my mind that the right thing to do now would be to brake on the dirt road waiting for us beyond the berm, hit Haggai with both hands, get out of the car and walk home. A huge bolus of rage had formed in my chest, a seething heart of anger, all mixed together. First, anger at myself. For carrying out the reckless instruction given to me. For becoming an operational robot and not thinking about the truckdriver who might have been killed because of me. Then anger about the possibility that I could have died in a training maneuver within the borders of the country. At Haggai's irresponsibility. At Jerry's complicity, since he must have known what was waiting for me and kept quiet.

You want to hit me, and you're right, Haggai said, as if reading my mind. He extended his arm in my direction. *Hit me, Sally, let it out...*

On the far horizon of the field beyond the dirt path rose several rural houses. *Welcome to Mikveh Israel,* Haggai said, leaving his arm raised at me defiantly.

I kept silent. The silence in the car was thick and stifling until Haggai broke it. *These kinds of decisions will save your life in the middle of an operation, Sally. Think about it: effective evasion happens with a decision on the fly, in zero time, at the most illogical point for those who are chasing you. Imagine that you may have to drive at top speed, perform three or four more maneuvers like that and then drive for three hours straight. Let's say, from the center of Tehran to the shores of the Caspian Sea.*

I began to doubt my hearing. Tehran? The Caspian Sea? Was Haggai trying to impress me? Was he pretending to be aware of my upcoming mission or did he know something?

Haggai's words only agitated the storm already raging within me. The adrenaline was still pumping through my bloodstream from swerving in front of the tractor trailer. It would take another second or two before I managed to steady my breathing, gain control of my thoughts, and to remember that he was not a child. He was a veteran Mossad agent, an expert trainer who had seen much action in the field, one to whom other senior agents owed their lives. I had to trust him.

After two more minutes of flying in a cloud of white dust we approached an old and isolated country house on the outskirts of a village. The tiles at the entrance looked old, some broken. The land around it was neglected. Dust-covered purple thorns burst from the parched ground. The driveway had seen better days.

Sally, please stop by the yellow gate, Haggai said.

I braked and got out of the car, slamming the door loudly and walking away from him. I walked four times around the crumbling house. I didn't stroll; I hit the ground forcefully with every step, my foot striking the dry, hard ground with a muffled thump. I tried to vent the frustration, the pent-up anger, the latent fear. I tried to hold back the tears.

I turned the knob of the front door and entered the ramshackle building, only to feel as if I had moved from one reality to another. Beyond the heavy door which, from the outside, had seemed to be merely an ancient slab of wood, lay a cavernous space — without walls, flooded with bright neon light. The far wall was dominated by a huge screen. On both sides, the sterile space was filled with rows of computer stations.

Welcome to the virtual world, Haggai said.

I dropped into one of the swivel chairs scattered in front of the monitors. It was amazingly comfortable. I closed my eyes, wanting to sink into the sweet escape of sleep. I needed to get away from it all — from Haggai, from training, from the last quarter of an hour whose after-effects still made my heart tremble and my chest tighten. The bridled rage and frustration remained wedged in my throat.

Welcome to the Espinas Persian Gulf Hotel, Tehran.

It was Haggai, who surprised me with his perfect English, accent and all. He had his back to me, engrossed in one of the monitors set up against the wall. I felt that once we'd moved past that deceptively simple wooden door, he himself had undergone a metamorphosis. He became reserved, the rough speech of the operational driving instructor dialed down to low and refined. He suddenly spoke in polished English, immersing himself in the screen in front of him, embodying a role so different from the one I had known for the past two days.

So, what do you say about the Espinas? Would you like to stay there on holiday? he asked after a minute-long silence. Only then did I notice that the huge screen on the far wall had come to life, displaying the lobby of a luxury hotel.

Stand here, Sally, Haggai told me and pointed towards a small square that was glued to the bright granite tiles. *The software knows how to watch you and follow the movements of your eyes. The screen will lead you inside, into the bowels of the Espinas, according to whichever direction you look in. When you get tired of this hotel, we'll move to another*, Haggai explained.

Another hotel? I asked.

Haggai looked at me with a half-smile and tilted his chin towards the big screen. I raised my head and found myself facing the lobby of another hotel. He spoke again in perfect English: *Welcome to the Grand Hyatt, Doha.* He dove back towards the computer, his fingers running over the keyboard at an impressive pace. The monitor showed a split screen: on the right was a mirror image of the far wall, while on the left was a blue display of lengthy, rapid lines of code. Every time he pressed the Enter key, it shifted to show more lines, which seemed to be writing themselves.

I was completely surprised. I knew Haggai as a virtuoso driver, the best instructor in operational driving. I knew he would also be training me in firearms. However, I'd had no idea that he had the impressive professional knowledge that he demonstrated in the covert station at Mikveh Israel.

The next few hours were like playing three-dimensional games at a virtual amusement park. The huge computer screen was amazing. A slight glance to the right or left was enough for the lobby projected in front of me to adjust itself according to the direction of my gaze and begin to draw me in, further and deeper into the halls of the hotel.

And where are the tennis courts? I asked, unclear whether in amazement or defiance. Still, the moment I uttered the words, the lobby of the Grand Hyatt tipped itself sharply to the right and I began to drift virtually down a long corridor until I arrived at a glass door that opened on the side and allowed me to pass into the tennis complex. All along the route, small red dots flashed slowly on the screen. To my unspoken question, Haggai replied: *Pay attention to the circles. Each one represents a security camera that transmits directly to the control room of the chief of security and simultaneously to our control screens in Tel Aviv. They hired the best minds to overcome the loopholes in their security systems, but the live broadcasts to Tel Aviv continue, thank God. In Qatar, there is a security camera on every square foot. It's bad and it's good. As long as you are in the hotel complexes that we'll be training on, there will be several people keeping an eye on you. In Tehran, there are far fewer cameras and far fewer control rooms, but every third person you meet is collaborating with the intelligence services.*

Over the next two hours, I walked through the lobbies and corridors of two more Tehrani hotels, Hanna Boutique and Parsian Azadi. Haggai's deft control of the computer in front of him and his vast knowledge of these locations was comprehensive, surprising, and impressive.

We focus mainly on hotels in Doha and Tehran favored by hedonistic military officers, government officials and foreign businessmen, Haggai said. *Ones that have sophisticated spa complexes, tennis courts, and a lot of mingling with businessmen from the West.*

Psssh, what an investment, I replied without a hint of cynicism or sarcasm.

These images are from the last two months, observed Haggai. *You can trust them.*

I was enthusiastic and carried away. I didn't notice the hours that had passed until I glanced at the clock. *We've overdone it, Haggai. I have to go home,* I said.

Haggai confirmed. *You're right, but just before we leave here, here's a preview of tomorrow's training,* he said with his back to me. His fingers hovered over the keyboard in front of him and then he swiveled his chair towards me and gave me a mischievous and amused look.

The giant screen had returned to the Grand Hyatt precincts. At the top flashed several headshots that I recognized immediately — members of the Al Thani family, the ruling dynasty of Qatar. In the last two weeks, I had memorized more and more pieces of information about them, their roles and their ranks. I had scrutinized dozens of images, some of which were quite intimate.

I know them all, I said complacently, and then I got another surprise. The headshot of Colonel Nasser Al Thani, head of QSS (Qatar State Security), floated to the center of the screen and then disappeared, only to be replaced by the man himself, standing right in front of me in the lobby, in all his glory, with all his gleaming medals and insignia decorating his chest. I could see the stubble on his chin, even the uncontrollable tic in his right nostril.

I had already learned all this from reading the files and examining the images, but this time he stood in front of me at his full height, grinned at me, and then soberly extended his right hand towards me and said: *A pleasure to meet you...*

Now that he had emerged from his computer file, I realized that he was exactly my height. A flesh-and-blood enemy who needed to be smiled at to gain his trust.

Get to know this officer, said Haggai in a quiet voice. *He likes to portray himself as an officer and a gentleman, but behind that impressive chest full of medals beats a greedy, grubby heart. His cash cow is the Iranian steel industry. He has arranged several transactions to circumvent sanctions for a factory in Ahvaz, in Khuzestan Province. They paid him with several suitcases stuffed with cash, but not enough to satisfy his appetite. He's in contact with two other steel plants operated by the Iranian government. All three of them are of great interest to us, but we haven't been able to infiltrate them, despite the best efforts of the geniuses in Givatayim.*

When we left the building, I noticed two vehicles parked next to the house. In each sat a pair of young men in sunglasses, even in the late-afternoon dusk. One of them offered a symbolic salute to Haggai when he got in the car. *Now I'm driving and you rest a bit. You had a busy day with more than a few surprises,* he said in a soft tone, quite different from the one that characterized the driving and weapons training.

The return trip to Tel Aviv was also relaxed. He seemed drained too.

The next day's covert training focused on more and more encounters with avatars who greeted me, spoke to me, reached out, giving me a chance to get used to the thought of having ongoing conversations with them.

Towards two o'clock in the afternoon we moved to the range at a nearby base. Weapons training included becoming familiar with and trying out several new types of firearms. Much of the time I trained with a pistol, with and without a silencer. Haggai remained nearby the whole time, supervising every step of the training, but he passed the personal responsibility to Elon, who had a somewhat boyish face.

Sally, you're training so you won't have to use your shooting skills. If you need them, that's a bad sign. A very bad sign, he recited from time to time, recalling the mantras of Shimon.

During one of the sessions, I reflected on Jerry's words. *I know you, Sally. We could talk until we're blue in the face. Thinking about the children will tear you apart. But in the end, you will do what feels right for you, for the mission, the institution, the country. You can't fight it. We're now going through the same process, step by step, that we went through last time when we had to decide whether to go to Pakistan undercover, with a small child and an unborn baby, no less.*

After two more days with the avatars of Mikveh Israel and with Elon at the range, a surprise arrived. Field exercises were replaced by sessions at a new playground: a covert Mossad office on Ibn Gabirol Street, one of the main, busy commercial and residential streets in Tel Aviv.

I realized soon after I arrived that it was not the stylish office of another Tel Aviv startup. An old-fashioned, creaking, scary elevator took me to the fourth floor, where steel doors separated me from the space where I would spend the next few weeks.

Two doors that led me to the adventure of my life.

9

On Ibn Gabirol Street, an introductory lesson in
cyberspace

A rotting wooden door, looking like it might fall off, obscured the
first multi-bolt steel portal. Beyond that was a short corridor that
ended in front of another steel door that looked like it would have
belonged in a bank vault.

Opening it required biometric identification via a retinal scan-
ner. Beyond the steel barrier stretched a spacious room that looked
like a converted bomb shelter. It smelled a bit moldy. Gradually, I
detected light clouds of sweet and suspicious scents.

This was the kingdom of Bar Raveh. A young man with a boyish
appearance, maybe twenty-eight or so, wearing a wrinkled, faded,
tattered T-shirt and hiking sandals. A thin avant-garde beard ended
in a small braid jutting out of his chin. A golden earring with a tiny
blue stone hung from one of his ears and his cheeks were pockmarked.

Bar sat in front of a monitor and keyboard, playing them like a
piano — his quick and nimble fingers racing over the keys; the fast
clicking sounded like the continuous rustling of plastic.

His posture was lackadaisical: one leg folded tightly, resting
on the chair; the second leg thrown forward. He continued typing
at breakneck speed even as he looked at me and asked questions.
Sometimes he typed with one hand and with the other performed
a dance on his cell phone, firing off short WhatsApp messages. The
meetings with Bar started with silly questions about mastering office software and, from there, they slowly rose to surprising heights.
This kid knew what to ask and immediately understood when I was
trying to fake answers.

He was matter-of-fact and clever as a devil. He demanded to find out how current and advanced my programming skills were. Did I know how to search external and internal drives? Did I know how to find files with passwords? Did I know how to open password-protected files? What was my typing speed in English? Had I ever typed in Arabic? Was I familiar with mobile devices other than my iPhone? Did I know any financial apps?

As Bar's questioning progressed, I realized that they had already investigated my background: my programming studies, my work as an information systems manager at the Israel Electric Corporation, my activities in London. Between the lines I realized that he had also talked to Jerry to evaluate my experience with computers. Jerry, then, was in on the secret, but that didn't diminish the anxieties and doubts that plagued him.

After about a week in Bar's digital kingdom, when the daily schedule became increasingly harsh, I noticed a change in Jerry's demeanor. He did not look directly at me; his speech, which was already formal, now became more serious and thoughtful.

One evening when I arrived home totally bushed, Roy and Michael were irritable and irritating. They were looking for more attention. *And when your work only makes you only three hours late...* Jerry blurted out of nowhere and fell into a long, scolding, agonizing silence, the way only he knew how to keep quiet. His verbal statement trailed off, but what he left unsaid echoed in my mind: *Do you know what will happen here while you're gone for three months?*

I replied aloud to his accusatory silence: *You know I'll be back for three days every month! You're brutally putting me in an impossible position. You're playing both sides here. You knew in advance what they were cooking up for me, what I'll be expected to do. You've already discussed this with Shimon! You knew about the computer training and you provided them with information. But, above all, Jerry, you were with me during those sleepless nights before we made the decision.*

Jerry was silent, as was I. It was clear that we'd reached that conclusion together, but this was touching on the deepest and most painful scars of our experience in Pakistan. A chain of events that we both had not forgiven ourselves for. Not then, not ever.

There were many excuses. One of them was based on that term of art, operational circumstances. A juxtaposition of events and ideas that led us to a terrible decision. To leave baby Michael, all of eight months old, in Pakistan, and get out of hell for six weeks. If that hadn't been crazy enough, Michael had been left with our friend, the local chief of staff. An insane decision. Crazy, irresponsible, but still based on solid logic.

It was the only place Michael could be safe, I thought to myself.

True, Michael stayed with a nanny he knew very well. True, it was a joint decision, Jerry said in a low voice. But this does not make it any more correct, more justifiable. And yes, I agreed, but I'll never forgive myself for it. He spoke with deep sadness, in a tormented voice, as if placing a ticking bomb between us.

Jerry's words hit me mercilessly. It was the first time we'd dared to voice the pain that continued to sear our flesh. The first time we shared a conversation about it, with sharp words, with frankness. I saw him in agony. He, for his part, saw how the spring of pain bubbled up in me and turned my face ashen.

Jerry, I should resign. I'll ask for a meeting with Shimon tomorrow and let him know that I am withdrawing from it all, I said. *Both of us leaving the children and earning pennies... how stupid. In the private sector I could earn in two weeks everything I'd get from the Mossad over two years.*

It's your decision, Sally. I can discuss it with you, dissect, debate — but it is your choice alone, my love.

10

The extent of the knowledge I demonstrated surprised Bar. The latent tone of disdain in his speech gradually faded and disappeared. Still, there was another ocean of material I had to cover. I was seriously behind when it came to coding. I had zero knowledge of cybersecurity. My familiarity with mobile devices was limited. I didn't know how to dive into a personal computer and find hidden files on it. I didn't recognize the variety of laptops he presented to me. I didn't know the differences between a PC and a Mac. I had to recover and improve my typing speed in English as well. But somehow, I leapt over some of the pitfalls in Bar's classes.

I noticed that, during our training sessions, there was always the same young person sitting in the corner, back to me, long hair shimmering.

I stared at Bar and tipped my chin towards the observer with a silent question: *Who is that?*

Bar looked at the long-haired man and whispered: *That's Eliot. The real boss here. I learned everything I know from Eliot. Rock star... Total rock starrr...*

My question and Bar's answer were very quiet, but the chair at the end of the room slowly swiveled to face us.

Are you gossiping about me? asked the subject of our exchange, who turned out to have the face of an angel. Alabaster skin, beautiful but very delicate features, prominent cheekbones. Eyes like two translucent azure ponds. Someone hard to forget. Personally, I thought it was too much. I stared and found myself wondering if this rock star was male or female.

Then Eliot stood up, rising to the height of six-foot-one. Definitely a man. He crossed the room with long, springy steps and extended his right hand. Defying my expectations, his handshake was unusually powerful. It was also surprisingly lengthy, and he brought his left hand around to cup mine enthusiastically.

Eliot, Eliot, he said in a thin and gentle voice. His gaze was so profound and penetrating, I felt a shadow of self-consciousness. For a moment he seemed to me to be the same age as my son, Roy, but his piercing stare into the depths of my eyes and the mysteriousness of his appearance made it hard for me to process. What was I seeing? What did that intense look mean?

Eliot, a French name, I babbled, trying to conceal the awkwardness.

Ravi de vous rencontrer, belle dame.

Then suddenly, out of nowhere, I heard Bar answer Eliot in French, in a admonishing tone that sounded a bit mechanical to me: *Arrête tes bêtises, Eliot!*

It amazed me. I could rattle off a few words in French. I realized that Eliot had complimented me and called me a beautiful woman; I also understood that Bar had rebuked him for his silliness. Still, the Gallic sounds seemed out-of-place in this classified area, where I'd heard the tech wizards employ only excellent digital English and broken Sabra Hebrew for the past fortnight. I stared at Bar with a scolding look that expressed wordlessly: *How come I've been with you for two intense weeks and you've never even hinted that you also speak French?*

What? he shrugged, implying both understanding and apology.

Eliot returned to his chair, once again with his back to us and sinking into the screen in front of him. The silence from his corner was deafening now.

So much for my sorcerous reputation. Would I have to hand in my hat and broom? The two kids had managed to fool me.

Bar and I were left alone again with the exercises he tried to assign me. Eliot was present-but-absent in the periphery, his back to us, his face glued to his monitor. However, I couldn't forget the startling hue of his eyes and his bottomless gaze. The enigma he represented would continue to haunt me.

Well, how about some necromancy? See if you can defeat the blue screen of death, Bar challenged me and pulled me back to the world of reality and to my training. He picked up his laptop and handed it to me. The screen crackled with flickering blue. Long rows of numbers flew at breakneck speed from the bottom of the screen and disappeared at the top. It looked like it had suffered a murderous cyber-attack, as if no tap on the keyboard could revive it.

Want me to fix it for you in French? I asked Bar, unclear whether I was really angry or pulling his chain. Grabbing the laptop, I placed it on my lap and started typing quickly. I took care of the problem in short order. For a moment, I felt like twenty-year-old Sally, working in the electric company's IT department, improvising solutions in COBOL or in an assembler program on the company's mainframe computers. After about thirty seconds, I turned the screen towards Bar with a triumphant expression on my face.

Now you're the rock star. Where did you learn how to do that? Bar asked, examining the device in disbelief.

Are you really interested in how an antique like me understands computers, or are you asking out of politeness? I asked.

Bar looked at me briefly and answered: *I'm really interested, Sally. Politeness isn't my thing.*

My reply to Bar was relatively brief. I described in a few sentences how I decided to study programming when I was only seventeen and a half, how I received my father's blessing even though there were only males in the classroom at the Technion satellite campus. Still, that was enough to bring up the memories; my mind was flooded with the emotions of that impossible decision decades earlier.

To my surprise, Bar asked to hear the whole story anyway.

I explained to him how, like many Orthodox girls, I had sought an exemption from conscription on religious grounds. I had been light-years away from the world of computer programming, an obscure discipline then. Indeed, I seemed to have no chance of meeting the minimum requirements for the course; after all, what connection did I have to the real-world educational frameworks of information systems management?

Do you understand that, Bar?

The candidates for the course I read about in the newspaper came from classified electronics units in the IDF, along with two fighter pilots and elite combat support squads. The best and the brightest, who arrived with extensive and impressive prior knowledge.

Beyond all that, they were all boys. A cocktail of testosterone to which only the most adventurous mixologist would add me. I wasn't even eighteen yet, a light-haired slip of a girl from a *moshav*, naïve and inexperienced in every way. I hadn't served in the military, I didn't have a degree, I'd never had any education in programming.

Meeting the minimum requirements seemed like a pipe dream, especially since I also had to come up with the money to enroll in the course. Why bother to try?

But giving up wasn't in my nature. When I saw a wall, I had to scale it; when I saw a border, I had to cross it. I needed to challenge myself, against all odds and with absolute faith in my ability to succeed. There was no empirical mathematical or scientific formula to calculate how low my chances were of getting into the course, let alone passing it. Perhaps that required a supercomputer which did not yet exist. That led to my conclusion that my success had to be dependent on something else. I knew that I was good at practical subjects, logic, at math. I believed in myself and thought it was a perfect fit for me.

The instructors tried to dissuade me from this absurd idea. They said I wouldn't be able to keep up with the adults, the experienced, the ones with records — both military and academic — who had already signed up for that semester. However, they weren't prepared for someone who refused to surrender, who didn't know the meaning of the word no. So, they were left with no choice but to tell me yes. I returned to the *moshav* with the news that I had been accepted to study programming in Haifa, in a course that would be held three times a week.

My mother felt that her world was ending. For a start, she didn't understand what computer programming was to being with; what's more, she wanted to arrange a *shidduch* for me, marrying me off as soon as possible, in keeping with Orthodox custom, at least at the time.

It was my father, the tough *etrog* farmer, who was much more open-minded. He asked to read the material and come to a meeting with me at the Technion in Haifa to understand why he had to pay so much for this opportunity. After sitting through that meeting — and facing my determination — my father pulled out his checkbook to bankroll the entirety of the course. It wasn't easy, but he supported me and believed in me.

As it turned out, some of his customers were bigwigs at the Israel Electric Corporation. Towards the end of the course, my mother started to bully them. One of them was a senior executive at the IEC, who finally decided to give me a chance. Getting that job at the electric company was a life-changing event, the kind that realigns trajectories and determines destinies. The underestimated, unlikely girl from the *moshav* becoming a brilliant systems administrator — who would have thought? They ended up quite pleased with me. The IEC job allowed me to further my education at the Technion.

Fate continued toying with me, as it was by way of that job that I met Jerry. His noisy conversation with one of my co-workers, an old army buddy of his, in the office nearby was getting on my nerves. I admonished them, telling them that their shooting the breeze wasn't more important than my work.

That might have been the most momentous remark ever. Jerry couldn't ignore the assertive blonde who kicked him out of his pal's office. He resolved that he had to get to know her — i.e., me — better. I had made my own *shidduch*.

The rest is history. That was how my romance with Jerry began, that was how I got to London, that was how I got married, and that was how I became involved with highly classified operations for the Mossad in a hostile Muslim nation.

11

14:00 hrs.
Dueling confessions at Reviva and Celia, Park
Tzameret

My training was my life insurance, the basic conditions for my survival. There was a clear and present mortal danger inherent in the missions that awaited me, but I continued to have trouble focusing. I had disturbing thoughts that did not allow me to concentrate on my lessons. At first, they were just a nuisance. Later on, they became a real threat to the operational tasks that I was expected to execute, on both sides of the Persian Gulf, in regions where death was always a reasonable outcome were I to be caught. How could I live with the secret I kept from Jerry? How had Jerry acted when he played roles like Yiftach's, when he served as a field agent? I was training for the mission of my life — an edge-of-your-seat thriller the likes of which no one had ever directed before — so how dare I be preoccupied with the one and only kiss that happened during my training?

A poisonous cocktail bubbled up in me: flashes of jealousy, hints of guilt. A massive and demanding lie that grew and swelled between me and Jerry.

I would come to the conclusion that I had been right to veto Jerry's operational activities which might have entailed 'For the sake of the country, I went up to her room' situations. Then, a second later, I was angry with myself for even bringing this up in my dim thoughts and for turning my feelings of guilt into a hidden and baseless accusation against Jerry.

Amidst the surge of internal battles, the desperate need to share with someone what I experienced in the darkness near the Gulf of

Piraeus, the vortex that persisted in my thoughts, began to arise within me. The simple question was why didn't I share with Jerry the allegedly juvenile, allegedly innocent experience. I asked myself a lot of questions that I didn't know how to answer, and I grew tired of talking to myself. So, to whom could I unburden myself?

I dismissed my mother immediately. My friend Mira was not suitable either, I thought. She would develop feelings of jealousy, and I could not be sure of the sincerity of her ideas or notions. Yaffit was busy with a strategic procurement deal, updating me on the details so that I would understand why she did not have the time and mental strength to share the storm with me. I happily rejected two more friends whose discretion I didn't trust, and then I remembered the good and wise Racheli. Racheli was not a close confidante of mine, but definitely one whose discretion, judgment, intelligence and honesty I respected.

Racheli was sixty, maybe a little more, divorced for a decade. She was a gifted programmer who had been a partner in a hi-tech company and, after making her exit, she had begun dealing with cryptocurrency. She was part of the Pastel Parliament group, but a silent partner. Even at the smaller get-togethers we held from time to time in a cafe on Rothschild Boulevard, she held her peace.

Her skin was surprisingly smooth. A matter of luck and genetics. I would sometimes comfort myself by examining her crow's feet. She was also fairly thin. Her hair was usually blown out in a mane of bright, messy curls. Her eyes shone a deep blue.

A careful look under her baggy clothes would reveal that she had an excellent body and an impressive chest, even in her seventh decade. However, Racheli was meticulous in concealing that data. She never wore tight pants or cleavage-baring tops. She never came in hot pants or crop tops, like several of the women in our neighborhood who tried to defy their ages via the use of pathetic tools and procedures.

I asked myself if Racheli was up to the challenge I proposed for her. I thought back on the last few years and gradually realized that she had never talked about her dates, was never seen with a temporary partner. Nor did she participate in conversations where the girls spun heroic tales about casual hookups, or discussions drifting into graphic descriptions of stormy marital relationships. You could say that Racheli was the ultimate nerd. No one paid her mind when our talk turned to men or sex, though I, married for many years to Jerry, had little to contribute at those moments either.

I arranged a tête-à-tête with Racheli at Reviva and Celia, a cafe in Complex G of the Park Tzameret neighborhood in Tel Aviv. It was a convenient location for both of us. An innocent, relaxed, short meeting over a salad and a glass of wine — until suddenly the conversation turned into something else. Like an earthquake that hits with no prior warning.

It began with my story. I spoke to Racheli as if she were my reflection in the mirror. I thought that I would be excited, that I would be ashamed, that tremors would come over me, that refined electric currents would shake the vertebrae of my lower back, that my lips would be ignited for a moment by that heat, that a glimmer of a tear would emerge into the open air. But none of these came. Not even the hint of one. My mind replayed the events, my lips moved, my mouth intoned, but it felt like I was reciting a passage from a book and talking about someone else.

Racheli listened patiently to the twists and turns, while I was looking for a way to confide in her about the depths of the kiss with Yiftach, attempting to justify it as an operational necessity where I had no choice.

Her smile widened as I became entangled in quandaries and convolutions. As I began to describe the electricity of the meeting of our lips, she began to giggle. She had ironclad patience and impeccable politeness. She listened and listened and then prodded me: *And... Well, Sally, and...*

And nothing... Just a kiss that unsettled me.

Racheli shot me a look; I couldn't tell if it was amazement or disappointment. *Nothing...?* Over the next hour, she gave me one of the most important lessons in modesty I've ever received. Racheli started sharing her life story with me and didn't stop. I had come to share my secrets with her, but she was the one who managed to shocked me.

Gradually it became clear that the shy programming expert, the sexagenarian who kept quiet amid the piquant conversations of the Pastel Parliament, had an impressive record in several fields. She unfolded her jaw-dropping story to me, leaving me breathless. A light lunch over a salad and a glass of wine turned into a heart-to-heart conversation that lasted almost until the evening, until the placemat on the table had already been changed twice and we were both already on a fourth glass of Gewürztraminer.

It turned out that Racheli was quite a heroine. She had been recruited to assist the state in covert tasks related to her vast knowledge in the field of cybertechnology and the deep and unique expertise she had acquired in the field of cryptocurrency.

I also discovered that some of these tasks were not carried out in her posh office in the Atrium Tower near Elite Junction. Her discretion was admirable. She did not even hint at who employed her, which arm of the government, the people who were involved in the operations, or the targets of attack. Still, I gathered that the aim of her activity was to expose and eliminate the digital financial channel of the Revolutionary Guards. Racheli talked and talked, but she didn't utter a single name.

I listened intently to her every word. My initial aim had been to share my personal affairs with Racheli, intimate disputes, issues far removed from blockchain challenges; but something completely different happened.

As she went deeper into describing her activities, I realized that she could make a crucial contribution to complex international investigations. Those I didn't yet know I would be involved in up to my neck. And there, in the midst of that conversation, over a fine bottle or two, the seeds of calamity were also sown between Racheli and me, with consequences difficult to overstate.

12

The next stage of the conversation truly floored me. Racheli began to talk about sexual awakening in the golden years. I had read about this concept several times in glossy magazines, as well as two best-sellers translated into Hebrew; but in my mind, it simply hovered there somewhere between prattling folklore and science fiction.

Racheli's words sounded to me like a continuous quote from a piece in the women's weekly *La'Isha*, but that was only the beginning.

The next step swept me to a hidden cliff at Stella Maris in Haifa. Accessing the spot is perilous, but the view makes you feel like you're hovering above the waters of the bay, wings fully spread.

I returned home that evening, sat down on the balcony with the panorama before me, closed my eyes and recalled Racheli's words with uncanny precision. It was inconceivable that she had made up the tale or that she had heard it from someone else. This was her story.

It all started with a buttoned-up and boring work meeting shortly before Passover, Racheli had said. *I was sitting in a tiny conference room at the Dan Hotel in Haifa with three colleagues. The meeting dealt with some kind of investment from an American cybertechnology firm. Not much. Maybe thirty million dollars.*

One of the three was insanely smart, but dry as a muscat raisin. An utter genius, working for a company I knew well. He spoke and acted as if he had aged prematurely.

The second was an American with his head in the clouds who had been in Israel for two years. His speech was heavy, throaty; even though my English is fine, I didn't understand half of what he said.

The third guy arrived late. I looked up when he knocked on the door, and he was like Tom Cruise in the movie American Made. He was beaming with arrogance. As soon as he started talking, I said to myself, here's another fighter pilot in the reserves. You're familiar with that intonation, the hand gestures, the condescending Hebrew. And I have news for you, you know him well. Today everyone knows him. He's made his spectacular exit from three different startups. But then, three years ago, he was still completely anonymous. The most they knew about him was the nickname: Air Force G.

I listened to Racheli intently. My curiosity skyrocketed. Who was this Tom Cruise doppelgänger who had suddenly landed in my slim-cut Jägermeister shot glass? But it was impossible to stop her. It seemed that Racheli had waited three plus years for this moment to unburden herself. This personal conversation about matters of the heart and the body allowed her to release the dam of passion in her chest.

She went on: The meeting at the Dan didn't last long. Flyboy was quite full of himself, bragging about his famous wife and revealing a disturbing level of incaution in several of the things he said about blockchain technology. His imprecision screamed to the heavens. Even so, he possessed some quality I found impossible to ignore.

When the meeting ended and were on the way to the elevator, he addressed me directly, without preamble and without apology: If you're feeling spontaneous, I can show you the most exciting place in Israel. I promise you... I have no idea why. No explanation. I ought to have slapped him, or taken a token look at my watch and told him I was too busy, or shot him a caustic laser-like glare while reminding him of his wife, driving a pointy dagger between his eyes.

But a different answer came out of me. My body reacted differently and drove me forward with an energy I didn't know I had: I was spontaneous... and I was shocked at my own actions.

Two minutes later, coming out of the exit from the Dan's lobby, I had a second shock in store. There would be more to come, more than I could imagine, that day and that week and throughout the following months.

Flyboy pointed to a heavy and ornate motorcycle. We'll take off on that, he announced, in the arrogant argot of pilots, and handed me a helmet. Even an amateur like me recognized the front wheel protruding forward at an exaggerated angle and the silver handlebar grips sweeping back. I don't know what I found more shocking: the massive Harley Davidson or myself. I slipped the helmet over my sheep's mane, as if I did it several times a day, raised my leg and — a split second later, I was already thrown back, holding tightly onto Flyboy's waist, trying not to become airborne while he was surging forward at many, many miles per hour.

We'll be there in four minutes, he shouted, trying to get me to hear him.

I cursed myself, my lax discipline, the strange sense of adventure that suddenly gripped me. The motorcycle was too wide, it vibrated too much. I had to hug a strange man from behind, someone whom I'd met an hour ago. I was shocked at what he was doing. I was shocked at what I was doing. It wasn't me flying west on HaNasi Boulevard.

Eventually we got off the paved roads, crossed a parking lot and passed between two concrete pillars that blocked the entry of cars. From there we went down a narrow, steep and winding path between thorn fields of spectacular color. My gaze was captured by the contrast between the mesmerizing blue eyes of the cornflowers and the sharp thistles that emerged from them. It was a contrast that reflected that outing exactly, which became more and more bizarre from moment to moment.

At a certain point, I dared to think about asserting myself, to formulate the sentence of protest I would shout in the direction of the helmet in front of me; but then the motorcycle braked. I raised my head and felt that I was suddenly swept into a vast ocean of air, bluer than blue, horizon to horizon, having no boundaries and no point of reference, whose depth or breadth could not be estimated. I was left breathless.

I disembarked from the motorcycle gingerly, removing my helmet and letting my mane of curls play in the gentle breeze that came from the realms of magic.

For a moment, I feared that my feet would soon detach from the brown rock I was standing on and that my body would begin floating above the bay. I looked down for a moment and saw Flyboy, already sitting on the edge of the cliff, his legs swinging back and forth, like a small child on an adult's chair kicking tiny feet. Next to him was a silver thermos and two red plastic cups. But what happened then had nothing to do with the thermos or the glasses. I think I lost my mind for a moment.

I broke in: *Racheli, another minute of this and I'll wring your neck!* I had lost my patience, my blood raging in my veins. *Who is Flyboy?*

Racheli stopped her flow of speech, staring at me with a deep blue gaze and took a long breath. *Daniel Geffen.*

I thought I'd misheard. My eyes popped open violently and I bent my head forward, getting into Racheli's face, as if asking her to restate the name more clearly.

Daniel Geffen used to be my neighbor. A strikingly handsome man, very rich, very smart, very famous and very married. He made the top of the lists of both the country's wealthiest and the country's most successful high-tech entrepreneurs. He had done spectacularly well making his exit from three prominent startups, and then he had married Ramit, a premier influencer on Instagram. Their partnership was iconic in tabloid media, the quintessence of a dream marriage.

Still, a few years ago Geffen had found a window of opportunity to toss one or two flirtatious sentences at me, examining my reaction.

The shock I experienced intensified a minute later when Racheli continued to detail her experiences on that cliff, atop which no real boundary remained with no inhibitions in sight. No eye could observe them, except a pair of eagles circling above, completing huge orbits over the bay and above the overhanging rocky ledge.

13

Somersaults in my stomach at Park Tzameret

Two years had passed since I'd touched a man. No man had ever touched me so gently, Racheli said in a hushed tone. I'm sure about the timing because it was two years earlier, shortly before Passover, that I received a scar that would never heal. It was in the midst of a nightmare date. I was with a relatively young man at the time. He fancied himself a macho Don Juan, aspiring for a new chapter in life, and I was swept away into hallucinatory worlds. I wanted to believe him. I was flattered that a handsome man in his fifties was interested in a woman in her sixties — even thinking of formalizing the relationship.

But my bedroom witnessed one of the most pathetic performances I'd ever seen. Halfway through, as we were reaching the climax — well, he was at least — he started weeping. It took me a while to realize that the sounds coming from him were not moans of lust. Then he confessed that he had lied to me. He was very married, and he loved his wife, of course. A second later he broke away from me, sat down on the rug and burst into tears. I got into the shower, shoved two fingers down my throat and threw up the lies he had been pushing on me during the two weeks of our counterfeit courtship. I've been with married men, but never a worm like that — a cowardly, lying storyteller. God help him. What exactly did he think he'd gain from the deceit?

So, I can tell you that it had been two years since I'd looked at any man as a man. I wasn't able to trust anyone. I didn't respond to any courtship, I didn't go on any dates, I didn't touch anyone, I just couldn't. I plunged further and further into the depths of my work, escaping from my disgust. I sat in social circles where they talked about couples, relationships and intimacy, but I always put myself on silent mode.

Then, out of nowhere, came the flight to the cliff at Stella Maris. Daniel's right arm wrapped around me from the back, touching my bare hand and burning my skin. There were goosebumps all over my neck, my stomach, my breasts, millions of pores opening at their tips.

I looked slightly to the left and saw Daniel's eyes sparkling in the breeze coming from the north. I sent out a bent finger and wiped away the glimmer of a tear nearest to me. That tiny drop made all the difference. He was no longer an arrogant and careless pilot, but the surprising man who brought me to this dream.

Then we drowned in each other, bursting together on that rocky ledge. Small stones dropped from the cliff and fell down, a thousand feet of free fall towards the Cave of Eliyah.

It turned out that he, too, a famously married man who appeared with his wife on talk shows and told heroic stories about their perfect relationship, had neither touched nor been touched for at least two years.

He was really excited. No posturing. When I caressed his face, he shuddered. His life had longed for such a caress for too long.

Then came the moment we entered into an altered state, physically and mentally. We stopped being solid and became transparent to the environment, to the passers-by who walked along the deer trail, to the Air Force helicopters rushing north. We rolled from side to side in perfect harmony. Lips to lips, burning pelvis to burning pelvis, bursting chest to bursting chest. There was a rollover and another rollover, until we were floating naked between sky and sky, flush against the cliff wall. And yet we did not feel that we had reached the end, nor did we feel the light breeze that came up from the abyss.

It was two days before Passover. Glancing at my watch, I was amazed to find that the sudden explosion on the ledge had lasted about five hours. And what better way to usher in the holiday of liberation! What freedom!

It's been going on for two years, Sally. Two years of legendary, epic, never-ending sex. I don't know where I get the strength to carry out my management duties for the company, flying abroad and standing in front of audiences and lecturing — and giving my children all the love and attention they need, even taking a weekly shift with my crazy granddaugh-

ter — while at the same time persevering in this infinite marathon of passion, with no limits and no reservations.

At least for now, it's not all finished for us, Sally — but I'm going crazy. I don't understand where all this was before. I don't understand how for two whole years before I made the most basic and foolish mistakes, punishing myself because of the stupidity of another.

I took a deep breath, once, twice and two more times. I listened to Racheli in a kind of daze, not just from what my ears heard, but from what I had absorbed with my whole body. Somersaults in my stomach, the back of my neck tingling, my diaphragm balling up, deep breaths that I felt one by one. Still, I wasn't ready for the next phase of the conversation, which plunged even deeper, out of the blue.

Racheli so wanted to tell me. It was like a fire in her bones and, at that moment, when she asked the waitress for *something a little more edgy* to drink, she had already begun to unravel the most profound secrets hidden within her for too long.

I didn't think a woman my age, married for so many years, a mother of two young men, a young grandmother, could be so deeply embarrassed by stories about sex. Racheli, a silent member of the Pastel Parliament, talked about lovemaking in every possible way and from every possible direction. Turbulent and unrestrained, without blushing, without hesitating even for a moment. As the conversation progressed, my reputation as an all-seeing, all-knowing sorceress crashed. At no time during the Pastel Parliament meetings did I give Rachel an ounce of credit and I always treated her perpetual silence as a form of criticism and condescension.

And I couldn't prevent the thought from sneaking up on me. *How naive and conservative I am about intimacy. How ignorant I am,* I told myself quietly.

Then, as part of the open and honest conversation, I told Racheli this too. *I don't know anything, Racheli. I don't know anything.*

Racheli and I said our goodbyes without words, but we knew for sure that this conversation had not yet exhausted itself — and it was to be continued.

Something significant had occurred between us in those hours and I felt I needed to prepare her for the fact that I was going to disappear for a few weeks.

A few weeks? Racheli asked and looked at me with her wise eyes. She was not stupid, but reconciled herself to accept the forced answer I improvised.

She approached me and hugged me for a long time. An unusual embrace.

Good luck, friend. Good luck, she whispered in my ear.

I was impressed that she understood more than met the eye.

14

13:30 hrs.
A fateful meeting thanks to Iacocca, on a British
Airways flight

There was nothing suspicious or untoward about being in business class on a luxury flight to Qatar on British Airways.

I had brought *Iacocca*, the autobiography of Chrysler's legendary CEO. Four hundred pages that were supposed to sharpen my business English and contribute to the new cover story I'd assumed. But somehow, even the simplest task sometimes becomes complicated. Iacocca's beaming, self-satisfied face jumped out from the book's cover and drew the attention of a relatively young Qatari businessman.

Waves of a fine cologne emanated from him. Probably Christian Dior's Sauvage, one of the most expensive scents in the world.

Dressed in a three-piece Zegna suit, he looked about forty years old, polished, full of himself. The juxtaposition of an English-speaking, green-eyed blonde and the autobiography of a multi-billionaire piqued his interest. In a moment he went from just a neighbor in business class to a potential stalker, a real risk.

Then, for the first time since I started training for missions in the Persian Gulf sector, the penny dropped. I suddenly understood the true significance of putting a blonde widow, a lonely businesswoman, in the position of being surrounded by men with a macho Mideastern mentality. On one hand, it was an excellent cover story for the type of operational activity I was in store for. On the other, I began to doubt the wisdom of utilizing it in cities like Doha or Tehran.

After the lesson I'd learned in Islamabad, this time I changed my identity from Sally Amir to Jessica Stone. Back in Pakistan, I had used the careless cover of an orphan with chestnut hair from the godforsaken town of Vardø, Norway; that had turned out to be too clever by half. It almost ended in utter disaster.

KISS, KISS, Shimon Eitan had berated me with obvious anger. *Keep it simple, stupid. Don't pretend to be from the middle of nowhere. Haven't you learned anything? Didn't you have Sally stick her head in the lion's mouth back in Islamabad? Did you portray her as being born in a tiny town in Norway hoping that no one in the world would find out that she'd never set foot there?*

Shimon was usually relaxed. His manner of speaking was quiet, charismatic, captivating; it inspired respect. It reminded me a lot of Jerry's speech. Still, it was evident that he had no patience for fools.

He approached the job of constructing the cover story with reverence. He spent hours on every single detail, stressing out the whole team, sending every bit of information to a couple of brilliant investigators who worked with us. These detectives did some fact-checking to ensure my grand mission wouldn't collapse over trivia. At the same time, our team designed two professional websites, provided Google-able news items, excerpts and mentions of the two companies I started managing after I became a widow, along with details of the philanthropic activities undertaken by me and my late husband. They also invested in my social media presence, mainly on LinkedIn.

The world is small... tiny... miniscule... Even at the other end of the world there will be someone born in that desolate Scandinavian hamlet. Do you understand that? The bigger the target, the better. Go big. A large city, a huge neighborhood, a crowded business, said Shimon, his tone growing more intense as he pontificated.

That's how Jessica was born. A 56-year-old British widow of Scandinavian origin with straight blonde hair, thin and well-groomed eyebrows. Expert in cybertechnology, the digital world and mobile communications. Mother of one — Bill, 18, who'd gone to study in China.

Two years earlier, she — i.e., I — had stepped into the shoes of my late husband, George, a real estate investor, after he died of a heart attack. In the last decade of his life, he had also begun investing in cybertechnology, both offensive and defensive. George and I had been engaged in philanthropy for years, donating to disadvantaged populations including refugees and immigrants from developing countries.

It was impossible to exaggerate the importance of this cover story which opened the door for several sensitive and complex operations when I was alone. Alone...

The tasks assigned to me this time were considerable. The tennis matches in Islamabad were child's play compared to the challenges that awaited me this time in Doha, with the possibility that I might also reach Tehran.

I held *Iacocca* as if I were reading it, skimming the lines of the chapter 'Trouble in Paradise', but my thoughts were somewhere else entirely. I memorized over and over the story of my late husband, George, that we had fabricated. He was London-born and bred, wildly successful in the field of real estate, operating a network of offices in Canada, the United States and the United Kingdom. The company he founded and managed, SCRS, had been transferred to me upon his death. The technology company, Gstone, also came under my sole ownership.

The office in London was a real, living, breathing thing. Helen, secretary and office manager, a 35-year-old single woman with a melancholic look, was convinced that she was running a functional office with the worldwide portfolios of SCRS and Gstone. We gave a lot of thought to the communication she would have with corresponding offices in the United States, Canada and Latin America. We designed a work schedule for her, assigning her real tasks.

In the two months leading up to the flight to Qatar, I called Helen every day, practicing my name, Jessica Stone, practicing business English, and memorizing answers to questions I might be asked about her. Along with the daily roster of busy work for SCRS and for Gstone, I would ask how she was and share with her the difficulties of being a widow. From time to time, I switched to girl-talk and personal matters.

After each of our conversations, I forwarded summaries of my meetings by email and WhatsApp with a list of tasks to be performed; I also requested a performance report for the previous day's tasks. In addition, Helen helped me with the philanthropic activities, donating to various causes. The company's computers already had folders and documents dating back several years, and a significant contemporary record was also slowly being compiled. Most of the tasks Helen received were idle. Both companies had impressive websites, but all the phone calls, letters and emails she sent moved within a closed circuit among several offices operated by the Mossad throughout Europe, Canada, the Cayman Islands and the United States. Some of them served an actual purpose, such as buying office equipment or a planter for the lobby, donating to charity or other trivialities.

In order to substantiate the firm's activities, two deals were also sewn up. First was the purchase of an old apartment building in the heart of the City of Westminster. The seller was a man named Vasily, British citizen of Russian origin. The name of that scary man with tattoo inscriptions on his body, hands and neck would come back to me later in a threatening storm that I had not foreseen, that I could not foresee. Helen was asked to assist in all phases of the purchase and was commended for her performance.

At the same time, a deal to sell a software package to the Pakistan Army was completed, and negotiations were underway to sell the package to two countries in Latin America. Gstone's cybertechnology was real and had fascinating capabilities. The finest virtuosos of Israel's elite units created a cyber-monster that worked with impressive efficiency. Along with its offensive capabilities, it inserted a back door that the buyers could not identify in any way. The back door came to life at a chosen time, after the software had been installed on the purchaser's computers. From that moment on, our good guys had access to the computers that used the software, to the enemy's cyber-defense schemes — and to the attacks being planned.

Helen did a great job on this deal as well. She had no way of knowing that unseen hands helped close the final details. There had been several reports planted in the UK financial media about Gstone's success in marketing its cybertechnology. *The Financial Times* published a story about Gstone's successful deals with two major armies, but the names of the countries were not revealed in the article. In the financial sections of several newspapers, analysts reported that the company was considering an IPO on Nasdaq. All calls to the office phone or to Helen's cell phone were tapped twenty-four-seven. It was my lifeline. It was the channel to call for help if one of my missions went awry or if I found that my life was in danger. It was the way to intercept conversations or any attempts to investigate my affairs.

The messages I memorized to convey to Helen were elegant in their simplicity. There was a logic in them that allowed me to remember them easily, even if I was in distress or under duress. Beside Helen, there was also my old friend, Gretchen, from Germany. She was kept in reserve for truly dire situations.

I came to the assignment in Doha as Mrs. Stone, with my original blonde hair, loose and flowing to beyond the shoulders, a sharp and precise part in the middle. I was without glasses and with thin, well-groomed eyebrows. It was a huge relief, after Mrs. Travers had arrived in Pakistan with heavy gold-rimmed glasses, wild eyebrows, long bangs that hid most of her forehead and a meticulous brown bob with dull blonde streaks. I hated every moment of that look, but in Pakistan I was better off not being a licentious blonde.

I sank deep into *Iacocca* — although, contrary to the instructions I'd been given, my thoughts wandered to my sons, Roy and Michael. Then I fell asleep in front of the open pages, hoping that the young man in the suit would return to his business. It was a hopeless expectation.

I know this book by heart, I've read it several times. What chapter are you reading now? he shot in my direction and gave me a curious look.

Trouble in Paradise, I answered and turned the open book towards him defiantly, as if to prove that I was telling the truth.

A shocking chapter, he replied immediately. *Ford demanded that Iacocca fire a manager, just because he wore tight pants and was suspected of being gay.*

The words of my stranger surprised me. I hadn't made much headway in the chapter yet, but I squinted at the beginning and easily recognized the fourth paragraph and the word homosexual, which was repeated several times. He was right, my new suitor. He did know the book and its contents very well.

Amazing, I replied and returned tired-eyed to the opening of the chapter. *These Americans were, until recently, racist, homophobic, narrow-minded. I'm not sure that the public in Europe or the Mideast knows these disturbing facts.*

Eventually, I fell asleep for real, with the paragraph about Henry Ford's homophobia bearing down on me with full force. I was crushed by fatigue and fell into a deep sleep, despite the heavy cloud of anxiety that surrounded me, my longing for my two beautiful children, my raging pulse, and the million questions that came and went in my head, as if I hadn't practiced for three months every comma in the cover story, as if I hadn't prepared myself for a prolonged separation from the children and from Jerry.

When I opened my eyes, I saw the entire business class in gear for landing. The passengers packed up their things, shoving gifts they'd picked up in the UK into their carry-ons. Women touched up their makeup; the men took off their canvas shoes and slipped into their leather ones. *Why are they in a hurry?* I asked myself. *We still have almost an hour before we land.*

The only one who sat in his place without moving, his tie and suit unruffled, was the man who loved Iacocca, who had given me a special look. He positioned himself so he could meet my eyes. When he managed to catch my gaze, he extended a hand to shake.

Charmed. I'm Hamid… Hamid Al Thani… he said. His words were left hanging in the air. Al Thani, the ruling dynasty in Qatar since the 19th century. The one whose details I went over and over at Mossad headquarters and in Mikveh Israel. I had read about Hamid in only one of the reports. A few idle sentences without a headshot. I wondered: Was he indeed a member of Qatar's ruling dynasty? Was he close to the top? Was he trying to imply something?

I offered him a small, polite, restrained smile. *Jessica... Jessica Stone...*

It was clear that there was less than an hour left until landing, but it was important for Hamid to advance in his random introduction to me.

Do you live in London?

Yes, I live and work there, I replied, trying not to sound evasive and at the same time not encourage him too much.

I fly to London at least twice a month. I have good reason to. His gaze, fixed on me, lowered. He sent a tense finger to his upper lip and placed it under both nostrils, as if blocking them. It was obvious that he was trying to hide his excitement. It was also obvious that he was looking for an opportunity to talk.

Then he slowly looked back at me. Something of the arrogance that surrounded him melted. He reached into his suit jacket, deftly pulling out a business card and handing it to me. His fingernails were thin, long and delicate, almost like a woman's. His hand remained in the air in front of me.

I reached out both hands, grabbed the card and pulled it close for a thorough inspection. In golden ink, it identified him as *Hamid Al Thani, Coordinator of Procurement and Technology.* Floating above the text was the emblem of Qatar, which I had memorized for quite a while during my classes. The name of the nation in English and Arabic surrounding a yellow circle with a sailboat — a dhow, to be specific — and two date palms on a sea nestled between a pair of crossed scimitars. I murmured my appreciation at the bespoke card and I already heard him asking which hotel I would be staying at in Doha.

Grand Hyatt, I replied, and immedi0ately received a flurry of approbation.

Excellent choice, Mrs. Stone. Excellent choice. All the important people in Doha love to hang out at the Hyatt's pools, spas and tennis courts.

I kept silent. That, precisely, had been the intention.

Mr. Al Thani, I see that you are in charge of procurement and technology. That's what I'm here for. One of the companies I run deals with cybertechnology and communications. But what does it mean to be the coordinator?

Hamid, Hamid. Please, Mrs. Stone, my name is Hamid. We may dispense with formalities.

Jessica, Jessica. Please, Mr. Al-Thani, my name is Jessica. We may dispense with formalities. I echoed his words and managed to elicit a light chuckle from him.

It's been a pleasure speaking with you, he said, getting serious for a moment and turning to me. *Jessica, give the business card back for a moment...* I gave him a questioning look and held out the card I still had in my hand. Hamid took it with one hand, pulled out a golden fountain pen from his inner pocket, opened it with a deft twist, wrote a number in the empty space at the bottom of the card and blew gently on it. *Please, Jessica, this is my personal phone number. The number on the card is for the office line, and it goes through the secretary and through too many ears.* I looked at the upgraded card as well. Hamid's handwriting was fluid, yet round and precise. Next to the phone number he also wrote the word *Personal* in small letters and drew a thin line under it.

He went on: *I still owe you an answer. As procurement and technology coordinator, I venture abroad: throughout the Gulf, and on to Egypt, Jordan, Iran, Pakistan, Sudan and India. I listen to their needs, and then I present them with the latest technologies from Western companies. I try to match the suppliers with consumers.*

That set off alarm bells for me and my heart trembled at the golden opportunity. Learning the secret phone numbers of Qatari, Iranian, Jordanian and Saudi intelligence targets was one my priorities. The nature of Hamid's activities also excited my imagination. *Traveling around all kinds of countries, including Iran,* he said nonchalantly, flooding me with thoughts about how to develop this relationship.

I wanted to continue the conversation, but that proved impossible. A tiny air pocket pinned us both back into our seats. Nimble flight attendants asked all the business class passengers to return to their seats and fasten their safety belts until landing.

I relaxed in my seat and talked to myself. *Well done, Jessica, well done, but stay alert. It's too good to be true.*

I muttered to myself in English, following the rules that Shimon drilled into me in English throughout the training. *Mrs. Jessica Stone, you speak in English, sing in English, dream in English, cry in English. Say goodbye to Sally, to Hebrew, to Jerry, to Roy, to Michael. They do not exist for now, until the end of the operation.*

A small vein would swell along my right temple in response to Shimon's mantras. This dictum was particularly maddening. I was furious. I wanted to yell at him, but I knew he was right. Jerry and I whispered in English even in our most intimate moments in Pakistan, when the children were asleep in the other room, when darkness fell over the land, when our doors were locked with four bolts.

When the landing gear struck the runway, many of the people in business class hurried to get up and get organized. In the slight commotion that ensued, Hamid disappeared from my sight, though I searched for him.

I was left with a nagging anguish. It was a wonderful, golden opportunity for me. Every agent's wet dream.

Still, some warning lights flashed at me. The occasion had been created on the initiative of the other party and not on my initiative. The chance came too soon. Hamid was not on the list of people I had learned about in training. Above all, the opportunity that fell on my doorstep was way too good to be true.

Too good to be true, I sat and muttered to myself again and again, *thank the Lord.*

15

9:30 hrs.
Forbidden photography and getting into trouble
at the Grand Hyatt Hotel

Hamad International Airport was spotless and brand-spanking new. It had only opened a few weeks before. It was impossible not to be overcome by its power, beauty, and efficiency. It was clear how it had earned the title awarded by the financial papers: the best airport in the Middle East.

However, for me, it was a battlefield. I walked in eyes open to the dragon's fire-spewing mouth.

The ground crew, modestly but fashionably dressed, hurried towards the business class passengers, each wheeling a duffle or suitcase behind her. My cute purple piece of luggage was served to me with record speed as I walked towards passport control. I looked straight ahead and took a breath before standing in front of the border control officer, this time with Jessica Stone's British passport.

Then my attention was drawn to the left, as most of my fellow business class passengers crowded in front of the huge screens showing the Al Jazeera news broadcast — left in Arabic, right in English. The lead story was about the three teenagers kidnapped in the Etzion Bloc of the West Bank, with a map of the area displayed. The case had led to an international uproar even before I left for my flight. Apparently, there was no connection between it and my mission focused on the Iranian nuclear issue. But in the seething heat of the Middle East, everything touches everything. My heart foretold evil.

I looked around, half looking for Hamid. He was not in the group of business class passengers. I scanned the hall from end to end, then noticed his suit. He was walking away from me towards the VIP line, accompanied by two men in suits who bore twin black leather suitcases for him.

The scene of dozens of people assembling around screens to watch Al Jazeera repeated itself even after I passed passport control. The border control officer examined my face thoroughly, looked at the picture in the passport which he held in his right hand, typed with his left hand, lowered his glasses a little and stared at the screen in front of him for a long time. A few seconds in total, which seemed like minutes to me. Finally, he placed the passport on the table and stamped the first real stamp on a passport loaded with fake ones.

There were also crowds in front of the TV screens in the lobby of the Grand Hyatt, the lovely hotel with the spectacular facade where I was to reside in the coming weeks and which had been carefully chosen — because of the prestigious tennis tournaments held there; because it was especially loved by the elite of Doha; and because, in the secret control rooms of the Mossad in Tel Aviv, every inch of the hotel and its surroundings were being monitored in real time. During training, the adjacent beach was also mentioned as a possible escape route in case of entanglement. Within a few weeks, it would go from being an alternative way to get out of Qatar to an actual rescue operation. Sailing to the heart of the Gulf on a luxury yacht, then taking a speedboat to a merchant vessel secretly owned by an Israeli.

Here, on the wall next to reception, there were four huge screens. Two broadcast in Arabic and English from Al Jazeera, two more in English from the BBC and CNN. Many of the visitors sat in leather armchairs, reading newsflashes on their cell phones. I stood there with everyone, focused on the English-speaking screens, listening to the never-ending flood of reports about the kidnapping of the three teenagers. Things were repeated ad nauseam, until the BBC exclusively broke the news about Salah Sirhan, a Hamas member from Gaza who had left through the Rafah crossing and had since disappeared. An image of his face was prominently displayed: square face, messy bristly beard, prominent mole on the right side of his forehead.

The next morning, I went down to the main lobby about half an hour before breakfast. I was exhausted after the direct flight from London and a sleepless night. Tormented by nightmares, I couldn't keep my eyes closed and I no longer had the patience to sit in the room.

It had been a night of longing for Jerry. I'd tortured myself with questions. Why was I not cuddled up with him now, under cozy blankets in our bedroom? Why did I need all this? I wasn't even a full-fledged Mossad employee. Didn't they have enough skilled agents?

As I drifted towards an answer, I repeated a phrase of Jerry's that echoed in my mind. *You're battle-tested and you have courage, Sally. That's a rare combination.* He added: *I'm proud, Sally, very proud of you. You're a special woman.*

In moments like this, when Jerry and I had been required to be brave, my thoughts went higher and higher, to the loftiest spheres, to the meaning of life. Massive concepts such as vocation and fulfilling a national mission were swirling in my mind. My religious Zionist education served as an excellent basis for these ideas. My *moshavnik* parents pushed me to dream of something bigger, without fear. They taught me that you don't come into the world just like that. Each of us has a role. Acknowledging this gave me strength to do the right thing and to believe, with complete faith, that if I did something not to get a reward or prize, but because I believed in it, I would succeed. *If you set goals for yourself for the benefit of the nation and of society and not just for yourself, you will see blessing and success in all your doings,* my mother used to recite as a mantra.

When I finished these valuable reflections, I came back down to earth, to reality, to the battle between me and myself in the operational matters at hand. Numerous disturbing thoughts flew through my mind. The meeting with Hamid was the result of his stubborn initiative. Why would he give me his personal cell phone only an hour after meeting me? Doubts pertained to Mrs. Stone, a lonely blonde woman in the Qatari capital. There were also minor qualms troubling my mind regarding my primary mission, to get close to key figures in Qatar State Security and the Ministry of Interior. How would one even start?

An efficient waiter appeared the moment I sat down at a table. *One of my bodyguards?* I asked myself instinctively, then immediately put the thought out of my head. *That's not allowed, Sally. It is forbidden.*

I had chosen a table that would allow me to see the entire lobby and, at the same time, close enough to the huge windows through which I could view the spectacular pool complex, the square islands of grass with palm trees planted in the center, and across to the beach. *Bravo to Haggai and his covert teams,* I thought to myself. His 3D visualization in Mikveh Israel also included this fascinating spot.

I needed coffee. Strong, double, lungo. I sipped it slowly, studying the structure of the lobby, comparing my 3D training with the reality on the ground: the location of the visible and hidden security cameras, exits and entrances, the passageway to the tennis courts, the path to the beach, the location of the toilets, the discreet route to the service elevators, the more modest seating areas at the back of the spacious hall. I forced myself to focus on moving from the virtual lobby to the real lobby. Even this preoccupation failed to dim the understanding that crept up through my subconscious to the forefront of my consciousness and awareness. *You're on your own, Sally. All alone. You only have yourself. Many eyes follow you, near and far, but there's no one by your side. Alone in this tiny country which fosters warm relations with terrorist organizations, a country infested with Iranian agents, a country many of whose leaders loathe Israel, a country full of men whose imaginations are sparked by the sight of a lonely blonde.*

It was in no way akin to the operation in Pakistan, where I was not the lead agent. Jerry was by my side most of the time, looking at me, reassuring me, touching my hand when necessary, whispering a tip, sharing his vast operational experience, kicking me under the table, stopping me from forbidden emotional reactions.

With this storm still running through me, I noticed an unusual crowd near a table in the back of the lobby. I immediately recognized that the table had been placed in a dim and far corner, under the security camera. Three men in red-and-white keffiyehs sat at the table with their heads together. Four other men stood around the table, facing out. I thought they would sit down shortly, but they remained standing, scanning the surroundings. It was transparent; they were security men and bodyguards. I pulled out my thin and handsome MacBook from my bag, which could also capture images from the back, placed it on the coffee table at an angle that would allow me to view the far table in the back, and began typing vigorously.

After less than a minute, a young man emerged from the elevators, holding an unusually thick attaché case. He quickly walked towards the group. The bodyguards stepped in and looked towards the trio at the table. One of them raised a hand in greeting to the young man, stood up, rolled back the kaffiyeh on his head a little and stepped forward for a traditional hug. This fraction of a second was enough for me.

The man who stood up to meet the newcomer was undoubtedly Salah Sirhan, with the square face and the mole on his forehead, who disappeared less than a day after the story broke about the kidnapping of the teenagers. He'd absconded from Gaza through the Rafah crossing, and all the Western networks reported that he was a key suspect. The recognition stunned me in the microsecond when his face was visible, my blood roiled. The entire world was looking for him, but here he was, with me in the lobby, in a territory infested by Iranian agents. Conflicting thoughts and ideas churned in me like a tempest in the heart of the ocean. *I must not report. I must report. It's dangerous. It's my duty. It's a calculated risk. It goes against Shimon's rules. It's a reality. I must ignore them. It's easy. It could endanger me and my mission. Someone might be plotting to hand over the kidnapped boys to the Iranians. That's complete nonsense. Handing them over to the Iranians would be a major national disaster. It's none of my business, I'm here for other reasons.*

I keenly felt Jerry's absence in those moments. I had no doubt that he would have held my hand in his, closed the laptop with his other and offer me a fake smile of reprimand. I could guess the next sentence Jerry would whisper, a staccato imperative: *We get up from here and forget what we saw.*

But Jerry wasn't there, and I was infuriated. Salah Sirhan was a scoundrel with Jewish blood on his hands. Added to this was the connection made by the BBC commentators between his disappearance from Gaza and the kidnapping of the boys, as well as the suspicion that the boys would be handed over to the Iranians. Ron Arad had been shot down over Lebanon in 1986 and, three decades later, his fate was still unknown. What if there were three more of them, God forbid?

All these conflicting thoughts were pushed aside by several facts: the guy with the thick beard did not look Qatari or Palestinian. The particularly heavy briefcase was placed before Sirhan. The men behind the keffiyehs clung to sunglasses even in the darkness of the lobby and made an effort to hide their faces from the people around.

My laptop mouse flicked teasingly at the Gmail icon on the desktop. I decided to click on it and drafted an email to my good friend, Gretchen in Berlin. A long and gossipy text about the great flight from London to Doha and my intention to go skiing in a few months. Every fourteenth word in the email was genuine. The long and chatty message was intended to convey one short sentence that floated between the lines: *Salah Sirhan is in the lobby of the Grand Hyatt in Doha, surrounded by men; he has received a heavy briefcase, potentially full of cash.*

I signed the email with emojis of hearts and smiles — and four innocent-looking squares. They were four images, with sophisticated, uncrackable encryption, of the protagonists of the scene, captured by my versatile MacBook and not visible on any control screen in Tel Aviv.

There was no soft-pedaling my actions. The truth was sharp and harsh. I violated explicit instructions and cautions that I'd memorized over and over again. I was endangering myself, I was endangering the entire operation, I was endangering the Mossad. I could scold myself, but at the same time I was convinced that many operational decisions stem from emotions. Sentiment is more determinative than cold and disciplined consideration.

This dilemma came up in several of my arguments with Jerry. He insisted that in operational activity one must completely neutralize emotion and act coldly and detached from any sentiment. I always denied it.

Now the moment of truth had arrived, and I was no longer sure of anything. I ordered another cup of coffee and proceeded to vigorously type my instructions to Helen in London. Adrenaline was surging in me, but I had to look like a relaxed businesswoman killing time until breakfast. When I got halfway through the document, I noticed the silhouette of someone standing next to me, just at the point that allowed him to look at the laptop screen. He waited for me to finish typing and look at him. I realized this was no waiter. I raised my head with a half-smile. He was a tall, broad-shouldered man wearing a suit. He gave me a polite smile.

A storm arose in my mind and body. Had this man appeared by chance, just as I finished typing the encrypted message? I didn't believe in coincidences.

Hello, Mrs. Stone, he said as he leaned forward, his suit jacket opening enough so I could see the butt of his gun in a leather holster. The glinting steel hit my eyes and sent my pulse soaring; but in that split second I also saw an employee ID attached to his belt. It was the hotel security officer. *I'd appreciate it if you'd accompany me, it won't take long,* he said, and even the little grin was wiped from his face. I got up from my seat, violating another rule from my training. I glanced out of the corner of my eye at the security cameras covering the corner where I was sitting.

Did the good guys somewhere see and understand what was happening to me?

16

11:06 hrs.
A secret room in the Hyatt, a tight ball burning
in my chest

The security officer strode briskly towards the long wall at the end of the lobby, making sure I stayed in his line of sight. I really didn't care for this situation anymore. When we got near the wall, a heavy curtain reaching the full height of the wall began to move. Beyond it yawned a long and wide corridor. This hallway had not appeared in any of the briefings or in any of the virtual training that I'd undergone at Mikveh Israel. That fact bothered me a lot.

A second after we walked in, I heard a rustle. I glanced back. The two parts of the curtain moved towards each other, shutting behind me and cutting me off from the control screens in Tel Aviv. At the edge of my throat, various quips that I thought of addressing to the man leading me into the unknown rose and fell. Some were assertive, some jocular. But I held my peace. I reminded myself that I was a British citizen on a business trip; there was no reason to feel suspicion or pressure.

I counted in my heart the number of doors we passed. After the sixth door, the security officer stood in front of a double door with bright metal decorations, knocked on it twice and gestured for me to enter.

The door was opened immediately by another man wearing a suit. *Please, Mrs. Stone, come in.* I felt as if there was a tight ball burning in my chest. My pulse quickened, but I tried to keep my lips from stretching into a slight smile. After three steps, I easily recognized Hamid Al Thani sitting behind a heavy walnut table. He raised his head from a pile of documents, smiled, stood up jauntily and walked towards me with his hand outstretched. I breathed a sigh of relief. The ball was melting away. Of all the things I remembered about my encounter with him, foremost were his well-groomed nails and that fraction of a moment when the mask of self-confidence peeled away and I saw his vulnerability, longing for a listening ear.

Please, please, what will you drink, Mrs. Stone?

Water, only water. And while you're at it, I would appreciate an explanation of what I'm doing here, I replied in an assertive tone. One of the men in the room hastened to bring a silver tray holding a long-necked crystal jug adorned with gold. Next to it stood two matching crystal glasses. There was also a large coffee pot on the table and porcelain cups next to it.

Everyone else in the room quickly moved away from the table and scattered.

Hamid and I were left alone in the room, and it felt isolated. The smell in the air was of fresh plaster. This whole wing was completely new, so it had not appeared in any briefing and was not part of Haggai's playground.

This is a fine example of how the most thorough training and the most detailed intelligence can lead you astray, I noted to myself. After all, such a mistake could cost me my life.

Alongside the unpleasant odor of the renovation, there was a present, penetrating smell of sweet coffee, the unmistakable Qatari version, unique in taste and aroma thanks to the addition of cinnamon, saffron, sugar and cardamom.

First of all, Mrs. Stone, I owe you an apology for kidnapping you from the lobby. Maybe we were too dramatic, Hamid said as he chuckled and pressed his outstretched palms together in a jovial, apologetic gesture. *I also owe you an apology for disappearing upon landing at the airport. I had to be on time for a well-attended meeting with our interior minister, who also happens to be my older brother. You know you can't be late for meetings with the minister.* I was about to answer, but Hamid continued without taking a breath. *I've apologized twice, but I must do it once more. Next time I promise to host you in a place a little less spartan than the new office wing of a hotel.*

I smiled at him, effectively clearing the small cloud that was standing in the room. The brother of the minister of the interior, responsible for military intelligence, who had taken up a significant part of my training.

This also sounds too good to be true, I told myself.

After sipping the water and the coffee, Hamid said: *There are no secrets on Google, and there are no secrets in Doha, either. I understand that you have a real estate firm in central London and a company that deals in advanced technology in the area of information security. The papers are cheering for you, too, Mrs. Stone — sorry, Jessica. You have fallen to me from heaven. I am interested in both fields and both of your companies.*

I smiled a little. *Not information security, Mr. Al Thani — sorry, Hamid — but defensive and offensive cybertechnology.*

Hamid's English was excellent. Two degrees above the English proficiency of most of the figures Jerry and I met in Pakistan. One grade above my excellent English. He knew the difference between the two areas of expertise and had also mastered the nuances of cybertechnology. I realized that he had done his homework and absorbed every morsel of information online regarding me and the two companies I ran. I assumed that he or his men also made several phone calls to the office in London. The investment in Helen had paid off.

As soon as he gave me a chance to speak, I complimented him. *Your English is excellent; you even have a hint of a British accent.*

He looked at me with satisfaction, his pride apparent. *Four years at the London School of Economics take their toll, even on a mediocre student like me*, he said, trying to be modest. It was clear that when he talked to me face-to-face, he had no inclination to stroke his ego. I was more silent than I am used to in such social situations. It was evident that it was important for Hamid to lead the conversation. He did everything to quickly end the small talk phase and get to other topics. I had no idea what those other subjects were and, once again, a slight crack opened in my image as a fortune-telling sorceress.

The following morning, at a meeting in the lobby near the hotel's tennis courts, it became clear what issues Hamid wanted to discuss. Again, I was wrong.

I get the impression that you are one who knows how to be discreet, he said.

In real estate and cybertechnology, it's impossible to succeed without absolute discretion, I replied, adding: *I hope you don't think women are any less discreet than men.*

Half-an-hour later, we were already in the middle of a tennis match. He had strong opening strokes and was well-versed in techniques, but I led in most of the games. That was intentional. It was important that in and around the hotel they start talking about the British blonde who beats men on the court.

As it turned out, my random meeting with Hamid served as a short-cut, saving me a lot of tennis matches. It opened up possibilities I never dreamed of and, in retrospect, also shortened the time of separation from Roy and Michael. All this in the first two days of my stay in Qatar.

It was a goldmine, in all senses of the word. Hamid was personally connected to the richest businessmen in Doha. By virtue of his family affiliation, he also personally knew generals, members of the government and senior government officials. By virtue of being a procurement and technology coordinator, he came and went from countries I wanted to know more about. In addition, it was clear that he was widely loved and respected, not only as a member of the Al Thani dynasty.

Bringing *Iacocca* on the flight thus proved to be an inspired move. However, along with the fast-paced developments, there were small latent threats that I hadn't yet noticed.

17

14:30 hrs.
Durrat complex, strategic dating in the
hornet's nest

Hamid seemed thoughtful and troubled even after beating me in the last game. He lingered before entering the lobby by the tennis courts, moved away a little, made an apologetic gesture with his head and started shouting into his cell phone. A high-volume conversation with nervous hand movements. I suddenly recognized something else in the polite, refined, delicate-fingered guy.

After about a minute, he came back and approached me, faking a smile and muttering apologies. We sat panting at a small round table for two. I ordered a double espresso. This time Hamid settled for mineral water with ice.

This is the best champagne there is, he said, waving his crystal glass aloft.

Trouble in paradise? I said jokingly towards Hamid, trying to create some kind of intimacy.

The words cut through him like a laser beam. His body froze. He slowly raised his head and sent me a meaningful look. *You are a smart woman.*

It took me several seconds until I connected the sophisticated question with the name of the chapter in *Iacocca*. I almost hit my forehead with an open palm to express my embarrassment or to chastise myself for the hasty and insensitive statement. *Stupid, stupid*, I told myself. But I held back.

I prayed that the topic would pass from our conversation, but it didn't. Hamid did not want to move on. He was desperately looking for a sympathetic ear — not Qatari, not Muslim, not part of the quagmire of his aristocratic family. It was quite clear that he was desperate if, after such a brief, random acquaintance, he was willing to share with me — if only by implication — his frustrations, his troubles, the problems he had in Doha and London. He even sent a modest hint about an intimate matter, one that in Qatar could also end in tragedy. *It's not trouble in paradise, it's trouble here and now,* I thought to myself and supported my chin with my left fist, forcefully preventing myself from blurting out an inappropriate answer.

You seem like a good woman to me, he said suddenly, without any prior preparation, adding the compliment of the good woman to the compliments of the wise and discreet woman. He said these things with his gaze lowered, then raised his eyes and fixed them, moist and sad, on mine.

I had already reached my second cup of coffee and drank it as slowly as possible. Hamid had already finished off the entire water jug, but neither of us made any signs of rushing anywhere.

My company, Gstone, could be of interest to your brother, I said, trying to break the heavy silence that stood between us.

Hamid replied with a huge smile: *I have four brothers, and all of them will be interested in your technology. Which one do you mean?*

Oh, I didn't know you had so many important siblings. I meant your older brother. You said he was the interior minister, if I understood correctly. I would be happy to meet him.

Hamid thought a little, then answered: *No, Jessica, don't meet with him. I have a much better idea for your business.* He waited a bit, trying to draw it out, but he was enthusiastic and in a hurry to get to the point. *I will ask that you be included in a maiden flight that leaves the day after tomorrow from Doha to the beautiful Durrat resort complex in Bahrain. We are inaugurating a new Airbus line that we purchased, and launching a tourist route to the magical southern shores of Bahrain. Durrat is a magnificent location, like something out of a dream, and many foreign businessmen will be on the flight. It will be a day of fun at the expense of the state.*

My thoughts were running wild. I immediately understood that

Hamid was giving me a dream opportunity, but I was not required to use my imagination. He began enumerating, with his rapid, enthusiastic patter, the wonders of the flight for me. *Think, Jessica. All the elite of Doha in one fell swoop, not to mention some of the important foreign businessmen staying at this hotel. You can gobble them all up with one bite,* he said in a triumphant tone and demonstrated the opportunity with a theatrical gulp of water. He was pleased with his own brilliance.

Hamid's enthusiastic descriptions were modest compared to reality.

The event was the launch of a line of new, fresh-out-of-the-package Airbus A320 airplanes purchased by Qatar in a huge deal, and the inauguration of a domestic tourism route for the rich and connected. The destination was the Durrat complex, built on a fan of artificial islands designed in the shape of fish.

On the flight were the elite of the Qatari government, military officers in uniform, local businessmen in custom-made suits, military attachés and foreign businessmen who lived in Qatar or were staying there for extended periods. Most of them were guests of the Grand Hyatt. All these were also joined by about twenty of the bored wives of the local VIPs, some wearing a niqab, the traditional veil that covers the whole head and face, except for the eyes. Some wore looser traditional clothing. There were also four children with them who did not seem overly interested.

I looked around and, for a moment, I felt like I was in Imelda Marcos's shoe closet. Treasures upon treasures. The flight was full of everyone I could dream of for the sake of my mission. *Shimon will think I'm delusional,* I thought to myself, imagining the moment when I would sit with him at the Mossad headquarters and describe my Bahraini excursion. After all, when he had tried to persuade me to accept the mission, he kept coming back to the same idea: *You have a rare talent for making personal connections quickly and efficiently...*

At a mini-cocktail held in the terminal, I quickly became a star. Hamid introduced me to more and more people, and then — a real treat — he led me to a tête-à-tête with one of his four brothers, Colonel Nasser Al Thani, Head of State Security, Qatar's intelligence and security bureau. Subordinate to the Ministry of Interior, it was responsible for internal security and intelligence as well as foreign espionage. I had memorized that, getting to know him well. I could recite every detail about him fluently. I knew his height. I looked into his face from a distance of six feet, and even reached out to his extended virtual hand. Yet I asked naive, really stupid questions. About his rank. About the duties of a colonel in the Qatari army. About the multitude of insignia and decorations on his chest. I displayed complete ignorance when I clearly knew all the answers to each of the questions.

During my training, I learned every detail of his life, his habits, his political positions, his ambitions, his weaknesses, his family members, his betrayals, his secret connections with Iranian intelligence and the web of corruption linking him to the Iranian steel industry. I could also recite in my sleep the names, ranks and positions of three of his friends in the Revolutionary Guards. When they tested me in Tel Aviv, I knew how to describe even the strange tic that ran through his right nostril. Even his avatar had it. But in reality, it looked even stranger and scarier. *I heard you play tennis better than men,* the colonel teased me in excellent English. *It would be an honor for me to play with you,* he said, the right side of his nose crinkling up.

Sincerely, Colonel, the honor would be mine. I think I can offer you a significant challenge, I replied with a smile. *We might also be able to talk about the technology developed by my company. It's unfortunate that only private companies benefit from its capabilities. Our technology is innovative and revolutionary. It can help countries guard their oil and natural gas infrastructure and prevent unnecessary wars.*

The mention of natural gas was a powerful guided missile, fired straight to Nasser's heart. This touched the bare nerve of the Qataris — their paranoia about their natural gas reserves, 850 trillion cubic feet, third in the world.

When it was time for boarding, Hamid paid another debt. He held my elbow gently and directed me towards a tall and relatively older man. *Mrs. Stone, please meet Mr. Majed Al Thani, Minister of the Interior.*

Minister of the Interior and your brother, I said defiantly.

Minister of the Interior and his elder brother, emphasized Majed, unclear whether he was chiding his brother or mocking himself. Still, he turned to me with a smile on his face. The avatar had been accurate, an almost frightening resemblance. Majed was dressed in a starched white dishdasha, the traditional jalabiya made of light wool. On his head was a keffiyeh, also white. He had a pleasant look, very tanned skin and a wrinkled forehead. His posture was impressive, his handshake a little too strong. I knew every detail about him as well, including his corrupt deal with one of the senior officers of the Revolutionary Guards.

Mrs. Stone is here to promote her business, Hamid told his brother. *Her company sells fascinating technology. I think you'll find her very interesting.*

Hamid was more efficient than he could have imagined. It was important for him to impress me with his connections, his influence, his access to the elite of the elite. I still couldn't figure out why he was trying so hard.

I got the impression that he was smarter, more educated and sharper than his two brothers. Nevertheless, one of them was an important minister, the other a colonel in the army, and Hamid was only a 'procurement and technology coordinator'.

As time passed, the mystery intensified and deepened.

On the way to the plane, I quickly met Hamid's two other brothers, Hassan and Ali. Both were significantly younger than him and married. During the next day they were revealed to be devoid of style, devoid of tact, devoid of Western education. Still, both bore the title of deputy minister. Someone or something had left Hamid behind, outside the circles of power. My suspicions continued to grow.

Hassan and Ali turned out to be wild men. Rude, noisy young people, disrespectful to the flight crew and others in the group, smoking even when they were asked not to, disturbing those around them, reacting violently when they didn't like something.

My intuition screamed that Hamid's strange status had to somehow be related to the secret mission which had brought me to this hornets' nest.

I was right, although I still had no idea why and how.

18

Another drama in the air, somewhere between Doha and Durrat

The next two days were heaven for forging critical connections, even as I had to carefully edge my way around gaping chasms which endangered my person and my mission. The flight turned out to be a more significant event than I could ever have hoped for. The passengers were an uncommon assortment of Doha's best and brightest. In addition, each acquaintance I made advanced my chances of succeeding in the mission for whose sake I'd willingly walked into an active volcano.

The atmosphere was relaxed, and it became even more so when we arrived for a day at the picturesque beaches of Durrat, especially when we settled into our opulent suites next to Golden Beach. The somewhat tight social circles loosened up. The guests went to the beaches and to the swimming pools with a complete sense of freedom, away from their onerous positions, away from the discretion and caution required in military command centers or government offices. My personal Eden.

They all mingled with each other. The doors in the hotel worked overtime at night; but even during the day, connections were made and impromptu groups gathered to converse and laugh. Military personnel mixed with civilians, foreign businessmen associated with local officials — and London's Mrs. Jessica Stone interacted with them all. Even with the four children who'd come along. Playing tennis helped, maybe being blonde helped too.

However, Hamid helped more than anything else. He was indefatigable in arranging meetings for me. He did it for his own reasons;

he had no way of knowing what my reasons were. After returning from the glittering event, two more days would pass until Hamid found the time and place to amaze me, to deepen our relationship and to reveal another layer of skin, delicate and wounded.

But to get to that conversation, I had to survive three hours of terror in the sky. Airborne horror again. It was perfect déjà vu. Closing the cosmic circle, one might say, of the Gulfstream trauma. Otherwise, it would be hard to explain how, for the second time in four months, I found myself aboard a plane as it experienced a mechanical emergency. Again, it was a technical fault that was discovered in the air before landing — but that where the similarity ended. This time it was a real fault and a real danger. This was neither a prank nor a malicious psychological test by my teammates.

My fellow passengers were quite ill-prepared for the challenge: sunburnt, pleasure-drunk and exhausted after the never-ending succession of attractions, meals and parties lavished upon us, leaving us not a minute to rest.

We had been in the air less than forty minutes when, as our landing in Doha approached, disaster threatened to strike. The wave of apprehension on the plane started in the section where the uniformed military sat, passing through the government officials and finally reaching the area where I was sitting, next to the mothers and children. I pulled out the English-Arabic phrasebook I'd practiced with in Tel Aviv, trying to interpret the words and phrases whispered, then spoken, even shouted throughout the cabin.

It was clear that they were talking about an aeronautic malfunction and a delay in landing, but that didn't require a great command of Arabic. From the plane's loudspeaker came a series of messages in Arabic and English, which elicited screams of frustration from some of the mothers and heartbreaking cries from the four children. The cascading messages came out one after the other at an unbelievable pace, as if the flight crew had stockpiled them silently and then fired them all one after another, with barely a minute between them.

We anticipate a slight delay before landing...
Our landing will be delayed by half-an-hour, please remain calm...
We ask all passengers to sit in their seats, buckle up and wait for instructions. Please stay calm...

Every message that came out of the loudspeakers was accompanied by a heartfelt *Inshallah*. Each update raised the level of anxiety, increased the intensity of crying and worried voices, fueling the children's outburst even more. The initial forty minutes of the flight were well behind us, and the extra half-hour the pilot spoke of had also passed.

Two of the mothers sitting next to me screamed at the flight attendants that they had to take their children to the bathroom. Even by the door of the lavatory at the front of the plane, where the generals and VIPs sat, an impossible queue stretched as tensions were growing. Absurdly, the plane actually flew smoothly. There was no turbulence, no air pockets, no disturbing vibrations, no unusual noise. A smooth, pleasant flight, one might say, were it not for the ominous broadcasts from the flight deck.

The more the children wailed, the more their concerned mothers cried. What really stuck in my craw was the disconnection between the front of the plane and the back, where the women and children were seated — as if they were aboard two separate aircraft. As an Israeli living in the developed world, this stung me, to the point of pain.

I looked for Hamid and his two older brothers. They were the most senior figures on the plane. My gaze wandered up the rows until it landed on the epaulets of the heroic colonel with many decorations on his chest, Nasser Al Thani. He sat in his place, petrified, his dark complexion turning gray and white. His eyes were closed and his lips were shaking. Maybe he was praying.

Two seats away sat Majed, the eldest of the Al Thani brothers, the honorable and all-powerful minister. At one point, he got up, walked towards the cockpit door and knocked on it. The door opened a crack. There was a short conversation with a lot of hand movements that indicated stress and nerves, then the minister returned to his place. He looked worried.

I knew myself. There was no way I would stay in my seat and do nothing in such a situation. I released my seatbelt and walked briskly towards the front of the plane. Lots of eyes followed my determined stride. None of them realized that I actually suffered from a fear of heights. I arrived near the seat of the huddled official, bent down and whispered: *Minister, I understand that there is a problem. The children and women need to be calmed down somehow. I am ready to help with whatever is required.*

Majed raised his eyes, shocked and startled. *We do have a problem, Mrs. Stone. They cannot deploy the nose landing gear,* he replied in a kind of rare tribute to Qatari society. *The solution is a belly landing or a water landing. We will get out of this alive, but it is not a simple matter at all... Any assistance you can offer to the mothers and children would be a kindness. Please do as you see fit.* Majed's English was quite good. He also controlled his speech and seemed much braver than his brother, the colonel. Many eyes followed the whispering between us.

Thank you for the information, I'll do what I can, I replied quickly, then headed back to my seat. The children's bawling had increased, until it sounded like one continuous wail.

To my right sat Noor, the pregnant wife of the heroic Colonel Nasser, and her seven-year-old daughter, Salma. To my left sat Rittal, the minister's relatively older wife, with Ahmed, about the same age as his cousin. In the row behind me sat two ten-year-old girls, Jamila and Amal, who were silently weeping. Their mother, Yasmin, was paralyzed with fear. She was the wife of the Minister of Transport, Abed Al Atrash, a man who knew everything the State of Israel would like to know about maritime traffic in the Persian Gulf. He was not on the flight.

In my homework on Qatar, I learned that polygamy in the peninsular principality is more common compared to the other Gulf countries; some men there have three, four or even more wives. But here there were three wives of three men, and I became extremely curious. Were their husbands monogamists, or were these simply the favorite spouses of each man, respectively?

From that moment, I became a kindergarten teacher for four children screaming in terror and a nanny for three frightened mothers. Noor spoke incredibly good English. I asked her if she could help me with the translation. She agreed. I offered a smile and a kind touch to Jamila and Amal, encouraging them to move to the free seats in our row. Then I sat down with my knees on the floor of the plane and put my cell phone on the seat. It was in flight mode, but it had some children's games and cartoons that I'd saved for the benefit for my friend Ronit's kids. Noor helped with the translation and explained each of the games. I created a kind of competition between them. The cries slowly subsided.

A hysterical flight attendant demanded that I go back to my seat, but she calmed down when she noticed the absolute silence that prevailed in the children's section. She gave me a small grin and turned to deal with the cursing and urgency in the line to the bathroom.

The children were besotted with the blonde nanny who suddenly began to play with them and relate to their plight. Some of them tried to make an impression and spoke the few words of English they had learned in school. When I exhausted the digital games, I moved on to tell them a story about brave children on some fictional flight. I spoke quietly. I ad-libbed. I improvised. I connected the tale I wove about the brave children on the plane to the stories that I used to tell Roy and Michael. It somehow worked. Whenever I paused to take a breath, I stroked their heads in turn. Ahmed, then Salma, then Alma, then Jamila. They looked at me gratefully. Happily, they understood most of my story in English. Noor helped me translate the rest.

After about twenty minutes, which seemed like an eternity, there was another futile announcement about landing delays and another idle request for the passengers to stay calm and in their seats.

The children remained quiet and close to me, asking to hear another story, which yielded another quarter of an hour of silence. The three mothers stared at me with adoring thanks. Under the auspices of the nightmare on high, a friendship was born between three Qatari mothers, devout Muslims all, and a strange, blonde Western woman — an outsider.

However, the deepest alliance was formed with Noor. Two wives, two mothers, two partners in covert contempt for the colonel's cowardice. She acted as an interpreter. She was the link between me and the terrified children — and she happened to be the frustrated wife of my main target, determined before I left. Nasser was responsible for internal and external intelligence and espionage, along with what we called in the briefings 'his steel startup in Ahvaz'.

I'm not sure how long it took, but I had to get up for a moment to stretch my legs which had started to fall asleep. As I straightened up, I looked back at the men's section. Colonel Nasser was still praying. He was in complete shock. Nothing but a ragdoll wearing a uniform, cut off from everything going on around him. Majed looked straight at me and gave a thumbs-up as a sign of thanks and approval.

Hamid gave me a small grin, clasping his palms together to indicate gratitude much as he conveyed contrition. There was something cute about the way he smiled, reacted and communicated.

The plane continued to glide silently in a circle. The minutes ticked by one after another. Loud and even violent confrontations festered by the lavatory. Hamid's two younger brothers were at the center of the shouting, a maelstrom of agitation, cursing and raised hands.

19

10:10 hrs.
The women form an alliance in the air, as the
seeds of betrayal are sown

I sent a small smile back to the men's section and had reassumed my post as the flying kindergarten teacher when the PA system crackled to life again. I already recognized the sound of the beginning of an address coming from the speakers. I wondered what stupid idle message would play now. To my surprise, it was actually a calming call. *Ladies and gentlemen, we are preparing for landing. The problem with the landing gear has been fixed, praise Allah. We will land, Inshallah, in a few minutes. We ask everyone to take their seats and fasten their safety belts.*

Three hours of anxiety came to an end. I rose, returned to my seat, closed my eyes and stopped the tears. My calves seemed to disappear, my thighs burned with thousands of pinpricks, and from my knees came a searing pain that hit me in waves, waxing and waning with the rhythm of my heartbeat.

Suddenly I felt a hand gently grasping my left shoulder. It was Rittal, who looked into my eyes and was silent. She was grateful. Later on, she would become a friend — in a sense — and I would be invited to visit her home. The visits would take place once Majed had left for work.

A little while later, I felt another hand on my right shoulder. Yasmin imitated Rittal's gesture. She looked deeply into my eyes and thanked me quietly: *Shukran, shukran...* She seemed to know only snippets of English.

Last but not least, Noor stood up — defying the rules — and I rose to meet her. She hugged me for a long time. I felt her belly tightening against my stomach. It seemed to me that I also felt the movements of the fetus in her womb. Noor didn't say a word. She just tightened her embrace more and brushed her nose. She wept, then raised her head a little and kissed my hair.

I closed my eyes as I sat down once more. I needed a window of time alone. To breathe a sigh of relief, to relax, to digest the three hours that had passed, to understand what happened to me operationally during this interval, which no intelligence expert could have prepared for.

However, instead of relaxing and analyzing the situation, anger began to develop in me. I was furious with myself. How was it possible that in all this drama, which could have ended in the worst possible way, I'd taken care of four other children without giving a second of thought to my own?

Twenty minutes later I fell deep into another seat. This time it was a luxury lounge chair made of leather in the arrivals hall of Hamad Airport. I put both hands over my eyes. I became engrossed in the black cloud deep down inside me and entered into a kind of meditation which turned the absolute blackness into purple, yellow and blue clouds intertwined.

I couldn't say how much time passed until I removed my palms and opened my eyes, surrendering them to the blinding light of the terminal.

Hamid sat in the padded armchair in front of me, waiting silently and patiently. There was something new in the look he gave me. *My dear Jessica, I already told you that you are a good, smart and discreet woman. What more can I say now?*

This was his way of flattering, saying thank you, implying that our relationship had gone up a notch. His question was worth more than any other superlative. Our relationship, which was only four days old, had become tighter and deeper.

Another day would pass, unbearably long hours, until Hamid and I would be together again, alone, in a closed room. Until we sat facing each other, away from prying eyes, out of the range of security cameras, beyond the effective range of eavesdropping sensors. He was no secret agent, but he had mastered all the tricks of the trade, and he maintained iron discipline to allow us to meet again in the new and hidden section of the Grand Hyatt.

Your performance on the plane was amazing, Jessica. You managed to highlight how cowardly my brother the colonel is, and how rude and mean my two younger brothers are. Resentment and contempt for his brother added to the mystery of his junior position — despite his wisdom, despite his education, despite his style.

This time there were several trays on the table. Lots of water, fruit and crackers. As the conversation continued, they also brought in dishes of food under silver cloches. An aromatic mixture of thyme, mint, cinnamon and saffron rose from them, which whetted my appetite. Hamid tried to find out what I prefer to eat.

Don't order anything else for me. I'll follow your lead, I replied.

Underneath the silver cloches were the best Qatari delicacies. Majboos rice, chicken thighs, tomatoes and onions. A plate full of zucchini stuffed with rice, swimming in a lake of yogurt and redolent with garlic and mint. Two plates of harees, a ground meat dish mixed with wheat grains. In a fleeting moment, I went from indifferent to ravenous. It was the first time since taking off from Heathrow that my appetite roared back to life. *I'm starving,* I apologized.

I devoured the detectable dishes to the last crumb. Hamid looked at me amused. He held knife and fork with his delicate fingers and skillfully separated different food components on his plate. Chicken separately, rice separately, vegetables separately. I followed his obsessive-compulsive dining, still focused on my own bingeing.

Beyond hunger, there was deliberate intent in it. Sharing a meal is just one operative technique to form a closer bond with a person of interest. I knew it intuitively, I knew it experientially, I knew it well from the training over the last few months. It always worked, and it worked this time too. When our plates were nearly licked clean, Hamid pulled his chair towards one of the corners of the empty hall where we sat. Then he motioned for me to do the same. I sat down in front of him. Chair to chair, no table between us.

That's better. This is an ideal location for a tête-à-tête, Hamid said and sent me a small, sad smile. *I will begin with a small confession,* he continued almost in a whisper as if, even in this remote corner, in this hidden room, after all the evasive maneuvers, he was afraid that he would be heard.

I feel we hit it off right away, you and I, Hamid began. It sounded like a speech he'd been preparing for quite a while. *I have never encountered such lightning chemistry in my life. You can fly to Europe for years and never have an interesting or meaningful meeting, or you can have such an encounter in a single flight. In the meantime, Jessica, I also did some homework on you, on your businesses, on the generous help you give to refugees and the needy. It's certainly admirable.* I looked at him with a small smile on my lips and a curious look in my eyes. *Getting to know you, Jessica, fills me with happiness,* Hamid continued in the same breath. *But it's important for me to be honest with you and put the truth on the table. I have been looking for a long time for a relationship like ours.*

I'm doing this because I need your help. Some personal help, which I can only get from someone who is not a religious Muslim, who is not involved in the quagmire of Qatari politics and does not belong to my nosy family. My intuition say you can help.

Here it comes, I told myself. *Here comes someone who has left no trace in the training, the briefings, the background materials of the ruling family. Hamid, procurement and technology coordinator, flew under the radar of all the agents, investigators, eavesdroppers, professional hackers from Unit 8200 and sleuths digging up background information.*

I listened to his every word and remained silent even after he finished speaking. Silence is golden. It was clear he had a lot more to say.

What an understatement, indeed.

20

8:30 hrs.
In the hidden wing of the Hyatt,
a shocking secret emerges

Almost immediately, Hamid solved the mystery of why the chapter 'Trouble in Paradise' in *Iacocca* meant so much to him. The issue which weighed so heavily on him was homosexuality. A relatively easy topic for Western ears, a matter of life and death in a country that operates according to the principles of Sharia and judges its citizens according to these laws.

However, Hamid did not want to have a moral, philosophical discussion about being gay. He immediately moved on to practical aspects and detailed what was bothering him. He flitted from one topic to another. As he spoke, I remained silent for the most part, nodding my head, murmuring words of sympathy, tearing up, blowing my nose repeatedly until Hamid pulled out a folded, ironed cloth handkerchief from his pocket. Like Western gentlemen of old.

His trust in me was absolute. He told me about the partial ostracism from the ruling family because he refused to marry a girl who had been affianced to him. This brought shame on his entire family who had to endure menacing speculations implying his demurral stemmed from his sexual orientation.

This also explained why his uncouth and uneducated younger brothers stalked the halls of power while he was limited to the un- glamorous job title emblazoned on his business card. *Procurement and Technology Coordinator*, he once again spat with contempt at the role he'd been forced to accept, which illustrated how all his brothers, cousins and even his distant relatives were allowed to take part in a huge orgy of nepotism — holding various government jobs with creative names of real or fabricated positions; wielding titles and assignments which served only to guarantee huge salaries, business cards, luxurious offices and limitless expense accounts.

The conversation continued for another three hours, which passed in no time at all. Hamid turned out to be a wonderful storyteller. His linguistic and intellectual capacity meant that I neither wanted to nor could stop listening to him — or tearing up at his predicament. His English was somewhat literary, colorful and deep, but this was neither fiction nor fantasy. Hamid told his life story, full of pain, which could have become — without adaptation, without filters — a cult series on Netflix.

Hamid's partner and beloved was Karim, a distant relative, only twenty-four years old, who was 'suspected of homosexual perversion', as the Qatari authorities put it. Other calumnies were heaped on him, including false accusations of pedophilia. All these swelled into a monstrous indictment. If he had been tried according to Sharia law, he could have suffered a long prison term, flogging, or even sentenced to death by stoning.

So Karim had to disappear. When the authorities interrogated his associates, they all repeated the same rumor: Karim had fled Qatar to an unknown destination. The authorities did not buy this answer and initiated an exhaustive search for him.

The truth was that he'd sought refuge in a safehouse, an apartment in Al Wakrah, about ten miles south of Doha. Hamid and three of his confidants were the only ones who knew about it, the only ones who knew how to avoid any surveillance, the only ones who could reach him, get supplies to him and see to his needs. And this is how the mystery of Hamid's operational abilities was also resolved; my suspicion that he was part of a dark and dangerous system disappeared.

Karim's descent to the underground lasted seven months. His and Hamid's working assumption was that the moment he left the hiding place he would be captured and arrested. In Al Wakrah, there were too many suspicious types in plainclothes who were sniffing around and asking questions.

During those months, Hamid flew to various cities in Europe, as his job title provided a good cover. From each of these waystations, he proceeded secretly to one destination: London.

Specifically London? I asked in one of the few occasions when I broke my silence.

Hamid's answer spanned over an hour of excitement, his tears and mine, and silence from both of us. The dramatic heights expressed over the previous two-hour conversation seemed trivial compared to the next chapter in the story revealed to me. *About two months before the accusations against Karim exploded, we flew to London together and to initiate a surrogacy procedure with my sperm and an egg donation,* said Hamid, choking back tears. The loud crying continued until I got up from my chair, went over to him and grabbed his shoulders, trying in vain to calm him down, to convey warmth and empathy. The surrogate, it turned out, was a British woman, a resident of London of Emirati origin, who would carry to term the future daughter of Hamid and Karim.

When we met on the flight, Hamid admitted, *I had just come from spending two days with Nadine. That's her name, our secret and amazing daughter. Her surrogate mother is raising her for the time being. You must understand that I am torn. Happy to the core at being a father, terrified at the possibility that Karim will be caught. I'm devastated that he can't come out of hiding and move to London with me, to raise our daughter together. But most of all, I am sad and despondent that we will never get to raise Nadine in Qatar. This country is ten thousand years away from the day when a gay couple will be able to raise a child here.*

It was all a bit too much for me. I asked to go to the bathroom, where I burst into tears. This wasn't a game. This was not part of my impersonation as an agent. My face was red as fire. It was already clear to me what Hamid was thinking of asking me. It was already clear to me what could be achieved from this rare combination of circumstances, with a desperate procurement coordinator roaming around Iran.

I returned to the corner of the empty hall with my face flushed from crying. From that moment on, all the dams opened. Hamid understood that he had to fire all his guns at once, to lay out precisely what he needed from me, without mincing words. This time I was able to accurately predict what came next.

Putting all his cards on the table, Hamid detailed his dream of being reunited with his lover and their child, somewhere on the globe, in a hidden place, where they could live their lives and peacefully raise their daughter without either of them being seized and hauled back to Qatar. In order for this dream to come true, it was vital to elude any kind of surveillance; to get Karim, wanted by the local police, out of the apartment where he was hiding; and to whisk him safely out of Qatar, and from there to London.

Jessica, you have excellent sources in London and you love to help people in need. You can help me smuggle Karim out of Qatar and into London; you can arrange a new address and new identities for us. That's your part. As for mine, I will sell your software to every country I visit. I have friends and secret partners, and I'm good at sales. Believe me. And when I am grateful, I'm even better.

Boom. Hamid had placed an atomic bomb on the table. He had no idea with whom he was dealing. He made the plausible assumption that a kind-hearted British businesswoman who had sympathy for immigrants and disadvantaged populations would do everything to help him — and at the same time promote her business and make a lot of money. This is what the legions of businessmen who had passed through or lived in Qatar had successfully done. For this purpose, Mrs. Jessica Stone came to Qatar too.

If you help me, concluded Hamid with a theatrical flourish, *you will be a very rich woman — and I will be the happiest person in the universe. Mrs. Stone, isn't that a win-win situation?*

I mumbled something and Hamid continued talking, but I was no longer listening. My thoughts flew forward, to the next step and the one after that, in this divinely fortuitous chess game I had stumbled upon. Still, I was most bothered by the question of how I'd manage to encrypt such a complex message and how I'd convince Shimon to give the green light to such a sensitive ground operation which, clearly, never arose in any of the scenarios we considered or rehearsed.

Then I thought of Jerry, and his absence gnawed at me. Here I had a golden opportunity, so why wasn't the number-one spy standing by my side, the world champion in recruiting double agents? It was a hypothetical question for that moment, something that could not be changed, but that did not reduce the intensity of the frustration and the depth of the anxiety. Thinking about Jerry's abilities and trying to guess what he would have done facing the enormous challenge before me gave rise to a burning longing, especially at a time when my full concentration was required. Inside, I understood that whatever I did next would have substantial consequences for the success of my mission.

21

10:30 hrs.
At Colonel Nasser's house, scheming in
the dragon's maw

Paralyzing fear gripped me during my first visit to Colonel Nasser's
house. His wife Noor and I had become friends during the plane incident. In actuality, I became a secret ally to her frustrations and
her loathing of her husband. At the same time, Noor, without her
knowledge, became my ally and accomplice in the secret mission I
planned to carry out in her house.

In those moments, I suppressed the moral arguments against
the betrayal of my new friend who had put her trust in me. But once
it was over and we returned to safe harbor, I tormented myself non-
stop. Nasser embodied the macho archetype in the region, though
he never married another wife. He also felt like a colonel in his own
home, in his daily relationship with Noor — and even in his behavior towards their daughter, seven-year-old Salma.

*Did you see how the heroic colonel turned into a ragdoll during the
flight?* Noor asked me. She spoke to me in a half-whisper as we
sipped coffee together in their spacious living room. This was not
the only time when Noor put herself and me on the same front
against her husband, father of her daughter.

It was weird. I was supposed to overcome the fear. To focus on
strengthening the relationship with Noor in order to achieve my
primary objective: to install malware on the computer that Nasser operated from a private room in his house, to crack his security
passwords, to get his correspondence lists and to locate the secret
cell phone he used.

I was supposed to perform the exact same tasks at Majed's

home, as he was Nasser's boss. His wife, Rittal, my other friend from the nightmare flight, had already sent me two imploring text messages in broken English. *Please come visit me after my husband goes to work,* she wrote, attaching hearts and smileys. In the third message that Rittal sent there were warning lights and hints of jealousy. She mentioned the fact that I'd paid Noor three visits, while I hadn't found time for her.

I answered her immediately: *Dearest Rittal, I would be very happy to visit you. May I come tomorrow morning?*

That's how I found myself in the home of the Minister of the Interior as well. Rittal gave me an introductory tour through the massive residence. In every room and every corridor I noted fixed cameras on the wall. She showed me, with obvious pride, her son's room, the kitchen, Majed's personal study — and also the master bedroom.

I expressed my admiration volubly. I praised her impeccable taste in designing the room and selecting the color scheme. When we entered the bedroom I lingered on the wall-to-wall carpet, the curtains, and then also on the wall where the security camera was placed. *What, you record yourself in your boudoir?* I asked Rittal, giggling naively and slapping her on the shoulder.

She looked at me and burst out laughing. *Of course not! Mrs. Stone? The cameras only activate when the house is empty. I would never allow security personnel at the ministry to watch me or my child. And certainly not here!* she said with a blush and a sweeping gesture taking in the huge double bed that took up most of the room.

Your balance sheet, Mrs. Stone, isn't looking so bad so far, I said to myself after the first visit to Rittal's home. *You have formed a very strong bond with three important women. All three feel they owe you. In addition, you have a rapport with their four children, and even visited the bedroom of two of your prime targets. Tomorrow morning you're invited to visit and tour the house of the third 'friend'.*

It was time to commit to memory, for the thousandth time, my list of tasks and the bits of data which I had to recite reliably, even in my sleep. We were interested in Colonel Nasser Al Thani that stemmed from intelligence data detailing his close and covert connection to senior IRGC officers, as well as a secret and highly lucrative relationship with the steel industry in the Islamic Republic. The Iranians needed the help of Nasser and dozens of other collaborators across the Persian Gulf to bypass the severe sanctions imposed by the West, to aid their steel industry — vital to military development — and to advance their nuclear program. Nasser and his ilk thus became a lifeline for certain Iranian military units and the race towards a nuclear bomb. And they were willing to pay a pretty penny for that assistance, deposited in secret accounts in third-party countries.

As Majed was Nasser's direct superior, all intelligence activities of Qatar's tiny military were under his control. Israel's best and brightest had tried and failed to crack the security around Majed's personal computer, emails, phone calls and private cell phone. Yasmin's husband Abed also came up in the briefings, but only cursorily. He was not a target worthy of much time and energy, we thought. It would take a few more weeks to realize how wrong we —Shimon, the full surveillance and research team and I — were. Abed Al Atrash's computer turned out to be a treasure trove, a direct conduit to several key elements in the IRGC. He was not a member of the Al Thani dynasty; in fact, he outdid them all in pure avarice and perverse sadism.

Acceding to Yasmin's requests, I finally graced her with my presence, only to encounter one surprise after another.

I hadn't realized how striking Yasmin was during our airborne adventure. Silky smooth skin — a milky complexion, fairer than most of the women I saw there. She'd won the genetic lottery, her eyes large and prominent, shining in phosphorescent olive green. My gaze was locked magnetically to her beautiful, pale face and the emerald orbs that dominated it. I couldn't look away, nor could I ignore the sadness of her look, a silent plea for help.

Then there was her distinctive scent, a light cloud with a pleasant aroma, yet devoid of any manufactured perfume. I tried to decipher what I smelled and the only phrase which came to mind was *the fragrance of innocence.*

Yasmin kept silent for a long time. We looked at each other, warily studying each other, until the dam broke and she couldn't stop talking. She revealed to me her deep loathing of her husband. That wasn't the only sobering detail she told me. Within the hour, she pulled me close in a sororal embrace and whispered, her mouth inches from my ear, a most startling secret:

My broken English is just a show for Abed and his informants, Yasmin revealed, apologizing for the performance she'd put on aboard the Airbus.

I stared at her in genuine real surprise. I had failed to recognize that Yasmin was faking it. Why would she? A few minutes later, that became clear as well.

So Hamid told Abed that you deal in real estate in England, she said after her domestic servant had finished bringing us water, coffee, nuts and sweets. *Shukran, Amina,* she dismissed her without lifting her head.

I deal in real estate all over Europe, I corrected. *It's a major firm that my late husband and I started many years ago.*

Yasmin could not hide her admiration and curiosity. *I have a friend who is looking for a house in England or anywhere else in Europe, but it is a discreet matter. Can you help her find a property?*

That's my job, Yasmin. That's exactly what I do in my business.

Great, Mrs. Stone, great! So, can you help my friend? She is looking for a home for herself and her two children, she said.

Who is the friend? For what purpose is she looking for a house? I asked naturally without any deliberate intention.

Yasmin blushed at the question, looked down and hesitated for a long time. *She's a close friend of mine, since childhood. And her husband is violent. Really sadistic. He abuses her, but also beats their children. She is determined to leave Qatar and relocate to Europe, but this requires maximum discretion. If anyone finds out about her plans, it will end very badly. The cost might be her life.*

I get the impression that you have a very brave friend. How serious is she about fleeing Qatar? I pressed gently. The answers to questions I hadn't yet asked flitted through my mind. Yasmin's giant green orbs were pleading. She took long sips from the glass of water in her hand but maintained her silence. I broke it to say: *If you have a computer at home, I'd be happy to show you some beautiful houses for your friend.* At this, Yasmin's olive-green lakes swelled with tears.

We walked together towards the sanctum sanctorum, her husband's study. As minister of transport, Abed knew more than anyone about the civilian and military traffic in the waters of the Persian Gulf, not to mention his close, though covert, relationship with several senior IRGC officers.

Every agent dreams of the sort of golden opportunity that then fell into my lap — certainly for anyone trained, like me, to infiltrate the personal computers of Qatar's elite. Abed's PC had remained elusive to the hacking geniuses back home; neither military intelligence nor the Mossad could crack that nut. He connected to the internet randomly and for short periods of time under other profiles. The only chance to access his computer, emails, files or cell phone was simple and somewhat primitive: human intervention, i.e. manual insertion of spyware.

Yasmin and I settled in front of the computer in the minister's tiny study, very close to the master bedroom. I opened the SCRS website, looking up between keystrokes. The security camera on the wall did not move left or right, nor was the red indicator lit up. We seemed to be safe. I proudly presented Yasmin with a selection of properties SCRS offered, asking what her friend's price range might be.

Meanwhile, I went back three months in my memory to one of the discussions about my cover story. Shimon had listened as patiently as he could to the staff's descriptions of the cybertechnology company I had supposedly inherited from my late husband. It was obvious that he was not happy. After about an hour of twisting and turning in his chair, he exclaimed: *Friends, Mrs. Stone is also in real estate! A broker, buying and selling apartments in the UK and throughout Europe. The Qatari appetite for property there is insatiable. If Mrs. Stone can offer them that, she will be sought after; some will be far more interested in real estate than cybertechnology.* I suddenly realized how smart he was and the value of his many years of experience.

Yasmin looked with sparkling eyes at the homes displayed on the computer screen. *They must cost millions, but my friend has only modest resources as she has to operate in secret,* she said quietly, shyly. She was whispering again. She only has £800,000 to spend.

I asked Yasmin if we could bring in our glasses of water, which we'd left in the other room. *Min fadlik, min fadlik, Mrs. Stone,* said Yasmin, running to the doorway and calling to Amina, who was in another wing of the house taking care of her two daughters. *I'll go get us water and some refreshments,* Yasmin said and ran towards the living room.

That gave me a small window; it would have to be enough. In my left palm I held the special USB device prepared for me by the boys from the special operations department. I slid it along the monitor, in a way that wouldn't be visible even if the security camera was on. I also made sure not to bend my body to the side. Male met female, and I slid the drive into the socket.

At the same time, I activated the mouse with my right hand, entered the C drive, quickly found the folder I was looking for and perused it. *Bless your crafty hands, Bar,* I thought in those seconds — in Hebrew, a gross violation of procedure. Still, I was grateful to the talented Tel Aviv kid with the weird beard. For two days he put me through the wringer, not letting up until I had displayed the requisite skill in finding hidden folders, as well as sliding in the USB drive without bending over. I counted in my heart about thirty seconds. That should be enough for the bastard device to crawl into the bowels of the Minister of Transport's drives, transforming the new, imperceptible files into an invaluable reconnaissance tool, leaving no fingerprints and arousing no suspicions. Of course, there was already my spiffy real estate website. Just opening the page flung wide the gates of the desktop before the tech geniuses in Givatayim but, to be safe, we also took the other actions. It was clear that sitting in front of this computer, in the heart of the fortress that was Al Atrash's home, was a once-in-a-lifetime opportunity.

At some point, the twentieth second or so, I felt a large shadow at the door. A surprising cold crept up the back of my neck. *How long have they been there? Did they see me put the USB drive in?* I asked myself.

I decided to take the route of nonchalance. *Yasmin, my dear, you startled me. How long have you been standing in the doorway?* I said, a toothy grin on my face as I turned around. But there was no one there. Perhaps a shadow had passed by the large window, causing my heart to skip a beat. I looked back at the computer out of the corner of my eye as I extracted the device and slipped it back into my jacket. In the meantime, the connection was off and running; the Honorable Minister's computer had been successfully connected to the sophisticated server of the real estate website for some time. When Yasmin came back, I suggested that we look together at more houses for her friend, but this time in Manchester. That would buy even more quality time to link between Abed's PC and the SCRS server.

Tell your friend that, with the amount of money she has, I can get her a much more spacious and much more luxurious flat in Manchester. Come, I'll show you. I have a beautiful selection of properties there. If you want, I'll send an email to Helen, my secretary, right now, and ask her to prepare a list of properties up to £800,000, both in London and Manchester.

Shukran, shukran, Mrs. Stone, Yasmin said and hugged me from behind. A lasting embrace. I felt her heart beat with strength and excitement soaring to new heights. The scent of her innocence rose again, only emphasizing my betrayal of her. A slight feeling of nausea inflected my operational tension and maximal concentration, which also affected my thoughts. *Taking advantage of a desperate woman...*

I immediately went to my Gmail inbox and started typing as I quietly read the text. *Dear Helen, how are you? I am now at my friend Yasmin's house. She is the wife of the Qatari Minister of Transport, Abed Al Atrash, and is looking for a house in England for her best friend. I sent a detailed email about ten minutes ago about properties I am looking at for her. The handling of this matter must be carried out with absolute discretion.* This email, like all emails to and from Helen, was captured and analyzed in real time. I ended the email with a few hearts and three thank-you emojis.

We returned to the living room, resuming our conversation. Yasmin got down to brass tacks, detailed plans and technical questions about the procedure for purchasing property, distributing payments and dealing with any additional costs her friend might incur. Her caution was waning, leading to some pronominal confusion — even referring to her mysterious friend in the first person. The more we talked, the more enthusiastic she became about the options I presented for her friend. *Nice, nice, that sounds great,* she said, looking at me meaningfully, communicating with her eyes.

The truth was obvious. Yasmin's sudden interest in English real estate was about her. She had plans, she had the required amount of money, and she also had the courage to act and escape from her gilded cage along with her two daughters. Great, great, she said about every idea or tip — until her eagerness abruptly vanished. The milky complexion of her face paled even more. Her eyes darted back and forth as her cell phone vibrated with several message. She read them in alarm.

Mrs. Stone, my husband will be back shortly. I don't know what happened but he and his two aides are on their way here. He's never come home so early. She hurried to clear the table, grabbing cups, saucers and leftover refreshments to head to the kitchen. Her hands were shaking. It was glaring that she did it all on her own, rather than summoning the maid. *It's imperative that my husband not learn about my friend's search for flats in England. Please, Mrs. Stone, please!* Her voice trailed off as tears filled her olive eyes.

I grabbed some plates and pieces of cutlery and started moving with her to the kitchen so that we would have time to conclude our conversation. As I walked, I told her: *Yasmin, we are women. We must look out for each other. I am, first of all, your friend. Of course I will keep it confidential. Discretion is a very important part of my profession. It is impossible to buy and sell real estate if you cannot maintain confidentiality. I won't talk to anyone about what we did, what we talked about, and certainly not about your friend...*

Yasmin was silent, her shoulders shaking. I hugged her like you hug a daughter. *I will do anything to help you, Yasmin. Anything,* I whispered. *I'll also give you Helen's phone number. You can call and talk to her whenever it's convenient for you. Helen is a hardworking and very talented girl. She will help your friend, trust me.*

Shukran, shukran, she said for the thousandth time, *but please, you must leave now. My husband will arrive with his aides in ten minutes.* Her look was one of gratitude and appreciation.

It was another one of those moments I agonized over. At the moment of truth, I only thought about my mission and what it required. But in quieter times, in my hotel room or on the flight back home, I found myself in an internal debate about manipulation, about deceiving one who trusted me as a confidante. There was the broad, automatic response that this was what being a Mossad agent meant. No two ways about it. Just a role to play, I had to convince myself. When it was over, I'd have to give up the duplicity and return to my family's bosom, completely free of the deceit, treachery and pretense. Either that or lose my mind.

22

In front of the target's computer, sharing a
secret with the enemy's wife

My mind was roiled by tension. The minister's early return home prompted a whirlwind of thoughts, along with some gusts of paranoia. Did he still have the means to see or hear what was going on in his home? Was it possible that the ostensibly dormant camera above the computer was, in fact, active?

My taxi back to the hotel got stuck in traffic and I had a lot of time to try and analyze the sequence of events at Yasmin's house. My head was about to explode. Then there was a persistent vibration from my cell phone. Yasmin's name appeared on the screen and with it rose another tsunami of anxiety. A second later I heard Yasmin's voice: "*Mrs. Stone, shukran, shukran.*" She spoke again in awkward and broken English: "*It was a pleasure for me telling with you about growing children. My husband has come home with a headache and high fever. He rests now. Come to me again sometime, please, Mrs. Stone.*" The whirlwind in my mind suddenly dissipated.

And, at the same time, the traffic jam cleared, picking up speed on the way to the Grand Hyatt. The smell of jasmine filled the cab. I had nowhere to escape.

I closed my eyes and thanked the Holy One, blessed be He, for watching over me and giving me the courage to carry out the task. The pilot program was a success, Jessica. Now you have two more computers in two more houses to tackle.

My thoughts sailed forward. I was racking my brain for ideas for my next move. How could I convert my frequent visits to Noor into operational action?

As if on cue, the cell phone vibrated again. This time Noor's name appeared on the screen. The relationship with her had gone from zero to a hundred within days. Since our airborne adventure, I had been to her place three times and we'd had prolonged, soulful conversations in the enormous living room.

I was twice her age. I could be the mother she hadn't had since she was ten. She treated me as a confidante and ally in matters between her and her husband, as well as childrearing and pregnancy. She already had a child and was twenty-five weeks pregnant with the next, but her level of knowledge was zero. Noor thirstily drank every word that came out of my mouth.

The message that flashed on the screen was brief and innocent.

My friend, I must speak with you. Please come tomorrow morning. Love, Noor.

Her relationship with the colonel was strained. He turned out to be a difficult person, to say the least. An ultra-conservative man who dismissed her, her personality, her wisdom, her excellent spoken English and the fine English literature she read. He vetoed every step Noor was interested in or thought of pursuing. He didn't hesitate to beat her if she said something which belied her status as a woman. With his screams, he dismissed her thoughts of studying for a master's degree and threatened to slap her if she continued to bring up the idea. Unlike many of his friends, Nasser had not taken three or four wives. However, he indulged wildly and openly with everything that moved and gave Noor pathetic, transparent and insulting excuses to justify his absence from home — sometimes for whole nights, sometimes even for a day or two.

Noor became addicted to our conversations revolving around giving birth, about raising children, about educating them.

You have experience. You succeeded in your mission. I envy you, she told me time and time again.

These confidences advanced my goals and the mission for which I had come to her house, but they also tore me apart inside. Talking about kids and parenting were a breach of discipline and all prohibitions; all I could see was a huge screen filled with images of Roy and Michael, light-years away from me. Only a two-hour flight, but completely in another universe. Again, I suppressed the question that stubbornly nettled me: what kind of mother was I?

I learned from Noor that many of her friends had a shared dream: to covertly stockpile funds in an American or British bank account and to flee Qatar. The deeper our conversations went, the more I tried to figure out if Noor, herself, shared that fantasy. When I felt ready, I asked her directly. Noor's eyes filled with tears. She ran out of the room without answering. When she returned to the living room, she approached me and extended her arms for a brave hug. With her head close to my ear, she whispered quickly: *Rittal and Yasmin, my two best friends, are looking for ways to get out of here with their kids, but they don't have the courage.*

How would one go about it? I responded.

It has already happened, more than once or twice, stressed Noor, but everything is kept quiet.

Much later, once I was safely home in Tel Aviv, I would eagerly devour every morsel of information about the escape to Europe by Princess Haya bint Al Hussein of Jordan, second of the six wives of the Emirati prime minister and ruler of Dubai, Sheikh Mohammed bin Rashid Al Maktoum. She finally got her divorce at age 45, but that was only the beginning of a bitter custody battle. I read and cried about her as if she were my lost daughter. The same was true about Noor, Rittal, and Yasmin.

I could not stop my mind from drifting to comparing and contrasting our life experiences. How blessed I am, as a Jewish woman and as an Israeli, as opposed to my friends for whom I leave a place in my heart!

The year before Princess Haya's escape, another member of Sheikh Mohammed's household, his daughter Latifa, made an attempt. She was caught off the coast of India and forced to return to Dubai.

The images haunt me. I cannot help but recall the similar scene of horror on the occasion of my return flight from Tehran.

But back then, I had no idea that terror would be a part of my mission.

23

16:00 hrs.
At Nasser's house, sharing intimate secrets
and betting the whole pot

I would love to visit you, I replied to Noor immediately. We arranged to meet in the late afternoon, about an hour before Nasser returned from work. When I arrived at their spacious home I was surprised to find her lying in bed, her cheeks hot, her eyes red from crying, and her forehead glistening.

I touched her with the back of my hand. Her forehead was hot, covered in cold sweat. I sat down in the chair next to her and she launched into a heartbreaking monologue. After a few minutes I was up to date with everything I needed to know. I listened to her with one ear. The rest of my attention was focused on the golden opportunity that had presented itself: to work my magic on the colonel's computer.

Her summary of the previous day was disturbing and depressing. Noor hadn't been feeling well. Colonel Nasser returned from work late and ignored her fever, chills and tears. He was angry, irritable, bitter — and louder than usual.

After about two hours of agitated phone calls, he got into bed earlier than his wont, approached her from behind, silenced her sobbing cries with a cruel smack to her head, forced himself upon her with unusual ferocity and then turned over to sleep.

Noor related this all in a whisper, her hands close to her face, covering her nose and mouth tightly, her eyes closed. This was her way of revealing the most horrifying violation she had experienced, attempting to stop the tears about to burst out of her while simultaneously evading me — my gaze and my reaction. I reached out and took her two hands in mine, squeezing to show my empathy and my encouragement.

This morning, Noor whispered through the two sets of hands over her mouth, *the heroic colonel woke me up and informed me he had to fly to Tehran for two days.*

At this point, all the dams failed. Noor turned her head away from me and burst into heartbreaking sobs. I grabbed both of her hands again and tried to calm her.

She clearly felt alone, despite all the help she had around her: the Sri Lankan nanny who looked after Salma; the kitchen staff who took care of cooking and cleaning, including serving refreshments to guests; the strong young Filipina who was constantly around her, at her beck and call.

Still, the colonel's message broke something in her. His blunt and violent style was nothing new. The insensitivity was a constant element in their relationship, but this time everything was different. Noor was contending with the pregnancy, the hormonal changes, the conversations with her friends. Nasser was clearly dealing with hidden agendas that were driving him crazy and making him more aggressive than usual. A thought crept into the back of my mind: did this have anything to do with his disgraceful behavior when we faced our challenge in the air? After all, it had been devastatingly public, taking place in front of the critical eyes of some of Qatar's top brass as well as the astonished eyes of foreign businessmen and their wives. It's not beyond reason, I thought to myself, that the cowardly behavior of a senior uniformed officer of the Qatari army had become a national embarrassment that had to be dealt with.

About an hour later, the door of the house opened with a crash. Colonel Nasser entered, roaring into his iPhone and pulling open his uniform as he walked to the refrigerator. Two maids ran towards him, asking what he wanted, but he chased them out of the dining area with a shout and rude hand gestures.

From the armchair at the end of the living room, I followed his progress. When he noticed me, his shouts and gestures ceased at once. He buttoned up his uniform, straightening the row of medals on his chest and looking at me in surprise. I've caught him in conduct unbecoming yet again, I mused.

Oh, Mrs. Stone... I didn't know you were here. I apologize, Mrs. Stone, the colonel muttered, stepping toward me with his hand outstretched. I gave him a piercing look and, at that moment, I knew what my next step would be.

Colonel Al Thani... I said and left the rest of the sentence hanging in space. *I came today to visit Noor and found her upset. Her pregnancy is progressing, and that's not easy. I know it very well. This is exactly what happened to me at this stage. She has some heat and chills, but mostly she needs support and love.*

Nasser looked at me with embarrassment and curiosity. The silence hanging between us was heavy. He reached into his shirt pocket, pulled out a Marlboro pack and tried to extract a cigarette from it. His fingers were shaking. He tried one more time, then decided to give up on the idea, put the pack on the table and pushed it away from him, as if convincing himself not to smoke in front of me.

Colonel, I understand from Noor that you have an important mission outside of Qatar. I'm prepared to stay with her and Salma at least until tomorrow evening. What do you think, Colonel Al Thani, would that be alright with you?

Nasser looked up from the table with unusual slowness, allowing me the opportunity to scrutinize his face from such a close proximity. The tic in his right nostril twitched repeatedly at an abnormally high rate. His face remained menacing, but his eyes were somewhat off. He looked beaten and depressed. *Mrs. Stone, can you afford to miss two days of business meetings?* he asked, speaking slowly and cautiously, patiently awaiting my answer.

I don't have anything scheduled for tomorrow, I replied immediately, without a second thought. *The first meeting, the day after tomorrow, will only be in the evening, so it's no trouble. I can stay here until you return. But the decision is all yours, Colonel; I defer to your wisdom, respectfully.* My heart trembled. I was betting the whole pot but, in this case, it was necessary.

It would only take a few more minutes for the idea I had raised to become an actionable plan. Nasser would walk briskly to the bedroom and address Noor in a soft voice, the kind she hadn't heard in years. He would be interested in her well-being, ask what she thought about my staying with her until his return, receive an enthusiastic, grateful reply from Noor, and return to me with a triumphant expression. That was how I scripted it, and that's how it happened. A feather in my cap.

Did you hear, Mrs. Stone? Noor agrees. It is our honor to host you in our humble home. I will always remember your kindness, he said, throwing open the gates for me to betray him and Noor. It was a naive thought to have, both in my profession and under the circumstances, but it was there, raising its head and taunting me.

After Nasser left the house, the Al-Thani family's army of servants mobilized to serve me. They escorted me to the suite the colonel had assigned to me, which included a bedroom, a full bathroom, and a balcony that looked out over the eastern horizon of Doha. They showed me a closet full to the brim with new nightgowns, still in their original packaging. They let me choose the color of the brand-new towels and equipped my bathroom with a full set of soaps, shampoos, toothbrush and toothpaste.

The closet also held new packages with brand-name underwear in my size. *You can host a battalion here and allow everyone to choose which silk or velvet robe they want to wear,* I told Noor, managing to squeeze a slight smile from her. She was weak, but went out with me to the living room. The staff of servants showered us with delicacies, putting out small plates with a broad selection of hummus, tahini, salads, pickled and spicy side dishes and, finally, many types of sweets and tea with mint.

I see that your mood is already a little better, I told Noor. *We can wave goodbye to Nasser. He must be looking at the cameras. It's reassuring to know that he can be in Tehran and still know what's going on with you and if you're okay.*

Nasser can't see anything. Nor can his whole horde of miserable soldiers and aides, Noor replied with shocking acerbity. Her tone was sharp and venomous. She added: *Last month I got tired of all these cameras and demanded that they stop watching me and Salma. That's no way to live! Any junior officer can stalk me in the kitchen, in the living room, on the way to the bathroom?! But I really blew up when I discovered the cameras in our bedroom.*

Blew up? What do you mean? I asked.

I threatened to grab Salma and a suitcase and go back to my parents' house, Noor replied, a shadow covering the slight smile she'd had since she'd gotten out of bed.

And what happened...? I asked with obvious curiosity.

Noor got up and motioned for me to follow her, striding towards the front door of their huge house. There was a closet recessed into the wall by the entrance. The wooden door opened with a soft click. There was a cabinet containing an electrical panel, the size of two shoeboxes. Its cover was loose and askew. Beyond it were dozens of thin and colorful electrical wires which had been sliced. *Here are all his cameras,* Noor said, agitated, running her fingers over the spaghetti of cut wires. *This whole country is manic about security footage. There are more video cameras than people here. Soon we will have cameras over every toilet and bathtub as well.*

We returned to the living room with both of us laughing, loud and loose. *I'm glad to see that you're feeling better,* I told Noor; and, in the same breath, I launched my spiel: *If you've got a computer here, I could show you a little about my business in the UK. We offer the most beautiful homes in London, Manchester, Leeds and other cities. You won't believe how many houses we sell to Qataris. But everything is discreet. Either they buy confidentially or they use a third party. Last week I sold a very large house to a certain lady from Doha, and I have no idea who she is!*

Noor burst out laughing. *I have three laptops, but when Nasser leaves the house, I prefer the computer in his study. Great Internet connection, huge monitor, excellent speakers. It's a pleasure.* Five minutes later, we were already in the holy of holies, the colonel's personal study, which shared a wall with the bedroom. We got online and started browsing the real estate galleries which the tech guys had stocked on the SCRS website. They had done a wonderful job.

Noor was quite enthusiastic about some of the houses, inquiring about prices and the availability of houses near those purchased by some of her husband's friends. After about thirty minutes of perusing real estate porn, I deployed my drinks-and-snacks ruse.

Oh, Razane isn't around now. I sent her on errands all over town so we could have a quiet morning to ourselves. I'll go make us a tray, Noor said, leaving me the time needed to take out the USB device, plug it into the appropriate port, and take a look at some of the folders on the C drive — all before she came back with a platter full of refreshments.

At a certain moment during a virtual tour of one of the houses in London, Noor held my hand, looked at me and said with obvious fear: *Nasser can never know that we've been on his computer. You get that, right?* I felt a tremor in her hand. Then, she added shyly, in a whisper, that we ought to wipe away our tracks. She surprised me with her mastery of the ways to clear cookies and delete browsing history. *I do this every time I surf on his computer, then open my laptop for display in the living room,* she giggled.

I listened to her and couldn't help but notice how much she had in common with Yasmin in her attitude towards cameras in the house; her covert, taboo browsing on the husband's computer; and her fraught relationship with her husband, the father of her children.

24

18:20 hrs.
Forbidden tears and forbidden longing in the
taxi to the Hyatt

This is too easy. Is my success becoming a liability?

Those were the thoughts which struck me after visiting Rittal, following my two-day stay at Noor's.

Tap, tap, tap — like the pecking of a woodpecker on a dry tree trunk. I thought I was losing my mind. I closed my eyes and held my head with both hands, my palms covering my ears, two fingers on my temples. I pressed with all my might in a futile attempt to stifle the disturbing thoughts, harrowing scenarios rising and falling before me with the syncopation of a nightmare. Nevertheless, I was determined to hold it together, lest the cabdriver catch my emotional turmoil in his rearview.

The worry began to gnaw at me the moment I left Rittal, after another long and meaningful social engagement with a friend I'd only met a few days before.

Rittal greeted me with an unbounded hug. My intuition told me that she knew about my time with Noor and Yasmin. Still, the embrace was emotional and the enthusiasm was earnest.

By that point, the framework of the visit had become routine. Sitting in the living room, talking about personal matters, telling a story about selling a flat to a large family from Doha. Rittal's barely contained curiosity led to an offer to browse the SCRS website. Entering the minister's private study, being left alone in front of the computer, inserting and removing the USB drive; deleting cookies and browsing history, as the desperate wife adjures me to keep it secret.

However, this time there was an exception. As I reached for the USB drive, a chest of drawers with golden metal handles caught my eye — beyond the computer, an arm's length away. None of the drawers had a lock or keyhole. I couldn't stop myself, and I didn't. I couldn't spare a second for a second thought. Rittal had walked away towards the kitchen, announcing that it would take a while because she was preparing some surprises for us.

I quickly reached for the top drawer and pulled it to me with my pinky, without the pad of my finger touching the wood. The carpentry was impeccable. The drawer rolled out soundlessly. Inside were neat stacks of documents, a bag of rubber bands, a stapler, and puncher. Deep in the drawer, beyond the pile of documents, the barrel of a gun peeked out. I closed the drawer with a light push and immediately pulled out the next one, which was almost completely empty aside from a Samsung Galaxy that lay there dead. There's his secret mobile, I hummed to myself. I automatically reached into my right pocket, pulled out the Galaxy I had brought with me, grabbed the cell phone with a handkerchief I had in my left pocket and turned it over. It powered up. I quickly connected the cable and darted a look behind me. Rittal had not yet returned. Whatever surprises she was whipping up in the kitchen, it gave me the seconds of grace I needed before plunging back to into the real estate porn of the SCRS website.

It was clear that Rittal, just like Yasmin, had organized a full day of tasks for her maid and her nanny. Each was sent to opposite ends of Doha with endless shopping lists for food, household goods and children's clothes. The security cameras were not operational at the home of the Interior Minister. Rittal volunteered that the cameras switched on only when she and her husband were away. *Majed is an important official*, she said casually, *but I'm not ready to live in an aquarium. The cameras are just there to keep tabs on the staff. They've stolen cash and jewelry several times this year.*

And yet, I tormented myself. It's too easy, I said to myself. Same old, same old. You've become addicted to the rote — which is diametrically opposed to your training! Routinization is bad. It's very risky... and very reckless...

I went over every second, from the hug to the conversation in the living room, from the USB sleight-of-hand to my unassuming exit. Yeah, same old, same old — but it wasn't only my infiltration techniques which were becoming too familiar. The emotional whirlwind was also an encore performance. Getting into the taxi only to be overwhelmed by guilt at my betrayal of trust. This time, Majed and Rittal were the victims of my duplicity. I was proud of my achievement, but my conscience jabbed at my chest incessantly. I tried to convince myself that I was deceiving a good and innocent woman for a greater cause. I pulled out all the well-worn arguments about the welfare of the homeland, but it was futile. The pain from the dagger of shame persisted and intensified, until two large tears rolled down my cheeks.

It wasn't the only reason I had to cry, either; the unbearable traffic jam left time for me to reflect on Roy and Michael, my longing for their voices, their faces. If I'd been safe, I could have used my cell phone to call them or just to look through their images, their funny and touching expressions. But I was very far from anything resembling security; even thinking about them or Jerry or our home in Tel Aviv was a serious misstep, utterly against the rules. For now, they do not exist. How bizarre, how cruel, how contrary to the laws of nature.

Alongside calming thoughts, I recalled the agreement with Shimon and the rest of the team: they wouldn't make use of my infiltrations in Doha until I was already out of harm's way. That was the deal. It was my life insurance policy as I carried out these crazy missions. But this deal, too, was somehow broken.

25

9:00 hrs.
The blonde defeats the colonel at the Hyatt
tennis courts

A day after breaching the interior of the interior minister's home, I returned to the tennis court — a routine I could safely fall into. I sat in the sumptuous lobby of the complex and sipped coffee. This was the first coffee for the day, as I had skipped breakfast at the hotel. I couldn't eat a crumb.

While luxuriating in my armchair, I watched fresh newcomers and panting players, but my mind was elsewhere. I had crossed quite a few tasks off my list: the confidential number of a member of the Al Thani family; full access to the private phone of the interior minister; and entrée to three personal computers belonging to three senior Qatari officials — two ministers and a colonel. I ought to have been flying sky-high but I felt like I was weighed down, the pressure on my chest making it difficult for me to breathe. Or maybe I had achieved high altitude, owing to lungsful of air that I was gulping down like I was scaling a mountain. Arguably, I was. Every success brought me closer to the summit, to the day when I could stride through the departure terminal of Hamad Airport and return to my life. But every operation I completed also brought me that much closer to the moment when I could shed all disguise and pretense.

I looked towards the automatic glass doors that separated the lobby from the tennis courts. They opened and closed with a soft whisper, but this time a familiar figure came through them; it took me a moment to recognize him without his uniform and chestful of medals, but it was Colonel Nasser Al Thani. He was decked out in trendy Nike gear, a towel over his shoulder and a racket in hand. Chastened after his shameful behavior on the plane, grateful for the help I gave his wife, and curious to hear of my own exploits on the court, he quickly covered the distance from the door, sat down in the chair opposite me and indicated with his fingers to one of the waiters that he would appreciate a ristretto.

This time I sat right in front of him, not far at all. He had a handsome face, but his skin was pitted and scarred from years of battling stubborn acne. Faint wisps of mustache erupted from the deep crevices along his upper lip and cheeks. There was something heartbreaking about his insistence on sporting facial hair, but his overall appearance was somehow still aesthetically pleasing. I studied his face for a long time, finding it difficult to reconcile it all: his attractiveness, his senior position, his paralysis during the airborne disaster, and his cruelty as a husband and father — according to the little I'd heard from Noor. Sometimes you think you know someone's personality just by looking at them, but you haven't got a clue, I said to myself. Nasser met my gaze for a while until he worked up the courage to swallow and ask, with a hint of embarrassment, if I wanted to play with him.

I accepted, but I fell victim to one of the classic blunders: I, Jessica Stone, the British blonde, wiped the floor with the decorated Al Thani scion in every match. Sheer operational logic, not to mention everything I learned about the psychology of the Qatari man, ought to have told me that was the wrong move. I only realized it when we got back to the lobby, over coffee. I had wounded Nasser's pride yet again. One time too many, after the humiliation on the plane and the assertive conversation at his house.

We have to play tomorrow too, he said. *I am very tired today.* I thanked God for this window opened, so I could rectify my error.

You work extremely hard, Colonel. A two-day business trip, all that flying... you must be exhausted. Get some rest and we'll meet here tomorrow at ten in the morning. My work meetings don't start until after lunch, I answered and breathed a sigh of relief.

Fortunately, I only won the second match the next day. From the third onwards, the colonel's winning streak was uninterrupted. Once I put my mind to it, it wasn't too formidable a task. I wasn't required to serve less powerfully or accurately, nor did I have to slow down my response time. All that was required to maintain his male dignity was to turn a blind eye to the lies, big and small, about whether the ball landed out of bounds or not, on the line or not. The boys running around, as well as Nasser himself, cheated brazenly. His two assistants and the ball boys groveled in front of him and confirmed more and more victories for him. I smiled to myself and said from time to time: *Well done, Colonel. No way I can beat you. You play brilliantly.*

At the same time, I struggled with the enigma. Nasser was intelligent, fluent in multiple languages, well-educated with two university degrees from the States. Was he oblivious to the deception? Was he incapable of noticing how lopsided the results were? After the previous day's defeat, could he really imagine that he was good enough to 'beat' me so soundly?

We finished around noon. We sat down to catch our breath and drink something cold in the magnificent lobby. The conversation flowed, but Nasser kept relegating it to the personal level. So-called sophisticated statements with touches and allusions to intimacy. It was borderline bizarre. He knew how close his wife, Noor, and I had become, yet his advances were transparent and juvenile. Compliments on my appearance, on my opening serves, on my 'masculine' play. Eventually, he shifted into high gear and began to drop hint after hint. I was alone in a foreign land. He was interested in my business. What were my plans for this afternoon and evening? I elegantly sidestepped his romantic serves, refusing to volley, even as I tried to spare his male ego. Eventually, I was saved by the bell — or the ringtone.

The jingle came from his tennis bag. It was a different ring from that of his high-end iPhone. Indeed, he pulled out a completely different device from his bag, a twin of what I'd seen in

Majed's drawer. Nasser answered briefly, hung up and placed the phone on the table between us. My studying with the phrasebook allowed me to understand that he had asked not to be disturbed again at that number.

Samsung Galaxy, I thought and breathed a sigh of relief. I have the right cable. The silent device placed between us immediately brought me back to the erstwhile lessons with Bar in Tel Aviv. Repeated practice that seemed troublesome and unnecessary. Oh, how wrong I was about that talented boy. *This must be Nasser's secret spare phone,* I realized. I needed to improvise. It was time to start acting. I assume a pose of befuddlement. I started turning over the things in my bag. I felt the pockets of my jacket. I bent down and looked under the armchair. I stood up and looked around.

What happened, what did you lose? Nasser asked. I continued to scan the surroundings, avoiding his question; then I sat down in the armchair with a nervous movement and muttered lowly: *I'm so scatterbrained. How dumb of me, I forgot my phone in the room again — and I have to call my friend in Germany!*

Nasser's iPhone rang and he pointed to the Galaxy, gesturing for me to take it. Then he put his palm over the iPhone and whispered: *Please... feel free...*

I picked up the Samsung, mouthing: *Thank you, thank you, thank you, you're a lifesaver.* Then I got up from my seat and called Gretchen, my best friend in Germany.

I started the conversation speaking more loudly than usual, while walking in circles around the table. I told her about leaving my phone in the room, playing tennis with the delightful Colonel Nasser, who was kind enough to offer me his cell phone.

Nasser's conversation continued. He placed his right palm over his heart in an apologetic gesture. I also sent a hand to my bosom in thanks and continued talking to Gretchen. We were discussing our planned ski vacation. I waited for my moment — within sight of Nasser, but far enough away, and directly beneath the security camera. I needed a single moment in the dead space between cameras to connect the compatible device to the Samsung, count to thirty, and then slip the device back into my pocket. This all-too-transparent operation, silly sleight-of-hand in broad daylight, was in no way similar to anything I'd trained for. It ought to have quickened my heartbeat, sent my blood pressure soaring, painted my face bright crimson, popped beads of cold sweat from my pores. There was always a possibility that another security camera existed and was recording me without my knowledge. It certainly would have been more likely than the serpentine complex of rooms behind the lobby wall, which was not mentioned in any briefing and did not appear in the 3D simulation.

I had every reason in the world to be on edge, but the exact opposite happened. Some kind of strange, somewhat senseless peace came over me. I felt an inch taller; I was proud of myself, allowing myself to do the forbidden and think of Jerry in Hebrew. What would he think of me? How would he react? How would he himself have acted in those moments? I sat down again in front of Nasser, placed his Galaxy on the table between us, looked into his eyes and offered him a prolonged gesture of gratitude with both hands. His conversation continued for a few more minutes.

I had to talk to my friend Gretchen in Germany to coordinate our vacation in the Alps two weeks from now, I told Nasser.

The vacation was part of the cover story built for me and also the explanation as to why, sometime soon, I would have to return to Europe. I told the colonel about the expected departure and felt a hint of relief. *I'm scaling another cliff*, I thought. *The summit is almost in sight.*

Oh, how wrong I was.

26

18:30 hrs.
Green meets blue on the path from the Hyatt
to the beach

The business meeting scheduled for the afternoon was a pre-arranged ruse. The day before, shortly after the tennis matches, the phone vibrated with a call from Billy Adams, the American representative of an Austrian cybertechnology firm. That was the cover for a Mossad agent who was supposed to meet me if I needed to deliver sensitive, extensive and complex information — e.g., Hamid and Karim's thorny dilemma.

We arranged a meeting in the most visible place, in the center of the lobby, in front of all possible security cameras. As usual, I was a little early. I wanted to survey the location and its environs, committing to memory how to get out of there as quickly as possible. A matter of caution.

Then, at the designated time, to the second, Billy Adams made his grand entrance. He recognized me without difficulty, walking briskly towards me, holding out his hand. I got up and extended my own hand. *Hello, Mrs. Stone, have you had lunch yet? I would love something vegetarian, if they serve something like that here.* That was our coded opening sentence.

Hello, Mr. Adams, I have never ordered vegetarian food here, but they have everything you could want. Even Indonesian food.

The identification phase went smoothly, but I knew immediately that it wasn't any Billy who came to meet me, but Giora from my Greek test flight. Trustworthy, fair-haired and handsome. This time he sat right next to me, without the drama of a plane about to crash, without a heavy mahogany table hiding his body. He was indeed strikingly attractive, taller than me by a head, solid, with a pair of eyes that pierced me like deep blue lasers. His forehead was unwrinkled, his mane of hair running over it, though there were two patches where that was starting to thin. His light-brown complexion stood in fascinating contrast to the hue of his hair and eyes. I was under the impression that he had tanned a lot since I saw his face on the plane. His English was fluent and incredibly clear, but the German-Austrian accent was evident. *So how old is he? Forty-five, I bet,* I said to myself.

Billy smiled as if reading my mind. *Feel free to guess, Mrs. Stone. My age is a trick question.* Refined, polite, nonconfrontational. There was something very calming about the way he spoke, listened, asked and answered. Still, there was something unsettling about the conversation. Eventually I realized what it was: he looked me straight in the eyes and at no point turned away.

We started the conversation at a table covered by four different cameras. I spread paperwork on the table and presented him with a laptop presentation detailing the wonders of cyberspace, as presented by Gstone.

Billy, i.e. Giora, was an excellent actor. He expressed curiosity and wonder, pointing at the screen and perusing the papers I placed in front of him. Everyone who watched our conversation was convinced that it was a serious sales pitch, with millions on the line.

Then he suggested we go for a walk along the path leading to the beach. This was also planned. As we stepped outside and started moving east, he said in English: *God willing, you can stop selling Gstone and start selling Hamid.* I gave him a complete overview of how I'd met Hamid, his position, the countries he visited to sell software and weapons, his personal background, his tragic love story, his resentment and contempt for his older and younger brothers and the entire ruling family in Qatar. I also expressed his readiness to do anything to get himself and Karim to Europe to raise their baby together.

Giora showed no enthusiasm. He must have asked two hundred questions. He raised doubts, expressed paranoia, rephrased the same queries over and over. He was testing how convinced I was of the truth of all the details, trying to undermine my confidence as well.

We walked slowly. No hurry. By the time we reached the beach, we were talking about the deal Hamid could strike in order to extricate Karim and get them back to their daughter. *And what exactly is he able to provide in return?* Giora asked. The conversation was becoming exhausting. It was the fourth, maybe fifth time that he'd asked me to detail Hamid's commitment. One question after another. It was clear that Giora was mainly motivated by Hamid's connections in Tehran.

The light of the sun, which had been blinding during the stroll, dimmed a bit. We continued to talk as we walked; then Billy suddenly stopped, grabbed me with both hands and gently pulled me to stand facing him. His blue gaze was fixed on the green in my eyes, examining them.

It was a strange positioning, arousing curiosity, arousing passions. *What's happening here?* I asked myself, shifting to high alert.

Billy persisted with his piercing blue gaze. *Now tell me please, Mrs. Stone, do you believe Hamid completely and utterly, without a shadow of a doubt?*

I breathed a sigh of relief. Giora did not intend any inappropriate act. He also knew how to choose a location that would not be seen by any camera. I looked down and saw that he held his fingers to blood vessels in my wrists. I assured him: *I am one hundred percent sure that Hamid is not lying. He is in real trouble and will do anything he can to for his lover and for his child,* I said as I met his piercing gaze with one of my own.

Billy ran his tongue over his upper lip as he considered this. *Just one more question, Mrs. Stone,* as I was still hooked up to the human lie detector, *are you convinced that it is worth risking our people for this operation?*

My answer was quick. *Extracting Karim from Qatar is well within the capabilities of an organization as competent and efficient as the Mossad.*

For a moment, there was silence save for our breathing. Then I broke it: *Billy, I am convinced that Hamid will fulfill his obligations. He's a strategic asset. He has great connections in Doha, Jordan and Iran. In Tehran, his links are beyond our wildest dreams.*

I went on: *These are not mere business relationships. Mansour Najifi, his close friend there, is a cyber whiz in Unit 455 of the IRGC. I get the distinct impression that there are no secrets between Hamid and Mansour — who is still single at forty. He even knows about Karim, and Hamid knows Mansour's lover. I couldn't tell you his name; that wasn't in my briefings. But Hamid's aid is priceless; he has the skills and motivation to help us, far beyond what we could have planned for or simulated.*

Above all is his love for his little girl, hidden somewhere in London. The distance from her breaks his heart. You should see his eyes when he talks about her. You should see his eyes when he talks about Karim. It's not every day you have someone who volunteers, who will help us infiltrate the most sensitive Iranian targets — out of love and out of pure self-interest.

I saw a big smile appear on Giora's beautiful face for the first time. Combined with his flawless facial features, it made him maddeningly attractive. He released his grip on both of my hands very gently, until they were straight at my sides. Then he straightened to his full height and looked me up and down. His eyes were no longer probing lasers, but a pair of calm lakes, glistening in a soft and caressing indigo.

You're wonderful, Sally, you're wonderful, he said quietly in Hebrew, bent down a little, held my head gently with both hands and kissed my forehead.

It was a kiss of appreciation, but it sent me sky high. I wonder what Giora might feel now from my wrists. My pulse would take him aback. Then, even before I had finished digesting the excitement of the compliment, his lips came down to me once more, stopped in front of my forehead and planted another kiss on it. This time it was more persistent. I was surprised.

The first kiss was for Operation Hamid, I surmised quietly, *but what was that?*

Giora's smiled soberly. He considered his answer for a while. *Your information about Sirhan rocked the Mossad to its core,* he said in a whisper. *There was a great fury, a great worry as well. Some supervisors thought that your lack of discipline was endangering you and the entire operation; they demanded that you be sent home. Others argued that your carelessness imperiled your fellow agents in the region.*

Well... I haven't heard anything about it, not even a hint, I replied.

That's because Shimon believes in you. He ignores all the background noise. Believe me, Sally, he fights for you like a wounded bear coming under fire. But then it turned out that the information you passed on was golden. Once we knew Sirhan's location, we checked who was with him and who he was in contact with. We recognized all the faces in the photos you sent. It had nothing to do with the abduction of the boys; it was an arms deal, transferring Iranian weapons to Gaza. Fortunately for us, unfortunately for him, he's a creature of greed and lust. He recklessly indulged with several young women, including a minor related to the Al Thanis. At the same time, he tried to arrange a nest egg of millions for himself in a Western country. That attaché case was not full of clothes. We had a few people here on standby. We exposed him and let the guys from Hamas and the Qatari authorities do the dirty work. Along the way, we also torpedoed his deal in the making. And it's all thanks to you, Sally. All thanks to you.

I slowly raised my arms and held Giora tightly, with my head resting on his chest. It wasn't an embrace. I held on to him. I hung onto his sturdy body.

I felt my legs fail. Too much excitement, anger, pressure, fear, longing, regret and surprise. Everything mixed together in me and became a deadly cocktail, sapping my last erg of energy.

Giora wrapped me in his long, strong arms. We continued to stand there for a while longer. The darkness around us became thick. The only glimmers of light were from the distant lampposts reflected in the waters of the bay.

No one appeared on the path leading from the hotel to the bay and marina. We stood there alone, limbs intertwined. My ear, pressed against his chest, absorbed his heartbeat, which was fast, rhythmic and powerful. My senses and my thoughts became a lie detector too, and I discovered the truth: he was emotional, scared, overwhelmed, lost — and, above all, in need of a warm hug from someone he could trust in this near-far country.

Part II:
Luck, Fate, Miracles and Loss

27

Plotting Karim's rescue in the Grand Hyatt lobby

As I returned to my room, I was on edge, my emotions raging.

When I'd bade goodbye to Giora, the thought had crept into my head that I might never see him again. My encounter with him had provided a moment of sanity, a piece of home in the depths of this madhouse — and I desperately wanted more.

Billy-Giora's professionalism instilled confidence in me. The compliments he showered on me at the end of the meeting were sincere and filled me with pride. The two kisses on my forehead still burned with an intensity that showed no sign of subsiding. My conviction that Hamid, Karim and Nadine would be reunited soon was growing stronger; it was a virtual certainty. Still, my impatience made the next two days interminable; I hardly breathed or closed my eyes.

After my second sleepless night in a row, with the laptop open in front of me in the lobby, an encrypted message arrived containing the code words I had coordinated with Giora. The message lifted me sky-high: a long rambling email about the details of a cybertechnology deal contained the relevant information and confirmation of everything I could have hoped for.

Another operative had taken over the Karim rescue brief and he'd already met with Hamid the previous night. The operative had talked to him about their mutual acquaintance, a certain British businesswoman. Karim was required to maintain discretion and not tell anyone about the meeting, not even the entrepreneur from London. This strange demand was intentional. The operative wanted to make sure that Hamid was convinced that I was an innocent businesswoman and that he was able to maintain discretion and compartmentalize. Even from Mrs. Stone. They negotiated Karim's extraction from Qatar by sea after Hamid established connections between the British businesswoman and relevant parties in Doha and Tehran. This exchange, proposed by Hamid, would be carried out slowly and carefully. Once Karim was in a safe place outside Qatar's borders, Hamid would be recruited for a limited period and trained how to make good on his deal. The operative formulated a long-term plan: finding a haven for Karim, Hamid and Nadine, while Hamid continued supplying the goods for at least a year.

The combination of the news regarding Hamid and Karim and the meeting with Giora had me out of sorts. I went down to the tennis courts, trying to hide the euphoria that gripped me. I sipped coffee, enlisting all my acting talents. When I ordered my second cup, Hamid entered the lobby dressed in a resplendent tennis outfit and walked straight towards me. It was natural. We had been seen here together for the last few days, playing tennis in front of everyone.

He grabbed the cup of coffee served to him, lifted it towards his mouth and took advantage of the moment when his lips were hidden to say a short sentence. *One game, and then you need to head back to your room Jessica. Get ready because we're flying to Tehran. Something short. Three days in total,* he said quietly and slurped up all the coffee in one gulp.

I stared at him, full of questions. Thousands of thoughts ran through my head. *I have to report... Have to report...* I felt like my mind was about to combust, but I made sure to smile and chatter idly. About the weather. About yesterday's game. *I'm tired, so we'll only play one game today.*

We played a short but energetic game in front of the legion of security cameras and a few curious eyes, and then we went back to the lobby sweating and panting, leaving a few minutes apart.

The walk towards the elevator and from there towards the room became a real task. I felt a slight weakness in my knees. I mistakenly wandered past the bank of elevators to the western wing of the hotel. Inside my head, a storm raged. Flying to Tehran had been part of my training program, but it was no longer theoretical. That shattered the dam of my anxiety. Small thoughts which had accompanied me since taking off from London had become tiny cracks, extending until they touched and released the flood.

Through clenched lips, I spoke to myself. *What are you doing, Sally? What the hell are you doing? Your achievements in Doha are impressive. The computers and cell phones you infiltrated in Doha have given the control rooms in Tel Aviv access to computers and cell phones in Tehran and Natanz. It's a dream come true. It ought to be enough...*

My door was half-open. The maid was pushing a cart with cleaning supplies and fresh towels inside. Once I entered the room, she closed the door and delivered a short and precise message from Hamid. The next half-hour was a whirlwind: a coded email to Gretchen, a short conversation with Helen, a hasty shower, some breathing exercises in front of the mirror to relieve my tension. I got dressed and pulled out my favorite piece of luggage, quickly filling it with three light suits, two tennis outfits, a makeup kit that hid connectors for several types of cell phones and *Iacocca*, which held two slim flash drives.

The walk back to the elevator and the main entrance of the Hyatt was easier. The internal debate continued, but this time it was focused on the question of what could go wrong over three days in a luxury hotel in Tehran. *Just three days, on hotel premises,* I wrote in the message to Gretchen.

As the maid sent by Hamid had told me, a taxi was waiting by the entrance, the driver large, bald and dark. Less than half an hour later I was standing on the scorching asphalt of a remote patch of the airport. The taxi had let me off next to a Gulfstream whose engines were already whining. Once again, me and a Gulfstream plane on an isolated runway. *This is becoming a habit,* I smiled to myself.

Thirty seconds later, a black Mercedes S600 with tinted windows stopped next to us. Hamid emerged, tilted his head towards the airstairs and began walking towards it. He swiftly skipped up the steps, without any gentlemanly gestures, without 'ladies first,' without a helping hand at the bottom of the iron steps. *Too many eyes,* I surmised.

A man stepped out from the plane to grab my luggage and motioned to me to come up. Eight iron steps to Tehran. I waited for the wave of anxiety to wash over me again. Light sweat on my forehead and back. Stress, tightness in the chest, a storm of thoughts that would give me no peace. But it never came. I was as calm as if I'd overdosed on benzos.

As the door shut and the Gulfstream began trundling down the runway, I discovered a new Hamid before me, so different from the fragile and tearful figure I'd met in the secret office complex. His tone of voice turned from pleasant and caressing to rigid. His speech became matter-of-fact, exact, and efficient; no hint that someone had met with him, not a word about the agreements they had reached. All of him was now dedicated solely to one mission. To fulfill his commitments, to seize the opportunity that had come his way and to move towards the day when he and Karim could live somewhere with Nadine, their collective treasure.

Still, I noted the small, stubborn droplet of sweat hanging on his right cheekbone as he sat down. The air was redolent with the same scent that had tickled my nose on the Airbus flight from London to Doha. It was the same Sauvage fragrance by Christian Dior, but this time it was infused with the faint odor of fear.

28

10:30 hrs.
Aboard a Gulfstream again, a briefing
before landing in Iran

The flight seemed too long to me — seven hundred miles — but Hamid made use of this time to brief me on Tehran, on what was prohibited and what was permitted in the Islamic Republic. He elaborated on the Espinas Persian Gulf Hotel where we'd be staying, about the bubble of hedonism going on below the surface. The corruption of the Iranian government drained into halls and suites and spas and tennis courts. He explained the high-level intrigue between loyalists of the ayatollah on the one hand, and of the president on the other. He elaborated on the senior IRGC officers, pretending to be fanatically devoted to an extreme interpretation of Islam even as they conducted business under the table, earning fortunes discreetly deposited into secret bank accounts. Then he talked about the young tech whizzes, geniuses in computer science and cybertechnology, who harnessed their talents for the glory of the Revolution while demanding to be treated just like their analogues in the West, demanding freedom of action, higher wages and improved conditions within a liberated hedonistic lifestyle, without religious restrictions.

I listened attentively to every word that came out of his mouth. I asked many questions about the hotel and what was going on there, even though the Espinas had been part of my training program, even though I knew the complete and precise answers to each of my queries.

I opened by doubting the veracity of his descriptions. You must be exaggerating, I said, even though I knew he was embellishing nothing. I asked carefully about his friend Mansour Najifi and about Muhammad Reza Moslehi, the two Iranians he was going to introduce me to. It was a careful probing that conveyed a semblance of indifference. Two more customers, nothing more. *What is the essence of your relationship with this tech whiz Najifi?* I asked. *What did you tell Moslehi about me? What does he expect? How good is his tennis game?*

Mansour Najifi is like a brother to me; we're very close, he explained deliberately, looking at me to see if I understood. *Moslehi is no friend of mine, but I've been doing business with him for five years. He is a Muslim fanatic, but still greedy and a skirt-chaser. Thanks to his lust for money and women, he owes me quite a lot – and I know a little too much about him.*

The longer Hamid spoke, the greater my admiration for the accuracy of the information I received during my training. Haggai knew how to get down to the finest details when I interacted with the avatars at Mikveh Israel, and my experience in the field had an uncanny similarity to the virtual plane. Two of the six characters I'd encountered on Haggai's magic screen were indeed Najifi, star of Unit 445 of the Revolutionary Guards' cyber directorate, and Moslehi. There was no trace yet of the four others.

Each and every sentence uttered by Hamid aroused in me another wave of admiration for the service provided by unseen hands, for the unglamorous, lackluster work carried out by an army of shadows. A bunch of brave people who took pictures of the hotels, mapped the security cameras, questioned every bit of information about the people I might meet and captured the high-quality images to create life-size avatars — making sure to take full-body photos, so handshakes were possible. I tried to imagine how many agents and collaborators risked their lives to facilitate the investigation, the mundane yet essential toiling which had resulted in the thick binders I memorized before the flight to Qatar. I knew every jot and tittle of Moslehi's bio – number two in the IRGC's intelligence division, responsible for cyber-defense of nuclear activity. I knew about the complete dichotomy: his loyalty to Islam and the IRGC on the one hand and his addiction to a life of debauchery, fornication and lucre on the other. I knew of his corruption to the last decimal point, even the secret Swiss and Manx bank accounts where he stockpiled his ill-gotten gains. I knew the types of technology that interested him. I fully understood why he was eager to achieve success at all costs. I even knew how he justified his hypocrisy, telling himself that his exploitation served the ends of the Islamic Revolution.

Most importantly, I knew about the pathological battle of egos between him and the number one in intelligence. These intricate details were supposed to give me an extra layer of protection while I played in the lion's cage. In case of entanglement, I was supposed to pull out my cell phone in front of Moslehi's astonished face and show him photographs and documents that would have made it clear to him that his fate was in my hands and not the other way around. You put that in your toolbox hoping never to use it, Shimon insisted and reiterated. *I know I've already told you, but I'll say it again.*

Alongside the exhaustive and comprehensive information that I committed to memory, many pairs of eyes which had been on me in Doha would be on me in Tehran as well. Some of them moved as shadows in the hotel itself, through the lobby, down the corridors, alongside the spa and around the tennis courts. They were hotel guests, waiters, janitors, maids, cabdrivers in the never-ending queue in front of the hotel doorway. Several other pairs belonged to the occupants of the control rooms in Tel Aviv, sitting at their computers. They watched me in real time through the fixed cameras at the hotels.

With their keeping such a close watch on me, what could possibly go wrong?

29

17:00 hrs.
Settling in Tehran, readying a wasp sting

For once, I had an uneventful flight. Landing at Mehrabad Airport was pleasant. Our smooth exit was unimpeachable testimony to how connected and valued Hamid was. It only underscored how serious a failure it had been for my preliminary intelligence to omit him. A third strike, as it were. For all their admirable research, my trainers hadn't uncovered Hamid's secret family, his secret wing of the hotel, or his secret associations with Iranian powerbrokers.

After a refreshing shower, I changed from the yellow pantsuit into fancy sportswear and went down to the lobby. I was dreading my maiden appearance in tennis togs. Tight, white shorts in the heart of the Islamic Republic? What would the Supreme Leader think?

My concerns proved to be way off. Throughout the central lobby and the corridor leading to the tennis courts were women wearing as little as I was, if not less. Tourists and locals churned in and out, a virtual parade. I began to breathe a sigh of relief.

Hamid pointed to others wearing white and wrapped in towels and robes. *They're on their way to the spa.*

I see them, Hamid, but what does all this mean?

It means defiance, Jessica. They're sticking their tongues out at the authorities.

As we were talking, a young man in a navy-blue three-piece suit approached us. No tennis or spa for him. He wore a bristly beard several days old. His shoulder-bag was leather, thin and elegant. He walked straight to the table I shared with Hamid. His direct, piercing gaze, his well-manicured nails, the subtle wink he offered

Hamid — all these augured well for my debut deal on Iranian soil. When he reached us, he turned away from Hamid and offered a handshake. He stood unusually close, staring at me with mischievous shining brown eyes.

A pleasure, Mrs. Stone, he said, but his gaze remained unbroken. His speech was quiet and pleasant. His cumulative scent was refined, intriguing, surprisingly inspiring confidence. His full hair was swept back and gelled. His eyebrows were too thin and precise to look natural.

I realized right away it was Mansour Najifi, Hamid's close friend and confidant. I was supposed to relax in his presence, yet I felt uneasy about associating with this cyber genius who served the Revolutionary Guards, with all the evil and all the murderousness and cruelty that the IRGC represented. *They may look nice, smiling and good-hearted*, Haggai intoned during the long hours I spent with him and the avatars in the Mikveh Israel base. *But you must not judge them by appearance. In the blink of an eye, that veneer of humanity can vanish.*

Mrs. Stone, Hamid never stops talking about you and the software you sell. I'd love to hear some more about it. But I am equally interested in your other business; I've heard you offer the best houses in London.

I sell software and houses only to those who play tennis with me. I have no idea where I pulled that from. It was spontaneous. A verbal outburst unprecedented in my practice or training. Najifi had alerted my senses, underling the obvious. I was sticking my head in the lion's mouth, and I had to do my best to carry out my mission quickly, efficiently and sterilely before those leonine jaws snapped shut on my throat.

I wasn't the sort of agent who scales, grapples, punches, kicks, drags, shoots, detonates or infiltrates a computer system in a secret enemy facility, escaping in disguise in a burqa. Not at all. I went there to be a little wasp, stinging quickly and deftly, injecting my venom by infiltrating a device or selling my malware — and to disappear before anyone realized.

Mansour grinned at my ultimatum. *Hamid has revealed to me all your secrets, Mrs. Stone.*

So you know that my opening serve is invincible, I taunted him.

We'll see soon. I need to change, and then I'll meet you on the court, Mansour replied with a smile that was just as provocative.

My encounter with Najifi was another occasion to sorely miss Jerry. His X-ray vision, his ability to see through it all and reach the core of the issue in a split second, the way he'd dig his elbow into my waist subtly until I snapped out of my complacency and confronted the gravity of a situation.

Fifteen minutes later, I was deep into a sweaty match. Najifi was an excellent player — surprising, intelligent, much more skillful than Hamid. It took an exceptional effort to escape defeat. I stretched the limits of my abilities and won it in three games, just by a point. Every time I made contact with the ball, I felt like I was saving the country. Actually, myself.

Our game was the talk of the town, or at least of the tennis complex. Quite a few eyes followed us. The rumor about the blonde tennis player spread like wildfire. That was good. That was bad.

Our next match was in the air-conditioned lobby with its light-blue-painted walls. We took a moment to catch our breaths and sat at a table adjacent to the massive picture window at the front. He brought his elegant leather bag to the table, pulled out a thin ASUS and began to tap away with a rhythm that recalled Bar or Eliot. *Just a moment, Mrs. Stone, I have to log in and respond to some urgent emails. I've been offline for an hour and everything is falling apart in the meantime.* His fingers were strong but delicate. They seemed to have been designed for precise keystrokes. When he sank into his small screen, he seemed to forget the world, the hotel around him, me. His pupils narrowed slightly.

He read the emails to himself with his lips pursed, in a kind of continuous hum. I secretly thought I would have given a lot to know whom he was writing to and what he was writing. I looked at him briefly and sank into my cell phone, conveying indifference to the passing time and his dive into the depths of the laptop. After a few minutes, enlightenment shone on me and I dialed. *Helen, darling, how are you? I'm in Tehran now!* I spoke quietly, but still loud enough to be heard on the other side of the coffee table. Helen was happy to hear my voice and started asking questions about how I was doing and if I'd found some clients. *They're interested in two flats in London and one in Manchester*, I answered as I looked at junction of ceiling and the wall. Mansour was in his world, I was in mine, but he finished before I did. *Just a moment*, I motioned to him with my right hand and placed it on my chest. Mansour signaled *OK* and waited. By the time I was done, he was staring at me with obvious curiosity.

Mrs. Stone, Hamid says you have dream homes in London, he said.

Correction, Mr. Najifi. I deal in real estate in every major city in the UK, plus several in France, the Netherlands and Germany. Does that pique your interest?

Instead of an answer, Mansour turned the laptop screen towards me and looked at me expectantly. *It's not for me, Mrs. Stone, he explained. I have a friend who is interested. Hamid says that you are discreet, that I can trust you even with my eyes closed, and I trust Hamid with my eyes closed. He's Qatari, but I consider him a brother.*

I felt an electric current run down the back of my neck, spreading along the vertebrae of my spine. The IRGC cyber-star was handing me a laptop, active and online, less than two hours after meeting me. Was this an opportunity or a nascent catastrophe? The chance to fulfill my mission or a trap? Could anyone in Tel Aviv see what was happening to me?

I ignored the screen turned toward me and kept talking to Mansour as if I wasn't interested in the laptop. I was interested in his friend, looking for a home in Europe. I was curious where he'd learned to play tennis at such a high level. I asked him to tell me how he knew Hamid. I wanted to know where his family lived. A relaxed chat. Small talk that hid the storm raging in me, obscuring my primary goal: to dive into the laptop offered up to me with puzzling generosity, with utter carelessness, by a computer whiz. I was shocked by the casualness, not to mention Najifi's negligence. Then came the gnawing anxiety that parched my throat. *It's so easy, Sally. Actually, too easy. Actually, suspiciously easy.* The thoughts flitted at the speed of light in the space between my temples.

My question about Mansour's family hovered in the air until he abruptly said: *I have no family, Mrs. Stone. Hamid is my family.* Then he fell silent. The answer exploded into the space between us like a stun grenade. Mansour looked at me with sparkling eyes once he'd uttered the statement. One short sentence which became a turning point. Now I understood some of the thing's Hamid had said during the flight to Tehran, about brotherhood and closeness and sensitivity. Another lacuna in my briefings and training: I'd learned about Najifi's formidable position and skills, but nothing about his personal life. I'd had no idea that this would be his succinct and shocking answer to all my questions.

We kept quiet. He was shocked by the openness he showed to a foreign citizen he barely knew. I was shocked because suddenly I'd been hit by déjà vu. Mansour was confessing that his family had banned and banished him, just as Hamid's family had dispossessed him of all signs of royalty – and for the exact same reason. *Oh, why, why, why?* A low moan came out of my mouth as I misted up. A brutal sentence. *I have no family...* Such harsh words. How much pain! And what an opportunity for me...

The déjà vu deepened. The IRGC tech whiz suddenly seemed fragile, exposed, thirsty for affection and warmth, desperately looking for help. Just like Hamid. It was absolutely real, without the slightest hint of deceit. This explained his recklessness and negligence in front of me.

Now I began to run my own calculations. How desperate was he? How loyal to Hamid? How involved was he? How far would he go in exchange for helping him and his mysterious friend looking for a home in London? *Chalk up another victory for Iacocca,* I told myself. Another burgeoning success in Tehran.

Meanwhile, the charged conversation with Shimon at Mossad headquarters in Tel Aviv crept into my mind. The words luck, fate, destiny flickered in large Hebrew letters on the center of my forehead, breaking one of the strictest precautions I'd absorbed. *Don't speak Hebrew, don't even think in Hebrew.*

Mansour's laptop screen was still facing me, calling me to take a look at it, but I didn't spare a sliver of a glance. My eyes were fixed on his; my questions piled up and his answers became increasingly stark, sincere, searing my heart and soul. There was everything there. Family ostracism. A threat to his very life. A loved one who'd gone underground. Secrets that had become a millstone around his neck, used by his boss, who envied him and hated him for his outstanding talents. Mansour talked and talked, and every extra minute brought us closer — even as the shame sprouted inside me, burning like acid. Here was another person whose weakness, whose distress, whose brokenness allowed me to take advantage of him. To abuse his trust in me. To betray him.

I couldn't contain it. My heartburn bubbled up again, like after Hamid's agonized confession. Like after the visit to Yasmine, as she hung all her hopes on me. Like on the way back to the hotel from Rittal and Noor.

Mrs. Stone, you must forgive me, but you remind me so much of my dear mother Soraya. I think you are about the same age. I miss her so much. We haven't spoken in eight years. She's not allowed to meet with me, or even to talk to me.

Mansour's words hit me hard. For a fleeting moment, it seemed as if he had been listening in on my internal conversation, with the caustic shame of my dyspepsia climbing up my throat. I kept quiet. I inhaled two deep breaths of air to stifle the growing burning and looked into his eyes, as if asking him to continue. My interest seemed sincere, and it was. I got carried away. My heart went out to this unfortunate young man.

Mansour, are you not afraid to talk about such topics? My question hovered in the air for a while. The punishment in Iran for homosexuality can range from corporal to capital punishment, swiftly executed.

I already told you, Mrs. Stone. Hamid is like a brother to me. He told me who you are: a caring soul, trustworthy. I understand from him that your life is not easy either, that your husband recently passed away; yet you volunteer to help refugees.

That's right, Mr. Najifi, that's right...

You already know almost every detail about me, Mrs. Stone. So please call me Mansour and let me see what you've got for sale. How does that sound?

I pulled the ASUS towards me and started typing quickly. First, I went to the SCRS website and started looking for apartments that would suit Mansour's 'friend.' Every move I made I explained for Mansour's benefit. *Here is my company's website... Here is a selection of flats in London... Here are our properties in Manchester... Here's what we have to offer in Birmingham...*

Connecting to the SCRS real estate website should have been enough. The site knew what to do, inveigling itself into the innards of every network that linked to it. However, that required a min-imum amount of time to allow the digital foxes of the Mossad to breach the fences. My fingers hovered over the keyboard, trying to imitate the rhythm of Bar, attempting to keep up with Mansour's pace. There was no chance of that, but my speed was impressive enough. As we moved from London to Manchester, I surreptitious-ly clicked my mouse, adjusting the settings twice. While shifting from Manchester and Birmingham, I used ipconfig/all to locate the MAC address of the laptop's communication components. I copied all the data and transferred it to the 'Contact Us' panel of the SCRS website. So be it, just in case. Just in case the data transfer from the computer was halted for some reason. The good guys in Tel Aviv received a real-time alert about every message that reached SCRS in London. This time it included the MAC address in 48-EUI format, one of 281 trillion possible addresses. They also got a live broadcast from the depths of the laptop's guts, in the heart of Tehran. I had no idea if it was a laptop that Mansour used for covert affairs as well or just for entertainment, gaming and surfing social media. I couldn't tell at that moment whether the connection was transmitting to Tel Aviv the names of contacts, emails, classified documents, images and lines of code, or just a collection of bland and insignificant personal matters.

As I was diving into the screen, I noticed a silhouette approaching our table. I half-looked and noticed Hamid. *Do you know how long you've been here?* he asked good-naturedly, patting Mansour's shoulder.

Mansour shook himself, as if from deep slumber. He straightened up in his seat and glanced at his watch. *You're right, brother. Two hours, and I didn't notice. But your timing is impeccable. Mrs. Stone has properties in London to show me for Daryush.* I straightened my head slowly and looked into Mansour's eyes. He gazed back at me, with a tiny, imperceptible nod. This was the friend who needed a home in the UK. His eyes spoke to me. His exhilaration was transparent.

Hamid remained standing, about six feet from the table, and motioned for his friend to approach him. Mansour got up and hugged Hamid for a long time. A lively conversation ensued between the two. They whispered to each other, but the movements of their hands indicated the great excitement that gripped both of them. Then they returned to the table and sat down to my right and left. Hamid started telling him about the wonders of Gstone's cybertechnology, then proposed a tactical order of actions for selling the software to the department that Mansour managed. *It's got to go through me,* Hamid explained. *I have permission to sell software and equipment to the unit where Mansour works. For you, it would take months.*

Mansour listened in silence. When Hamid finished, he explained why he couldn't wait. *I have to show results to my boss, Mohsen Khodaei. He's abusing me, threatening to expose my relationship with Daryush. It could end in disaster.*

I knew Khodaei very well. I even shook his virtual hand in front of the screen at Mikveh Israel. He was a bad man, extremely cruel, deeply religious, and extraordinarily competent. Far from the bubble of escapism and hedonism of Hotel Espinas, he was number one in the unit and commanded a group of about ten cyber-talents such as Mansour. He was highly valued but lacked a binary mind. He had been given command of the unit thanks to his absolute and long-standing loyalty to key figures in the leadership. The gears of my brain turned at top speed. I had to promote the introduction of Gstone into Unit 445's computers, the secret heart of the IRGC. This was potentially an enormous breakthrough, fortuitous for sure. I prayed that the open laptop in front of me was operational. Naughty me, praying in ancient and forbidden Hebrew, in the midst of a clandestine operation in Tehran.

I listened silently to the heated conversation between Hamid and Mansour even as I tried to be as unobtrusive as possible. I turned my body aside, immersed in my cell phone, distancing myself from the ping-pong of the conversation between them but recording every nuance of Mansour's anxieties and committing to memory every argument Hamid raised. My entire mission could be at stake.

So, what do you say? asked Hamid and lightly patted my shoulder.

I beg your pardon, I wasn't listening; I was working on my upcoming vacation to Germany and Switzerland. I turned back to the table. Mansour had folded in on himself, eyes downcast, head bent, palms holding it. Hamid summarized the conversation that had gone on behind my back, which I already knew by heart.

I was in no hurry to reply. I massaged my temples with circular motions and remained silent. Hamid and Mansour were waiting for me to speak. The proposal I drafted fell on attentive ears and met Mansour's hidden needs. Gstone could help him in the power struggle with Khodaei, exposing his boss's well-concealed corruption and burnishing his own status as the wunderkind of Unit 445.

I don't want to hurt him. I just need some trump cards to ensure he'll no longer be able to threaten us, Mansour said in a quiet voice, his palm obscuring the movement of his lips.

The agreement we reached had an excellent chance of success, alongside dramatic risks. I listened to Hamid's plan and nodded my head. By the next morning Gstone would be safely housed on Mansour's computer within Unit 445's headquarters.

I ought to have felt satisfaction, pride, happiness, but a night of regret awaited me as I tossed and turned. At the same time a wave of anxiety rose in me. I had no one to consult. I didn't have a shoulder to cry on as I voiced the torments of my conscience for betraying Mansour. There was no Jerry by my side to offer his professional opinion. Nor were Bar and Eliot there to reassure me, to convince me that I had acted correctly, to guarantee that Gstone would not be visible to anyone in the department except for Mansour.

But would it truly remain undiscovered? Alongside Mansour, there were nine other brilliant minds in the department. First-rate high-tech professionals. The best of the best in the Persian-speaking world. Most of them had studied at the finest universities in the UK and the US; most of them were fueled by an ideology of hatred for the West.

This thought made sweat pour from my pores, over my forehead, down my back. I felt like I was on fire.

With a hysterical motion I cast off the thin sheet that covered me. Then I peeled off the thin T-shirt I was wearing and ran to open the window. I had to suck in lungfuls of air lest I suffocate.

30

10:05 hrs.
Doffing the chador for Western sanity in a
Tehran sports complex

Cruel. A monster on two legs. Sophisticated. Avaricious. A skirt-chaser. These were the descriptions of Colonel Muhammad Reza Moslehi related during my training in Tel Aviv as well as in Hamid's briefing on the flight from Doha to Tehran.

Moslehi was number two in the IRGC's intelligence division, which reported directly to Supreme Leader Ali Khamenei. He had tremendous power. He was considered a success story and scared me more than all the other figures whose names, images and finest intimate details I'd memorized. His success was overshadowed by two factors. In parallel with the Revolutionary Guards' intelligence organization, there was another intelligence ministry which was subordinate to President Hassan Rouhani and constantly strove to be bigger, smarter, and more efficient. Iranian redundancy was a feature, not a bug. Another obstacle facing Reza Moslehi was his immediate superior, Brigadier General Javad Rezaei, the commander-in-chief of the intelligence division.

My short-term espionage mission slipped through the cracks of these redundancies, divisions, and battles of ego. It was devoid of Hollywood action scenes — stakeouts and surveillance, karate and parkour, poisonings, explosions and assassinations. Until that point, it had been car chase-free too, unlike my Athenian excursion.

I had always imagined Reza Moslehi, resplendent in the dark-green parade dress of a full colonel in the Islamic Revolutionary Guard Corps, three ten-sided stars on each shoulder, medals shining on his chest. But the encounter with him was in a completely different uniform: white, bright and short.

Hamid had called to inform me that Moslehi would arrive at the spa and sports complex at 10 AM. A few minutes earlier, I had already settled in at a round table at the far end of the lobby of the complex. It was packed not only with foreign tourists, but locals who drained into the Espinas to inhale an hour or two of Western sanity, free of the black chador.

Tattle of my grueling and close match with Mansour had spread like wildfire, prompting Moslehi to come and challenge me. A few seconds before ten Hamid entered the complex from the tennis courts. Reza Moslehi entered from the large glass door of the main lobby. A moment earlier three bearded gentlemen in black suits, looking like three avatars cast from the same production line, entered through the same door. They made no effort to hide their earpieces. Each occupied a corner of the lobby, hands crossed over their suit jackets, close to their concealed firearms.

Hamid introduced us each in turn: first me, then the colonel, then himself. He smiled contentedly. We chuckled and sat down. Hamid spared us the embarrassment of polite handshakes and began to do what he knew best: sell.

He placed a slim ASUS Zenbook on the table, turned the screen towards us and began to lecture methodically about the groundbreaking technology. The presentation, most of which he had received from me, included an article from The Financial Times about the sale of the software to the Pakistani army and the news about a pending deal with two militaries in South America. I looked at Hamid in astonishment. He had known Gstone for three weeks but talked about it as if he were part of the development team. He was precise about the technological nuances and spoke enthusiastically, with a real shine in his eyes. Throughout, he offered subtle and well-crafted hints to the colonel, who was locked in a fierce struggle with his superior — who himself was competing with the president's intelligence unit. Hamid's presentation was impressive and efficient. Every sentence, every word, brought him closer to rescuing Karim and reuniting the two of them with Nadine.

Reza Moslehi listened to him in silence. He was undoubtedly impressed, but it was evident that the software did not interest him at the moment. He was focused on a specific challenge: beat the blonde. *Mrs. Stone, I am extremely interested in what you have to offer in cybertechnology; but I am here this morning to play tennis. Will you do me the honor?*

It would be my pleasure, Colonel. I'd love to get some exercise too; I haven't had any this morning. But are you sure you want to play against me?

Reza Moslehi's smile shone through his thick, graying beard. A fair-haired peer of the fairer sex could not be a threat! We set out for the court.

I walked heavily, my mind swirling. What was I to do in the face of such an opponent, a cruel and bloodthirsty Muslim fanatic? My inclination was to let him win the first match, to defeat him in the second and then to request that we go back to the lobby to rest.

As we began to play, a question began to nettle me, a surprising one which I'd never dared to formulate earlier, not even in the deepest recesses of my brain. Could it be that my Jerry couldn't resist the temptation, that he had gone to the control room and was watching me right now? Was he standing there looking at me? Was a monitor now displaying a close-up of my face to him? Was he enjoying as I trounced the Iranian spymaster or was he disappointed that I couldn't help myself? It was a strange thought, but quite logical. Jerry was at the top of the Mossad. All departments were open to him. The control room was just down the hall from his office. These thoughts broke my focus and gave the colonel two easy volleys, but no more. I stuck to my plan. Moslehi beat me in the first game, I won the second, and then I asked us to go back for a drink in the lobby because I was very tired.

Hamid wasn't there. Reza asked for a pitcher of cold water and a ristretto. I asked for cold water only. We caught our breath — I easily, he with some difficulty. He continued to gasp and wheeze for a while and even indulge in the short, damp cough of heavy smokers. To break the silence between us, I complimented him: *Colonel, you're an amazing player.*

Oh, you are an amazing player — and a smart woman, Mrs. Stone, he replied and poured himself another glass of cold water. *I would love for you to come and visit me at my home tomorrow at noon. There is an adjacent tennis court there. We can find out who wins in the end...*

I listened carefully and was angry at Hamid for leaving me alone with this frightening man who was now inviting me to his home. It was an unexpected development, certainly one that deviated from Hamid's promises prior to takeoff from Doha. *Just three days, on hotel premises,* he'd told me, and I had added in my own head: *Just within range of the cameras and the people watching me.*

I sipped my water to kill time. I scanned the lobby in a forbidden and futile attempt to identify who was on the lookout for me. They all seemed to be guests or hotel employees. None of them looked towards our table. *Thank you for the generous invitation, Colonel, but I have to check with Hamid what he's planning for tomorrow. Give me your phone number and I'll keep you posted.*

My pleasure, answered Moslehi and began to dictate his mobile number to me. I saved it and immediately dialed it. As I did, the number flew all the way to Tel Aviv and back. Reza Moslehi picked up the cell phone in surprise.

There, now I know I've got the right number. And you can save mine, too. Our relationship has moved to the next level, I said with a prolonged smile, although the weight upon my chest remained, perhaps even intensified. My anger at Hamid also increased. I took another swig of water, then caught sight of the lobby door swinging open. Hamid strode toward us.

The three of us were not reunited for long. The colonel said he had to go back to the office on an urgent matter. His bodyguards abandoned the corners of the lobby and clustered around him as he opened the wide glass door.

I skewered Hamid with an unrelenting look, laser-like. *Where did you go? Why did you leave me alone with this psychopath?* I fired at him and did not hide my rage.

Jessica, it'll be fine. The colonel's house is like something out of a movie, one of the most magnificent in Tehran. You'll have fun. The colonel endeavors to impress every visitor from the West who comes to Iran. He is a true patriot. It is important for him to show foreigners that not everything is dark here.

31

9:30 hrs.
On the way to Lavasan, Tehran in its full beauty and full ugliness

There was nothing leisurely or fun about going to the colonel's house. It was one surprise after another, almost all unpleasant. I was angry at myself for agreeing to the outing, even though Gretchen had sent me a reassuring, congratulatory message. Decoded, it said: *Good for you. Visit your new friend. Work on your connection. Eat, drink, play tennis.* That was it, nothing more.

As I left the hotel, a shiny black Mercedes was waiting for me with a smiling driver standing by the open door, greeting me in perfect English. In the back seat sat Hamid, tapping away on his laptop. *Good morning, good morning,* he said without taking his eyes off the crystal screen.

The morning drive lasted about half an hour, from Hotel Espinas to the upscale enclave of the Lavasan neighborhood.

Hamid was insanely busy but smiling, loose, calm. I was a bundle of nerves but made an effort to put on a relaxed facade. *Hamid, I hope we won't waste time on this trip. I came here to sell, not make courtesy visits.*

Hamid was engrossed in whatever he was typing. His manicured fingers flew across the keyboard. He replied, without looking in my direction: *Jessica, you can trust me. I'm cooking up at least two Gstone deals here – and your real estate business won't suffer either. The colonel is a senior officer, quite prominent, and he very much needs the technological solutions you offer. All he thinks about is business and profit. You'll see; he won't hold back.*

The drive showed us Tehran through tinted windows, in all its hues — all its beauty, all its ugliness, all the signs of the fanatic dictatorship that had crushed the people beneath its heel, all the buds of rebellion and liberty that sporadically and stubbornly appeared nonetheless.

The streets were crowded and noisy. Unbearable traffic jams, three IRGC checkpoints. On the sidewalks swiftly moved swarms of black tents — tens of thousands of women in raven outfits under the watchful eye of the morality police. At the intersections pairs of soldiers in desert camouflage carried assault rifles. The sides of buildings displayed huge portraits of Khomeini. Here and there were traces of graffiti by brave subversives.

At the first checkpoint I felt a wave of cold go down my back. I sank deep into my laptop, pretending to be busy.

Just keep working, Jessica, everything is fine, Hamid said quietly and calmly. Then he rolled down the window. A soldier, assault rifle slung across his chest, leaned down. His beard was black and full. His cap cast his face in shadow, but his eyes smoldered. His speech was gruff.

From the few sentences in Persian that I'd learned in training, I gathered that Hamid wished the soldier a good morning and a good day by the grace of God, or something to that effect. The soldier did not smile or return the salutation; instead, he demanded our papers. Hamid pulled his fancy leather wallet out to present a plastic photo ID.

This is my magic card, he said with a smile once the soldier handed it back. *I'm a member of the household here — an honored guest of all the senior officials.*

Hamid's confidence was validated at the second checkpoint as well. Precisely the same ritual, the camo-clad corpsman sending us on our way. Yet I couldn't help but note out of the corner of my eye that two soldiers had violently torn a tearful woman out of a fancy jeep in the parallel lane. Her head covering fell off, revealing a woman of about thirty with a glossy complexion and a smooth, long mane, black as charcoal. One of the soldiers grabbed her hair and slammed her down on the hood of the car. The other soldier hit the back of her legs with a short club. Blow after blow, until the young woman collapsed onto the asphalt.

As our Mercedes accelerated away, Hamid remonstrated: *Focus on your work, Jessica, it's not our business.* His gaze was fixed on his laptop. Despite what he said, I couldn't look away from the spectacle on the other side of the window. The Mercedes moved forward, but I rubbernecked, unable to avert my eyes from the horror, a cruel reminder of where I was and why. *You ought to be focused on your own affairs,* Hamid said in a tone that contained a hint of reproach.

We drove past crowded, dusty, distressed neighborhoods and on towards a spacious residential area. The road became modern; two lanes in both directions, with flowers, plants and trees in the roundabouts. Now there were private homes with gardens on detached and semi-detached plots, a taste of the bourgeois; I could not help but think of what we called *Bneh Beitcha* back home. Jessica Stone ought to call it something else but, before I could think of it, the houses became mansions, increasingly elegant, with imaginative designs, high fences, guard posts. *This cannot be Tehran. Maybe Beverly Hills, the Hamptons, Bel Air...*

Then came checkpoint number three and things got complicated. The soldier looked angry, took Hamid's magic card and summoned an officer to come check it. The officer glanced at it, turned it over to the other side, shook his head and spoke into his walkie-talkie. The other soldier opened my door, vigorously and anxiously motioning at me to get out of the car. Hamid got out and tried to argue, but the first soldier was determined and gestured for me to stand up and present my papers. I tried to reconstruct what had just happened, what had alerted the two soldiers, why Hamid's ID card had been taken for inspection in a wooden shack several yards from the guard post. I gave the soldier my passport and examined him closely. He looked like a child. Maybe twenty, with a thick black beard and bright eyes. He didn't know a word of English, aside from *Passport... Passport...*

I sent a questioning look at Hamid who was standing on the other side of the car. He grinned, but I felt it was a show. He was troubled. *This has never happened to me,* he said, miming an apology.

The boy in uniform leaned forward as he flipped through the passport, back and forth. He had no idea what he was looking for. As soon as his gaze was turned away from me, I surreptitiously positioned my cell phone so I could scroll through my list of outgoing calls. I squinted down, clicked on Reza Moslehi's name and prayed he would answer. The soldier glanced at me, considering me, but then went back to idly flipping through my passport. Another glimpse showed that my prayer had been answered, as well as my call.

I brought the cell phone close to my face in a flash and said aloud, in Farsi, *Hello, Colonel Muhammad Reza Moslehi, how are you?* The soldier whipped his head up as if he'd been bitten by a snake. Hamid, whose head had been fixed on the ground, raised his head too and his astonished expression quickly broke into a big grin.

Two minutes later we were already in the car again after the pair of soldiers and their commander begged our pardon profusely, and after Hamid's magic card had been returned to him with a host of additional apologies.

I sat down in the backseat and closed my eyes. Shortly after, the Mercedes faced a barrier at the entrance to a spacious and regal manse. *This is our colonel's house,* Hamid said. Genuine surprise spread across my face, which only intensified when the Mercedes passed through the gates and the entire estate was revealed to us. *It's one of the most beautiful houses in Tehran,* Hamid said, *but it's not in the premier league. Wait until you see the houses of the ministers, the military chiefs, the allies of the Supreme Leader.*

I packed my laptop into a thin leather case, put it in a larger bag I had brought with me, and asked the driver to keep it until the end of the visit.

32

11:00 hrs.
In Lavasan, photos of the family
and theHermit Kingdom

As I surveyed the estate, it seemed that Moslehi had done everything possible to impress me.

The garden in front of us seemed to go on forever. It was very
cleverly designed, as if it were the natural continuation of the huge
living room with an extremely high ceiling. The adjacent wall of
the house was glass, drawing in the infinite greensward with its
meticulously landscaped trees and rounded fountain. A wooden
deck spanned the entire length of the wall; ornately designed tables were loaded with delicacies. To the right of the lawn stood a
regulation-size tennis court with a fine, chain-link fence around
it. Some distance to the left, the vibrant green turned to sparkling
blue, a beautiful oval swimming pool like an unblinking eye. Three
couples in minimal swimsuits were swimming and slipping into it
via a translucent slide.

The waiters were all fluent in English. They were resplendent in
their three-piece suits, a light shade of gray. There were also three
waitresses, their headscarves large and colorful sitting nonchalantly atop the most fashionable hairstyles.

I struggled to reconcile it all: the heedless extravagance; opulence;
flamboyant fashion; the copious food, music and drink — and on the
other side of the chasm, the dark, crowded, screaming and dusty reality I'd studied in Tel Aviv and witnessed throughout the ride.

One of the binders on Iran I'd been assigned for homework described the morality police. Its officers had, to date, fined or arrested
(or worse) three million women for inappropriate clothing. Yet here

the family and friends of one of the senior members of the IRGC defiantly violated every last dictate of modesty!

Shiraza, the colonel's wife, looked younger than him by two decades, perhaps more. Her face shone bright white with a slight natural blush that flared up whenever she laughed. Tall and thin, she wore a startlingly scarlet pantsuit, cut wide and long. Her delicate silk headscarf, in subdued yellow, repeatedly slid back revealing her wavy hair, light brown turning to blonde at the tips.

I'd like you to meet my wonderful wife, Shiraza. When we met, she was an actress and model. He nodded and turned to talk to Hamid.

Shiraza beamed as she touched her face. The chemistry between us was immediate, a lightning connection. *Come, I'll show you around our humble abode.* She grabbed my hand to give me a private women's tour.

We walked out of the spacious living room into a hall that led to a separate wing. Opulent chandeliers hung from the ceiling. The walls were covered with paintings that looked like originals to me.

At the end of the corridor was a parlor, smaller but no less striking than the main sitting room. In one of its corners stood a carved walnut table under a full array of spot lighting which sent rays of light slanting down to glint off of dozens of picture frames. These were rows and rows of photographs, though few featured the family. Most of them featured Colonel Muhammad Reza Moslehi at various promotion ceremonies, on training maneuvers, in battledress with groups of officers, on visits to various sites.

Some of these pictures date back to when we first got married, when my husband was a junior officer; the newest are from this year, Shiraza proudly said, pointing towards a cluster of framed photographs at the front end of the table. I expressed a polite interest in them. *Spectacular, spectacular,* I mumbled and then it hit me. One of the pictures showed the colonel next to a group of officers with almond eyes and prominent cheekbones. Another showed him with civilians, similar in appearance. I realized with a start that I was looking at photographic evidence of the Tehran-Pyongyang axis. I had to act quickly, so I whirled around to compliment my hostess: *What an intimate and cozy space you've made here. I'm sure that you deserve the credit for the refined design.* I touched her shoulder gently to express my appreciation.

Thank you, Mrs. Stone, Thank you. This parlor was indeed my idea. I cannot stand that cavernous sitting room. It's not much of a living room; it's just for our distinguished guests — or should I say, his distinguished guests.

It's amazing, absolutely amazing. You have exquisite taste. May I take your picture in this wonderful space, the artist alongside her creation?

Oh, Mrs. Stone, you flatter me. Feel free! Remarkable, you've been here all of half an hour, but I feel like I've known you for years.

I took two steps back and aimed three quick clicks at Shiraza: one vertical, focusing on her; two horizonal, one capturing as many of the photographs on the table as I could, the other a close-up of the two North Korean pictures.

Look at this great shot! You can see the beams of light coming down from the ceiling. It's just like a painting, I gushed. I showed her the first image, capturing her in her full stature and full beauty, without any background.

What an amazing photo! Send it to me, Shiraza said and gave me her cell phone number.

We moved on to the magnificent kitchen and laundry room, finally arriving at the bedrooms. It was then that I asked Shiraza where the bathroom was. I needed to take a breather, relax and review my work.

Before I flushed, I sent Gretchen the two horizontal images. My cell phone camera has been upgraded, which would allow the gang in Tel Aviv to isolate each of the photographs I'd captured in my two cross-sectional snaps.

I left the bathroom to find Shiraza had been joined by her husband the colonel, as well as someone new, in uniform. The three ten-sided stars on each shoulder told me he was a colonel too. My heart skipped a beat.

33

13:00 hrs.
Infiltrating the home computer at the
colonel's house

There you are! I couldn't figure out where you'd disappeared to. Let me introduce Colonel Haider Al Muhammadi, said Moslehi.

Muhammadi looked older than his comrade. His face was wrinkled, a large scar running from his left temple to the center of his cheek. On his nose was perched a pair of thick-framed glasses. His widow's peak was aggressive, leaving huge swathes of his forehead bare except for the strange narrow strip in the middle.

Haider is a close and dear friend of mine, Mrs. Stone. He is extremely interested in the real estate you're offering. Hamid says all the Qataris are crazy about you. I just hope you have something left for your friends from Tehran as well.

I laughed, trying my damnedest to make it convivial, continuous, convincing. *Colonel, these are the finest homes on the market. Best of the best. I can show you as many as you'd like.*

That sounds great, said Moslehi, leading us down the hall past the bedroom. At the end was a mahogany door with brass accents. *Be my guest,* he said as he opened the door. *This is my study.*

I stood a few feet behind the pair of colonels, my legs refusing to move. It was as if my blood turned to lead, flowing down to my feet and weighting them to the rich carpet. Should I dare surf once again to the SCRS website? How many times had the prohibition been echoed by Bar, Eliot, Haggai, Shimon and Jerry? *Don't get addicted to routines. Alter your modus operandi. Improvise. Innovate.*

I had a second or two to decide what to do before my dawdling in the hallway would begin to seem strange. I blinked briefly, praying for inspiration. It failed to appear. So I opened my eyes, forced myself to put one foot in front of the other, and entered the room which now became crowded. I had no choice but to put on an encore performance.

Moslehi sat down, turned on the computer, then offered me his chair. I sat in front of the screen, typed in the SCRS URL, and started scanning properties in some UK cities. Our online experience needed to last at least twenty minutes in order for the masterminds in Tel Aviv to get what they needed without leaving a trace.

In practice, our browsing lasted almost an hour. The two colonels vied with each other to see who could be more enthusiastic about the more expensive apartment. The competition was great for me. At one point they stole my seat to flit between the finest urban properties in Britain, France and Germany, eager as two small children. Shiraza and I looked at each other and smiled at the juvenility of the two senior officers. She reached out to me again and said quietly: *Let's go back to the lawn, to the open air.*

Two hours later, after some prolonged girl-talk about childrearing, hugs and mutual commitments to visit, I offered my heartfelt thanks to Moslehi. After exchanging looks with Hamid, I started walking back to the Mercedes.

My humble host followed me. *Thank you, Mrs. Stone, for honoring us,* he said, reaching out to me for a warm handshake and staring at me closely. *It's been a while since I've seen Shiraza so happy. Thank you so much,* he continued, enlisting his other hand as well. *I'll see you tomorrow at the Espinas sports center. You owe me a game,* he continued, my hand still sandwiched between his and his eyes still fixed on mine.

You owe me a game, Colonel. I have to improve the balance sheet when it comes to you. I don't like a draw. With a light giggle, I extricated my hand and turned to disappear into the backseat of the Mercedes.

34

11:00 hrs.
Monstrous cruelty at the sports
and spa complex

My hopes were dashed. I thought that the colonel would have more important operational tasks than a mere tennis match at the hotel. But at a minute to ten his three bodyguards had already entered the complex and, precisely on the hour he entered, resplendent in his white tennis outfit, striding straight toward me.

Today is payback, he said. I noticed that his smile was somewhat dampened. He seemed tense, annoyed, angry, depressed. Some combination of these.

The foray onto the tennis court didn't last long. I won two games, which was a mistake. I had no idea why I chose to beat him. Perhaps I needed Jerry to subtly pinch me and keep me from my worst impulses.

We were both out of breath after our brief but vigorous game. I asked for a jug of ice water and started chewing an ice cube when suddenly, without warning, the colonel bent over to me and spoke in a whisper: *Mrs. Stone, you are probably impressed by my refined speech, my American education, my luxurious home, my expensive clothing, my skill in tennis, but do you have any idea how cruel we can be?*

I stared at him astonished. I kept quiet for a while, and then I whispered back: *Why would you say such a thing, Colonel? I thought I got to know you. I was extremely impressed with Shiraza. I don't see anything cruel in your character. You are very nice people. Why would you say such a terrible thing in this lovely place?*

Moslehi smiled in a way that frightened me, pressing a finger hard against the center of his cheek. *We are particularly cruel towards those suspected of espionage or treason.*

His words cut me apart. A cold wave crept up my leg. There was an awful pounding in my temples, but I gave him a thin, confused grin. I had a split second to decide what my answer would be. I stole another moment by gulping my water. I imbibed a large ice cube with a theatrical flourish, biting into it and saying, mouth half-full and smile at one-quarter: *I hope, Colonel, that you aren't saying these terrible things just because I beat you in tennis.*

The colonel did not smile and continued to talk as if I had not spoken. He began to voice atrocious, graphic descriptions of the capture of a Western businessman suspected of espionage. *We put him in an ice water bath after slicing him open from nipple to navel, not to mention copious cuts all over his face and all other parts of his body. Then we started pouring increasing amounts of salt and vinegar into the ice water.*

Oh, I objected, *oh my god! Why are you telling me such frightful stories first thing in the morning?*

Moslehi insisted on continuing. He went into great detail about the incisions on the body of the suspected spy, from stem to stern. He described the screams produced by the ice bath. He detailed the additional torture that was carried out while the infiltrator was still in the water, to get out of him who had sent him to Iran.

I knew I shouldn't sound indifferent to the horror story, but I didn't want to seem too shocked. Still, my brain began analyzing the situation and trying to understand what the colonel was trying to tell me, why he was illustrating all these atrocities to me. Regardless, one conclusion was undeniable: I was in clear and immediate danger. My cover might be blown, I might be captured, I might be executed. Body, soul, mind — they were all on autopilot, as I frantically searched for an escape hatch.

As I considered all this, my thoughts retreated to the words that Ohr Barkan had told me: *Sally, you were born beneath the sign of the pine tree. According to Chinese astrology, this is a symbol of perseverance.*

The pinecone can survive at sixty degrees below freezing in Siberia, but it also survives the heat of a kiln. It can tolerate a range of hundreds of degrees — and you are as strong and enduring as it is. In addition, you were born on the last day of the Chinese astrological cycle. This is a rare date that occurs only once a century!

Ohr's statements seemed ridiculous compared to the imminent danger I was in; but the symbolism of the pinecone's durability managed to calm me down.

I forcefully shunted that train of thought, returning to my reality in the heart of Tehran. Moslehi was still talking, macabre enjoyment on his face. He went back to recounting the blood-curdling screams of the torture victim — and the woodpecker went back to rapping powerfully upon my brain. *Tap, tap, tap.*

As he went on I began to think that, in his distorted way, he might be seeking to bury my incriminating visit to his little acre of hedonism, contradicting the principles of the distorted Islam he represented in his position and at his rank. Perhaps he wanted to hide the paradoxical nature of his Islamic Revolutionary Guard Corps zeal and his juvenile enthusiasm for Western real estate. It was also possible that he wanted to cultivate a triumphant masculine image of himself, which meant he needed to punish me for my dismissal of his romantic advances from the intimate look he tried to share with me — to the aggressive, intrusive and prolonged handshake — out of Shiraza's sight, far from the eyes of his friends.

All these were reasonable options, suiting the colonel's personality profile and his crude machismo; but there were other possibilities which arose in my mind, ones which might pose much greater difficulties. Maybe Shiraza had told him about how I played the shutterbug at his gallery of framed photos? Had my broadcast to Tel Aviv from his home computer been intercepted and decrypted by his geek squad of subordinates? Maybe Hamid's Mercedes had hidden cameras? Perhaps Moslehi's unit had carried out an in-depth investigation to find out more about Gstone?

Even worse, had Nasser from Qatar called up Reza in Iran, colonel-to-colonel? I felt like I was losing my grip on sanity. I'd wondered hundreds of times if my Doha routine hadn't raised some alarms. Could it be that Nasser was utterly unaware of my activities? All it would take was one security camera that I'd missed once while infiltrating a home computer. So did the two officers maintain a working relationship and update each other? Was there a connection between Moslehi's horror stories and something discovered in Doha? One thin crack in my facade could have cost me everything.

As the conversation progressed, I realized that I'd never know for sure what caused Reza's motivation; I was driving myself to distraction, but it was all in vain. A minute ticked by, another, and then my mind issued a pithy, precise imperative: *Mrs. Stone, get out of here now.*

I gave the colonel a small, embarrassed smile. *Colonel, this conversation has really gotten out of hand.* I knew that, from that moment on, a timer would begin counting down. It took my most impressive acting to appear nonchalant, lest I expose a hint of anxiety or a change in behavior. Why wouldn't an innocent British businesswoman be disgusted, let alone stressed out by the colonel's tales? I begged his pardon and said I needed to go to the restroom for a moment.

On the way, I pulled out my cell phone and dialed my friend Gretchen. *Hey, we spoke just yesterday, how are you?* I asked if she would be able to join me next week on a canal cruise near Norwich, England. My phrasing, wording and choice of destination sent a sharp, clear and urgent message across the ocean indicating the highest and direst state of emergency.

Gretchen chuckled for any listeners and said she would be happy to join me; but the startling message she conveyed was that I had to leave posthaste; the mission had been completed, but I had to be extricated quickly, within twenty-four hours at most.

When I returned from the bathroom, I walked rapidly back towards the table where Moslehi had been sharing his sickening stories with me, addressing him from some distance and at considerable volume so that anyone in the immediate vicinity could her me clearly. *Colonel, I'm famished. Won't you treat me to lunch?* The simple request conveyed a number of messages without my having to voice them: *I'm not scared. I'm not rushing anywhere. As far as I'm concerned, nothing has changed. Your graphic tales of torture sound exaggerated and don't concern me at all. Above all, you still have a chance to seduce the widowed blonde from England.*

Reza Moslehi looked at me for a long time; it was unclear whether he was shocked, disappointed or still hopeful that he might get me in bed.

We ended up having an extravagant luncheon, featuring the finest delicacies of Persian cuisine. We talked a little and, even in that little, I tried to say things that might encourage him. *Shiraza tells me that you are an excellent husband and a great father,* I wove in at one point. Towards the end of the conversation, I threaded in: *Wish me good luck, Colonel.*

He looked up slowly, not hiding his confusion. *Of course, I wish you the best of luck,* he murmured, aiming a quizzical look at me.

You see this swelling, I said and randomly touched the skin of my neck. *I'm supposed to fly to England to have thyroid surgery. It's a simple but sensitive surgery I've been waiting two years for. Finally, I learned yesterday that I've been approved. I'm optimistic. I will fly to England for two weeks, then come back here to continue our business.*

Moslehi listened in silence.

The next morning, I went down for breakfast in the hotel garden. I dined alone. I was nervous and agitated, but I made sure to walk vigorously and confidently, beaming small smiles at everyone around me.

My thoughts ran to-and-fro. The omelet was divine, but I couldn't swallow it. I drank another glass of juice, then another coffee. I wondered what my distress would set in motion and when.

One of my fellow guests caught my attention: a man dressed in a white, shiny, elegant kandura, his white ghutra encircled by a traditional black agal. The smooth, loose fabric looked like a mix of silk and cotton. *Ah, another visitor from Qatar*, I told myself. He was sitting about six feet from me, facing me. A thick, shapely beard defined his face, his eyes hidden behind dark lenses.

Chapeau à lui on the Chopard sunglasses, I quipped, but then I jerked back as if a sniper's bullet had hit me. His right hand reached for the small cup in front of him, grabbing the handle with two fingers. As he lifted the demitasse, he extended the index finger of his left hand to pin its bottom. He upended the cup to gulp down its contents summarily, then coordinated the vessel's descent with his index finger, until it rested on the table once more. I adjusted my position so I could scrutinize him without turning my neck. I lowered my head but continued to squint at the man in white. My immediate reaction was not one of suspicion, but outrage. I watched him as he executed the maneuver yet again — just as he had on the Gulfstream from Greece.

I felt the blood draining from my face. I tried to pick out what physical features I could that weren't obscured by the kandura and ghutra: his forehead, his eyebrows, the few hairs that stuck out, the palms of his hands, the thickness of his fingers. It didn't take long. I knew for sure that the man at the table closest to me was Yiftach.

He raised a hand and motioned to one of the waiters, who hurried over. He spoke in a relatively loud voice, a sabra with flawless Arabic — the effortless rolling of the tongue, the accent authentic, the inflections convincing, with all the modulations and variations and intonations characteristic of the Gulf. His speech reminded me of what I'd heard at several meetings I had attended in London and Dubai. He was particularly good at what he did. Perfect, perfect, the thought passed through my mind. *Now I've discovered the fourth language he speaks*, I told myself, suppressing a grin.

As I pondered how to take a step towards him, a light-haired man dressed in a gray three-piece suit, but with the same sunglasses, approached Yiftach. It was Giora, AKA Billy. He walked to the table briskly, lifted his glasses to his forehead, and extended a hand to Yiftach.

35

10:30 hrs.
The rescue squad appears in Tehran

I got to my feet, flustered. It was clear that Yiftach's appearance in Tehran and his rendezvous with Giora were related to the coded message I'd sent the day before to Gretchen. It was no coincidence that the two of them were meeting here, right in front of me. Ostensibly, this should have put me at ease; here were two professionals looking out for me — but the opposite happened. I put two and two together and realized how dire my predicament was.

I started down the gravel path from the wellness center to the main lobby. I wanted to run the distance as fast as possible, but I held back. I walked naturally and slowly, with performative ease for the cameras lining the trail. I needed to appear relaxed. *Where would the British lady be rushing to at this time of morning?*

Halfway to the automatic glass doors I heard steps crunching in the gravel. Someone stepped behind me at a faster pace than mine. It was clear that he was trying to catch up with me, that I was the target he was aiming for. I kept looking forward, maintaining my moderate pace, and waited.

My pulse accelerated as the rustle of footsteps approached me. He came from the right, and then I heard *good morning* in English with a slight German accent. *Good morning, Mrs. Stone.* It was Giora. I couldn't mistake his voice, his refined speech, the shadow of his Austrian inflection. A quick side-eye affirmed my conjecture, along with his perfect profile. *How do you feel, Mrs. Stone? It's a great morning for traveling,* he said, as he quickened his pace and was swallowed up by the automatic doors. I smiled and continued walking calmly despite the cyclone tearing through my mind. A moment later I was in the air-conditioned lobby. While walking towards the elevators, I surveyed all the tables and armchairs around me. There was no trace of Giora's tailored suit. He had simply evaporated.

The elevator whistled its way to the fifth floor, where the stainless-steel doors parted to reveal the long and somewhat poorly lit hallway. I pulled out the magnetic card and walked towards Room 522. I thought I would need to unlock the door, but it was already open, as evidenced by the slit of light. Another round in the horrific game I'd been playing since the day before. From the terrifying conversation with the colonel to Yiftach's appearance in a beard and white robe, Giora's portentous small talk and now my half-open door. I felt silly. Was I supposed to go inside and dispatch whoever the interloper was with my bare hands? I extended my finger gingerly to push the door slowly, breathing a sigh of relief when I discovered a hotel maid in a light blue uniform and matching hijab standing next to the double bed and spreading the duvet.

Sorry, I murmured. *Sorry, please go ahead,* I continued and motioned for her to finish her work. The cleaning lady gave the duvet one last tug and turned towards me with her finger resting on her mouth. In a flash I recognized the mesmerizing amber fountains in the eyes of Anat, the flight supervisor from the Gulfstream. She motioned with her hand towards the glass door, which led to the spacious and shaded balcony and began towards it. As she walked, she removed her blue uniform to reveal an impeccably tailored, fashionable fuchsia dress underneath. In the next step, she pulled off the blue headscarf, loosening the waterfalls of her amber hair. She looked stunning. Anat beckoned me to sit in one of the chairs at the glass table and admire the view. Then she closed the glass door and sat down in front of me.

The tempest swirling within me increased. Yiftach, Giora, now Anat —everyone was here, in the heart of the City of 72 Nations. A massive storm seemed to be looming. I sat down in the chair opposite Anat, completely overwhelmed. Still, I felt enveloped. Protected. We were getting the band back together, the Gulfstream gang reunited in another country, in a different reality. Surrounding me

— in the garden restaurant, in the lobby, in the room — giving me a hug of confidence.

It reminded me of things that Shimon told me in one of our early conversations, when I had not yet consented to go on a mission alone in an enemy country. *Always remember, Sally, when you go on a mission in an enemy country, you are not alone. You're not some superhero who's going to save the country single handedly. You're just one gear in a huge clock. Always, always, 24/7, our agents are in the field beside you. There are those who watch over you, there are those who lay in wait for something to happen. There are many good people who do exactly what you do, but with other people. They surround you, Sally. Tourists like you, cleaners and custodians, waiters, taxi-drivers, bellhops and tennis instructors. Remember that they are there, but never try to guess who's who. Make no effort to identify them.*

Anat's English was excellent. The shadow of her German accent did not take away from her eloquent and charismatic speech. She spoke English even though we were alone, with the glass door of the balcony closed, with the awning shading us and hiding us from the other balconies. Anat spoke in English, and I replied accordingly. Just like the conversations in English that Jerry and I had in Islamabad, even when it was just the two of us, completely alone, in the double bed, deeply immersed in each other. *Under no circumstances, never, no matter how sure you are that you are alone, you do not speak any language except English.* This was one of the ironclad rules that Shimon repeated so many times I was tired of hearing it. Then came Bar, who repeated similar instructions regarding programming languages, WhatsApp messages and emails.

Anat made every effort to look relaxed, nonchalant, but it was apparent to me that she was hiding the heavy pressure she was under. She fired at me an incessant sequence of instructions in very short sentences, with a gap of a breath or two between each directive. *Listen carefully and commit it to memory. It must all be in your head. No notes, no reminders. Your flight is tonight. Your new passport is Dutch. The woman who entered on it shares your height and build. She arrived two weeks ago by air and left quietly on a ship through the Caspian Sea.* Anat gave me some important tips and made it clear that they would help me on the way out. *Passport control at Mehrabad will be staring at the blue screen of death,* she assured me. The shadow of a grin stretched across her face. *And you can look forward to additional assistance, I promise,* but she didn't elaborate.

Towards the end of the surprise visit Anat asked me for all my technological accoutrements, including the laptop and all the hardware for connecting to the computers and cell phones of Hamid, Nur, Rittal, Yasmin and Colonel Nasser. Then she went over to the cloth bag she left on the carpet by the door, pulled out a laptop and a cell phone identical to mine, and said: *Here you go, toys for the next two days. The cell number is the same and most of the content is the same. The laptop, too.*

She was ready to go, but I tried to tell her that maybe I had made a mountain out of a molehill. Perhaps I was just paranoid, perhaps the colonel was a straightforward sadist whose macho self-image was insulted.

Anat listened to me patiently. *You mustn't take unnecessary risks, Mrs. Stone. You only know a small part of an exceptionally large picture. Other things have happened, which I may share with you when we're both swinging on the porch of a retirement home.*

What? I asked. *No hints?*

Your colonel in Tehran and the Qatari minister of transport will be out of the picture in the near future, she said in her slow and soothing voice. *Both are suspected of undisclosed prohibited transactions with a German businessman who works with the Iranians. You'd better not be here when they're interrogated. Aside from that, madam, you were too efficient. Almost all of your tasks were completed in less than four weeks. Neither Shimon nor anyone else predicted such a pace. The optimists estimated about two or three months...*

After all these compliments, Anat told me one last thing. It drove me so mad I wanted to scream.

36

12:00 hrs.
Talking about classified access
on a Tehran hotel terrace

You see, Mrs. Stone, you've got to make yourself scarce. Dramatic things have been happening on both sides of the Persian Gulf. A steel plant near Ahvaz has suffered a devastating explosion. Several leaders of the industry have been arrested on suspicion of espionage or negligence leading to the disclosure of classified information. That's why Nasser connects to the Internet once or twice a day, and has been for some time. He sends classified emails without bothering to encrypt them. He has lost all his discretion. Gstone was active for over an hour every day, scooping up everything we wanted: access to the steel factory in Khuzestan, to two mainframes in secret production facilities, and to the private computers of some of the biggest executives in electricity production and industry. It's a dream come true.

I felt a hurricane within me, gales of rage at Anat's revelation, threatening to throw me off balance and elicit an uncontrollable series of shrieks. I took some deep breaths and then stunned her by whispering fiercely in Hebrew: *Anat, that isn't what I agreed to. This violates everything we arranged! Are you listening? The consensus was that they'd start running the programs and taking advantage of the backdoors only after I was gone!* I was so furious, I was tripping over my words. I gasped. It was the worst kind of anger I'd ever experienced — the betrayal; the unparalleled affront leaving me feeling overwhelmed and helpless.

Anat matched my fury. *Are you speaking Hebrew, madam?* she rebuked me in English, embellished with a German accent. *You have to trust Shimon. He would never put you at risk. He knows what he's doing, and moving up the timeline wouldn't have happened without his autho-rization. You can be sure that he made a methodical decision based on the gravity and urgency of the situation...*

I went back inside on leaden feet. I felt as if tens of thousands of white-hot pins had been stuck in my legs. I dropped into the arm-chair heavily, closed my eyes and held my head in my hands. I had to calm down. I continued to sit there for a long while after Anat reclaimed her chambermaid persona, leaving the room with a cloth bagful of my treasures.

When I had finally gotten my heart rate and my thoughts under control, I went down to the main lobby to find the concierge. His badge identified him as Anwar, and he wore a three-piece suit and a broad, toothy smile.

Something has come up, I explained to him. I have to fly to London for a few days to deal with a medical matter, but I'll be back soon. This triggered a barrage of well wishes, blandishments and sympathies, straight out of the hoteliers' arsenal. I offered a hand to shake, a yel-low-brown EU banknote in my palm. Anwar professionally trans-ferred the 200 euros to his own pocket as soon as we broke contact. *You see, Anwar, I trust your discretion and professionalism. I don't want anyone prying into my private affairs. So, if anyone asks, just say I've got some business meetings for a few days. I'm counting on you!*

I walked out of the Espinas. I found a Mercedes taxi waiting for me, VIP with a minimalist sign atop it, the license plate ending in 224. Just as Anat had promised. I sat in the air-conditioned car, ask-ing the driver the question she'd given me. I got the corrected an-swer and replied: *OK, thank you. Take me to Lavasan, please.*

The driver skillfully sped through the streets of Tehran, weaving his way from one lane to the next on the highway heading toward the airport. He also performed several minor evasive maneuvers. Some distance from Mehrabad, the taxi turned onto a narrow road that split off from the main route. After about an eighth of a mile we pulled into the private garage of a one-story house. As the taxi came to a halt, the large door closed behind us, bathing me in darkness. The driver got out, and so did I. I came around to the front of the car and, thanks to the headlights, I recognized him in a fraction of a second. My chauffeur was the bullnecked man from the Gulfstream. *Hail, hail, the gang's all here.* He hadn't changed a bit. He still clung to his hat and sunglasses, even though we were in a gloomy garage. He clung to his silence too, even though we had arrived at the safehouse.

From the front, my hideaway looked like an ordinary residence. Anyone who entered through the front door would see a fashionable living room with quality parquet floors. At one end of the expansive space was a well-stocked kitchen. At the other end was a passageway to the bedrooms.

Looks can be deceiving, though. My brawny buddy led me down an innocent-looking hallway to an unassuming door. He opened it, motioned for me to enter, closed it behind me, and remained outside.

I found myself backstage, for lack of a better term; it might as well have been the hair, makeup and prop room behind a Broadway curtain. Racks upon racks of shirts and suits, dresses, skirts and blouses. Two dozen disembodied heads stared at me from a long table displaying a variety of wigs, hairpieces, headgear and eyewear. Three chairs were arranged in front of a long, well-lit mirror.

I had time to review all the many components of the large space and admire the vast selection of costumes, cosmetics and accessories. As I was taking a closer look at the collection of sunglasses, some branded, some modest and generic, the door opened again. A young, petite woman with a meticulous bob entered the room, dressed in a sleeveless T-shirt. Her bare arms were adorned with exquisite tattoos of birds and mysterious figures. *Hi, Mrs. Stone! I'm Dana. Have you enjoyed waiting in the wings?* she asked in fluent Hebrew and with evident humor. Then she went to the end of the room and picked up a passport and an enlarged color photograph. Both showed a bespectacled, black-haired woman. Please meet Alicia Janssen from the Netherlands, she said and waved the picture in front of me. Alicia was my age, but she looked more like an aunt than a mother. Her hair was smooth, charcoal black, but her hairstyle was a bit too much, bangs covering her forehead. She had huge glasses with thick, golden metal frames.

Forget it, I won't cut my hair, I declared.

The young woman's look sobered immediately. *We are not playing around here, Mrs. Stone,* she admonished me. *I determine what happens in this room. By the time you leave here you'll look like Mrs. Janssen. You'll be Mrs. Janssen. Bangs, hair the right color and length, the glasses a perfect match. I need to add a few more years to you...* She pointed to one of the chairs in front of the mirror.

I sat down submissively and closed my eyes. The fatigue, tension, fears and stress of the last four weeks had drained into my chest. I felt like I couldn't breathe. It was a panic attack. My body was trembling all over. I hugged myself forcefully and sobbed loudly. Dana came and embraced me from behind. The petite girl had tremendous strength. I felt it, but her hold was full of empathy, thoughtful. She injected new energies into me and managed to stop the tremors that shook my body.

You are allowed to cry, Sally. You are allowed to let it all out. You're great. Just take a deep breath, she said in a half-whisper, surprising me with my real name. Her comforting words and the solace of my real identity were my first steps back to my life, to normality.

Still, I felt I couldn't stay there another minute. I wanted to be home. Now. To wrap my arms around Roy and Michael, to hug Jerry and not let go. Then I wanted to shut the blinds, wrap myself in my blanket and curl up in my bed, in the dark, not leaving for at least a year.

About an hour later I was already on my way to the airport, properly transformed to dowdy and raven-haired. My driver was a burly man of about forty who appeared to be Iranian born and bred. *A local asset,* the thought flashed through my mind. *Or maybe not...*

His impressive driving skills were second to none. He performed two continuous evasive maneuvers, switching lanes with surprising efficiency. His earpiece was receiving messages informing him which intersections to avoid and the location of IRGC checkpoints.

As we neared our destination, he flipped open the sun visor, looking into its mirror to match eyes and spoke to me in English, in a surprisingly clear voice. *Well done, Mrs. Janssen. Well done.*

These were the first and last words I heard from the anonymous chauffeur. There was an implicit compliment in them, an attempt to tell me that he knew a little more than just operational driving. These short words sent a subtle shiver down the back of my neck and compounded with Giora's two kisses on the forehead, Anat's words, and the whisper that accompanied Dana's hug. Each was a token of gratitude, and I needed them all so much.

Every time my Iranian driver tapped on the gas, I edged closer to freedom. I looked at the reflected image of the City of 72 Nations and felt in my heart that I was bidding it adieu, and not arrivederci. In fact, until sanity returned and they learned to make do with a little less Dieu, I never wanted to see Tehran again.

We passed a roundabout and suddenly came upon a long traffic jam blocking the service road to the right of us. The snarl started somewhere on the southern horizon of the road we were traveling on and continued all the way to a gas station about an eighth of a mile away. I asked the driver what was going on.

It's an interesting story, Mrs. Janssen, he replied and adjusted the sun visor again. Then he added: *The gas stations have been offline since the middle of the night. The pumps don't work and, instead of the gas price, the displays just show an inscription in Farsi attacking President Hassan Rouhani.*

All the gas stations? I asked in genuine amazement.

Yes, Mrs. Janssen. All the gas stations. State radio says it's the work of the Zionists. The opposition websites praise another successful cyberattack by the Mossad.

Cyberattack? I asked. The question hung, unanswered, in the cabin. My driver, who knew how to compliment Mrs. Janssen, was also aware that this was an idle question. With one final burst of acceleration, we reached the curb by the terminal's automatic doors.

The driver got out, opened the trunk, and pulled out my favorite purple piece of luggage. He grabbed my other large purple trolley as if it were full of cotton balls. He placed them in front of me, got back in the car, and sped away.

37

13:22 hrs.
Cyberattack on passport control at Mehrabad

I found myself once again at Tehran's international airport. So close to home and family, yet so far away. Just one more successful passport check and it'll be over.

What happened next was easy. Too easy. Our good guys, the cyber wizards from Givatayim, did what they do so well. The immigration officials' computers had been disabled. As promised. The passport control officer repeatedly leafed through the huge pile of printouts continually placed in front of him until he finally gave up. He dumped the heap of papers with an annoyed thump; with the same degree of force, he stamped my Dutch passport. He did it with resignation, already pointing at the next in line before I'd realized I had made it. I thanked him with a smile and grabbed my two purple suitcases, following the digital signs towards Emirates check-in.

A tall flight attendant watched as I entered the cabin. She saw a black-haired lady sitting down in Row 15 of the Airbus, straightening the golden spectacles on her nose and putting a slight smile on her face.

Relax, Sally, just smile and relax. With my return home imminent, I allowed myself to break protocol and call myself by my real name. I no longer had an ounce of patience for the artifice of Mrs. Alicia Janssen.

Then, out of nowhere, and with terrible timing, I suddenly recalled the alluring scent of Yasmin; the faint vapors tickling the tip of my nose, sneaking into my nostrils and inching upwards. The scent of innocence had now become a symbol of my betrayals of my friends and associates here and in Qatar. It sat there between my eyebrows, the furrowed wrinkles in the middle of my forehead and the center of my thoughts. It wasn't just that smell, but the sight of Yasmin's eyes, the huge, olive-green lakes with the transparent curtain of tears that flooded over them as she looked at me, to the depths of my soul.

It was one torture too many. I needed to muster all my mental strength to focus and overcome the last hurdle on my way to freedom.

We were ready for takeoff. The flight crew were belted into their special seats. The pilot announced thirty seconds until our departure, but we missed that deadline. Then the PA system crackled to life, releasing a torrent of messages, chilling as an ice floe, incendiary as a lava flow. *On behalf of the captain, we apologize. There will be a slight delay in our takeoff at the request of the authorities*, the speakers said in what seemed to me like a terrifying shout. The passengers on the plane were sweating in their places nervously. Some of them also raised their voices and yelled protests.

It took a while, but eventually two IRGC troops in their stupid bill caps and camo entered the plane and stood at the flight attendants' post. One of them was holding a large photo. They began to advance, row by row, alternately looking at the picture and comparing it to the faces of the passengers. As they made their way through the cabin, working their way back, I felt my pulse accelerating, anxiety spreading to every cell of my body. By the time the pair passed the fifth row, my left cheek had already become ice cold and completely stiff. I raised my right hand and massaged my cheek with light, subtle motions. From time to time, I stuck a finger under my glasses to rub my eye as well, to complete the display of fatigue.

Now the pair had reached Row 8. They carefully considered seats a, b and c, then moved on to the rest. They were already close to me. Too close, I thought.

As the soldiers advanced one more row, I thrust my hands into the pockets of the bright-colored jacket I wore. I pulled out wireless headphones and jammed them in my ears. Enya poured into me with force. The honeyed sound of bells allowed me just a sliver of relief. My icy cheek began to thaw, slowly returning to life. I faced a clear and present danger, but I had to maintain an air of nonchalance.

However, my mind wasn't cooperating; it was churning out myriad questions: Were these Moslehi's men? Had the Qatari interior minister discovered something unusual in his home, then passed that information on to the Qatari security services, who had updated their colleagues in Iran? Had Yasmin bowed to pressure and spilled the beans to her violent husband? Was there a security camera in one of the Doha homes I'd infiltrated that had captured my intrusion? Was it possible that someone had deciphered the encrypted messages flying between my laptop and Gretchen? Had Anwar the concierge reported my suspicious activity? Could someone have followed my car to the safehouse? Was my magnificent house of cards, built in record time, about to collapse before me? Would I be caught with a counterfeit passport and ersatz identity? Why, oh why was I flying commercial to escape the Islamic Republic, instead of zipping away on a speedboat through the Caspian Sea?

So many questions — none of which I could possibly answer. So I closed my eyes, plastered a calm expression on my face and mainlined Enya's lyrics:

Taking the stars
So far away
Everything flows
Here comes another new day

The singing was supposed to regulate my breathing, my pulse, the rhythm of my thoughts, but time stood still. The quiet on the plane became oppressive and threatening. I broke down and opened an eye just a smidge. The troops were three rows away, but something detained them there. Their gazes ping-ponged between the photograph and the far end of the row, faster and more furiously. They whispered among themselves. I struggled to contain myself, staying still in my sleeping position; but I continued to peer through my lashes at what was going on.

They were six feet away now. I could see their faces. I could count the bristles of their scraggly beards, examine every wrinkle at the corner of their eyes. The more deeply I looked at them, the more I became convinced that their gaze was more embarrassed than enthusiastic. It became apparent that they would rather not find whoever they were looking for.

It was zero hour, an instant before disaster, time for a quick conversation with God, for brief and hurried negotiations. In another second they would arrive at Row 15, waving the photo. I marshalled all the encouraging words I used to say to myself in moments of crisis; but those ideas ran smack into the images of Roy and Michael and Jerry and my two parents, all bumping into each other. They jostled each other, the collection of beloved faces and the collation of prayers and requests from the Creator.

And then it happened. One of the soldiers hunched down and forcefully grabbed a niqab-clad woman. Two little girls sat next to her, similarly dressed. The veiled woman sobbed, trying in vain to grab the armrests, the seatbelt, anything which might save her.

I watched the spectacle as the pressure upon my chest slowly dissipated, replaced by waves of anguish and empathy.

The woman entreated, then sobbed, then begged in a voice that tore through the silence in the cabin. Finally, she surrendered to the strong arms that pulled her out of the row. They dragged her and her daughters along the aisle, towards the exit and an uncertain and undoubtedly grievous fate.

38

23:00 hrs.
Second metamorphosis in a day at Heathrow

Four minutes later the door was shut and the jetway detached. The captain apologized profusely and multilingually for the delay; the flight attendants echoed the sentiment with conciliatory and sheepish grins.

Despite the hasty exit, I would be returning to my children, to my Jerry, to my parents, to the landscape I'd loved since childhood and to myself.

After landing in London, I underwent a metamorphosis once again, this time in the opposite direction. I washed the black out of my hair, put the glasses in their case and went back to my tailored clothes.

I called Jerry and spoke to the children: talking, crying, laughing in joy and pain. I swore I would never leave them again. I promised that in a few hours, we would meet again in Tel Aviv.

All the televisions in the terminal were broadcasting the breaking news on a loop. Time and again, experts assessed the wave of cyberattacks on Iran's gas stations, power plants and steel mills. The video captured by the security cameras at the steel factory flashed on the screens repeatedly, with an emphasis on the moment of the explosion in the heart of the system. Each channel had tech experts in the studios. In stone-faced interviews, they offered their professional opinions, the consensus being that the sophistication of the offensive was far beyond the capabilities of pirates, hackers or opposition forces. I watched the television trying to escape the cyberattack stories from Iran and the Persian Gulf, but the only respite was MTV.

The next day I was already at home. Literally. I breathed deeply, filling my lungs and my soul with the air of home. Then I enveloped Roy and Michael in a bear hug, refusing to let them go. I inhaled their cheeks and their hair and their palms and their closed eyes.

Then I embraced Jerry, powerfully, unrelentingly. Jerry looked at me with an admiring look. His compliments didn't need to be verbalized. He didn't have to make pompous speeches to illustrate how proud he was of me, how much he appreciated my performance. After all, Jerry's adulation came from the best of the best. He had done it all, breaking all the records for operational success at the Mossad. I knew him well. His seriousness and professionalism wouldn't have allowed him to give out laurels and ribbons he didn't really believe in. Certainly, when it comes to a critical operational activity that could determine the fate of a nation. Still, I recognized a trace of gloom in his eyes. He was happy and grateful and felt relieved at my return but, deep beyond his pupils I deciphered something else — disturbing, stubborn, unnamable, unknowable. What few words Jerry did convey sounded, at least to me, like nothing I've ever heard him say.

That's it, Sally. That's it. We're finished. We're done. No more taking lead roles in spy thrillers. We've done our part for God and country. That part of our life is over. You've done far more than anyone could ask. Far beyond anyone's expectations. More than you can possibly know now. You may never know. He finished his speech, fell silent for a while and then added: *I was skeptical, Sally. So skeptical. And now I admit I was a fool.*

Precisely then, the phone rang. In the midst of the whole celebration of the reunion, even before I realized that I was in a safe place and that Colonel Muhammad Reza Moslehi wasn't lurking behind my bathroom door to dunk me into a tub of ice-water and salt, the cold and brief call came from Shimon's office. *You must report immediately.*

What ensued in the following hours and over the next few days and nights was a nightmare which outstripped my experiences in Doha and Tehran. I would have preferred a conversation in the sports complex with the bloodthirsty colonel over the interminable conversations with a growing cast of characters, most of whom I'd never seen before. Debriefing.

Now, don't get me wrong, there were hugs and there was praise and there was applause on several occasions. I was congratulated for my performance and there were superlatives about the effectiveness of the operational activity. There were professional compliments from Shimon which raised me sky high; and there was his insistence on invoking the realm of the spirit too, as he pontificated about the lady with incomprehensible abilities and immeasurable luck and pluck who carried out the mission in a quarter of the allotted time. Again, that word: lucky.

Still, these congratulatory exercises exhausted themselves rather quickly as the debriefing went on and on, longer and longer. I was ordered to answer a non-stop barrage of direct questions. They sat in front of me and filmed and recorded and wrote down in notebooks and notepads every sneeze or throat-clearing.

What does the living room look like in Yasmin's house?
What is the color of the paint in the room with the computer?
Is Hamid in good physical shape?
Where exactly is the secret door in the lobby of the Hyatt?
How many cameras were in the lobby of the sports complex at the Espinas?
How far can we trust Hamid?
In your opinion, is it feasible to recruit Najifi?

I got home exhausted, enervated in body and soul, and asked Jerry to go for a walk in the park with me. I was suffocating, unable to sit in a closed room anymore. For two days I'd seen only walls, shuttered windows, sealed security doors. I'd listened to an endless gush of stupid and annoying questions, I told him angrily. I was ranting, looking for sympathy.

Jerry hugged me and remained silent. He knew every little fragment of my cross-examination. He knew about these interrogations that lasted longer and were much more difficult than usual— but he was loyal to the Mossad.

Walking alongside Jerry infused me with new energies. I felt it even though our hands didn't touch, even though our shoulders were a distance apart. The energy that lingered in the narrow space between us was palatable. The park's trails, jam-packed with runners, walkers, riders and rollers, solidified my sense that I had returned to a safe haven.

The breeze blowing over my face was something that had only entered my forbidden dreams during the nights in Doha and Tehran. It was a kind of high for me.

Then I noticed something strange. After about an hour into our stroll along the Yarkon river, I noticed that Jerry — king of the world, the paratrooper, secret agent number one, my rock, my private James Bond — was lagging behind me. I looked at his face and recognized some sort of fatigue he was trying to disguise. His breathing was irregular. He was panting when all we'd done was walk. We hadn't run even five feet. I looked into his eyes and recognized the shade of gloom I'd noticed the other day. *Something is going on, Sally, something is going on.* I gave Jerry a pointed, probing, demanding stare. He caught my gaze and looked down. I filed this fact away for later, though it never left me.

I needed to find another opportunity to catch him. I worked at it. More than once I asked him to take an evening walk with me around the neighborhood. *I've got to get some air, Jerry. If you don't feel like walking to the park, we stay close to home. We can just go around the block...*

I knew every mark and line on his face. I could easily anticipate any response. He'd turned me down twice with the flimsiest of excuses, so I knew the third time would be the charm. He would force himself to concede and accompany me. But when the time came, he was more stubborn than usual, more evasive than usual.

I desperately improvised. *Do you want me to go alone, in the dark? Let it be on your conscience if someone assaults me!* I said, trying to provoke him.

He chuckled at that. *What has Agent 009 got to be afraid of? Are you kidding?*

The bout of giggling became contagious, and I joined in. We both fell apart. We needed that, the relief of howling with laughter. But, after a few seconds, the exercise turned hollow. It was performative, an attempt to deflect and obscure. What the hell is Jerry going through? What was he hiding from me?

Then the suspicious dots appeared. Red spots, all over Jerry's hands. *It's nothing,* he would say and go about his day. Was I more annoyed or worried? Hard to say. I photographed his hands — despite his protests, which were also uncharacteristically weak. Jerry knew how to object when he wanted to. I sent the images over WhatsApp to doctors I knew at Beilinson Hospital who would allow me to pester them with personal requests, whose integrity I trusted. But that went nowhere. The replies were contradictory, vague, and sometimes evasive. The most common opinion was that it was some sort of allergy.

Less than a month after my return, I began to notice patches of skin on Jerry's arms that had hardened and scarred. Reddened, puckered, raised blood vessels around them as if they were trying to break through the skin. It looked bad.

Then spots began to appear on his face as well. *There's no way you're leaving the house like that,* I told him, trying to enlist another reason to convince him to go for tests. When he insisted on going out, or when his presence was essential, I did his makeup. I smeared foundation on his face, trying to hide the spots. It was pathetic. The foundation might have obscured the discoloration, but didn't fool anyone. Everyone who knew him noticed his face and his palms peeking through his jacket; they all knew something was wrong with dear Jerry, and they tried to figure out what it was.

Consider all this an introduction. It was the most minor of

events, a trifle compared to what was awaiting us up the road. Not that I had any clue about what we were in for, as I was still in a whirlwind after my debriefing at the Mossad.

39

The astrologer's mysterious and
questionable prediction

Meeting with Ohr Barkan, my astrologer and mystic, turned my insides out. An unbearable conversation, completely different from anything we'd experienced over the last decade. I knew every flash of his eyes. I understood every wrinkle on his forehead. I could give a pointed interpretation of the intonation in his speech, which ascended roughly and then dove down into a whisper. But not this time.

Eventually, after a prolonged silence, he unglued his eyes from the computer screen and looked at me strangely. His speech was thoughtful, hesitant.

I don't understand...
I see that a quiet time awaits Jerry...
Very, very quiet...
Everything is calm...
Very, very relaxed...
Tranquility...
A new beginning...

I felt it coming. I saw Ohr was indecisive. He was unusually ill at ease — stalling, pausing at length between words. Many months would pass — and many storms — before I understood what Ohr was actually saying or trying to say.

Nevertheless, I trusted him. Ohr devoured more books than anyone else I knew. Reading was his lifeline. He sped-read, in Hebrew and English. He devoured, with sincere interest, all sorts of texts:

philosophy books, publications in the field of alternative medicine, every word that popped up on the Internet or in a new book about Western or Chinese astrology.

His ability to connect all of this to his network of intuition was a rare thing indeed. Every encounter with him was a meaningful, thought-provoking experience, impetus for action. His eloquent speech, embellished with morsels of Chinese wisdom, energized my thoughts, encouraging me to get out of my routine. Mystical utterances became decisive, razor-sharp instructions.

I wasn't alone in the deep experiences I'd had thanks to Ohr. There were many, many others. Men and women from Israel and around the world found themselves on waiting lists. Some of them waited weeks, even months, for the opportunity to have a face-to-face conversation with him. Others compromised, sufficing with Zoom or WhatsApp video calls.

His eloquence was captivating. His associative world and unbound knowledge produced flowing, touching, precise and compelling conversation.

This time, however, there were loud silences that spoke volumes.

A quiet time... Calm... Tranquility... What, in God's name, could be calm or quiet about Jerry's routine, which was always fiery like lava? I angrily thought to myself, what could possibly be calm in the marathon of operational tasks required by his investigations? What damned serenity was there in the days that turn into nights that turn into days?

There were moments when I questioned everything Ohr said; and then, I would reconsider. Over the years, and up until this encounter, Ohr had never been wrong. It seemed that it was precisely for this reason that Barkan had become the oracle of many, many members of the upper echelon, the elite and the wealthy. The sort of person to whom one made pilgrimage to unravel enigmas from the world of emotion and the sphere of business in order to listen to smart advice. To get a surprising, if not amazing, perspective on decisions required at life's crossroads. Ohr maintained complete discretion. He never mentioned or gave away the names of those who came to him. However, through conversations with acquaintances I had sent to him, I heard, bit by bit, the stories of the rich and powerful, the titans who refused to make any personal, business, professional or intimate decisions without first checking with Ohr for his take on it and what Chinese or Western astrology had to say about it. He deservedly acquired his status; his clientele was drawn in and became hooked on his insights and life-changing conversations; his sensational revelations that they could never have imagined before hearing it from his lips in his characteristic staccato: thinking, insight, thinking, insight. And always with humility.

It hadn't taken long for me to become a close friend of Ohr's. I loved listening to and learning from him. He analyzed and explained global processes with great wisdom.

At no point did I tell him about Jerry's illness. He hadn't heard from me that my James Bond was crumbling before my eyes, about the red spots that horrified me, about the light in his eyes that was slowly dimming. Ohr certainly didn't know anything about the worldwide research I pursued to find answers. Still, out of nowhere, he emphasized two topics in our conversation, each of which stood on its own. One was the issue of calm and serenity in Jerry's life. The other was the matter of men who pop up in my life and then vanish.

I kept quiet. Silence was uncharacteristic on my part, as well.

When Ohr finished speaking, we settled back into our armchairs. You could cut the tension with a knife. Me, slowly connecting his insights with the anxieties that had been gnawing at me for several weeks, Ohr with words he thought of saying but kept in his throat.

I must take another walk in the park with Yaffit, I thought. *I must.* I rose from the armchair vigorously, eager to disconnect from the dark thoughts that crept into my head and get out of there quickly.

Ohr could sense my urge to dash but was completely immersed in his cell phone, plunging into the depths of the secret language of Chinese mysticism, imbibing fragments of words.

You know Sally, there's something else here that I haven't seen before, he said suddenly. He spoke slowly and calmly, as if afraid to alarm me. Again, his confident speech was fragmented. He hid more than he revealed.

There is something here that you and Jerry are about to make public. Something massive, perhaps even global...

It seems strange to me...

This doesn't add up...

After all, this isn't your style, nor his. You are the exact opposite. But it looks like you're preparing something that requires exposure...

It's happening in Israel...

But I see it happening all over the world...

40

11:20 hrs.
Metzitzim Beach, Tel Aviv, strong desire
for entire world to know

The day after my magical mystery meeting with Ohr, I had a day off from the investigative hassles at Mossad headquarters. Jerry wasn't around either. He was stuck in one of his frequent urgent work meetings. He was again involved in an international investigation that dominated his time, his thoughts, most of his attention. I sat on the armchair in our living room facing the view and was struck by the smallness of it all, from living room to kitchen to the bedroom hallway: stuffy, narrow, confined. The warm, embracing atmosphere of my home suddenly smothered and suffocated me. I tried to tidy up the dining room table but stopped after moving the first piece of mail. I took out a bag of rice and some spices from the pantry, but left them on the countertop, untouched. Water was dripping from the faucet, but I didn't have the strength to cross to the other side of the room and reach the sink.

I felt empty. Everything seemed meaningless to me. Banal. I could leave my house without checking the peephole to see who might be lurking outside. I could walk to the elevator without scrutinizing who else was in the hallway. I could make lunch. Too challenging. I could go to the local supermarket without checking for security cameras, purchase a set of aluminum pans. Another ridiculous challenge.

With robotic movements, I took the elevator down to the parking lot. I was driving like an automaton as well. Looking ahead, eyes on the road, sidewalk in my peripheral; but my thoughts were not there at all. I had to subdue the nagging feeling of emptiness that consumed me. I was angry at myself for going back to normal with the kids and Jerry, only to find myself unfulfilled. I had to try and understand what I was going through. What Jerry was going through. I drove until I found myself on the seam between Metzitzim Beach and Hilton Beach. A relatively empty spot.

I sat on the yellow sand facing the blue water as the eastern wind smoothed the smallest of ripples. The water hardly moved, except for tiny waves that gently broke on the shoreline. I scooped up delicate grains of gold and let them drift on the light eastern breeze which caressed my head and face, watching the handful of sand slip through my fingers.

I suddenly felt the urge to share my experiences with others. To tell them what it had felt like. Try to explain how it happened that I became a different woman from the one I had been. Other axioms emerged: I'm neither Wonder Woman nor Sean Connery; nevertheless, something had definitely morphed and mutated within me.

It was important for me to write, to say that anyone can do remarkable things. I wanted millions of women to feel that they could do the unbelievable, to give them a strong belief in themselves, to convince them that they could shatter the glass ceiling over their heads.

There was an active volcano within me, but the lava flow was being halted by the Mossad's endless over-analysis and interrogation. It would be much better to document it myself, to direct everything through my slim laptop. I could recreate the scenes I'd experienced, turn the chapters of my life into the stuff of Hollywood spy thrillers.

I decided to tell the world about the moments of horror and the moments of satisfaction, about the successes, about the failures — and also about the near-disasters. To show readers that women are capable of carrying out hair-raising secret missions as efficiently as a grizzled James Bond. To tell a story that would give hope and inspiration to a moshav girl on the fringe, show her she could achieve the unbelievable. I wanted to share with my readers the steadfast struggle that was my lot, between my duty as the mother of two children and my allegiance to my country. To present, in the most tangible way, the crazy alchemy between the world of action and the world of instinct. I thought it was important to examine whether events shaped me and my destiny, or did I shape them? Was it free will or fate?

I felt a powerful urge to tell the whole world how a young, unskilled woman could accomplish incredible things. Everyone needed to know that they could change the world for the better, if only they believed in themselves.

Start writing, Sally. Start writing here and now, I told myself. I bent over to pick up my bag, brush off the sand, and pull out my slim laptop. It had waited faithfully for me in Tel Aviv, closed and sealed as long as I was Jessica Stone. I opened a new Word document and let the text take over. It was kind of magical. The events, the images, the words, the anxieties, the emotions — they vibrated, they stirred, they rushed forth. Ideas were born between my eyebrows, fighting for a place at the front of the queue. I was spinning amid the flashes and fragments of random memories and words that need to be turned into sentences. *Articulate, be clear, present a character, tell a story.*

My fingers typed at a speed I'd forgotten I was capable of. Faster than the pace of my thoughts. I ignored typos, misspellings, unnecessary spaces. Corrections seemed like a nuisance to me. They impeded the flow of ideas.

Most of all, associative memory amazed me. It was efficient, powerful, obsessive, uninhibited and ruthless. I retrieved a moment from my Greek odyssey and that instant led me to a fascinating chapter about the whole ordeal which, in turn, recalled four high-stress situations on four other flights. I remembered the chase by the military jeep on the outskirts of the port of Piraeus, and that reminded me of when a giant van had plowed into my car with murderous intent, threatening to turn me into roadkill.

At the time, I'd denied what happened there. I repressed the facts and freed myself from liability. I argued with Jerry. I fumed when he took a scalpel to my conduct in Europe, all the ways I had put myself in peril. Hindsight now allows me to acknowledge that the driver of the Ford Super Duty had tried to kill me in broad daylight, in the heart of Tel Aviv, on a busy street an eighth of a mile from my castle. Precisely here, on the soft sand, facing the waves that began to pile up, I recalled that fraction of a second when I looked in the rear-view saw a huge shadow swallowing the back of our family Mazda. It was a double cab monster pickup with a high stainless-steel bumper. This wasn't a rear-end by an inattentive driver.

All this took place in the midst of the investigation of the impostor Rabbi Ben David. Another one of those times when I was stubborn beyond measure — and brought the danger to our doorstep.

Jerry had been furious. He'd been collecting information meticulously, running the exercises to know when I had to pull up stakes, when the other side's countermeasures endangered me, when the threats stopped being subtle and became lethal. I was bad at these analyses; I jumped over five sawhorses in a row, opened doors that screamed 'No entry!,' drove the wrong direction up one-way streets. I justified my actions on the spiritual and moral planes, even as I walked down the track towards an oncoming locomotive.

Looking back, there could be no doubt about the intentions of the Ford driver. He'd shoved my Mazda forward with a forceful, deliberate impact. I could hear the rear crinkling, the back window cracking, all as the engine of the Ford screeched and accelerated. A fraction of a second more, and I'd be mincemeat.

But the Ford braked for a moment, slowing considerably. That was the moment I mashed the gas pedal to the floor and propelled myself and the Mazda out of the silver jaws of steel, out of range of annihilation.

I looked ahead and saw a patrol car with flashing blue lights parked in the opposite lane, a hundred feet away from me. The other driver must have seen it too. He braked a moment away from a noisy assassination before the watchful eyes of two cops who just happened to be there.

In the midst of feeling terrified, the memory of the kiss with Jerry in the kitchen came to me and, even before it faded, a similar scene stubbornly and insistently arose — locking lips with Yiftach in Greece. I tried to separate them, begging one to wait for the other. With each in turn, I snuck a sentence into the surge of thoughts. Along with the memory of the events, all the emotions and sensations pulsed in me too, as if they were happening at the very moment I was writing on the beach in Tel Aviv — and not a year, or three, or five earlier, in Athens, Islamabad, Doha, London, Washington. Depression, love, longing, anxiety; moments of sadness and of uninhibited laughter; smells, vibrations of passion, pores open with sweat, stubborn tears.

Write about your fears as well. Be real. Don't try to fool them with stories of heroism. After all, no one will believe them. Even as the word 'fear' entered my mind, a sense of anxiety permeated each and every cell of my body and threw me back into Row 15 of that Airbus on the tarmac at Mehrabad, as the IRGC men checked the seats ahead and slowly moved towards me. I had been one row away from the ayatollah's grasp, a second away from personal disaster, a hairsbreadth away from a shameful failure on a national and global scale, narrowly escaping bringing eternal shame and infamy on the Mossad.

It was from the abyss of this reconstructed memory that I emerged, the call to record and recount growing ever stronger in me.

I enjoyed the writing process. At times I felt as if I was working on someone else's biography. *Who would even believe me? It's even hard for me to digest that I've been through all this. I recapitulate memories that sound like fantasies.* A different type of trepidation gripped me as I imagined others reading what I'd written. *Will Jerry and the kids scoff at my idea of writing about what I went through? They know me better than anyone else. Speaker is a role I embrace, but not author.*

A Mossad memoir was more suited to Jerry, the world-conqueror. He often found himself in situations straight out of a Hollywood blockbuster. He read thousands of books, underlining and writing notes in the margins, studying them in depth. He could have written three more scripts, in the first person, for the perdurable 007 franchise.

Still, the magic of writing overwhelmed me like a virtuoso lover. It captivated me and wouldn't let go. It was the first text I had ever composed. Until then, I had only written lines of code. I felt it flowing.

I thought it was interesting, but I never imagined that it might become a bestseller in Israel and around the world. I didn't dare think in such terms. I certainly didn't go as far as to contemplate it being the first book in a series.

I had not the slightest clue that Jerry would only glimpse the first edition of the book and no more. But the trickle turned into a flood that brutally swept me up a week later, along the road to the village of Champagne in western Switzerland.

41

11:15 hrs.
Going up to Champagne, the secret agent
struggles to breathe

We were halfway to Champagne, along the shores of Lake Neuchâtel in Switzerland, facing what seemed like an other-worldly, primordial landscape covered in mist when our lives were turned upside down.

We emitted steaming exhalations into the perfect air we breathed. We relished the quiet. Jerry expressed admiration for the view, but it was transparent. He was looking for excuses for his slackening pace, the pauses getting longer and longer. *That's it, Sally. Jerry has a serious breathing problem.* Paratrooper, officer, experienced covert agent, weightlifter, black belt in judo, healthy as a horse — but my man was hiding something, expertly. *And Sally, you saw, you heard, you disregarded one sign after another and repressed them — expertly. Enough playing around*, I told myself. *Jerry has trouble breathing.*

The warning bells were peeling away, in concert with the sound of cowbells from some nearby hill. I stared piercingly at, and never took my eyes off, the man I had loved all my life. I left him no escape route; and then he turned to me and said words I could never forget: *Go ahead. I'll catch up later. I'm going to take my time. The view here is spectacular.*

I turned my head towards the road leading up to Champagne and began to walk slowly up the incline. Stinging tears welled up in the corners of my eyes. It was a mask-off moment. A point at which all the games stopped. *You need to start moving, Jerry. It'll be dark in two hours,* I said into the air, increasing my pace. *I can make it to Mi-*

chael's house, grab the car and make it back here in ten minutes. I knew that if I offered that to Jerry, he would be hurt and start arguing with me.

My estimate was accurate, but it still seemed like an unbearably long time before I could get behind the wheel of our rented Mini Cooper. Compact, powerful and speedy, it gobbled up the twists and turns coming down the hill.

However, as I slalomed along past the fifth turn, I noticed for the third time that a red Audi was behind me. It was matching my pace but keeping its distance. An Audi A5 Cabriolet convertible. For such a winding road, it was quite a large and heavy vehicle. The driver was young, wearing dark sunglasses and a tight-fitting shirt, his pompadour playing in the wind — but his face was grim. I slowly tapped the brakes. The Mini Cooper slowed down. A split-second glance told me that the driver was shadowing my moves. He didn't overtake me, nor did he speed up.

As I made the next turn, I caught sight of Jerry. He was sitting on a boulder by the side of the road and looked exhausted. I passed him until I found a shoulder wide enough for a U-turn. Then I turned around to race back up the road. But, as I approached Jerry, the red Audi burst into view. I could see the driver clearly, and he didn't look young anymore. There was a small video camera mounted above his dashboard. His eyes set on Jerry and me, even meeting my gaze; he pressed on the gas and accelerated — not down the road, but towards us. I had seconds to save us both from being crushed to death. In the space between heartbeats, I veered towards Jerry's boulder. My beloved blinked in surprise, but his reflexes took over and he jumped out of the way, just before I stopped inches from the rock. I caught one more glance of the Audi driver as he decelerated for a moment. Realizing he'd missed his chance, he straightened out the convertible and roared down the hill away from us.

Jerry stared at me, clearly shaken. *What the hell, Sally?* he asked as I took off. There was no longer any room for doubt. Jerry was exhausted, depressed, winded. On a mission, Jerry would never be panting like this; on a mission, Jerry would never struggle to get his bearings. The merest glance would have told him that the Audi was trying to kill us. He would have anticipated my evasive maneuver, realizing that my only move was to veer towards the rock, deflecting the attacker from crushing us.

Everything is fine, Jerry. C'mon, they're waiting for us at Michael's, I said, diverting the conversation from the obvious fatigue that gripped him, from his panting, from the murderous red Audi which had popped up from nowhere on a Swiss road. I drove quickly, and there was silence in the small cabin. Words were superfluous at the time, although what was left unsaid lay stagnant in the air. Clear, hard, painful.

The next day, two old friends of mine from America joined us — and they brought their new boyfriends. The first was Linda Fillmore, clever and vivacious, whom I'd gotten to know quite well during our six-year sojourn in the States. While Jerry was stationed there, overseeing everything the Mossad was doing in North America, he worked closely with her husband, a senior officer in the CIA. The surprising, vibrant Linda was independent and opinionated, with a sense of humor. She was a phenomenally successful realtor, imprisoned in her marriage to Martin.

Jerry and Martin had a lot in common, in terms of their missions and operational interests; but they found a common language in their leisure activities as well. They were both into weightlifting, both had a black belt in judo, both played tennis — though I was still better than either of them.

Now Linda had arrived in Switzerland with someone else. He was five years her junior; most important, he was not Martin.

The second, Eleanor, had brought an even younger beau. Much younger. It was a new fashion that I was slowly becoming aware of: powerful women with younger men. The rules had changed. Sex was the new Botox, one of my friends had told me.

Eleanor Glick was a world-renowned researcher in the field of autoimmune diseases, developing drugs for rheumatological conditions. I missed her, how wise she was about life, her wide-ranging experience as a medical professional, research scientist and founder of several biotech companies.

But most of all, I was fascinated by her personal, private stories. Eleanor was a volcano of lust. She was more instinctual than any other woman I'd ever met. She shared some of her secrets with me, known only to her, to me and to God. More than once, when she told me about one of her exploits, I stared at her, embarrassed. I recoiled and withdrew a little, taking time to digest the details she'd poured out before me.

However, on this occasion, amidst the almost spontaneous plans to meet up in Champagne, Mount St. Eleanor erupted in full force, spewing bubbling lava, both threatening and disheartening. By this I mean that she brought her eldest son's best friend on her Swiss vacation. In short order, she dumped her husband of several decades — Thomas, Jerry's best friend — for a brilliant young man who'd been on this earth fewer years than her marriage lasted. Shocking!

The truth is that I'd been having a hard coming to terms with the situation ever since I'd learned about it. Did I really have a right to judge her? Her decision looked like madness to me, but what if I reversed the genders? Would it result in anything more than a raised eyebrow if a man were to date a woman the age of his daughter? Then why should society be more critical of the reverse situation? On the contrary, you could make a better case for a woman going out with a man half her age! After all, women have a longer life expectancy, and we know how to maintain ourselves and our sexuality almost indefinitely. It's only logical for the centuries-old mores to be reevaluated. All it requires is to examine reality with open eyes and an open mind.

For Eleanor, it all happened at the speed of light: splitting up with her husband of 30 years, hooking up with the young man, confessing the relationship to her son, Peter, a computer genius who adored her unconditionally and saw her as a role model. That was before those closest to her could even blink; before her son figured out what was happening behind his back. I certainly couldn't wrap my head around it over the course of the three-hour Skype conversation in which she spun the whole fairy tale for me.

Even weeks later, I was still struggling with it. I really liked Eleanor, but I wasn't sure I could accept this new version of her uncritically, without getting into moral and moralistic arguments with her, without trying to find out what Peter felt. I closed my eyes, as if to escape for a moment the warped spectacle but, in the dark, I was assaulted by a nauseating image, picturing Eleanor holding my own Roy in her embrace. I was about to vomit, as my subconscious assembled a tableau that effectively and economically conveyed the absurd phenomenon that my friend's life had become. I opened my eyes in a panic, only to find a WhatsApp notification on my phone: *Linda and I are flying to Switzerland tonight. We ought to take advantage and get together. If that works for you, we can find a motel near town. But we're not coming alone...*

My natural inclination was to formulate a creative excuse and avoid the charged gathering. I didn't relish seeing Eleanor with her new lover, as young as my kids. What would Jerry think upon discovering that his best friend Thomas had been betrayed and replaced? Even worse, Linda wanted to come with the man she'd chosen over Martin, whom Jerry liked and admired. I knew Jerry. I could easily guess how he would react, how much he'd disapprove, how he'd probably storm out of the house in protest. Still, another consideration lurked in the back of my mind. I wanted Eleanor to observe Jerry and give her own diagnosis, instead of the stuttering guesswork and blind hypotheses I'd encountered thus far. I'd alluded to her several times that something had happened to Jerry's physical health and that I was worried, but nothing more.

After about half an hour of hesitation, I had to decide. On my cell phone, a laconic text message appeared from Eleanor. Three question marks.

Eleanor, I would love for the three of us to meet, I wrote immediately, but can you leave the boys at home, at least this time... I waited a few seconds and added another text message. Three exclamation marks and three thank you emojis.

I was apprehensive about Eleanor's reaction. She knew how to be direct, often blunt. But as always, she was also smart, quick to pick up on things, savvy. Second later, she texted: *Agreed. I love you and I get you. Can't wait to see you.*

I waited impatiently for the moment when we would meet and whisper how much we had been missing each other. Eleanor is the kind of friend it's easy to reconnect with, even after a long time apart.

It would be two more days until Linda and Eleanor landed in Switzerland, and another two hours before they made it to Champagne. I kept thinking that meeting Linda and Eleanor might be problematic. That I would have to tell them some cover story that sounded convincing enough to explain why I'd been incommunicado for a month, a fiction justifying my protracted cellular silence.

However, when the time came for our confab, my anxieties proved to be unfounded. Eleanor and Linda were smart enough not to ask unnecessary questions, not to try to extract information I wasn't at liberty to disclose. I breathed a sigh of relief, but the challenge arose from an unexpected direction.

A few minutes after reuniting with Jerry and me on the lawn of Michael's house — hugging, kissing, gushing, joking a bit — Eleanor turned to me. *Sally, where's the restroom?* she asked, looking into my eyes, grabbing my hand under the table and pressing it tightly.

I took the hint. After I pointed and she went indoors, I followed her. She came up to me and embraced me again. It was weird. I thought we'd reached the quota of hugs on the lawn, but she was squeezing me again with unusual intensity, while we were alone, in a hallway far from all the happenings outside. As I was pressed against her grip, she brought her mouth close to my ear and quickly whispered: *Sally, I've seen what Jerry looks like. I saw the back of his hands too. That's all I need to know that he's in bad shape. We need to run some tests...*

No more tests, Eleanor. We've been groping in the dark for two months now. Just spit it out. What did you see?

Eleanor's strong embrace became even stronger. *I suspect that Jerry suffers from a horrible disease known as scleroderma.*

The shock of her revelation reverberated in the air between us, in my ears. *What is that terrible name? Something to do with multiple sclerosis? Does it cause memory problems? What does that have to do with what Jerry is going through?* I demanded, my voice rising so it sounded like a yell at the end.

Not a memory thing, Sally, absolutely not. It is an autoimmune disease that damages the skin — and, in severe cases, it can cause harm to internal organs such as the lungs or kidneys, or affect the blood vessels. Or, God forbid, a combination of all of these. Often it results from elevated levels of stress or tension. The blood vessels stiffen, and the consequences can be catastrophic.

Stress and tension? I thought and almost yelled again.

There's no time to waste, continued Eleanor. *What tests have you done already? Be as specific as you can. I could also use the names of the doctors who examined him.*

I felt ashamed. I didn't have ready answers, even though it was a matter of life and death. Jerry's life or death. *We did some tests, we consulted some doctors, I spoke on the phone with some experts. But to tell the truth, I gave in to Jerry, who refused to undergo a thorough examination.* I felt like I couldn't breathe. My head was spinning. It took effort to inhale enough air to keep from collapsing in her arms.

Eleanor, let's cut to the chase, I whispered in reply. *We ran from the truth. We didn't do the right thing. We should have gone to the hospital for comprehensive tests, but we didn't. We didn't do blood tests, either. I haven't dragged Jerry to the best doctors I know. I didn't do what I know how to do best — break walls. No, Eleanor, no... no... no...* I said with growing frustration, answering questions she hadn't yet asked.

As I was speaking, the import and meaning of the conversation struck me. I already wanted to escape Eleanor's grip, free myself from her whispers and run into a room, lock the door behind me, and dive into the depths of Google. What the hell was scleroderma anyway? I'd never heard of it, except when my daughter-in-law, Lucia the medical student, mentioned it once. Eleanor went on talking, but I wasn't really listening.

The initial Google results were depressing, explaining that scleroderma is a chronic autoimmune disease in which collagen accumulates in the connective tissues of the body. Seventy to eighty percent of patients suffer lung damage, in varying degrees of severity. The disease manifests in fatigue and shortness of breath, even at rest. I looked for treatments, but it stated that the condition is incurable. Eleanor had told me as much. But this sort of answer was not in my lexicon. No such thing. I would find a way to fight the damn disease and give Jerry the quality of life he deserved.

42

18:00 hrs.
A conversation in Yarkon Park with
my dear friend Yaffit

My life had been turned upside down. While my nightmares had once featured scenes from Doha and Tehran, there was a new subject permeating my dreams. I couldn't stop thinking about the consultation with Ohr Barkan. The conversation at Michael's home just compounded my anxiety, quickly becoming a life-changing and fate-determining event. My internet searches became obsessive and, as they progressed, my nightmares became worse.

I created a new folder on my laptop called *General*. I made some new folders, placed in them dozens of Word documents and called them creative names. I named one of the subfolders *Lectures*.

It was the code name I fashioned for all the websites, links, studies and articles from medical journals dealing with the strangely named disease that had taken our lives by storm. It was also the folder where I saved emails that I began to receive from several senior physicians I was friendly with.

The information that flowed in from all sides was disturbing, frightening, depressing. The doctors, some of them renowned department heads, answered directly and to the point. They had no reason to censor their answers or think twice. I presented my questions as interest for a childhood friend from the *moshav*. The answers were also sharp, honest, painful. Dr. Jonathan Kahane said that he preferred not to refer to Jerry's symptoms by familiar scientific names. *I'm still in the learning process*, he said, leaving me with the ridiculous cumulation of data from the desk of Doctor Google.

Red dots on the face... White fingers... Shortness of breath...

Raynaud's phenomenon causes fingers to turn white and a sensation of freezing...

Mighty Jerry feels cold even when it's not so chilly...

New symptoms were appearing fast and furiously, but I duly recorded them all.

A few days later, I rang my best friend Yaffit. She was the only person on earth, apart from Jerry of course, with whom I could share my most innermost thoughts, talk about illnesses, and unpack some of the worries that were keeping me up at night.

Yaffit was also my regular partner for walks in the park. We would stroll for hours and talk. I arranged to meet her there. It afforded us maximum privacy and time for continuous conversation, stress-free, as we ambled along the bank of the gently flowing, supposedly calming Yarkon river. Only her, me and God.

We were both daughters of religious families, and we both carried similar values into our secular lives. We both made a leap from a traditional home to the heart of a society so far from religion. I had conversations with her I couldn't have with any other friend. We talked about faith and the important things in life as if we were talking about the morning news.

Yaffit knew me very well. I didn't have to say much, explain, or make excuses. She realized faster than I could have imagined that this walk would not be about fitness or intimate experiences. The understanding between us was almost automatic. It was a special bond, a rare one. Our conversations accelerated from 0 to 100 in a fraction of a second. A statement, an utterance, a look, an intonation — and we were off, plunging into unimaginable paths. We didn't feel the passage time. Two businesswomen from similar backgrounds, goal-oriented, curious, assertive, forgetting about ticking clocks, about time and prior commitments.

What made our connection so special? Faith was definitely a part of it, the strength of our common religious Zionist background. It was a constant presence in our conversations. Beyond that, we were both entrepreneurs, turbocharged women, opinionated, ambitious, fearlessly working our way up in male-dominated spheres. We were dedicated mothers as well, connected to our kids with an inextricable symbiotic bond, much deeper than anything I observed among my other friends or family members.

I've rearranged everything to clear out a whole morning to walk with you, said Yaffit in her clipped manner. I'll meet you at the entrance to the park near the post office, at the corner of Pinkas and Weizmann.

Yaffit's answer afforded a smidgen of relief. She was a successful entrepreneur, insanely busy. A force of nature in several sectors of the Israeli market, including ones predominated by men. It didn't bother her. Quite the contrary.

Her schedule was always incredibly intense, filled with twenty meetings or calls every day. Everything was urgent, everything was super important. It was not a pose. Yaffit was truly busy, but she'd cleared out a morning with zero notice.

As I thought about how and what I would tell her the next morning, another thought struck me. I need another conversation with the perspicacious Ohr, who sensed part of what I was going through but couldn't arrive at a definitive, accurate conclusion.

Undoubtedly, Jerry's illness drained all my mental and physical strength. I was a warrior who always believed in goodness and in the Creator. But somewhere, in the unfathomable depth of my consciousness, a seed of anxiety began to germinate, thinking about the worst outcome of all. Then time began to factor in. I had a tough time deciding whether the exceedingly long conversation with Yaffit encouraged me or depressed me. She, for her part, gave me her all. She listened to me with a grave face and found creative ways to wipe her tears away without my noticing it. From time to time, she asked something in a quiet voice, her moderate speech attempting to sound neutral.

I knew Yaffit. She did everything so as not to worry me. When we reached the edge of the park for the second time, she was ready for a third without breaking stride. She didn't peek at her watch. She didn't tell me, 'well, this is it,' and terminate the conversation when we finished another round. Somewhere in the third lap, a new element joined our conversation. She became very optimistic. *It's all in heaven's hands, Sally. Doctors are not prophets. There is always hope, and there are always miracles. As long as the candle burns, it is possible to set things right.*

That's right, that's how I feel. I stopped at a nearby bench. I normally had the strength to walk many more miles, but I felt that my body weight was increasing with each and every step. My legs refused to continue.

The meeting with Ohr was scheduled for that afternoon, the second in a week. I tried to rest before it, after completing three whole circuits of Yarkon Park; but I couldn't close my eyes. A deviation from our usual discussions lay before us. Our previous conversation was the first since I met Ohr in which I'd hidden from him the real reason for my coming. But this time I thought I'd share all the facts with him. I felt uncomfortable. Hundreds of tingles burned in my back and palms until Ohr suddenly stopped, looked at me for a long time, and asked: *What happened, Sally, are you OK?*

This was another high point in our relationship, which included casual, everyday conversations.

We talked about me and everything that intersected with my life, but also about what was happening in the world. Politics, strategic moves, chess games between superpowers and debates in the personal sphere. Was a world war imminent? Ohr had always predicted, before anyone else, global processes. But I hadn't told him anything about Jerry's serious condition. At that point, only Roy, Michael and I knew about it.

I spoke confidently and fluently, without blushing, without batting an eyelid. At the last second, I decided not to put Jerry's prognosis in harsh and accurate terms.

Words create reality, Sally, I told myself, *so you'd better not say anything.*

Yeah, that's damn easy, I replied in my own mind, trying hard not to move my lips at all. Immediately after that, the figures of Hamid, Noor, Rittal and Yasmin came to mind. The people who approached me with an open heart, exposing themselves with naïve sincerity. I embraced them to my bosom only to betray them and carry out my scheme.

Ohr looked confused. Every time we talked about my life, about Jerry's life, about friendship, about my partners in my investigations, he saw clear, sharp, accurate scenes in front of his eyes. This time his vision was clouded by a massive thunderhead, casting hailstones of questions at him with shattering force.

Maybe we'll look at the Chinese map, he murmured, half to himself. Perhaps we should focus on Western astrology. Perhaps... Perhaps...

43

A princess of Monaco faces monstrous depravity

Jerry's disease was progressing rapidly, at a furious pace. At times, it was an express train flying towards the catastrophic end of the line, while I observed the inevitable collision in slow motion. I decided I wasn't giving up — I didn't have that in me. Even when facing a colossal medical challenge. Even when the best doctors in Israel and the world lectured me about an unforgiving, unbeatable chronic disease. Even when some chose to use the most dramatic terms.

My prolonged search brought me to *Cordyceps sinensis* capsules, the rarest and most expensive fungus in the world. The Emperor's Fungus was known for its ability to dilate bronchi, improve kidney function, encourage anti-inflammatory and antioxidant activity in the body, accelerate peripheral blood flow, balance the immune system and function as an antiviral and antibacterial — as well as fight cancer. Some of the medical experts smirked when I asked them about the fungus, sold only in China. Others shrugged their shoulders and remained silent, just being polite.

At first, I bought small vials and smuggled them straight from China to Israel. Then I shipped vials from China to the US, and from there to Israel. In a short time, the laughter froze even on the lips of the greatest cynics. The mysterious fungus helped Jerry. His condition improved for a while, but then his body got used to the magic and required increasingly higher doses. It was a monthly expense of thousands of shekels, but it wasn't just a financial challenge.

After a few months of near despair, the talented Dr. Kahane asked to see me in person and brought with him a ray of light. *Sally, there is a treatment for scleroderma. It's experimental, but it will probably be covered by the national health funds.*

The battle up to that point had been complex, as it would continue to be. It required emotional fortitude, pushing my soul to the limit, but I had hope.

Then the accursed disease took it up a notch without any apparent rationale, without our doing anything wrong. The splotches covered Jerry's face and arms but, again, I refused to give up. I applied layers of makeup to my man, straining to keep up appearances and to avoid intrusive questions at social events. We went together to the beautician who obscured the spots on his face and visible parts of his hands. Only in retrospect could I acknowledge how ridiculous and futile the entire process was, the subtle aspect of our denial.

In the meantime, Jerry's work in the private sector was proving as demanding as his role back at the Mossad. He insisted on running the five operational squads of our international investigative firm, Masada. Our clients were of the most wealthy and renowned and we had teams operating in the south of France, Switzerland and across Western Europe, in the countries of the former Soviet Union, and across the United States.

I tried to convince him to give up the business or, at least, to slow down. He tired quickly, contracting any disease that was around with alarming ease. I was crazy worried about him. I was also concerned about operational blunders that might occur, under the circumstances. Above all, Eleanor's words echoed in my ears: *Often it results from elevated levels of stress or tension.*

I tried to raise this issue with him, but Jerry is Jerry. Nothing fazed him. *Everything will be OK,* he would say — not out of arrogance or complacency, but from his profound sense of responsibility. His confidence was based on his decades of excellence, facing situations far more challenging than anything the private sector could throw at him. His career at the Mossad could have been fodder for three different Netflix series. He was able to rely on his reputation as well, as he was enthusiastically recommended by senior officials at MI5, the CIA, the DIA, and the FBI's most elite units. These were based on elite operations, involving customers from among the world's aristocracy and opponents from the crème de la crème of criminality. Jerry found it difficult to turn down such cases. Like so many of his colleagues, he was addicted to the roiling adrenaline: the excitement of being on a mission, matching wits with tactical geniuses, succeeding at ostensibly impossible tasks. Friendship also played a role; there was a residual esprit de corps among the veterans of the various intelligence services. If a former colleague made a request, it was imperative and undeniable. The projects themselves were also intriguing. They seemed to have been stolen from Hollywood's latest thriller or action movie.

That was how we found ourselves — together and separately — in the midst of a multibillion-dollar dispute over a Monégasque heiress and her inheritance.

It was Jerry's good friend, Martin — the husband Linda had traded in for a newer model — who connected him to a colleague, an active agent in Western Europe. Dangerous Russian mobsters had presented themselves as working for an international security firm. They became involved in the most sensitive of investigations, from the boardroom to the bedroom, using the process to extract vital information from their clients under the guise of confidentiality — only to turn around and blackmail the people who had hired them.

One mafioso had his used his perfect English and excellent French to present himself as an aristocrat closely related to Monaco's royal family. What began as a complex business investigation turned into a story of extortion, intimidation and the abduction of a fourteen-year-old girl — whose body parts the mobsters had threatened to send to her family, one by one, in order to prove how serious they were. It's the nature of investigation: you start by following one thread and, in short order, you find yourself unraveling a completely different scenario.

This is how I first became acquainted with the concept of digital extortion. I discovered that the most powerful and vile criminal organizations of the 21st century had carved out territories for themselves on the border between sophisticated cyberattacks and the classic, good old-fashioned art of extreme cruelty.

This was also how I learned of the turbulent lifestyle in a European principality covering an area of less than one square mile. In the midst of this operational whirlpool, a walk along the abyss, I was sucked back into the cyber-realm. Here, however, I wasn't focused on colonels, ministers and princes in the Gulf states; rather, I contended with tycoons, counts and princes striding down the corridors of European splendor, wearing a facade of culture, grandeur and refinement as I faced off against the most vile of criminals imaginable.

It reminded me of the terrifying conversation in the wellness center of Tehran. Again I was exposed to unimaginable brutality and savagery carried out with the kind of ghastly sophistication that could only have been born in the twisted minds of greedy sadists.

The truth was that nothing prevented me from turning down the projects which presented themselves to me, knocking on my door, one after another.

The sad fact was that Jerry wasn't the only addict in the family. I was excited by the thought of cracking the cases I was offered then — and I couldn't find the strength to say no.

44

Married to the Mossad flies off the shelves

Married to the Mossad was the surprise of my life. I'd never written anything before. I could never have imagined that the first book I put out, with the encouragement of my friend Yaffit — who just happened to be the owner of Steimatzky Publishing — would become, against all odds, a runaway success.

The proofreading phase exhausted me, as if I were running up a Himalayan slope. My energy was sapped, the air becoming so thin I had trouble breathing. My chest contracted painfully. Suddenly I discovered so many errors in my behavior over the years, along with so many sentences that I was not allowed to write; on the other hand, so many paragraphs seemed trite to me, unnecessary, meaningless.

Yaffit recognized my distress without my saying a word. She embraced me from behind as I foundered amid the sea of words. She whispered sharply: *It's a terrific book, Sally. Stop fiddling and fixing. The process has been torturous enough, overseen by enough pairs of eyes. You're not writing right now. Just checking that there hasn't been anything left in that you don't want to show to the whole world. That's it. Nothing more. There's a whole team of editors, proofreaders, typesetters and graphic designers to do the rest.*

Then came the four days between the distribution of the book to the stores and the first sales report. It would be banal to say these were the four longest days of my life, but they were. With every evening came another frightening ordeal. I heard my cell phone ring only to hear shouting on the other end. I imagined Yaffit's apologies. I closed my eyes, but the numbers appeared anyway, sales reports filled with column after column and row after row of the number zero. They presented themselves to me in turn, each more blatant and cruel than the previous one.

Then, one night, about an hour before midnight, it happened. My cell phone screen showed that it was one of Steimatzky executives. *Sally, do you have a bottle of champagne next to you?* she asked, a tone of triumph in her voice. *If not, go grab a bottle and pour some drinks for yourself and Jerry...* Silence, then I heard her say: *The book is flying off the shelves, Sally. Can you hear me? The first edition is selling like hotcakes. We're shipping whatever we have left in the warehouse, and then we'll warm up the presses for a second printing.*

I hung up and stood up in a daze, glancing around the dining room to make sure I wasn't dreaming. The strangulating nightmares galloped away as I realized it was all true. Jerry looked at me and understood everything even without my saying a word. Truthfully, he was torn. He would have preferred it if I hadn't chosen to write my memoir, but his love for me conquered all. I was important to him. My fulfillment was important to him. He was as supportive as he had always been — and he had always been happy for me when I succeeded. Still, Jerry, never afraid of anything, dreaded the wrath of Mossad officials. Cold calculation told him that the book should have never come to light, but he understood my drive to document what I had experienced, even as I found it hard to believe that they'd actually happened to me. And there was one more unresolved issue with Jerry. The cutting, burning question he'd posed to me at the beginning of project still lingered: *When did you decide to become a writer? Why be exposed? To satisfy your ego?*

No, Jerry, I feel the need to share what I went through, I replied. I want to prove that anyone can do remarkable things. That they should. That every person must take a break from their routine, their comfort zone, and contribute to the community, to society. It's not about ego at all.

Then the assault began. Calls to the cell phone and landline, masses of WhatsApp messages, more and more texts through Messenger. Friends and acquaintances, relatives, Jerry's friends from the Mossad, reporters — in print, radio and television. There were also a few calls from abroad and quite a few from blocked numbers.

Jerry would answer. *Say I'm busy*, I requested. Jerry understood. He too thought I deserved to enjoy a few hours of peace and quiet.

In the following weeks, the success of the book became a fait accompli. The sales report was good. Better than anything I'd allowed myself to envision.

The talk of translating the book into English came faster than I could have hoped. The calls didn't stop, either. I sat at our huge dining room table and began jotting it down — the only way to remember who called, from where, why, what they criticized or complimented, what they asked for or offered. I started with sticky notes, moved to a notepad and then to a notebook.

The balcony window was wide open. A gentle breeze came from the west. I loved closing my eyes and indulging in its caress. I loved peeking out from time to time towards the sea on the horizon, between some of Tel Aviv's new high-rises. The quiet was intoxicating. The notebook in front of me testified to what I was going through, the progression of my new baby. Then, suddenly, a stubborn vibration. My cell phone quivered in place, shaking the pile of papers on which it rested. *Another frivolous conversation*, I thought.

My energy had been depleted. I wanted a break from the flood of phone calls, many of which were idle; but this caller was adamant. The cell phone would not stop vibrating, nor the rustling of the papers under it.

I picked it up reluctantly. *Hello, who's this?*

My question was answered quietly, with a deep exhale. A harasser? *Hello Sally*, he said suddenly. He spoke in English with an accent I couldn't identify.

Hello, I answered with obvious impatience. *Who is this?*

I see that you are celebrating your new book. Good for you. Enjoy it while you can, because soon you won't be able to enjoy anything anymore. I'm telling you: that's a promise, Sally...

I listened to the end of the sentence and the silence that immediately followed. My head was spinning. Something strange was happening and I ran through alternative scenarios in my mind. Maybe someone with a bad sense of humor was pulling a prank on me? Maybe someone connected to the Masada investigation on the French Riviera? Maybe someone tied to my activities in Qatar?

OK, but who's talking? I replied, still refraining from attacking head-on, lest it really be some fool with a poor sense of humor. *You'll know who I am when the time comes. That's my promise,* the voice replied from the other side of the conversation. *In the meantime, I'll be watching you, Sally. I wonder why you picked that shirt today. Green with a big white design on the front. Really?*

I held my breath and my eyes darted down, as if to confirm what the caller had said about my clothing choice. He was right; that was what I had put on that morning before having my coffee at the dining room table.

My next instinct was to glance at the balcony. Beyond the railing were more than ten high-rises, scraping the sky west of the road we lived next to. Lots of residential towers, some of them taller than ours, and each of them adorned with hundreds of balconies and windows. *Excellent, Sally, you're a quick study,* the mysterious voice at the end of the line snarked at me. *You have just a few thousand windows and balconies to scan in order to find me looking at you...*

Then, a few beats of dead air until I heard a click and the call ended. I glanced at the time. 2:03 PM. I took deep breaths. Logic dictated that I call Jerry immediately and report what had just happened, but I decided to adopt my father's wisdom: count to a hundred before you react. I didn't want to dump this on Jerry while he was struggling with his own health issues, using all that was left of his strength to tackle the complex and cruel convolutions of the Riviera case. I stood up, went to the balcony window and stared for a while at the dense forest of residential buildings to the west. I pulled the curtains closed, then the drapes until the balcony vanished.

Then I dialed. Yaakov Lavi always made himself available for me.

He had a ringtone especially for me, one you couldn't miss. I imagined him leaping in the air and grabbing his cell phone in a matter of seconds, even if he were in the mid-operation, even if he were in negotiations, even if he were tending to his personal or private affairs. Yuval, I need you here and now, I said. I used the code name we used for emergency calls between us, whenever there was the slightest suspicion that someone was listening in on us.

My dear girl, what is it this time?

Yuval, I need you here and now.

That will take me six hours. That was the answer Lavi knew how to provide, even if he were busy in France or Italy or England. It was clear to both of us where I needed to go to meet him just before 8:00 PM, after all the necessary evasive maneuvers.

Our conversation ended and then my internal discussion began. *What should I say to Jerry? Where should I tell him I'm going tonight? How can I lie to him?*

I had all the reasons in the world to hide the truth from him; but, at the same time, all my anguish, all my doubt, and all my anger reawakened — all directed at myself.

45

14:00 hrs.
A mysterious sniper threatens the Amir home

The next few days were like a Category 4 hurricane, and it struck without warning.

The Monacan investigation became extremely complicated. Our Greek tech guy betrayed us and vanished, while Jerry's health deteriorated. I knew that the Chinese fungus begins to lose its effectiveness as the body grows accustomed to it.

Then there was our mysterious caller, who returned the next day, at the same time. *Do you think, Mrs. Amir, that curtains and windows will protect you? Think again!*

He spat it out word by word, remained silent for a bit, then hung up.

I recorded the call. I listened to it over and over again, in a futile attempt to place the accent. I raised my eyes heavenward to bemoan the awful timing of these threats. *Why now when I need every ounce of energy to fight for Jerry?*

The previous evening, I met Lavi at an apartment he rented on Arlozorov Street. It had been carefully selected; its location made it easily accessible, but it also allowed for the highest level of security and surveillance.

Lavi saw me through the camera mounted over the barrier gate and let me in. The heavy garage door opened, showing me two fairly wild off-road vehicles, a Mercedes Coupé upgraded for speed and a heavy urban motorcycle.

I hugged Lavi tightly. *My dear girl, what's going on?* he asked me, his reciprocal embrace giving me confidence.

Lavi was one of the people I trusted implicitly. A consummate professional. One of the few people in the world who knew about the severity of Jerry's condition. He fully aware of the complexities of the Masada investigation on the French Riviera. In addition, I had a vague suspicion that he knew where I'd been for the month I remained incommunicado.

And, as a professional, Lavi held his peace. Even when we talked about the anonymous caller, he gave me all the space to describe the problem and my array of concerns without rooting around unnecessarily, without making me name countries or cities.

The itinerary over the next few days made me slightly dizzy. It was a bit too much, even for me. I had scheduled several appointments for medical consultations. The first was with Dr. Dan Aravot, a world-renowned expert and the only lung transplant surgeon in Israel. The second meeting was with Dr. Mordechai Kramer, an internationally acclaimed expert in pulmonary surgery. Both were from Beilinson Hospital, the only facility in Israel to perform lung transplants.

Finally, I had an appointment with Dr. Yaron Barak, a prodigy, handsome and talented. I had helped sponsor him, as part of the Beilinson Friends Association, in his three-year training at Duke University as he honed his skills as a transplant surgeon, including studying artificial lungs. My conditions for sponsoring him were clear: he committed to come back to Israel and to send his kids to a Jewish school while in the States. Three years had passed, and now the circle was complete. My assistance had paid off, personally. Dr. Barak was my guardian angel, leading me through the entire transplant process.

I knew that I'd have to hurry home from my rounds at Beilinson in time to prepare for my daily call from my stalker. Lavi had promised to send me someone to deal with it. I still had a list of at least fifteen more errands to accomplish that day. I had to find a special medicine for my mother. Michael had told me he needed to consult me on an urgent matter. There were plenty of tiny trivial tasks as well. I had to reply, to inform, to write, to answer. I was supposed to be interviewed on Skype for a Jewish news channel from London. I had to talk to my lawyer, Blum, about copyright protection ahead of the book's translation into English.

I called a cabdriver who worked with me on particularly stressful days. *Victor, today you're mine, from now until evening. Don't leave me!*

He arrived at lightning speed, ready for the task. *Mrs. Amir, whatever you say. I'm here for you. If you're calling me, you must be under a lot of stress.*

The meetings at Beilinson were discouraging. Lung transplantation was spoken of as a last resort. The only variation among the medical authorities were how low Jerry's chances of survival were. Forty or fifty percent was the best we could hope for with his current poor condition. Disheartening, but unsurprising. Aravot and Kramer made it clear: Jerry's life depended on a particularly cruel roulette wheel.

From Beilinson, Victor took me back home and waited. Lavi's man was supposed to arrive at 1:00 PM and, indeed, the intercom bell rang three minutes ahead of time. The doorman informed me that some workmen had arrived, with armloads of equipment.

Three minutes later, a team of four men arrived at my door. The boss was Yarden, a 35-year-old guy with ripped jeans and a well-worn long-sleeved T-shirt. He had an aquiline nose and a short ponytail. However, his authoritative tone belied his disheveled appearance. He directed his squad professionally and efficiently. *Sally, right? Lavi told me a bit about you. We know how to deal with this stuff. We've already analyzed the logistics. You have two windows facing west, and my guys will take up positions next to them. Soon you'll open the curtains, and you're going to put on a show, just like you're taking a work call, handling papers we'll give you.* Yarden positioned a hidden camera on the table to face the balcony. I put some documents and notebooks on the table. *There are ten or more high-rises in the area; some have twenty floors, some have as many as forty. That means hundreds of windows and balconies — and the calls have lasted barely a minute.*

So where do you look first? I asked defiantly, but immediately regretted it.

Sally, I'm surprised at you. Think about it: You're on the 22nd floor. He watched you while you were sitting here at the end of the table, and described what you were wearing and even knew when you were squinting in his direction. He has to be in a nearby building, and he has to be above the twentieth floor. In fact, he's got to be in one of those three buildings, Yarden said, opening his laptop deftly and spinning it around to me. On the screen was a panoramic shot that showed the high-rises in the neighborhood. Three of them were numbered: 5, 6, and 8, and marked with arrows in blue and red. *We paid a visit to your roof this morning. The doorman let us go up to fix a satellite dish. We were there for barely ten minutes. It was enough to take pictures from the exact spot above your balcony window. After our little show with the curtains open, we can narrow it down more.*

No matter how unkempt he seemed, Yarden was clearly smart, experienced and proficient. Once the curtain opened, the hidden camera between us took pictures, one after another. *Click, click, click.* After about ten minutes, the whole group gathered in my kitchen and analyzed the photographs. The number of windows and balconies which offered our mystery caller a view of my outfit narrowed it down to only about thirty apartments.

He thinks he's clever, but we're smarter, Yarden said, pointing to one of the three buildings under suspicion. *I'm betting he's here.* He tapped the image of building number eight. *I presume he'll call again today at exactly 2:00 PM to deliver his speech.* His lips spread in a smile of satisfaction mixed with pride.

After that, it was easy. Too easy. The phone rang at exactly 2:00 PM. Yarden's team split up, taking up their positions at the two windows, in the kitchen and on the roof. Each had several apartments to scope out.

I tried to drag out the call. I gave the man on the other side the feeling that he was scaring me. I told him that I was willing to pay him as much as he wanted to leave me alone. I mentioned $100,000. He fell into my trap and cracked a series of prideful words. *It's not about money, Sally. Understand that this has nothing to do with money.*

I pulled the conversation in a new direction. *Yesterday you guessed which shirt I was wearing. You can't see anything, you're just a liar,* I said, and he went on the defensive.

Don't fool yourself, Sally. Yesterday you were wearing a green shirt. Today you went for yellow. I can even see more than that... He hung up.

Bingo! The shout came from the observer at the kitchen window. Building number eight, top floor, last one on the right.

Yarden motioned me to go to the edge of the living room and close the curtain. Then he came right up to me, looked into my eyes and put a hand on my shoulder. *You can breathe a sigh of relief, Sally. We passed on the info. Your job is over, and so is ours. There were already agents in place, next to each of the three buildings. Now, they're doing whatever needs to be done.*

Even as he was reassuring me, he was already busy moving towards the cases to pack up their equipment. The cases were black with molded gray foam interiors, uniquely suited to house the dazzling array of binoculars, cameras and other accoutrements. Yarden and his team unscrewed, retracted, folded and collapsed everything with stunning precision and speed. In less than four minutes they were already at the door, apologizing for any mess they might have made in my home.

Yarden had the last word: *Sally, we promised Lavi that we would put your mind at ease. That was our mission and I'm satisfied that we carried it out in full. I understood from him how important you are to him, and you have no idea how important he is to me.*

I sank into an armchair far from the balcony. I needed a few moments to digest everything that had occurred over the last two hours, to accept that the clear and present danger had dissipated as if it had never existed. I felt profoundly indebted to Lavi.

I closed my eyes and allowed every muscle in my body to relax. My hands covered my chest on the left side, protecting my heart as it raced.

I offered up a silent prayer of thanksgiving and asked for help for Jerry.

46

15:00 hrs.
At the Amir family home, a turning point
in our lives

The cell phone, perched on top of a pile of notepads and papers, started to vibrate. I was three steps away from it, but I couldn't summon the marginal energy to cover the distance. Maybe I was scared. I was struck by a sinking feeling that Yarden might have made a mistake. Perhaps the threat from the window in building number eight still lurked.

Finally, I gave in and went over to the dining room table. Jerry was calling, scolding me. *How long Sally, how long does it take you to pick up the phone? We've got to talk. When will you be home tonight?*

The Outlook schedule flickered on the screen of my Mac in purple, green and blue. There were even some timeslots in bright red, a sign of the urgency and importance of the meeting. I hadn't even left a window for regular breathing. The estimated end time was later than 9 PM, but I knew Jerry. I could read him like a book. He was clearly under stress, and he obviously needed to discuss a serious and pressing matter.

Unfortunately, I turned out to be right. When Jerry came home he practically fell into the armchair in the living room. That horrible disease was draining the last drops of strength from him. He looked beaten and weak, as I'd never seen him before.

Sally, you've got to take over the Riviera investigation. I'm not happy about it, but the facts are what they are. You know I wouldn't ask you unless we were teetering on the edge. You're the only one who could take the reins and drive it home. Otherwise, we'll have to tell our clients that we've failed.

Ice slid down the back of my neck and quickly reached my waist. Jerry wasn't supposed to involve me in anything dangerous. After my return from the Qatar mission, he had assured me that I was done. Even more concerning was his word choice. Jerry never spoke of failure while an operation was ongoing.

I looked at him for a long time. The grey cloud over him had become a black nimbus. I wanted to wrap my arms around him, whisk him off to safe space, far away off from the fate that awaited us and whose outline was already becoming increasingly discernible. I already knew that unbearable days lay ahead.

But Jerry continued: *Sally, you have to take over for me at Masada. Everything, Sally.* He closed his eyes and sank deeper into thearmchair.

The Riviera case was Jerry's main focus at the time, but running Masada required dealing with dozens of administrative and bureaucratic tasks — major, minor and trivial. Tasks I had no idea how to handle.

Jerry's plea that evening marked a turning point in our lives. One did not have to imagine or interpret what it meant. Jerry was weakening. He was acknowledging that the end of his life was drawing near.

Of course, the concepts of mortality and finality were never explicitly broached in our conversations. I'm sure he banished those ideas from the top of his mind, but they lingered, hovering in the eaves like a swarm of wasps.

The following weeks pulverized me. I had to crack open five voluminous binders holding all of Masada's essential information. The most important of these, labeled with an A, was crammed into a safe that hid beyond bookshelves in Jerry's study. Four other binders were locked in a filing cabinet next to his desk. On top sat a thin manilla envelope; it was blank, but I knew what it contained. A sheet of yellow paper, covered with Jerry's elegant handwriting, printed with his black fountain pen. The ornate and intelligent calligraphy moved me. It was what made me fall in love with him; it made me fall in love with him each time anew. The page was divided into two. On the right, the names of the agents Jerry directed; on the left, those of the main suspects in the investigation. Each name was assigned a code, linked to a file on his computer.

I sat across from Jerry like an eager student. The Mac was situated on the edge of the table, waiting for new input. On my knee I placed my favorite Kohinoor notepad. Jerry leaned back heavily, bracing his neck with his intertwined palms, and closed his eyes as he began reciting from memory. Every file had its own password. Jerry had a system for each of them, based on the subject, degree of importance, level of classification, and seniority.

And that was only the beginning. There were hundreds of hours of recordings that hadn't been transcribed yet. Surveillance videos in disheartening quantities. Hundreds of memos, texts, messages and emails.

Then there were the hard copies. One folder was filled with a surprising collection of newspaper clippings. Another held photographs, portraits and full-body images. Then there were two-sided pages filled with the org charts of two international gangs. Some of the names were circled in yellow highlighter, three exclamation points screaming next to them.

That's all you'll need to know to get up to speed. It's not much, he said, though it wasn't clear if he was voicing concern or sarcasm.

I knew inside and out every tone of his voice, every wrinkle as he pursed his lips, exactly how he chose his words, and the bitterness was evident to me. Jerry was furious about the timing. He was angry that a challenging case was slipping through his fingers. He was outraged at the disease that compelled him to clench his teeth and say goodbye to Masada. He didn't audibly express these sentiments, but I heard him loud and clear: *I don't deserve this, I don't deserve this...*

Jerry, as was his wont, had done an amazing job. No one could compete with his abilities to survey the board, concoct a strategy, utilize his pawns, deploy his pieces and play the game with finesse and confidence. He always thought big — huge, in fact — and was always three steps ahead. Even when the target of the investigation was a medium-sized tech company, he acted as if he were orchestrating an operation against Iranian intelligence. Sophisticated, careful, well-camouflaged, built with every imaginable failsafe for the agents in the field; there were rescue forces to extricate anyone who got into trouble, and reserve elements to back them up.

That was why Masada's rates verged on the ludicrous, charging three to four times what other firms did. That was also why only Masada could handle the most complex and challenging cases — and why Jerry couldn't afford to fail.

Yaakov Lavi coordinated all the detective work for Masada: from surveillance on foot and by vehicle, logistics and procurement, photography and wiretapping to physical infiltration, boring into walls, remotely penetrating computers and arranging safe passage at border crossings. Lavi had cultivated these abilities over many years. He recruited the best professionals the private sector could access. There were recent retirees from the Mossad, the Shin Bet and the National Counter-Terrorism Unit, as well as veteran and senior Mossad officials who offered their advice and connections. Lavi had shaped Masada into a mini-Mossad, a small, agile and exceptionally efficient private-sector intelligence service. Lavi was everything you could dream of in a project manager, the gift that kept on giving for politicians, governments, corporations and the elites in Israel and on both sides of the Atlantic. For any investigation I took part in, I always wanted Lavi by my side; he consistently amazed me with his uncanny ability to recruit squads of professionals uniquely suited for any given mission, in no time flat. Everyone trusted him and loved working with him, despite — or perhaps because of — the fact that he was demanding and uncompromising.

I'd love to take a peek at his phone and email contacts, I thought to myself.

Jerry was completely relaxed when Lavi was around. As was I. After all, just recently he had proven, once again, how good he was at solving complex problems in no time. Though Jerry had only been running the investigation for two months, Lavi already had his double-agents planted. Two women in their mid-thirties and a man of about fifty already resided in the neighborhood of Font-vieille in Monaco, inveigling themselves in the local high society, socializing with the residents of the neighborhood, swimming in the pools of private country clubs, sweating in the saunas, surfing in the sea. They had even managed to become frequent guests at the castle owned by the Dubois brothers, our main targets.

Two other operatives had been ensconced at black-hat cyber-firms in a high-tech office complex near the Riviera Marriott Hotel La Porte De Monaco. It was located in the Provençal town of Cap-d'Ail outside of Monaco proper, but still right next to the beating heart of the microstate, entrenched in an ocean of money and assets.

These are the best of the best, Sally. Veterans of elite cyber-units who have worked with us for several years. They bring with them not only technological genius, but high fluency in English, Italian and French. They are excellent infiltrators; they figure out how and where to penetrate without blinking. They also know how to connect with people in a flash, Jerry gasped.

My mind was in a tizzy, my stomach roiling. The names of Bar and Eliot seemed to echo throughout the room. Eliot's clear eyes stared at me, his intense gaze skewering me. *Bar... Eliot... They work with us?*

I threw the question out, but Jerry didn't answer.

With each day, his thoughts became more disconnected and the sequentiality of his speech diminished. Cognitively, he was unchanged. His memory was as clear and as accurate as ever. His intelligence amazed me even after so many years together. But he was tired, very tired. Blood transfusions every few days were supposed to help him, but each treatment was ineffective after twenty-four hours, lasting less and less. The paratrooper, the genius, the weightlifter, the judoka — he was fading before my eyes, becoming closer and closer to reaching his limits.

The two companies in Jerry's crosshairs were Black Roy and Static York, active in the south of France, Switzerland and Vienna. Registered in the Caymans, both appeared to be legitimate software companies. *They appear innocent,* said Jerry in his tired voice, *though they're anything but.*

What can they do? I asked, and immediately regretted the question.

Whatever starts with an ingenious and immaculate infiltration ends in blood and indescribable malice, Jerry replied slowly and quietly. Was it paranoia, an abundance of discretion that had become second nature to him, that made him whisper or the extreme exhaustion from scleroderma? *They connect to the victims' computers, networks, and cell phones. They collect precise digital information — and then go fully analog on hunting expeditions. These are cruel people, devoid of basic morals, without red lines, without restraints, Sally. Listen to me, I'm not exaggerating. On the contrary, I'm downplaying what they're capable of. It's difficult to put into words what they do to anyone they suspect of infidelity or embezzlement, or just to someone they're trying to extort. Worse than you can imagine, Sally,* he said and sank back into himself.

I went back to the binders, the audio files, the surveillance videos, the newspaper clippings. I inspected them one by one and made notations.

I slowly began to understand why the classified folder contained reports of criminal incidents on the Riviera. There was a collection of sophisticated thefts from gated estates and luxury houses on the edge of the upper Alps in the port district, from the houses overlooking the Bay of Monte Carlo and from mansions in the old quarter of Nice. Works of art, exorbitant sums of cash, ornate jewelry encrusted with the rarest of gemstones, and lots and lots of diamonds. The more I read from the press and in the summaries of the team leaders, the more it became clear to me what the common denominator was: they got in, took what they wanted and got out cleanly. These were the actions of super-professionals who had astonishingly accurate insider information: the combinations for safes, the codes for disarming alarm systems, and even the times when the homes would be empty.

Jerry explained that this was not a counteroffensive, but rather cybertechnology activity aimed at collecting information. He had not been recruited to eliminate the rising crime wave in the south of France. The purpose of his investigation was to assist an aristocrat who had converted to Judaism, her Jewish husband and their seven-year-old daughter. She needed our help fighting the greed of several members of other noble families in Monaco. I kept browsing through the file of news articles and discovered another brown envelope. It contained only four newspaper clippings. All of them were about criminals targeting the wealthy and highborn. Ostensibly, these were four different events, but Jerry had marked the articles lightly with a pencil, circling some of the passages. There was not a single article about the apprehension of the perpetrators.

47

The driver who took me to Ben-Gurion airport performed three basic evasive exercises, venturing up Hamasger Street and taking a sharp turn into a body shop. As we stopped inside the tin structure, I shot at him: *You're sure you're not overdoing it a bit?*

The driver paused for a moment and then turned around. *Mrs. Amir, you are in good hands.* He stared at me reproachfully. *I do exactly what Lavi orders me to do. My part is done; now you've got a new chauffeur.* He pointed to a dark van parked parallel to us. I noted that its engine was on, and its side door was wide open. To my chagrin, I had no choice but to do as he said.

A split second after I got in, the van sped forward and left through the back of the garage. Fifteen minutes later I was already in an airport tram with darkly tinted mirrors that was deftly gliding towards an unfamiliar hangar. Another hangar I've never seen.

The huge doors opened precisely as we approached. The narrow aperture barely allowed the tram to enter and closed as soon as we were inside. The driver glanced at me, though it was unclear whether in amazement or in pity. I immediately recognized what was awaiting us, the turbofan engines unmistakable: a Gulfstream IV. Not only that, but the identification number also told me it was my old ride from Greece, GS222.

I boarded the plane which was still empty and took a seat at the mahogany table. Within minutes, I had filled the cabin with Jerry's neat binders, manilla envelopes, markers, yellow and red Post-it Notes, sheet protectors filled with documents organized by subject, two light folders and my personal notepad.

Now it's my turn to hog the table, I thought. Our flight to Nice would provide a great chance to finish studying the information I didn't have time to memorize at home. *Quality work time,* I reflected. *No phones, no WhatsApp, no distractions.*

Time passed and I was still alone on the plane, satisfied with the work area I had organized, but our takeoff was delayed. I kept my temper in check, telling myself that, as far as I was concerned, we could sit in this hangar until tomorrow.

About an hour later, I heard voices by the stairs. I raised my head and pricked up my ears. At least one of the voices sounded familiar to me. Very familiar, but I couldn't quite place it.

A minute later, the smug face and shaved head of Alon, captain of my fake nightmare flight, emerged from the flight deck. *Mrs. Amir, are you our guest again? I promise that this time there will be no unexpected glitches.*

Ha, ha, ha, Captain Alon, I replied, trying to make light of his words. *There may be no glitches, but I've been sitting here for more than an hour. And why so formal? I'm Sally, not Mrs. Amir or any other title.*

You're right, Sally. One hundred percent. Soon enough you'll be joined by the two kids who have us all spinning on their little fingers.

Indeed, a minute later, a pair of laughing faces entered the cabin. They were unmistakable: the legendary beard and the wild mane.

I knew it! I knew it! I screamed with childish enthusiasm.

Bar came up to me and hugged me tightly. *It's my brilliant student! You deserve a huge hug!* He planted a wet kiss on my left cheek. Eliot stood alongside, waiting patiently. Then he stepped forward and, once again, offered his trademark powerful handshake; once again, with the second hand coming up to cover mine, while his translucent blue gaze pierced and penetrated deep within me. *So it was you,* I said in an attempt to free myself from Eliot's double grip and the pair of eyes that lanced right through me. *You're the genius tag team! Jerry and Lavi are always singing your praises. I should've guessed.*

Bar and Eliot moved towards the two armchairs next to the mahogany table.

I stopped them. *Guys, I made too much of a mess here. There are too many things you shouldn't see.* I pointed towards the two seats at the back of the plane, but my assertiveness didn't last long. *Fine, sit here. I need to understand what you're doing here. How did you end up as part of a private investigation? Are you the moles that Jerry placed in those cybertech firms in Fontvieille? What are you doing in Israel while the operation is at such a critical juncture?*

You don't want to know, Sally. We're up against a gang of sadistic psychopaths, Bar replied. *We're talking about the Orange Mafia, based in Vienna under the cover of a legitimate international firm.*

I was familiar with the way Bar spoke. He sounded reluctant. I got the impression that he and Eliot weren't sure what they could share with me at this point. *Sorry, Sally, we only talk to Jerry and Lavi.* They didn't want to insult me.

Bravo, your secrecy and discretion are admirable, I said. *You've gone to the best school there is. But there's a new sheriff in town. I'm running Masada now, which means I'm your boss too.*

Bar and Eliot exchanged looks, took a step forward and sat down across from me. Bar said, in a clear attempt to change the subject: *I've heard some stories about your visit to our cousins. I'm blown away by how proud you've made me. You're the best student I've ever had, but that still doesn't allow us to discuss a new investigation.*

I hear what you're saying, I told Bar, even as I stretched my hand towards a manilla envelope marked with the letter Z. Without looking away from them, I stuck my hand into it blindly, felt around a little and pulled out two A4-sized photographs. I placed them on the table confidently.

Bar and Eliot couldn't hide their surprise. They again talked between themselves, exchanging glances. The photographs showed a pair of men entering the doorway of a Black Roy office and a woman leaving the offices of Static York. *Maybe I'm confused? Do you work here, and you here?* I asked defiantly and reversed the order of the photographs. It was like revealing a full house in a poker game.

Then I added the coup de grâce. If you insist, *I will also pull out the photograph of Sabrina Strauss — or should I call her Sabrina Dubois, as she was known before she converted and married an Orthodox Jew.*

The mention of the name got through to them. It was undeniable. It was clear to them that I knew what I was talking about. They used their vantage point to examine the extra materials I had placed on the table. Among the piles of documents, what stood out was the org chart of the criminal gangs in the Riviera.

However, the wave of crime sweeping over the French Riviera and the Principality of Monaco did not interest us. The investigation I'd inherited from Jerry dealt with one family, with blue blood and green envy. Their lust for lucre could never be satisfied, never mind the mountains of cash and unending list of assets. Nicolas and Andre, the addled heirs of the Dubois family, were distant relatives of the Monacan ruling dynasty. The family had used its wealth to gain control of three of the dozens of banks operating in Monaco. However, the death of the paterfamilias Charles — from cancer, at a relatively young age — had created a schism, with the brothers trying to seize their sister's inheritance.

Sabrina was guilty of a great many transgressions. First, she had been her father's favorite child and his will had granted her a larger share of the inheritance than her two older brothers.

Second, she had dared to marry a man who did not belong to the aristocratic class. Instead, he was a theater actor from Paris. But the worst thing in the eyes of the family was that he was a Jew. And now she was one too! The brothers Dubois were greedy and grasping, unsatisfied with their vast fortunes. They wanted more. They also wanted the share that their father had bequeathed to their sister.

I had a hard time determining where the fine line lay between simple greed and antisemitism. *You've got my number,* I had shot at Jerry in the first conversation in which he detailed the nature of the investigation, causing a small smile to come to his face. He knew very well that seeing a Jew being hurt aroused in me all the motivation and anger necessary.

I looked at the list of the family's assets and their values and my eyes almost popped out of my head. I found it difficult to compute the number of zeros. Then I looked at what they'd tried to expropriate from the unruly heiress who fell in love with the wrong person. I was floored by the numbers here as well. Ostensibly this was an intra-family dispute that ought to have been resolved during a legal hearing, but the greedy brothers decided to speed up the process by hiring private investigators. In retrospect, it turned out they'd put a target on their own backs. The detectives dug up more Dubois dirt than the brothers would have wanted and some of that information, including intimate details, fell into the hands of a criminal gang. Nicolas and Andre had unsheathed a double-edged sword. It was cutting deep into them and their families, including their younger sister.

It's not child's play, Sally, said Eliot, staring at me with his blue, limpid gaze. *These characters are more dangerous than the bad guys you tangled with in the Gulf. The head of the gang is Dmitri Ilyich Kotiev, also known as the mobster of a thousand faces. He surfaces and disappears and pops up again in all kinds of places, each time with a different name, with a different cover story and new atrocities.*

So, is he the hardest nut to crack? I asked in reply, trying again to decipher Eliot's expression, the color of his eyes and the intensity of his gaze. *Not at all, Sally. Not at all. Dmitri is big and powerful, but he's only a capo. The godfather is Boris Ahmadov. He's a ginger, hence 'Orange Mafia'. He dominates the entire region, making everyone quake in their boots all the way to the Riviera and Monaco. According to what we discovered at Black Roy, Ahmadov is furious about the Dubois situation. He's ordered that anyone who gets in Dmitri's way be taken out. They just don't understand that if they try to listen in on whatever moves on the Riviera, they as well can be heard.*

48

0:00 hrs.
Orange Mafia in action at the airport in Nice

Two minutes before landing at Nice Côte d'Azur I realized that something was awry. Alon told us that he didn't know what was going on at the airport, but he had been asked to take another pass. *I just hope they let us land eventually*, he half-joked.

Eliot, Bar and I were riveted to the windows, looking down on the blue-painted runways. We could see dozens of cop cars flying along the tarmac.

As we turned north, I could see that Rue du Capitaine Ferber was filled with even more police vehicles. *Alon, you bastard, are you trying to test me again?* I roared towards the flight deck.

Alon replied with a twinkle and a big laugh. *I deserve that, Sally. I definitely deserve it, but this time it's the real deal. You cannot get this many units to show up for a distraction. The tower says we'll be able to land in a few minutes. They're assigning us a runway on the side without any cops on it.*

Nice Côte d'Azur Airport sits on the coast and kisses the Mediterranean Sea. It is the third- largest airfield in France, a point of entry to the entire Riviera. Aside from international flights, it also has an active helicopter line between the airport and Monaco's private luxury helipads. Still, the number of police cars had to be a record. I tried to think what could have triggered this turmoil on the ground. Bar, Eliot and I had no idea that somehow, we were responsible.

When we disembarked, Yaakov Lavi was there, along with a black van right next to the stairs. *Something big is happening here*, he said.

It has to do with the Orange Mafia. I don't know if it's specifically connected to our joker, Dmitri.

So is it good for the Jews or bad for the Jews? I asked, trying to lighten the mood.

Yaakov sighed. *I have no idea.*

As disquieting as that response was, I was given ample reason to trust Lavi. The next few minutes proved once again how connected, organized, and precise he was. An older border policeman led us down a long corridor towards a glass door that opened automatically. On the other side was a tiny office. A police officer asked a few questions, glanced at the passports, didn't stamp them, scrawled something down in his own records and signaled that we could move on.

We returned to the van and drove down a dirt road towards a side gate. As soon as we crossed the fence, a Range Rover roared up and stopped alongside us. Bar and Eliot got out of the car and vanished.

You're amazing. Amazing! I said to Lavi, who looked at me wearily. He seemed concerned and very anxious.

The drive from Nice to Monaco took about an hour. Our chauffeur may have been skilled enough to compete in the Grand Prix, but the jammed roads offered him no opening.

I was troubled by a thousand matters, Jerry first and foremost. My brain had already stitched together some kind of solution for the investigation in France. In addition, I had pointed questions about why Bar and Eliot were involved in a private investigation.

Meanwhile, I took in the spectacular scenery. On the right was the Mediterranean Sea, flickering in a multitude of shades of blue amid the boats that cut through the bay. On the left were the slopes of the mountains, picturesque villages and some castles of the rich and famous. Sean Connery, Bono, Tina Turner, Elton John. I'd been down this road dozens of times but never grew bored of seeing it. My companions, on the other hand, seemed infuriated at the slow pace of the journey. Finally, we pulled up to the Riviera Marriott adjacent to the Port de Cap d'Ail Marina.

I went up to the room to freshen up and change. Then I entered the adjoining room, a spacious suite that looked like an operations room. From previous cases, I knew it was the sort of set-up Lavi could arrange in no time at all. There was a trestle desk full of paperwork as well as racks of documents, photos and maps. One table was loaded with electronic equipment that I couldn't identify. I recognized the org chart of the Orange Mafia. Some joker had taken a marker and rechristened it the 'Ginger Mob.' At the edge of the suite, near the balcony door, sat a bulky man who kept his sunglasses on in the room and was immersed in the tablet on his lap. I walked past the whiteboards, glanced at the documents on the desk and waited for Lavi to address me, but he wouldn't stop texting and talking on his mobile, his hand hiding his mouth. Eventually he turned to me and said, *Your timing, Sally, is impeccable*, and hugged me tight.

I had missed his hug — and now he was giving me a compliment too? *I don't understand, Lavi. What does timing have to do with our investigation? Next thing you'll be talking about some special luck that I have, just like Shimon Eitan.*

Lavi knew Shimon well and had served under him for many years. The name brought a smile to his worried and tired face. *So Shimon also says that you are a woman with extraordinary luck? I thought it was just me. But that's beyond my pay grade, Sally. I am a little more practical and much less philosophical. I keep two feet on the ground. I don't have the faintest idea where luck ends and fate begin; when it's all about professionalism – and when it's also a matter of karma. I'm not at all sure that there is such a thing as karma.*

Yes, but... I hear a but coming, I teased Lavi.

But, as it turns out, during the four hours you were in the air between Tel Aviv and Nice, a world war broke out between the Orange Mafia and Solntsevskaya Bratva. Both were born in Moscow, both are mobs from hell, both have a strong presence in Vienna – and both have fallen in love with the Riviera region over the past year. There's a bucketload of money and property here and lots of naïve businessmen. They couldn't resist.

And how does all this relate to our project? I asked matter-of-factly, trying to bring the conversation back towards a professional discussion.

From what I hear, three of Dmitri's soldiers were killed during an attempt to take him out. Following the assassination attempt, a shootout took place, the likes of which France hadn't seen in years. Dmitri arrived at the airport in an armored vehicle and managed to board a helicopter. Hell if I know where he was headed. He was chased by three jeeps loaded with armed Solntsevskaya men. These are people who have no God. They think that the autostrada of the Riviera is a battlefield in Chechnya or Afghanistan. One of the jeeps tried to breach the terminal. Four armed mobsters got out, and there was a prolonged shootout in which two policemen were injured and the mobsters were all killed. Around the same time, three motorcyclists arrived in front of Boris Ahmadov's headquarters in Vienna and shot it up. They killed a guard and an unfortunate secretary on her way to work. Then they disappeared. Rumor has it that the big boss was in the building and was smuggled out of a back door. According to the info we received, he's gotten out of Vienna.

Anyway, there was a lot of chatter throughout the chaos, with zero comms discipline. They made calls to each other and to Vienna without any precautions, leaving our guys an opening you could drive a tractor-trailer through. What our geniuses had already implanted in their systems meant we had access to a treasure trove of information. What had once been blocked and sealed and cordoned off became accessible, more than we could have ever imagined. That's it in a nutshell, Sally. We haven't had the time to go through even a tenth of the material.

Lavi's words amazed me and made me happy. One of the ideas I'd come up with on the way to France was to provoke tensions between Dmitri's gang and their rivals so that he and his men would be so busy they wouldn't have the time to harass the Dubois family. I still had other arrows in my quiver but, even before I'd landed, Dmitri had found himself more preoccupied than he had ever imagined, mainly trying to save his own skin. Even his redheaded boss had more important things to worry about than our client.

Listen, Lavi, I've spent two weeks diving into all the files, documents, recordings and surveillance photos that Jerry dumped on me. I haven't slept properly since then. First, because there's a mountain of materials to wade through. Second, because the responsibility for finding a solution to Jerry's illness rests on my shoulders, and on my shoulders alone. Trying to balance his business and health concerns exhausts me, physically and mentally. This all lands on me, Lavi, precisely when I'm expected to be at my best. I feel paralyzed, because Jerry's always been my rock. I haven't shown even a moment of despair in front of him or even hint that he was asking too much of me while I'm fighting to save his life. The show must go on. But when I'm alone, I sit on the floor and fall apart. If Jerry hadn't asked me to, I wouldn't be here today. Period.

I clamped my mouth shut, and silence prevailed in the room. Lavi looked at me curiously and waited for the rest. And it came. Flowing out of me in one long tirade, barely leaving me room to breathe.

Look, I understand that the two boys you brought from Tel Aviv are deeply ensconced in Dmitri's tech firms. I understand that this gangster and his people are also a target of the Mossad. I understand that Sabrina's little girl is in danger of being kidnapped. I understand that the families of Nicolas and Andre are also in danger. I know and you know that, in the near future, I will be very busy taking care of Jerry, and I will still need to devote time to the management and paperwork of Masada. It's all on me, Lavi. Do you get it? It's all on me! Everything!

I put a stop to my logorrhea, sucking in air before I passed out. A slight cloud appeared on Lavi's face. He loved Jerry dearly. What I told him about the illness hit him hard.

Everything you said is true. I have only two small corrections, Lavi said in a quieter voice than usual. He was exhausted and sad. *First, the two boys are really three. They have a third partner, Oded, who lives in Israel. They're going to be billionaires, these guys. Together they founded BEO — that's Bar, Eliot, Oded. They're barely old enough to shave, but they've already developed the Hydra program for cell phone infiltration — and what they already know how to do is impressive. Second, the Mossad entered the picture only three weeks ago, after they intercepted emails* and cellular conversations between Boris Ahmadov's men in Vienna and Dmitri's headquarters in Monaco. It turns out that the redhead got his hands on an old Soviet workhorse, a monstrous Antonov An-124 Ruslan which works overtime on the Tehran-Damascus-Latakia line.

OK, Lavi, OK. Stop. It's nice you keep the Mossad in the loop. I don't want to know details, who updated whom, why and when. Please don't get me involved in this. I also don't want to know too much about Hydra. None of this matters at the moment. We've come here to solve Sabrina's problems. That's what we're being paid a fortune to do. Our role is to protect her family and make sure that her two antisemitic brothers don't steal her inheritance.

Correct, Lavi replied, so what do you suggest? The material accumulated on the Black Roy and Static York computers contains enough damning information to implicate the lovely duo of Nicolas and Andrei. I don't know what else the boys managed to find in the last few days, but I'm convinced that we already have ten smoking guns against them. Their blue blood will not save them from the clutches of the IRS, the European Commission, the partners they ripped off, the Orange Mafia – nor from local law enforcement. Lavi stopped talking and just looked at me – either curiosity or skepticism, it wasn't clear.

I saw some of the documents, Lavi. We don't need more months of work and risk to our people, and we don't need to charge Sabrina hundreds of thousands of euros more. I have a plan, part of which I composed in Tel Aviv and some of which I completed during the flight, I said and handed Lavi a white sheet of paper with my handwriting on it. Lavi read it hurriedly, his eyes sweeping back and forth. From time to time he scratched his head. Once or twice he put the paper on the table and highlighted something.

You wrote here that the plan depends on a single condition, but you didn't specify what it is.

The condition is that everything happens tomorrow. Starts tomorrow morning, ends tomorrow at midnight. Following the assassination attempt on Dmitri, this is my condition for the whole program. Tomorrow or nothing.

OK, that's pretty obvious, but how do we do it?

Bar, Eliot and their partner can gather all the information that already exists concerning the business activities of the Dubois brothers. At the same time, they will plant a delayed command on the companies' computers that will send all the incriminating material about Dmitri and his men to the local police and press, Interpol, the European authorities and the Russian security service. I'm sure they're also interested in what's going on in this neck of the woods.

By the time the material is released into the world, Bar, Eliot and your three agents from the prestigious neighborhood of Monaco will be in some pub in Tel Aviv, and Sabrina Strauss and her family will be somewhere outside France. If the plan works exactly — I mean, exactly — as we're planning it, Sabrina will be able to return home in a few days with her inheritance and without any threat.

Suppose it is possible. We'll have to determine the timing of each and every stage.

Look again. There's a sequence to what I wrote. I didn't put down a timetable, but that's the order. Start with number one early tomorrow morning and get to the last one by midnight. Dmitri's soldiers will leave no stone unturned trying to find out who penetrated their security and figured out where their boss was going. I'm anxious for our two young men. Go to them now, brief them, and give them the order to fly away the moment they've completed their task. Let them go to work in the morning as usual, then excuse themselves after an hour and vanish. We must arrange an escape route for them like only you know how to organize — but please, no later than tomorrow.

What do you take me for? Lavi asked, obviously offended. *There's an escape plan ready. I didn't think we'd need it right now, but two calls to Avishai and it's on. He takes care of every detail, from valve stems for the getaway vehicle to skipping passport control at Nice Terminal to refreshments on board.*

I got up from my seat, went over to him and gave him a long hug.

I'm leaving you in good hands, Lavi reassured me, motioning with his head towards the bulky man in the armchair. Then he put on his grey jacket and walked towards the door. *I'll brief Bar and Eliot on what to do tomorrow morning and where to go after they get out of there. I still have one more conversation with Avishai about our three jokers in the Dubois brothers' neighborhood. I'll be back in an hour. You can stay here — or you can go back to your room to rest.*

Lavi was already at the door and reaching for the handle when I fired a piercing and smart-alecky question at his back. *Tell me, Lavi, do you think Boris and Dmitri were attacked simultaneously just by chance? That it wasn't coordinated? Aren't you the one who told me you don't believe in fate, destiny, luck?*

Lavi froze. He put his hand on the doorknob, then turned around to face me with dead seriousness and only the tiny, almost invisible, shadow of a smile. Then he turned back to the door and left. *Good luck, Lavi,* I told his retreating back. Then I retired to peruse the desk full of documents.

Just minutes later, my head started to explode. Overwhelmed with anxiety, my breathing became heavy, my mouth was dry. My hands and back began to itch. A prickle of cold sweat ran from my forehead. I couldn't get hold of myself.

I got up from the chair and started walking around the suite, pounding with both hands against the wall every time I reached the end of the room. What if they catch Bar and Eliot tomorrow? What if they conduct a thorough search at the border? What if the computers produce an immediate alert about their plans? What if Dmitri's soldiers had already suspected them and the assassination attempt had only strengthened their misgivings? After pacing the room four or five times, I forced myself to stop and speak to the man immersed in his tablet.

Do you speak Hebrew? I asked.

The broad-shouldered guy raised his head and put a huge smile on his face. *Sure, Sally, how can I help you? Looks like you're going crazy here.*

Can you safely ring Lavi? I asked. My lower lip was shaking. The guy pulled out another cell phone from an inner pocket. I could hear the chimes as he pressed the numbers. I could feel the pounding of my pulse in my neck and temples. Then I heard the quick and short tones stating that Yaakov was not available. *Are you sure you dialed correctly? Could you have made a mistake? Are you sure this is Lavi's number tonight? Can you try again?* I fired the questions one after the other, breathless. The guy in the armchair got up, came over to me and dialed right in front of my eyes. The discouraging sound repeated.

He's not available. I know Lavi very well. This is not by chance, Mrs. Amir.

Do you know me? I asked.

We all know you here. You've become a legend, even if you don't know it yet. I hope you don't mind my saying so.

Thanks, thanks, I mumbled. *I don't understand what you mean, but the conversation with Lavi is more important to me than anything else now.*

He dialed yet again, holding the cell phone out to me so that I could hear. Once again, a busy signal in the silence of the room. *Sorry, Sally. I'm Raanan, by the way. It's very nice to meet you.*

I shook his hand, which was as warm and large as his body. I turned around towards the desk full of documents and suddenly felt overwhelmed, depleted, totally drained. It was the concern I had for the safety of Bar and Eliot; it was the anger I felt towards myself for not stopping Lavi on time. There was the fatigue I'd been storing up for the two weeks since Jerry had asked me to replace him. There was the deep, perpetual exhaustion that has accompanied me since we started dealing with his illness. I stepped with my last ounce of strength towards one of the armchairs, collapsed into it and leaned back, interlaced my hands behind my neck, and closed my eyes. I missed my healthy, strong Jerry, unconsciously adopting Jerry's signature pose.

49

7:30 hrs.

A perfect sting at Hôtel de Paris Monte-Carlo

The events of the next day could be summarized in a single sentence: it ran as smoothly as a Swiss watch. The plan we had devised the night before was carried out with utmost precision. *Just the way Jerry likes it,* I thought. I was proud of myself. Secretly, in my heart, I hoped to hear a compliment from my man, the strategic mastermind, congratulating us on the meticulous blueprint.

Lavi returned two hours later.

The waiting had been driving me crazy. A lot of scary scenarios came to mind. He still hadn't answered his phone. Finally, he arrived, panting.

He presented everything in order and we began to scrutinize every last detail of the plan for the next day: The weather. Traffic patterns during the various times we'd need to be en route. How many lanes each road had. The positions of the security cameras in the elite quarter of Monaco. The location of the closest police station.

Raanan turned out to be much more than just a heavy. As we finalized each step of the plan, he dialed someone, identified himself by code name and instructed the person on the other end of the line where and when to be the next day. His French was good, his English even better.

When it came time to map out escape routes, he consulted his tablet, reviewed aerial footage and suggested improvements. *These images are from the past month,* he said, not hiding his satisfaction. He also proposed his own ideas. A truck on standby as a possible roadblock from Monaco westward towards Nice. *That's on me. Sur-*

veillance of each of the entrances to the Black Roy and Static York offices, to keep an eye on anything out of the ordinary at the pivotal point when Bar and Eliot are in action. He kept track of the extrication team, as well as the backup squad; he knew the types of vehicles each group would be using, and they would all refuel before the start of operation.

It seems you had incredibly good teachers, I interjected.

He looked at me with some embarrassment. *From the best, Sally. I learned from the best. Someone you know very well.*

The words brought a flush to my face as my pulse quickened. It all came together in my mind, as the stories Jerry had told me about the young guys he worked with clicked into place. I raised my palms towards my chest to express a quiet thank you to him. Raanan mirrored my motions and plunged back into practical matters: The convoy's entry route to Nice. The side entrance to the airport grounds. The password for the guard at the gate. The abort code to cancel everything. The encrypted, one-time communication system to be utilized throughout the entire operation.

We went through everything time and time again, rethinking, refining and recapitulating.

It was already well past midnight when I asked Lavi to go over everything one last time so I could envision the whole thing, like a motion picture.

What actually happened was no different.

At 9:00 hrs., Bar arrived at the Static York offices. His company ID, clipped to his belt, had the name Anton Garnier on it. He gave the security a typical man-hug: a handshake, followed by a couple of quick slaps on the back and then the pull-in to whisper in his ear: *Hey, man what'd you get up to yesterday?*

The guard returned the hug with a hearty laugh, appreciating the interest in his social life. He sent Bar through without another glance and turned to the next employee.

At the exact same time, Eliot arrived at the headquarters of Black

Roy. His nom de guerre was Tom Russo. The inspection there was more rigorous. The magnetometer beeped. Eliot went back and re-entered. The magnetometer beeped once more. The guard winked at Eliot and released him on his way.

Both wunderkinds had invested time and energy in cultivating their friendships at the security desk, and now it had paid off. As Jerry said, they were experts at exploiting human connections.

At 9:05 hrs., Bar and Eliot sat down at their computer stations, slipped the special USB drives they'd brought with them from Israel out of their socks, inserted them into the ports and resumed typing vigorously. Business as usual, should anyone be observing them.

At 9:30 hrs., a sizable Evian truck pulled up at Sabrina's house in the ward of La Condamine. The side of the truck facing the house rolled open and Sabrina, her husband and their seven-year-old daughter quickly came out the front door. Each held a small suitcase, and they were swallowed up inside the vehicle less than five minutes after it pulled up. Less than a minute later, everything was rolled shut and the truck pulled out of the driveway — at a casual, utterly unremarkable pace.

At 10:00 hrs., Bar and Eliot left their respective offices, making sure to part from the guards with hugs and pats and slaps, as usual. They each used the same phrase: *Oh, man, I've got a splitting headache. I gotta get to the pharmacy.*

That would be the last time anyone saw Anton Garnier or Tom Russo.

At 11:00 hrs., the Dubois brothers arrived in the parking lot of the beautiful Hôtel de Paris Monte-Carlo, in the beating heart of Monaco.

Nicolas, the arrogant elder brother, pulled up in a red Ferrari 448 convertible. Andre was right behind him, in a white Maserati MC20. The hotel valets rush up to their cars, nimbly pocketing the keys as well as a fat tip. The brothers met by the bank of elevators on the way to the business lounge. They winked at each other.

It's a good day, bro, said Nicolas.

A very good day, Andre replied, whacking his brother on the buttocks, urging him to get moving.

At 11:05 hrs., the brothers settled themselves in a remote and quiet corner, languourously reclining in armchairs. They were anticipating a mystery caller, the one who had claimed he had documents they might find intriguing, featuring their sister Sabrina. He'd even sent two samples by WhatsApp. *There's a lot more where that came from.* That had piqued their interest, personally as well as financially.

At 11:08 hrs., the Dubois brothers were approached by an ashen waiter who placed two massive black backpacks at their feet. They looked quite heavy. *Regretfully, the gentleman you're expecting has been delayed a bit. He would like you to have these files,* explained the waiter and walked away.

At 11:20 hrs., the Dubois brothers decided that they had exhibited as much patience as etiquette required. They stuck their hands into the black backpacks and began rummaging around.

It didn't take long to realize that there was no compromising information about their sister among the files. Inside each backpack, atop the files full of papers, sat an unsigned letter. It was brief and to the point: *If you're looking for incriminating documents, enjoy. Should you persist with your attempts to seize your sister's inheritance, rest assured that these documents and several hundred similar ones will be delivered simultaneously to the royal family of Monaco; to the business partners you've cheated, distant relatives of the Grimaldi dynasty; to the Police Nationale; to the Office of the Prosecutor; to Interpol; to the newsrooms of Le Monde and Libération and major television networks. Read the documents here! We're watching you. If you should leave the lobby before four o'clock this afternoon, we will immediately release the first batch. You will sorely regret it.*

The brothers exchanged haunted looks. Nicolas came to his

senses first, reaching into the bag to pull out a document at random. He came out with a few pages stapled together. He lifted his glasses to his forehead, quickly perused the first page, lowered his glasses, then raised them again. Then he moved on to the subsequent pages with frantic speed and began to speak to himself in an incoherent whisper.

Andre looked at his brother, terrified, not daring to reach for the bag closest to him. *Show me*, he demanded, in a nervous, almost hysterical, tone. He grabbed at the papers in Nicolas's hands, but only got one page, torn off from the rest. Still, the single piece of paper was enough. It contained details of recent transactions made by the brothers, facts which should have been known only to the heir and the spare of the House of Dubois — and to God.

Andre's hands began to tremble and the paper between his fingers rustled. With an annoyed grunt, he placed the page on the table, then went back to pull a sheet from the bottom of the pile at random. His eyes widened with astonishment at the sight of his secret bank account statement. After all, not even his brother was supposed to know about it, nor his wife. The photocopy had certain amounts circled, and next to each was the source of that deposit, handwritten in exquisite calligraphy.

At 12:00 hrs., a FedEx truck entered Nice Airport, breezing past all the guard posts and heading down an auxiliary runway. Some of the police officers at the checkpoints saluted the driver with careless disregard.

At 12:03 hrs., the FedEx truck pulled up in front of a Gulfstream GS222, parked there with its engines on. From the truck emerged eight people: a young man with a beard gathered into a braid; another young man with a mane of long hair; a man wearing a black yarmulke; a beautiful woman with a great pair of legs in stiletto heels and a particularly short skirt pulling along a frightened seven-year-old girl; two women about thirty-five years old; and finally, a man of about fifty. The group climbed onto the plane and, a minute later, GS222 began to taxi down the runway. Confirmation for take-off was received within seconds.

At 12:30 hrs., the Dubois brothers were still riveted to their seats in the business lounge. They'd removed their ties and jackets, their shirts drenched in sweat. They fully understood what was sitting in the backpacks, as well as what was still out there. It had been an hour-and-a-half, but they couldn't leave. From time to time, one of the waiters approached them to find out if they were feeling unwell or wanted him to bring them something. They asked only for cold water. The maître d' of the lounge showed up and, keeping a safe distance from them, monitored their actions to ensure their well-being.

After another hour had passed, Nicolas began to speculate on how all this information had reached the hands of a stranger. He mumbled and rambled, but dared not openly say what was in his heart. He suspected that it all stemmed from the complacency, arrogance and negligence of the man sitting next to him.

Andre was much more direct. He held one of the secret agreements signed by the brothers, looked at Nicolas openly, and hissed through gritted teeth: *You're such a fool! I told you not to take the papers home, but you insisted!*

At 13:30 hrs., the Dubois brothers noticed that many of the occupants of the business lounge had crowded in front of the television screens, which were displaying a breaking news chyron in big, red letters.

Nicolas was rooted in place, lacking the strength to get up and walk four paces towards the throng. Andre marshaled his energy to stand and walk over, rudely pushing some of the curious crowd out of the way to get a clear view of the news anchor on France 24. The report was about thousands of incriminating documents simultaneously being handed over to media and law enforcement.

Andre felt his legs turn to rubber; the increasing crowd gathering towards the tv screen helped prop him up and keep him from collapsing.

The anchor went on to announce that the identity of the source was unknown but, as far as the editorial board, journalists and police could tell, the materials seemed to be authentic. Then she began to go through a few of the most damning pieces of evidence, as they were displayed behind her.

Snowden strikes again! shouted one of the spectators. *This is the handiwork of WikiLeaks.*

WikiLeaks c'est sûr! came a shout from the other side of the lounge.

Andre felt as if he were floating in another universe, as if he were actually in hell. The piles of documents in the black bags had blurred sight and sound.

Then the newsreader went on: The anonymous source has offered a wealth of information incriminating the Russian mobster, Dmitri Ilyich Kotiev. The unknown person claims to have thousands of additional documents in their possession, which may embarrass the royal house of the Principality of Monaco.

This was too much for Andre, who felt that the air in his lungs was running out. With agitated, jerky motions, he managed to clear a path for himself and collapsed back into the armchair opposite his brother. *Did you hear that, Nicolas? Did you hear?* he demanded in a hoarse voice. He took a bottle of mineral water and, instead of drinking it, dripped it over his balding head.

Many of those present in the lounge recognized the billionaire brothers and looked on in shock at their behavior. One of the attendees gingerly took out his cell phone and shot a short video, which went viral on TikTok within minutes.

At 13:35 hrs., a convoy of police cars could be heard, sirens wailing, rising to a volume that threatened to rupture the eardrums of bystanders. It seemed as if all of law enforcement in the south of France was converging, descending on the same targets. On the television screens in the lounge, the anchor explained, as if on cue, that the police were momentarily arresting affiliates of the Orange Mafia.

It was at that precise moment that our hulk, Raanan, began to feed hundreds of papers into a shredder on the makeshift desk in Lavi's suite. He also tore down documents, photographs and maps that were pinned to the corkboards. A few were carefully removed and filed in perfect order in a single binder.

At 15:00 hrs., a taxi with black-tinted windows entered the hotel's lower parking lot to pick me up for a speedy ride to Nice Airport. It gave me an hour of peace to relax in the backseat. I turned on the light to illuminate my Kohinoor notepad, which I gradually filled with brief lines of text, asterisks and annotations.

No doubt about it, I thought. *The investigation on the Riviera and the events of today in Monaco have to be part of my next book.*

The trip ended too quickly. I wrote vigorously in the notepad, but I had so much more to write.

The taxi entered the airfield, speeding towards the auxiliary runway I knew so well. We pulled up by a Westwind plane.

I ascended the stairs quickly, buckled up, and closed my eyes.

At 20:00 hrs., the Westwind landed at Ben Gurion Airport and advanced towards the familiar, outlying hangar. The pilot and copilot emerged from the flight deck and tried to wake me. First gently, then raising their voices, then shaking me by the shoulder.

I opened my eyes and saw a gleaming forehead in front of me. This time it wasn't Alon. *Thank you, thank you,* I said.

It was the deepest sleep I'd ever experienced. I got up and knew that the drama of the last two days was just an interlude to what was in store for me. I would be a period without a moment of reprieve, not even in the castle of my own home.

50

17:30 hrs.
Back to Tzameret Park, as my James Bond falters

I went for an afternoon run in the park while Jerry stayed home. He said he planned to water the plants, but I knew it was another creative excuse to avoid the outing without admitting his inability to keep up with me anymore.

Fifteen minutes later, my cell phone began to vibrate in the palm of my hand. It was the housekeeper. Something bad had happened to Jerry, I was sure.

I wasn't wrong. Jerry had fallen on the balcony while tending to our plants. She was hysterical, fearing he was going to die right then and there. However, by the time I got home Jerry had already regained consciousness. It seemed he'd passed out for just a few seconds.

Still, the time it took me to get back to the apartment allowed me some headspace to reach an understanding. It was clear that we had reached a new level. We were facing a life-changing reality. It would never go back to what it had been.

My sinking feeling proved to be accurate. That fall was the first of three. The second resulted in a fractured vertebra... and the fracturing of Jerry's confidence... and the fracturing of our daily routine.

Then there was a fall which happened as I stood just a few feet away. He walked to the refrigerator and opened it, and then I heard a loud whomp from the kitchen.

I ran in to see my Jerry lying on the floor under the table, and a scream came out of my mouth that scared even myself.

Michael, who had been visiting us, heard the alarm in my voice and ran in quickly from the shower.

Dad's dead! I screamed in an unfamiliar voice. It suddenly occurred to me that, with all of my covert activities, I'd never actually seen a corpse before me.

The seconds ticked by, each tearing at my flesh, until Michael lifted his father's legs. It seemed as though it took another million ticks of the second hand until faint signs of life crept back into Jerry 's face. The color slowly returned to his cheeks and he opened his eyes, looking at me with an understanding that required no words.

Among the many battles we faced was the struggle to preserve Jerry's appearance. The red spots were getting bigger and bigger. No makeup ploy could hide them anymore.

We had a wall full of ticking clocks, but then we added one more: the organ donor list. The discussion of a lung transplant turned us into prisoners awaiting sentencing, somehow both a distant as well as imminent concern.

Dr. Aravot, director of the Cardiothoracic Surgery Department at Beilinson Hospital, was fair in his assessments. He explained that there was no way of knowing when or if the right donor would be found for Jerry, but he said that we were first in line.

At the same time, I was wrapping up the loose ends of our investigation in France while handling the multitude of commitments related to my debut book. *Married to the Mossad* stayed on the bestseller lists, was then translated into English, and began to be snapped up in the United States as well. With success came demands and requests that I rejected, one after the other, on a variety of grounds: prior engagements for interviews, in Israel and abroad, lectures, and more.

Along with the enthusiasm for the book came a surprising wave of requests for mediation in the disputes of the top one percent. Most of the inquiries were from Europe. It was surprising; I never advertised. I was happy, nonetheless, because I knew deep down that I was good at it. I knew how to mediate, compromise, and engineer smart solutions to complex conflicts.

Every morning I composed a to-do list. Jerry, Jerry, Jerry. Promoting the book. Making sure that Sabrina, her husband and child were safe and well. Checking bidaily that the Dubois brothers were doing exactly what we ordered them to do. But I knew that I was in a race against time and that, very soon, I would have to abandon all my pursuits and devote all my time to Jerry.

I missed my man. I drew my strength from him, but he had none left for himself. I was constantly afraid that the Dubois brothers would be poisoned by their hate. They might become complacent about our threats, deluding themselves that the danger had passed, and then they might find ways to evade the tasks we had assigned them: To meet with the family's lawyers. To find a way to reverse their position and come up with a good explanation for why. To annul the instructions they'd given to private investigators to act against Sabrina. To stop surveilling her home and her family. To repeal the injunctions delaying the transfer of her inheritance. And to instruct the executors to implement everything in the will, as written.

I had told Lavi: *I don't trust them. Keep dropping them hints. Bombard them with WhatsApp texts, messages, emails and faxes. Blow up their cell phones and landlines, send letters to their offices; as far as I'm concerned, stick memos to their pizza boxes when they order in. They must be kept in a state of paranoia. They must understand that we're going to keep sitting on them — a week, a month, a decade from now — never letting up our tenacious guard. They must understand that their business is transparent to us, that we can see them even when they're on the toilet.*

I was proud of myself. I worked with the degrees of precision, perception and perseverance I learned at Jerry's knee. *Even when everything seems to be working out, you don't take your foot off the gas, you never become complacent, you never stop conducting yourself with Yekke perfectionism,* I quoted his words to myself.

At the same time, I had to continue to wage the battle against the disease with the terrible name. I had to speak with the best experts, to stay on top of them unrelentingly, to make it clear to them

I was willing to agree to any drug, any treatment, even if it were still experimental, still unapproved.

Then, suddenly, there was a breakthrough, one which gave me false hope. We all breathed a sigh of relief for a moment. Our ties to the Ministry of State Security had paid off. A Chinese business associate of mine told me about another species of cordyceps, the caterpillar fungus. The name and description were enough to arouse all of Jerry 's objections. He wasn't willing to listen. He thought I'd gone crazy, but even Jerry couldn't stand up to me when I had my heart set on something.

It wasn't easy. I refused to settle for less than the original fungus from the Tibetan Plateau, which goes from worm to plant and back again. I would, under no circumstances, accept the cultured, capsulated substitutes offered in Israel, but the Ministry of Health refused to approve the import of the drug. I had to use every possible connection to smuggle it out of China via the US and into Israel.

Jerry was skeptical, but he agreed to take the drug. It appeared to be a miracle cure. He began to feel better. After about two weeks, Jerry stunned me and announced that he was going to the gym. We were completely delusional, but grabbed onto the delusion for dear life. But then it turned out that the body became accustomed to the effect of the fungus, so we had to increase the dose every few days.

After about two months we had reached a dosage of thirty milligrams. It only helped for a little while. The treatment became unbearable. Jerry loathed the taste and refused to drink it. In our arguments, he looked at me with a piercing look and declared: *Sally, this is my fate. It's my life. I cannot swallow this crap anymore.*

The new situation freaked me out. I felt that a miracle cure was within reach, but we just couldn't grasp it. I refused to accept answers like *You have no alternative* or *It's impossible*. These phrases aren't in my lexicon. Instead, I bombarded every possible expert with emails, messages and phone calls. I was in contact with doctors from all over the world.

I even contacted a hospital in China, which specializes in Chinese medicine and serves only a closed circle of military personnel. I did everything to try and save my husband. We didn't skimp on money or effort. I just couldn't imagine my life without Jerry, whom I'd been with since I was nineteen. I turned on my stubbornness again. I took advantage of the great esteem that Jerry had among some of the senior Ministry of State Security officials and, within a few days, we found ourselves on a flight to China.

Jerry stayed in the hospital for about a month. His condition was stable but, when that month was over, we had return to Israel and to the reality on the ground.

My time away hadn't lessened any of my burden. The to-do list was unforgiving. Wrapping up the Monaco investigation proved more complex than I had anticipated. I had to cancel more and more speaking engagements in the US. I consumed more medical journal articles than a tenured med school professor.

My brain was a salad, a hodgepodge of operational matters, obscure autoimmune arcana and authorial malaise; while also feeling like I was missing out on the fun of being a bestselling author in America, every day left me feeling exhausted and utterly bewildered. As I confronted the race against time for pulmonary transplantation, I realized how little I really understood. As if it wasn't hard enough finding a donor — it had to be a perfect match, the lungs had to fit Jerry's chest be compatible with his body and blood type.

As I went over the exacting requirements, I found that my strength and faith were being pushed to their limits.

I prayed every day for a cure for Jerry, for a change in our grim reality. I reflected: *How small we are! How the wheel of fortune turns us upside down and inside out. This is the same Jerry who went to the gym, lifted weights, had a black belt in judo, could run and speed-walk with the best. A crack shot. A rock of stability. A well of intelligence. The subject of much admiration and the dreams of more than a few women. And now...*

In addition to all the challenges, there was Raynaud's phenomenon. The cold that made his fingertips blanch and look like they are about to freeze. Here's my Jerry, my super-agent, who needed gloves even in summer. The medical staff explained that the phenomenon was due to the constriction of the small blood vessels, preventing blood from reaching the extremities of his fingers and toes. For Jerry it was a bit too much.

I went back to Dr. Aravot, who was as measured as ever. *It is all in the Almighty's hands. I have no way of knowing when, or if, we will have a match. A family somewhere must make the difficult decision to donate organs at the worst moment of their lives, but that's not enough. The lungs must be a perfect match from the perfect donor, and the procedure must be carried out immediately.*

It was a game of multi-wheel roulette. Time was one factor, and the odds of compatibility after a successful transplant were another. After our initial discussions, I had been optimistic. We were told that there was a ninety percent success rate. It sounded promising. The debate was over location: should the surgery be performed in Israel or in the United States — specifically mentioned was Duke University Hospital in Durham, North Carolina. My dear Dr. Barak, who was still at Duke, was resolute. *If it were my own brother or father, I'd do it at Beilinson. That is where he'll receive the most dedicated and professional treatment*, he declaimed eloquently and poignantly. Further inquiries tipped the scales. We were convinced that at Beilinson Jerry would receive the highest quality care. Thoughts of hospitalization overseas dropped off the agenda.

The daily routine of waiting for the phone call became its own nightmare. After months in which nothing happened, a meeting was scheduled in America. A Hollywood film producer had read *Married to the Mossad* and fallen in love. Jerry and I decided that I'd fly to New York. It was a massive gamble that we wagered together. I started packing... only one suitcase for one short trip.

And then it came. It was ten o'clock at night. My cell phone vibrated. The second I saw the name Kramer on the screen I knew I wasn't flying anywhere that night. Dr. Mordechai Kramer was director of the pulmonology department at Beilinson. He was a renowned specialist in lung disease, a surgeon who'd performed hundreds of lung transplants. He wasn't calling to wish me good night. *I have good news and not-so-good news,* he said in a quiet voice, trying to be gentle, considerate. *The good news is that there is a compatible donor, with good, healthy lungs. The not-so-good news is that you have to decide right now — and Jerry must get to the hospital immediately.*

I inhaled all the air I could and remained silent.

Sally? Kramer asked.

I went into Jerry 's room shaking. He looked at me and we didn't need any words. I felt it was the greatest test of my life. Roy was in Vancouver, a transatlantic flight away. Michael was in Geneva, a full time zone away. I said to myself: *Face it, all you've got is you and God.*

Jerry, they're calling to say they have a pair of lungs for you, I said nonchalantly, trying to disguise the excitement that threatened to overwhelm me.

Jerry looked at me for a long time and was silent. After a while, he said, *Sally, I trust you. You decide. It's your decision.*

I began to enumerate the pros and cons. A kind of balance sheet. It was pointless. After the repeated falls, the fractured vertebra, the constant deterioration in his functioning, the repeated humiliations he was suffering, a lung transplant was the only logical option. Still, it was overshadowed by the stark odds. Our ninety percent statistic had, meanwhile, plummeted to forty.

Jerry drove. He wanted to hold the steering wheel on this significant ride. On the way, an argument ensued. He asked me not to let the children know. I said I had already promised to update them about the transplant. The die was cast.

Two calls were made in the car, to Vancouver and to Geneva. Then it was Jerry's turn to takeover. He was sharp and polished, the master strategist facing his most complex and dangerous mission.

His driving was perfect. His eyes were fixed on the road. His voice was steady. His words were measured.

Sally, everything is in order. You don't have to worry about anything. You know me. I have a will. All the important documents are organized in Yekke style. You know how meticulous I am.

I tried to protest, to lead the conversation in a more optimistic direction, but he continued to speak. Stable, articulate and cold, as if he were acting out a role. As if he were talking about someone else.

I'm not coming back from this, Sally. Let's be realistic. We have to face it. It's over. I've had an amazing life. I succeeded in everything I wanted to do, and the best choice I ever made was you. You are the greatest thing that has ever happened to me. What we have is rare and special. You are the only woman I could ever be with, and you've given me two wonderful sons. If I were to relive it all, I would make the same choices and follow the same path. All the way to the end.

My body was screaming. It was physically painful for me to hear that valediction from the driver's seat. I felt like I wanted to stop the car, tear up the script, rewind the movie. I wished we could go back home. Embrace each other. Enjoy being together for however much time we had left.

I looked at Jerry and saw him at his best. My man. Driving towards his death. Secure, well-rooted like a palm tree, controlling things, navigating calmly in the midst of a tsunami, wise, loving, having come to terms with his condition.

I wanted to shout in protest, but Jerry preempted me. *Sally, I want to call Yaakov and say goodbye.*

Whatever slim chance there had been to bring this horror movie to a halt, it then went up in smoke. Jerry's request to speak with his friend, lawyer and confidant, Yaakov Katz, meant it was really happening.

I closed my eyes and projected a better film in my mind. In the space between one breath and the next, I watched our life together play out. From the first moment I saw his handsome face, to our quickie wedding in London, eloping with no family present. I recalled our globetrotting journey, the world-wide path that we shared, both as ourselves and using fictitious identities. I remembered the births of Roy and Michael, the missions we carried out together and separately, and then the progress of the damned disease. I saw everything up until that very moment, as Jerry steadily drove us past the point of no return.

51

14:00 hrs.
The final journey at Hibat Zion Cemetery,
Emek Hefer

The names of most of the funeral's attendees were confidential.

The cemetery in Moshav Hibat Zion had never seen such a large assemblage of senior intelligence officials from across the globe. Some of the countries were mentionable, others might never be known. For Jerry's final journey, many of the attendees wore sunglasses or other accessories to obscure their identities. There were also a formidable cadre of bodyguards sprinkled throughout the crowd and over the grounds of the cemetery.

The funeral was a dignified affair. Among the guests were a great many men and women to whom the State of Israel owes so much. Friends, chiefs of the Mossad, heads and distinguished members of intelligence organizations from around the world — FBI CIA, MI5. There were senior agents of espionage organizations from across Europe, British members of parliament, and businesspeople from Europe and America who arrived on private flights.

Alongside the illustrious and famous were anonymous characters lurking in the shadows, the bold and daring super-professionals who had put their own lives in extreme danger to provide escort, protection and reinforcement to Jerry and me when we were spies in Kabul. There were agents whose exploits would have made for the finest Hollywood spy thrillers, real-life heroes, who had escorted, protected and backed me when I was a spy in Doha and Tehran. There were the best of the best, who had accompanied Jerry beyond the mountains of darkness, superstars whose missions ought to have been optioned for the most gripping onscreen drama — if it weren't for the fact that these operations could not be revealed for decades, if ever.

Jerry would have been delighted. He loved the Mossad and everything involved in his work there. The institution was an essential part of him — and all those who gathered in the small cemetery were an integral part of the fabric of his life.

The men stifled their tears. The eulogies were many, in Hebrew and English, but the microphone was reserved for those who could reveal their faces to an audience and speak for themselves and their positions.

Jerry had asked to be buried in Moshav Hibat Zion, the place where I grew up. I stood there and smelled the odor of the dug-up earth, the scent of the flora being trampled under the feet of the attendees. A surprisingly light breeze brought with it the citrus fragrance from the etrog groves and the clementine orchards. The sun was shining, but I couldn't feel its heat. The grief sat too heavily on my shoulders. Glistening tears stood steadily in the corners of my eyes like honor guards, dampening the sight before me.

My Jerry was at the head of the procession, in death as in life.

Already at the cemetery, when I was shrouded in a heavy cloud of mourning, floating and disembodied, I felt the warm, embracing, compassionate aura of the Mossad. I walked along, trying hard to digest the fact that Michael, Roy and I were indeed accompanying Jerry on his final journey. But I couldn't help but marvel at how the world's toughest and most effective intelligence organization graciously showed its mettle in the moment of truth, demonstrating such empathy, immeasurable concern. Organizing a complex and sensitive funeral procession with zero glitches. Chiefs and senior officials of clandestine organizations from dozens of countries arrived on beautifully coordinated flights. A well-oiled system took care of secure transport from the airport to the cemetery, and from the cemetery to our home for *shiva*.

Moshav Hibat Zion had never known such a funeral. A long stretch of black cars, men and women in suits and sunglasses. Cinematic. Every last detail of the *shiva* was seen to with precision, as if it were an operational activity beyond the enemy's lines. Subtle. Thoughtful. Meticulous. Sweet.

Just the way Jerry liked it.

I glanced at the people around me, even those who couldn't show their faces. The Mossad is not a place of work, but a way of life. Its members are principled and disciplined, with a strong work ethic and sense of purpose. They are engaged twenty-four-seven, three hundred and sixty-five days a year, saving lives and carrying out missions that have a direct impact on the survival of the Jewish people, in the diaspora and in Israel.

They came one-by-one. Some surreptitiously. Some asking to speak with me privately in another room. And they embraced my body and soul and re-introduced me to the man with whom I'd spent my entire adult life, the father of my children, the knight-errant of my dreams. In story after story, they revealed it all to me; they helped me understand how little I'd truly known about Jerry, his competence and his capabilities, the complexity of the missions he'd executed and his unprecedented achievements.

It was a contradictory and confusing process that stirred both my mind and my spirit. I was trying to digest the fact that Jerry was no more; that I was slowly saying goodbye to him. But, to my surprise, I was discovering these new, magnificent and majestic facets of him, hidden aspects of a man, every minutiae of whom I thought I knew.

And so it went throughout the week of *shiva* and the month of *sheloshim*.

Finally, the procession of visitors, embracers and consolers petered out, and then we — Roy, Michael and I — received an invitation to a personal, private meeting with the head of the Mossad. This time it was not a briefing before a clandestine operation or a debriefing after covert action. It was a modest event, in which the man at top of the pyramid shared with us another classified, extraordinary, unprecedented, certified triumph attributed to Jerry.

The tale was, by necessity, abridged and redacted, but it still proved to me, yet again, who Jerry was. The strategic mastermind, the poker and chess champion. Reserved and quiet, calm and relaxed, polite and refined, noble but modest, doing what needed to be done on a knife's edge, executing the impossible.

His was the sort of operation that no one could depict in novels or films — as no literary agent or movie studio would find it believable.

Part III:

A Second Chance
for Passion and Love

52

11:30 hrs.
Back on the kitchen floor

I lay on the kitchen floor of our apartment and closed my eyes. I felt the cold rising from the marble tiles as I sank into the hollow emptiness that echoed throughout our home. It was a futile attempt to recapture a hint of the hour of ardent lovemaking that Jerry and I shared on that very spot, on the eve of my departure for the operation in Qatar and Tehran.

I lay there, trying to evoke the skin-to-skin contact; the feel of holding his face with both my hands; the unbridled outburst of passion that stunned us both; his surprisingly firm arms that formed a wall around me, strong as steel and soft as silk; the words we whispered to each other.

All my attempts to recreate the scene failed, one after another. The coldness of the tiles extinguished the heat I strived to resurrect.

I called that time 'the empty days.'

The supportive visitors, consolers and embracers went back to their regular lives. It's the way of the world, the blueprint of life. I found myself, for the first time, without my two anchors. Bereft of my late father, who had always been by my side with his good advice, his peace of mind, his common sense, his down-to-earth wisdom — and stripped of my Jerry, my lover, my strength, my support and balance, my bodyguard. I tried to be strong. To do what was expected of me. And then the questions came to me: who am I anyway? How does one go on after such a terrible finale?

I'm a widow... Alone... My life is over... Changed beyond recognition... I'm getting older... Condemned to be alone... Without romance... With-

out passion... I'll never again experience a truth so profound and virtuous as I had with Jerry, like his love for me... I'll never again have a man who knows how to wrap me in his arms like Jerry... I'll never again be able to enjoy bursts of sensual pleasure like the ones I experienced with my one and only man, since the age of nineteen...

However, I still felt like a young girl inside; I wanted to continue experiencing life and love. I already knew deep down that I couldn't give all this up. All the words and the sentences and the thoughts and the anxieties mixed with each other and turned into a frightening tempest during my waking hours and while I slept, while I cried and while I laughed; when I was alone and when I sat with the boys and when I met my friends — when I was surrounded by true affection, by those who genuinely tried to help. Jerry would repeatedly pop up, looking at me from the corner of the room or from where the wall met the ceiling, extending an invisible hand to flutter over my damp cheeks, whispering comforting words in my ear. He was with me in everything I touched. He was firmly ensconced in one of the crevices of my soul, constantly lending me strength and examining every aspect of my surroundings. Jerry accompanied me everywhere I went, even when I dared to return to the embracing circle of the Pastel Parliament, to my truly caring, loving friends. I heard the girl-talk all around me, swirling conversations about this man and that, about dating and going out, about new beginnings, about falling in love, about disappointments...

But I found the chatter jarring. I felt that I shouldn't be listening to them, that it wasn't right for me to open up, that I dare not think that all this is now my lot too.

I was seeking refuge from the turmoil. Then came the offer to run away with my sons and daughters-in-law and grandchildren to celebrate Passover in the furthest place possible. A vacation at the Fairmont Mayakoba resort, its divine beach stretching along Mexico's Riviera Maya district, south of Cancun. For one short moment, I felt reluctant to think about celebrating our family Seder in such an opulent and glittery destination while the absence of Jerry was so acute and so palpable. But soon after that, I convinced myself that this was exactly what I needed. In fact, it ought to be more than an Amir affair; my friends would be there — Diana and her husband, Josh, Samantha and her husband, Jonathan, friends from the United States as close as family.

Riviera Maya looked just like a painting, a piece of heaven, and yet I walked on the sand at the beautiful beach and the tears wouldn't stop. From time to time, I felt I couldn't catch my breath. When I went back to my room and had to open a window. I thought I was going to suffocate.

Naturally, I had my two bodyguards. Roy and Michael, standing beside me, solid as granite, sharp as a cliff face, ready to crush any threat or cleave in two any obstacle in my path. Their intentions were commendable, but all their goodwill was not enough to disperse the great cloud of mourning that encompassed me.

Then, out of nowhere, the sun shone through, its rays calming me and imbuing me with new kinds of energies — literally and metaphorically. I walked around the pool aimlessly, big Chanel sunglasses on my face. I looked at the men and women who were lying there to tan or read a book, at the couples in love who cuddled and kissed in plain sight, at the ladies who were clearly lonely and seeking attention.

Initially, it felt oppressive. *I don't belong here,* I thought. *I shouldn't be here, certainly not now.*

However, I soon noticed that several of those lying on their sun loungers were holding *Married to the Mossad.*

It began with a slightly too-toned and too-tanned man. He was about forty, and he held it in front of him as he lay on his stomach. I saw the familiar yellow-gray jacket and smiled. *Nice. Another reader of the English version of the book.*

I went on to discover more men and women of various ages holding my book, with the picture of Jerry and me on the cover.

Here's another, and another. Here's a young woman reciting a passage from the book to her partner.

I had known for two months now that the English edition was selling well, tens of thousands of copies. The UJA alone had purchased thousands of copies. Before Jerry's death I had been interviewed by Fox 5 in New York, several other TV stations, newspapers and magazines. I'd been invited to lecture in Brazil and Argentina. All this, of course, was completely different from the insipid phone calls that reported sales progress, nothing akin to reading the Excel spreadsheets.

The feeling was great, and it increased with each new person I found enjoying my book — flipping through it, marking it up, reading it to a partner. It was a hit, even amid the scorching heat of the spectacular Riviera Maya. As I strolled, I caught sight of Roy and Michael walking slowly between the sun loungers on the opposite side of the pool. They looked at the sunbathers reading the book with the yellow-gray cover and then looked at each other with a smile.

I was making my way back to the pool area but, as usual, I couldn't help myself. I went back to the first man, lying there on his stomach with my book. Now he was already in a half-sitting position, leaning back, shielding his eyes with one hand and holding the book in the other. I stood in the shade of the umbrella above him and surprised him. *Are you reading Married to the Mossad?* I asked.

Yes, yes, that's the book, he replied, with his eyes still fixed on the pages. A second later, he raised his green eyes at me, looking at me with surprise. *Have you heard of it?* he asked curiously.

I smiled. I held back for a moment, but then I answered anyway. *I heard that it was very successful in Israel, but I didn't know that it was popular in the English version as well. I'm glad you're finding it interesting,* I said and caught with a half-smile the wonder that shone on his face. Lifting my sunglasses to my forehead, I said: *Have a good day, enjoy your book.*

I resumed the pleasure tour I'd unexpectedly embarked on. I felt like I was flying. Tremendous satisfaction, a feeling unlike any other I've experienced in my life.

I raised my head heavenward and addressed my man silently: *Do you see, Jerry? Do you see how many people are reading my book? And you didn't believe in this project...*

It wasn't the first time I'd looked up and talked to Jerry. Sometimes I did it twice in an hour. But it was the first time I'd tried to confront him. I could hear his skepticism, still ringing in my ears, after I'd announced my decision to write a book.

53

9:00 hrs.
At a remote Maya Riviera beach,
a suspicious figure on the horizon

My next move was neither wise nor prudent.

After a night of suffering, tossing and turning in bed, I left my room and headed towards the beach, striding northward with a pace that expressed frustration, embarrassment and anger.

A brisk walk towards the Blue Diamond Luxury Boutique Hotel took me a fair distance from the Fairmont Mayakoba, but I still hadn't caught sight of any vacationers or staff. No one was running along the water. I was all alone, with too many sand dunes at my back and too many ahead.

I glanced at my cell phone, which wasn't showing even one bar of reception. I was angry at myself for becoming complacent and violating one of the basic precautions I'd been taught. *Never put yourself in any situation where you are alone in a wide open space, with not a person in sight,* Lavi exhorted me when we were finishing up the case of Sabrina *née* Dubois and her brothers. *Wherever you choose to go, remember Dmitri Kotiev's name and his soldiers. If that doesn't scare you enough, then remember Orange Boris. Their men are in every hole, Sally, and there is no wall, no barricade, no iron gate, no bodyguard to save you from them. Get it out of your head that any place is beyond their reach.*

Yes, sir, I'd said and saluted him before boarding the Westwind. It was neither being a smart aleck or projecting defiance, just a way of saying I appreciated his concern. Now, less than three months later, I'd already broken the rules. I turned around to go back, increasing my pace until it turned into a jog. After about a hundred yards, I felt that the run was too much for me. My chest was tightening, my legs burning, and the fatigue was shattering. The combination of jetlag from the flight to Mexico and the sleepless night was a bit too much for me.

I switched to a brisk walk when suddenly a figure appeared in front of me, getting closer and closer. The sun was in my eyes. I had no idea who was walking on the shoreline and steadily heading toward me. I looked to my right, to see if there was any building close by that I could slip into. Nothing was there except for a few wavy sand dunes. I peeked at my cell phone. The screen was unchanged. Zero bars. I decided to keep marching forward vigorously, my eyes searching for a stick or a stone. The figure persevered, doggedly approaching me. I breathe a sigh of relief when I realized it was a woman walking slowly, not rushing anywhere. It took another hundred yards until I recognized Reggie — the breathtaking woman I'd reconnected with the previous night, after years of superficial acquaintance. She was Josh's big sister, and he and Diana were old friends that were more like family.

Diana had pulled me aside at the beginning of the evening. *Sally, you know Reggie, my sister-in-law. You should talk with her, get to know her better; you won't regret it. She has a rare personality; we've all benefited from her wisdom and sensible advice. On top of that, she was widowed two years ago for the second time.* She motioned her head towards a chatting group of women not far from us. I lifted my head and easily recognized Reggie. Not young, but her beauty radiated everywhere she went. Taller than average, poised, smooth skin, almost zero makeup except for subtle pencil touches around a pair of almond eyes. She had flowing blond hair, that I bet was natural, and a delicate smile. Her spectacular Chanel yellow pantsuit glided from her waist with perfect precision; it displayed a subtle décolletage, creating an elegant but impressive spectacle. The look was completed with a long string of pearls descending to her cleavage and ending in a blue stone, precisely matching the color of her eyes. She held a long-stemmed martini cup, sipping from time to time. She offered a small, measured smile to the men who had, as if by chance, found their way nearer to her. After a short while, I realized the dynamics of this secret dance taking place in the lobby. More and more men orbited an elegant path that eventually led them to pass politely in front of her, produce a smile, try their luck and start a conversation with her. Reggie's look left no chance for any of them.

Until that day, I'd always looked right through her, but now she piqued my curiosity and I was eager to test Diana's recommendation. Just then, she lifted her lashes to me and, at the same time, her martini glass in a symbolic toast. I raised my glass and replied with a similar gesture. A minute later, I took my leave of Diana and headed towards Reggie.

Hello, Sally, Diana told me about you and Jerry, she told me quietly. Her voice and tone enhanced and heightened the effect of her overall appearance and Diana's superlatives.

Hello, Reggie, Diana told me about you, too, I answered, echoing her smile. Her lips twitched and she raised her glass again, mixing more martini in with the martini she'd already swallowed. The conversation that developed was not long but, a minute after it began, we felt that we were there alone. It was the kind of rare and explosive chemistry that occurs only in the finest relationships. At one point she grabbed my elbow and led us to a hidden corner of the lobby. *Here's better*, she said, and the message was clear. Far from the parade of prying eyes.

Reggie was smart, businesslike, and direct yet compassionate. She knew I was a fresh widow, that my husband and I had been involved in classified matters, that we'd been together since I was very young. *I understand perfectly well what it means to lose the man of your life. Believe me, Sally, I have a lot of experience with this.* I raised my head to her with a questioning look. *I've been widowed twice, Sally. From the first love of my life, when I was as young as you — and from my second husband, who was the second love of my life. Fate paid me no heed, saddling me with two terrible losses. Soul-rending. I lost one man of my dreams, and then a second. I loved them both, in a way larger than life. I still love them, and now there is someone who is already proving to be the third love of my life. There are few people with whom I feel comfortable sharing all this; I feel like you're one of them.*

It was a sweeping, binding and amazing statement, considering our friendship was still in its first hour. We felt that we were about to succumb to the jetlag but wanted so much to keep talking.

Your life is not over now, Sally. It's just getting started. Don't let the people here tiptoe around you with somber faces. Jerry is dead, you are not. You are here, surviving, thriving, starting a new chapter in your life.

She paused and I looked at her, not knowing what I was supposed to feel. Maybe I was supposed to be angry about her words, to refuse to accept them; but, after all, she was someone who, just two years earlier, had been widowed, losing the love of her life for the second time — and had gotten back into the race, searching for the next.

I feel like I've known you for at least two years, I said after the third martini.

She replied with a meaningful look and hugged me for a long time. I know what you're asking yourself, Sally. I'm used to it, so I'll cut to the chase. I am seventy-six years old, she whispered into my ear, disengaging from the embrace to wink at me.

54

10:15 hrs.
At Fairmont Mayakoba, passion in
the golden years

As soon as I recognized her, my body switched from a defensive posture, readying to bolt, to one of total relaxation. *It's just Reggie, Sally. It's Reggie*, I told myself, managing to finally calm myself down.

Two minutes later, she was strolling up to me, wearing a Cavalli silk robe over a perfect swimsuit, giving her the appearance of a mermaid hovering over the sand. We approached each other and hugged wordlessly. That was the appropriate gesture.

Reggie explained: *I saw you go out alone early this morning. I was worried about you and decided to follow you.* Her concern added another layer to the rare bond formed between us in less than sixty minutes.

Thank you, I said. I grabbed her shoulders and moved her away to take a good look at her. She really was the picture of perfection. We were in full sunlight, on the beach, a foot away from each other, but her face was still wrinkle-free, without makeup except for the subtle kohl line around her eyes reflecting the shade of the ripples in the bay.

Reggie, what you told me yesterday was hard to hear and difficult to accept. I don't think I would have allowed anyone else to tell me that, I said as we began making our way back to the resort.

I saw no point in going through the whole rigmarole of manners and mores. What's the point? You deserve so much more than that, Sally, Reggie replied immediately and reached out to me. This, too, was the appropriate gesture.

Over the next hour, we spoke in ways that turned everything upside down for me: psychologically, emotionally, and spiritually. The things that were said between us changed my life. I listened to her words, I felt them, I sensed the warmth of her hand. Together they conveyed the depth and essence of her message.

I can clearly see the dynamics around you, Sally. People are walking on eggshells because they have been raised to wear a grief-stricken expression and prattle on with you about how wonderful Jerry was and how sorely he's missed. They don't do it for you, Sally; they do it for themselves. It makes it easier to for them to live with themselves, in an environment which judges them for how they interact with you.

Look, continued Reggie, *I've gone through two rounds of this. Once after Jordan, the first love of my life, died of a heart attack while out on a run. He was only forty-eight, Sally, five years younger than me. He was the most handsome man I'd ever seen, a legal eagle soaring among the most rarefied eyries in DC. Have you heard the term 'sexpert?' He was a true friend and perfect lover, even after sixteen years of marriage — and just brilliant, Sally. Oh, how clever he was. We were like two crazy teenagers with each other, until the day he died and vanished from my life, like a bolt from the blue. I found it hilarious, the serious pose he struck in front of people and when he would go to the office or hold business meetings. People actually bought it, Sally. 'Your Jordan... he's such a serious man...' they would tell me in a cultured voice, in a ridiculous attempt to compliment him and me. But, as soon as we entered our little temple together, we just became animals. It went on and on, and we never grew tired of it. We were each other's happiness. An everlasting gift. And then he was gone, and I couldn't put up with the anguished faces around me. Jordan's dead, not me, I told some of those hypocrites who insisted on the whole show. They stuck out their noses in the air before me, and I took a swipe at them.*

I listened to Reggie but thought about Jerry. And about me. About our relationship, and the show I'd have to put on leading up to the Passover Seder in two days' time. Reggie spoke from experience, freely dispensing her authorization and rationale in such contrast to the perceptions I had before flying to Mexico — and all that before she told about Fred, the second love of her life.

My wonderful Fred was six years younger than me, she continued, somewhat thoughtfully. *We were together until he was killed in a skiing accident in the French Alps. It suited him so much to die like that, doing what he loved to do. That, and love-making marathons. We were together for sixteen years. He was a one-woman man — and I was a one-man woman. I mean, when we were together... We both knew that we wanted to devour life, to drink it to the last drop, together. But we both knew it wouldn't end with us growing old and walking together into the sunset.*

And then it happened. The God of Destiny picked him from my life too — and again began the ritual I couldn't tolerate from the first moments, the tight-asses in Washington with their side-eye looks. You could hold a gun to my head and I couldn't say where they learned this from. From Mom and Dad? At home? At school?

When we approached the resort again, I could see that many of the beach goers were those who had come to share the Seder with me. I had half a mind to turn around and flee back towards the Blue Diamond. But Reggie told me: *If you continue walking straight, another two hundred feet, you'll see the angel of my dreams, version 3.0. I have the dating algorithms of Match.com to thank for that one. They did their magic for me, incredibly and decisively pulling me out of the spiral after losing Fred. Now, I don't need to tell you who the third love of my life is. Keep walking forward and you'll find him on your own.*

She stopped, let go of my hand and settled herself on a spare sun lounger. I felt it was a kind of test. I continued to march forward, examining the dozens of men and women I didn't know. I moved further and further until I saw him — and it was him, without a doubt. A man of about sixty, planted on the waterfront with his gaze locked. Nothing in the hustle and bustle around interested him. His profile was somewhat strange. A small ponytail held back the remnants of his smooth, brown hair. The rest of his head glittered in the sun. His chin stood out and he wore thin, round, golden spectacles. In the earlobe closest to me sparkled a tiny, almost invisible diamond. His had an aquiline nose, and the two furrows in his brow seemed to slice his face in half.

It was impossible to ignore this mix. He wasn't a conventionally handsome man, but there was something magnetizing about him — and I just wanted to keep looking at him.

It seemed that I could actually hear his thoughts. I stared at him with an appraising look, trying to use my witchy skills, which were a bit out of practice. He was, I decided, not a businessman, not a lawyer, not a politician, not a secret agent, not a realtor, not a retired athlete, not a film actor. He was too relaxed for any of these options. His gaze rested on the water caressingly, and the sea seemed to respond in kind.

I stopped about a meter from him and looked back. Reggie's blue spotlights were fixed on me and a huge smile shone on her face. She was happy that I had been able to identify her man.

Fifteen minutes later, in line for the breakfast buffet, Reggie hurried to catch up to me. *You couldn't miss my poet,* she said in a triumphant tone. *I knew you'd recognize him.* We moved a little further towards the jam spread. *Remind me to bring you a book from the room that you'll love,* said Reggie in a half-whisper. *I'll be glad for you to have it. I've read it fifteen times already. It's Joan Price's runaway bestseller, the one that Americans went crazy over.*

I'll gladly come to your room so we can make the exchange. I'll bring you my book, and I'll take the one you're reading. It's a fair trade.

Reggie nodded in agreement. *Married to the Mossad* was part of the briefing Diana gave her before we met. We parted, and went to have breakfast in the company of our close circle. I rummaged through the cabbage salad as if there was some secret hidden within it. After two measly forkfuls, I set it aside and smeared strawberry jam on a bun and switched to coffee. Roy and Michael, who knew every detail of my behavior, recognized the restlessness in me. They glanced at each other and then looked at me for a long time. *Boys, everything is fine. Are you enjoying your breakfast?* I asked in an attempt to dispel the cloud of worry above them.

Reggie's suite door was open a crack. I pressed lightly on it, and it swung open. Reggie sat at the end of the sofa and motioned me to sit next to her. She had already changed outfits and was now wearing a short wrap of red satin, tied with a matching belt. As she crossed her legs, the satin flowed like water, revealing a long, gleaming, sculpted limb that a statue would envy. *And she's seventy-six!* I thought to myself.

I put my book on the table and took the two that were lying there, both of them by Joan Price. Two runaway bestsellers — that is, by the standards of the American market. The first was *Sex After Grief: Navigating Your Sexuality After Losing Your Beloved.* I perused it briefly. Many of Reggie's words were suddenly cast in a new light. I hastily looked at some of the chapter headings, then looked up at Reggie. We both smiled at each other. *Better Than I Ever Expected: Straight Talk About Sex After Sixty* was the other.

Is this a book Fred bought you? I asked sarcastically.

No, Sally, this book came out in 2005. Fred and I had already celebrated a decade together. And we really did celebrate. He didn't need much encouragement, but it was important to me that he understand me better. Reggie went to the suite's kitchenette and came back with a pitcher full of some red beverage with numerous lemon slices floating in it. *Ginseng and lemons, nectar of the gods, the drink of desire,* she said with a smile and poured me a full glass. I started browsing through 'Sex After Grief', a book that had been published a few months earlier, but was already an ultra-bestseller. Some of the most intriguing chapters were 'Myths about Sex and Grieving', 'Solo Sex', 'Dating Again', 'Your (New) First Time'. I gave particular attention to a chapter called 'Friends with Benefits', a concept I'd heard of, though hadn't quite understood yet.

Joan Price wrote this book just for you, Sally. She was widowed and wrote it from of her own personal experiences, having already bombard-

ed the American market with this bestseller, 'Better Than I Ever Expected,' Reggie said, laying her hand on Price's book from 2005. I opened the cover and peeked in. The book was replete with pink and yellow Post-Its, while dozens of sentences were highlighted with neon markers. The topics included sex in the golden years, the body we live in, sex toys, return to the dating world, and much more.

Is that a promise? I asked Reggie, pointing to Price's contention that sex after sixty is better than it ever was before.

That is the reality, Sally. It's absolutely true, and that's why my skin is so good. Look at my face! I told my gynecologist in Miami about my sexual desire, and she just laughed and told me that sex at this age is the best and most effective Botox. Many of her patients say their sex lives have improved after the age of sixty, and even more after seventy. She said she is thinking of doing research on it. Maybe publish a book.

Reggie's words embarrassed me. A slight blush came to my cheeks. I was also happy to hear it, because I knew that I still had a burning desire like that which I had at age thirty. *But...* I said.

But the most important thing for you to take away from this vacation is how to use a dating app. You are going to love Match.com. It's not an app, it's a miracle. That's what it was for me, my personal salvation. Fred's death was a cruel blow. The second love of my life was also plucked from me in a flash; however, this time I was already sixty-five, convinced that my life was over. That I had no chance of anyone looking at me again that way, of finding me attractive. That I would never enjoy sex again. Then, in the midst of a cloud of depression, a friend suggested that I use the app. I thought she was insane. I downloaded it, reluctantly. Then, suddenly, it happened, as if by magic. Text messages started coming at me at a furious pace, amazing me. I got compliments. Men expressed interest in me, in my appearance, in meeting me. I was in shock. The text messages brought me to life and injected me with waves of optimism. I suddenly felt that I was still worth something. It was a huge surprise — and then my poet arrived.

The conversation with Reggie seemed like a hallucination for a few moments. I looked at myself from the side and couldn't believe I was giving it a chance. I sat with a woman much older than me and found myself starting to make excuses. *If I put myself out there on Match.com and someone from my friends or family discovered it, I'd have to bury myself alive. I wouldn't be able to go out in the street*, I said.

Reggie listened and offered me a small smile. *You don't have to schedule any dates. You don't have to respond to anyone. Just enjoy the feeling that you are worth something. That men show interest in you. That you still have hope.*

Then Reggie moved on to the next level. *Look, I did the math. I calculate I have 3,502 days left to live, including sleeping hours. You understand, Sally. That's what's left for me — and I want to enjoy the balance, every single day. Look what this app gave me*, she said, pushing her cell phone towards me and showing me the screen.

There was a waterfall of male interest: offering compliments, asking her out on dates, attempting to impress her, thirsting for a connection with her. As I scrolled down further and further, she grabbed her laptop, sat down next to me and started building a profile for me on Match.com. It was quick. A few minutes, and I was already in the game.

About an hour passed, which seemed like the blink of an eye.

I wrote a dedication to Reggie at the beginning of my book. I tried to illustrate in a few words the strength of the bond we made in the blink of any eye, my gratitude for her waking me up and bringing me back to life. I signed: *Yours, Sally.*

I got up to go. *I see that you are busy, Reggie*, I said, glancing toward the balcony of the suite. The semi-transparent curtain fluttered in the wind. Beyond the sheer fabric, a silhouette was visible.

Reggie got up, hugged me and pushed me towards the door. *Well, then, go already*, she said with a giggle.

I walked towards the door and threw another glance towards the balcony. The strong breeze lifted the curtain slightly and there stood Reggie's poet, buck naked, with his back to the room. His eyes were again fixed on the expanse of the sea in front of him.

I didn't sleep that night. My virgin profile on Match.com filled my mind and, soon enough, it began to make my cell phone buzz with a slow, measured, surprising drip of messages.

It was a start, but I had no idea where it would go.

I was lying in bed with my eyes closed, waiting for the next Match.com vibration, but it came from the front door.

I saw through the peephole it was Scott, one of the resort's senior managers. *Mrs. Amir, I apologize for delivering this message at such short notice, but management would be honored if you would give a talk to all the guests about your book tomorrow evening.*

I dithered a bit, but just the tiniest bit. *Scott, I would love to do that. Show me the venue, and I'll start preparing for it,* I said, and once more I looked at myself from the sidelines.

Twenty-four hours later I found myself in front of a packed audience — some of whom held copies of my book, some just out of curiosity. They seemed mesmerized by the tales of my clandestine activity in enemy countries, life there with two children, the moments of danger and the moments of horror. I even shared the tragedy of Jerry's death and my dilemma about whether to go to a resort in Mexico.

Technically, it was an audience of two hundred, but my focus was primarily on two attendees. Roy and Michael were perplexed, never having read my book. They knew only a few details about what their parents had gone through beyond the mountains of darkness.

I told with tearful eyes how I found out that I was married to the Mossad, how I was dealing with the death of the one and only man in my life.

When I finished speaking, I found myself surrounded on all sides. Dozens rose from their places — to converse, to complement, to ask me to sign the personal copies they'd brought with them. Among them were several women who introduced themselves as widows, some quite recent. A few women huddled around me, with tears in their eyes, feeling sorry for me, grieving for themselves;

however, most must have had a Reggie in their lives. It seemed for a moment that they were reading the same guidebooks, or perhaps just the ones by Joan Price.

I was engulfed by a hodge-podge of encouragement. *You deserve to live your life... Move on... Go to the apps Sally... Times have changed... We are in a different era... Always choose men younger than you... Nowadays, we women have many options... We are independent...*

55

Talking to Jerry at The Mark, Manhattan

The vanity fair continued in full force, shaking me, my thoughts, my feelings. It threatened to destabilize me again and again.

And, in the midst of this storm, I received a panicked phone call, out of nowhere. The caller had a deep voice, his speech short and matter-of-fact. *I'm sorry to bother you, madam, but I need to talk to Jerry right away. I was referred by a friend of his, Martin, deputy head of the CIA until recently. That was a while ago, and I procrastinated; but now this issue has become urgent. I don't have a minute to waste.*

The tears were springing up in my throat, but I swallowed them to respond to him in a matching businesslike tone. *Sir, Jerry is not available, but I'm his wife, and I can assure you that I can handle whatever you may need. Our company is available for you and for your needs, sir. If we meet, you'll be able to present the subject at hand and your requirements — and everything will be handled efficiently and quickly, to your full satisfaction...*

Suddenly, I was selling myself and the company. Something I'd never done before.

My words were left hanging in the air. The man on the other side of the line hesitated.

I heard the wheels of his brain working, considering how to proceed. *Martin said you are the best and most reliable. I also heard about you, ma'am,* he finally said. *I trust Martin implicitly, but I don't have time...*

What's your name? I asked.

Ben, my name is Ben Mitchell, he answered. He sounded like a businessman to me. Experienced, impatient, assertive. He knew what he wanted — and he was worried.

Listen, Ben, I happen to be in New York. If the handling of this affair is really urgent for you, you can meet me tomorrow at 4 PM in the lobby of The Mark. Then I can hear you out, although I cannot promise you that we'll take on your case.

The call from Ben came immediately after I landed at JFK. I was dead tired. The flights from Israel to Mexico. My first Seder without Jerry. Holidays at the mindboggling Riviera Maya.

The conversations with Reggie had shaken my soul and stirred my mind. The reactions of the women who listened to my lecture had been thought-provoking but exhausting and, finally, the direct flight from Mexico to New York, which proved to be a knock punch to the head. I owed myself a good few hours of sensory deprivation before I rolled back into any routine.

Indeed, I sank into the steaming bathwater in the suite at The Mark, Room 422, and fell asleep for a while. Then I wrapped myself in the luxurious The Mark bathrobe, fell into the king-size bed and plunged immediately into a deep sleep.

After a good number of hours, I was startled awake by the annoying trill of my cell phone, lying on the carpet. Michael, worried, had wanted to know how I was doing, whether I had gotten some rest, what I was doing, what I thought about the trip Mexico, what I had eaten, what I was thinking about…

It was not an unusual phone call. Roy and Michael had always looked after me but, since Jerry's death, they had blanketed me in additional layers of love, concern and empathy. I was so proud and impressed by my boys, who stood to my right and left like the two giant silver lions in the lobby of the Fairmont Mayakoba. They embraced me even as they bared their teeth to the world. They guarded me with all their might, making sure I wasn't lonely or bereft for even a split second. They did every last thing to prevent my being hurt or harassed or depressed.

I looked at my cell phone and saw that I had slept for five hours straight, but it was only 2 PM. I sent Michael a kiss of thanks and love and set the alarm for a quarter to four.

56

15:45 hrs.
Preparations in Room 422 for
a fateful meeting

My cell phone's alarm clock pulled me roughly from the depths. I opened my eyes, my batteries finally recharged. I couldn't have known that I was waking up to a reality that would have a fateful role, a significant crossroads in the path of my life. I blinked my eyes once or twice, stretched my arms and found that my bathrobe was wide open and sideways. I had slept soundly and deeply with my body exposed, freed from months of proper attire, the stuffy and staid uniform of mourning: from funeral to *shiva*, from *shiva* to *she-loshim*, through memorial ceremonies, condolence get-togethers and silent family meals, social gatherings in which I had to play the role of the broken widow. My instincts told me to relish this opportune recumbency, to sink into the satin bedding. But then I suddenly realized that the alarm clock had called me to meet a man urgently looking for Jerry, to whom I had to explain that Jerry would never be available to talk to him.

After many more minutes, I got up to a sitting position, surveyed the room and began to plan what I would wear. Four minutes before four o'clock I pressed the button for the elevator to the lobby. I was wearing tight black pants by Ralph Lauren, a black Armani shirt and a Taheri jacket. On my arm was a green Hermès crocodile bag, on my feet a stylish pair of Ferragamo sandals.

It was important to me that the doors open to the lobby at four on the dot, demonstrating the perfect Yekke punctuality that Jerry so embraced, and which I had learned to love as well. I stepped out to look for Ben, but that was no great task: in the not-so-large space there was only one person, leaning over his slim laptop and typing at jet speed.

I was surprised to see who was waiting for me. My reputation for guesswork took another hit. I had expected a corpulent man well into his sixties, but instead I found a man of about fifty, tall, fit. He was dressed in a gray suit and a magnificently tailored Zegna molded to every inch of his body. His jacket was open, revealing an elegant and well-ironed white shirt, bisected by a beautiful deep blue tie. It matched the hue of his eyes and his Gucci shoes. Every few seconds, he reached out his hand, fingers outspread, to comb through his cheeky, full coif. With every slight movement he made, a wonderful and refined mist of masculine cologne wafted from him.

He was tough and businesslike, speaking in a determined tone. Zero emotion, zero patience. The truth is that I wasn't very nice either. I wanted the meeting to end quickly, after he realized that there was no longer a Jerry, after hearing the price I'd quote because it was a huge job.

Still, I didn't want to burn any bridges. The referral to Jerry came from his good friend, a prominent man from the elite ranks of American intelligence. As the conversation progressed, I realized how wealthy the man before me was, how connected he was and, most importantly, what a big deal his case was, the urgent task he'd called about.

That was when I had to tell him that Jerry had passed away and that I would be the one to handle his investigation.

Ben was businesslike, even at that moment. I followed his gaze, the rush of thoughts that went through his mind, the light cloud that passed over his face, the way he made a decision.

I was impressed.

May I offer you my condolences, he said and fell silent. After a long pause, he added: *I was referred to Jerry about six months ago. His colleagues from the CIA were extravagant with their praise. These are people I trust. Martin also told me about you and Masada, but I had no idea that this morning I was going to meet you alone. I'm deeply sorry for your loss. I also understand why you were not in a hurry to agree to the meeting.*

And, with that, Ben more or less exhausted his sympathies and compassion. It was quite obvious that he was in a hurry. The rushed real estate deal in the eastern Riviera bothered him a lot. *This is an important deal for me and my partners,* he attempted to explain. *It involves the purchase of two high-rises on the border of the French Riviera with the Principality of Monaco. They're designated for business and commercial use. It's a lot of money, and we expect a large profit, but we have an issue identifying three of the managers of the well-known company. We realized something doesn't smell right about this deal. We've already transferred a down payment of $26 million. My gut says something's fishy,* he said, turning the laptop towards me.

I dove deep into the screen and realized what had bothered me about his words from the very beginning. The location mentioned by Ben was the exact sphere of action for the investigation Jerry had bequeathed me. Then I took a look at the Google map Ben had sent to my cell phone, just two feet away, and I was even more amazed. The two buildings that Ben wanted to purchase were part of a complex of three medium-rise buildings familiar to me from the previous operation. Within two years, they had come to house a dozen companies dealing in cybertechnology and cryptocurrency, run by entrepreneurs from France, Monaco and Italy, and assisted by a few brilliant Israelis, graduates of the elite 8200 cyber-intelligence unit. On my last case, Bar and Elliot had been imbedded in the two buildings.

I was in shock. I froze for a moment. The screen that Ben turned to me was filled with the headshots of three men and two other images that appeared to have been taken from far away using a telescopic lens. One French, one British and one Italian — allegedly. The Briton didn't look the part, his face more reminiscent of a Russian from the Central Asian region.

Can you show me a higher quality photo of this man? I asked. Ben pulled the laptop towards him, typed something, and turned the screen around to me again. Dmitri's face leapt at me from the monitor like a striking cobra. It was unmistakable, although it had changed a lot. His skin seemed darker, beneath a pompadour. A new swath of hair ran from right to left, with a patchy goatee and a half-hearted mustache. The bristles of the beard were a distinctive reddish brown, and the eyes were unmistakable. Small, close to each other, scheming. But most of all, the name at the bottom of the picture popped up at me. Piotr Volkov. I delved into the supplementary images, and the picture became clearer. the mobster of a thousand faces.

Ben, I never forget a face. The partner in the company selling you the buildings is no Piotr, and his last name is not Volkov.

What?! Ben asked. Light pores of sweat opened in the center of his forehead. He looked like he'd been whacked on the head with a sledgehammer.

Ben, you seem to me a nice and honest person, I said. *The transaction seems especially important to you, and I understand your predicament regarding the transfer of the down payment. The challenge you pose to me is fascinating. However, it is important for me to warn you in advance, so I don't waste your time. This is a very expensive investigation that will last at least two months. Masada's rate for a mission at this level is about $800,000 for the first phase. Take into account that special requirements may arise later on, requiring additional funding.*

Ben looked at me in silence. The recommendations he received from Martin Fillmore still resonated with him. On the other hand, the quote I gave him was much more than he expected. More than three times the rate I would have asked for under normal circumstances. We both knew that the cost of such an investigation was likely to go up; it might even triple itself. I'd thrown out a high and rough estimate only to get rid of him. I was not in the mood for any investigation, certainly not facing off with the Russian mafia. Certainly not in the face of crime tycoons like the head of the Orange Mafia — and like Dmitri. In any case, Jerry had begged me to stop with the private investigations. Even in his last days, when he knew inside that he was going to die, he took advantage of every conversation we had to talk about exactly that. *Are you crazy?* he would tell me. *You don't know boundaries; you don't know when to say no. When you fall in love with a project, God Himself cannot stand in your way,* Jerry would say and try to soften his words with a smile, as if he were asking for forgiveness.

However, when Ben heard the price I quoted he didn't blink. He wasn't the kind of businessman who would raise his voice, twist his face or make sarcastic comments about exorbitant rates. He tried to haggle but was eager for the deal to move forward. I slowly realized that he needed this interrogation like oxygen, but I still didn't understand why. After about an hour, we moved from background talk, technical matters and rates to practical issues. Lists, names, tasks, enemies, allies. Ben transformed into a robot before my eyes. He scanned the internet with the light touch of a virtuoso, retrieving data from Google, Alexa and LexisNexis. He accessed his encrypted files in the cloud and simultaneously dispatched three secretaries to three of the offices his company owned. One was sitting five blocks away from us in Manhattan. The other was sitting in a parallel office in DC. The third managed his company's branch in Nice. *Helen, please write down everything I tell you, in order of importance. Myra, you must quickly locate whatever data I request. This is your top priority. Actually, no — this is your only priority for now. Rachel, stay on the line with us and be ready to process any information that will be easier to access from England.*

Some of the secretaries' answers worried me. Some of them even worried me a lot. The longer the conversation went on, the more I moved on to my own inquiries. I texted the details of the three businessmen, their passport numbers and headshots to my friend, Yaakov Lavi, without whom I would not move an investigation even one inch. *My dear Yaakov, for me everything is always urgent, but this time it is really an urgent matter. Sitting in NYC with an important client. Need your help. Hugs!* I didn't have to write more than that. Yaakov had been a true friend of Jerry and also became a true friend of mine. He has already proven that, when it came to us, he was never too busy. He would not shirk, he would not hesitate, he would never ask how much he'd receive in return for his assistance. The trust between us was absolute. Even during the Marin affair, the main focus of my previous book, he was always available, always attentive, always efficient, with awe-inspiring abilities. Throughout our previous investigation in Monaco, he had proven that he had spy networks and operations at the highest level, the kind one could only fantasize about. But now, when I was left alone, with Jerry no longer part of the equation, he became even more loyal. Stood by me unconditionally, without words. A steel wall, no questions asked, no calculations, no conditions.

After about an hour of simultaneously working with me, his three secretaries and the Internet, I glanced at the series of emails Ben sent me. There were names, passport numbers, addresses of homes and businesses, telephone numbers, email addresses, scanned documents, land deeds in the south of France, and even headshots and social-media profiles of two of the trio of sellers. I used my mouse to transfer files, one after another. Send to Lavi, send, send — without even looking it over, I transferred everything to him, click, click, click. Ben watched me as I examined the information that came to me, laced his hands behind his neck and leaned back with a kind of overstated, theatrical satisfaction.

He seemed pleased with himself and then managed to surprise me once more. *Beautiful day today. After all this effort, we should go out for a walk in the park nearby, in the great outdoors, and breathe some clean air,* he said. *This is classic, crisp New York weather.*

It was unexpected, and an offer that definitely suited me. I thought that if I stayed in the gloom of the lobby for one more minute, I would lose my patience and just run away.

After two minutes we were already on the sidewalk next to the hotel looking for a break in the traffic to cross the road towards Central Park. The brisk walk gave me the chance to check out his shiny black Gucci shoes. Pointed leather loafers that did not stop him from walking fast and at an even pace. I got the impression that he was a runner.

A second later, my mind wandered to the rather stupid question: *What will they say if they see us? What am I doing walking in the park with a strange man?*

I never imagined that these questions would become marginal. That the encounter with Ben would lead to clear and present danger for me and my family.

57

At some point while crossing the road, I felt Ben take tight hold of my hand, pulling me after him. He effortlessly negotiated the narrow gaps between two clusters of cars speeding down the road and led us both safely to the far side, adjacent to Central Park. It was a nice act of mischief with a hint of danger, which surprised me and also made me laugh. After all, I love danger and adventure. Had Ben had any prior information about this? When we reached the destination he let go of my hand and began to walk quickly and resolutely to one of the narrow paths leading into the park. I hurried to catch up with him.

How do you know this area so well? I asked.

I used to live around here, not far from the hotel. My son and my wife live in that building, he said, pointing to one of the high-rises on the horizon to the east.

And what does your wife do? I asked. It was my natural and usual point of curiosity. With finesse, I regularly invade the private lives of people I encounter, in social or business activities — and also during operational activities. Over the years I have learned that it is a way to get closer to people and instill trust in them; I take sincere interest in their lives, in their troubles, and in their joys to draw information from them. To learn how to understand them better. Words are powerful.

Ben was silent for a bit, then responded mechanically. *Unfortunately, we're in the middle of a long, ugly divorce process. Joey, our six-year-old boy, is with her most of the time — and it hurts. I'm trying to fight, but so far I've lost most of the battles.*

Walking down the road was less melancholic. Ben amazed me with his extensive knowledge of every bush, flower or tree we passed by. He knew all the names, botanical families, interesting adages and tidbits. There was something flowing, fun and liberating in the conversation that ran on and on. That was also a surprise. The rigid, rough, unyielding businessman became human. The pain poured out of him. The armor of the terribly busy and resolute entrepreneur slowly peeled off.

So why are you giving in to her, Mr. CEO? I slammed him. *You don't seem like a sucker to me.*

He then unveiled another human side, this one even softer, even more vulnerable. *I don't have the strength for a legal battle and I don't have the energy to confront it. I still have a great appreciation for her and, beyond that, I am very, very worried about Joey. I don't want him to be hurt, or at least mitigate the emotional upheaval.*

You're going to fight with three sharks in France and spend almost a million dollars investigating them — and don't have the strength to fight to be with your son? I asked. Maybe I spoke too harshly, but it stemmed from sympathizing with his frustration at the injustice of it all.

As I was saying these words, my cell phone came to life, vibrating incessantly. I glanced at it and saw a series of manic messages coming from Lavi, one every fifteen seconds. Among other things, they said:

Run away from this investigation like it's on fire.

The Russian is the same Russian from the previous investigation, but under a new name.

Another new name, I ought to say.

This is not child's play, Sally!

He added an emoji of a fire-breathing red demon.

I reviewed the warning once, then twice, then put my cell phone back in my bag — and continued to enjoy my stroll with Ben.

A few minutes later, after heading down the right paths and turning in the right directions, Ben landed us at the entrance to an authentic and modest Chinese restaurant. What do you think? he asked, glancing into the dimly lit restaurant interior.

The truth is, I'm a little hungry. You hit a bullseye with your navigations, I replied with a smile. Ben smiled at me and then, out of nowhere, I saw him bending over, drawing closer to my face and planting a light kiss on my lips. Not something very romantic. Not something deep. Not something forceful. Something like a kiss of friendship, but on the lips. I stared at him, surprised.

What's that supposed to mean? Should I call the cops? I asked.

Ben offered a tiny grin and began to walk towards the back of the restaurant. It turned out that he knew the place and the menu well — and also the owner. Within a few minutes the table was already full of platters with delicious dishes of all kinds and two glasses of red wine. The food was great, the wine even better. The conversation was easy. I was interested in how the CEO of an international real estate company has such a good command of the botany of Central Park. Ben asked curiously, but not nosily, about my record as a private investigator with an operational record.

He was smart. The questions were clever. He had a good understanding of what he could feel free to ask what was better to skip. Talking about the operational skills Jerry and I had, together and separately, led to a conversation about my book. Jerry's and my track records, as well as the book and its success, were part of the homework Ben had prepared but not revealed to me until that moment. *The book has been translated into English. I have copies in my hotel room*, I answered almost automatically, not reluctant to show off a bit.

In that case, I'm not leaving you tonight without having a signed book in my hand, Ben replied, and his face was serious. He meant it.

When we got to the second glass of wine, I saw that the restaurant was getting ready to close. The owner and his young son began to fold tablecloths, clear dishes, and turn off some of the lights. On the other hand, at our table, things were just getting started. He was easy to talk to. Time flew by. My jetlag had disappeared like never before. There was an aroma of quality in our exchange. As time went on, I noticed Ben's eyes looking deep into my own. He didn't look down, he didn't look away, even when we talked about the less pleasant topics in his life: about the longing for his son, Joey, or about terrible deals in which he'd lost a fortune because the other side turned out to be shrewder. It was very apparent that he wasn't trying to impress me.

In the meantime, more and more WhatsApp rants were shaking the cell phone in my bag. I ignored the first three. On the fourth, I broke down and peeked. It was Lavi who was trying to get my attention, repeatedly. A single phrase at a time, with a trio of question marks or exclamation points.

Did you get that???
Do you understand???
Have you gotten away???
It's the man with a thousand faces!!!
From our last trip to Monaco!!!
A cyber-bomb is ticking!!!
He's not French!!!
He's not British!!

I had never experienced such a hysterical WhatsApp attack from him. Lavi was generally mindful, measured and moderate in choosing words during a conversation or in texting. But not this time.

A red light came on at the back of my mind.

I deviated for a moment from my disinterest and texted an answer to him. *I immediately realized who it was,* I typed quickly. *I recognized him right away despite the fake name, despite some changes he made to his face. You can't miss his ugly puss...*

Ben got up and arranged payment with the restauranteur. When he returned to the table, he came around from the right, approached me from behind, bent over and placed another kiss on my lips. The gesture somehow felt natural, appropriate for the setting — a continuation of the open and fascinating dialogue we had that evening.

Ben knew how to maintain the boundaries of physical intimacy, keeping it in the realm of a friendly, affectionate kiss; yet it was a little deeper than customary, under similar circumstances.

The weather was still comfortable when we left. A light breeze wafted over us as we walked back towards the hotel. When we got to the lobby, I asked Ben to sit and wait for me in one of the cozy armchairs while I went up to my room and brought him a copy of my book. Ben didn't linger even a quarter of a second. He said it was a waste of my time and, as it was, I looked very tired. *I'll go up, I'll take the book, and you can go to bed without going back down to the lobby*; and even before he finished speaking, he was already walking resolutely towards the elevator.

Three minutes later, he was standing at the threshold of my room. I dove into my purple rolling suitcase, gently lifting up a layer of shirts and pulling out a copy of *Married to the Mossad*. I held it up and began to search all around for a pen to autograph it, yet the dedication was written only several days later.

58

21:00 hrs.
Mingling streams and daydreams in Room 422

I can't find a pen, I said, my back to Ben. Then I tried to swing towards the door and smile an apology, but I couldn't turn around. Two strong, gentle arms grasped my shoulder. A subtle whiff of Signature hovered over my nose and a warm, delicate, thoughtful pair of lips clung to my neck. A moral dilemma suddenly arose in me. In a split second, I flooded myself with questions. *Stop? Get carried away? Do I dare go down that road that Reggie talked about?*

My body's involuntary reaction eclipsed any conscious thought or rational judgement.

My shoulders were pulled back. The point where Ben made contact was aflame. A slight, subtle chill ran up and down the vertebra of my neck, my head pulled back and to the side. I was trying to touch the rest of Ben, who approached me from behind. A split second passed before I began to formulate real words in my mind — something to try to describe what was happening in the stormy strait between his lips and the patch of my skin, the pulse flooding through the arteries protruding from my neck, the uncontrollable heat rising in my cheeks.

The book I'd pulled out of the rolling suitcase fell silently back into it. The hand that had dropped it rose unsolicited and bent back as if in slow motion, until my fingertips touched the front of his close-cropped hair, stiffened with shiny gel. This time it was a volitional and deliberate move. I wanted to comb through his hair with soft motions as if to convey: *This is consensual, I'm quite happy to indulge.*

Now his body held fast to mine, along its entire length. My

hand grasped his hair as my head reclined along the silky smoothness of his neck. The palm of his left hand crawled along my waist. The fingers of his right hand touched my ear and slowly advanced over my burning cheek until they reached the juncture of my lips and touched them gently. One of them slipped delicately into my mouth, simultaneously touching-not-touching my tongue.

Then came the silence. Something like the veil of quiet that comes when your ears become clogged, leaving you temporarily cut off from outside noises, from the imperfections of the universe. I felt that everything was raging in me: mind, heart and spirit. I felt it in the pores of my skin and the coils of my gut. I sensed the subtle tremor that permeated my loins, as well as the pupils that darted to-and-fro under mOy closed eyelids, which became increasingly moist.

I felt like I was about to lose consciousness. I was supposed to turn around. I was supposed to put my face in front of Ben's and look at him, bring my lips to his. But I didn't move. A fear crept into my subconscious; if I moved a fraction of an inch, if I disengaged for a second from the position that connected us, the magic would disappear and this moment of grace would vanish. I didn't hear Ben say it, but I'm convinced that the same concern whispered in the back of his own mind. We both surrendered to this inverted hug — after months, probably years of being denied, deprived, neither giving nor receiving such an embrace.

I felt protected. Wrapped in the armor of passion and desire. I was thirsty for it. I sucked it down into my soul and lungs, every fraction of a second. And so, a minute passed, five, ten; and still, Ben and I didn't budge, reveling in the circuit of electric currents, immersed in a daydream.

The next stage of that evening, which became that night, was replete with mysteries. I don't remember how I eventually turned around, and I don't remember how my lips reached his; nor do I have any idea how we got from the luggage stand to the depths of my king-size bed. It must have happened somehow. Maybe we just floated there, as we swallowed each other.

At that moment, we were already in a waltz that refused to end until the wee hours of the morning. One continuous being, braided like a challah, a body speaking to a body with a harmony I had never known before or, at least, had forgotten.

Still, there were brief moments that desecrated the holy. Into the heart of all the divine beauty and the whirlwind of emotions that swept over us, crept in simple, mundane, and shallow fears. The little anxieties of everyday life that intensified as we approached the moment of nudity. What would I look like to Ben, more than a decade younger than me, when I wasn't wrapped in the protective layers of my designer clothes? How could I not be worried that he might recoil upon seeing the real me? Without the armor with which I so meticulously presented myself to the outside world. Without the supportive undergarments, without tight pants hugging my thighs, without my neat hair in meticulous coiffure, without touches of concealer to hide the tiny wrinkles around my eyes?

The rush of intrusive thoughts ended in a snap. Time passed imperceptibly and, suddenly, we were already undressed and flying to other worlds. It was a casual meeting in a lobby, which turned into a walk in the park, which became a journey to the stars, which inaugurated a new era in my life.

As I consider the last few years of my life, I know one thing for sure: nothing that has ever happened to me, nor anything that might ever happen to me, could compare to this karmic collision between Ben and me. All this, despite the fact that it would later become a temporary, short-lived and fleeting tryst, never to return.

A good few more hours passed in which Ben and I remained in a tight and profound embrace. We fell asleep connected to each other.

I woke up after Ben somehow managed to disentangle himself from me, get up, dress and leave. I found a brief note from him: *Sally, you're full of surprises! I've never run away with my emotions the way I did with you. I'm shocked but happy. Unfortunately, some urgent mat-*

ters have arisen that require my immediate attention. You already know about some of them. I'll be back when you're rested and recovered.

I almost asked aloud: *He wants to come back?* Then I lay back and sank into the bed, which had become a mess. I only wanted a few minutes to digest the night and the note, but that turned into another two long hours.

Just before I fell back into a coma, I heard music that captivated me. It didn't spring from any speaker, just hovered delicately inside my head, clinging lightly to my shut eyes. I have no idea what I heard. Maybe it was 'Perihelion' by Vangelis, crazily ramping up higher and higher until it dissolved into very quiet bells.

It was hard for me to breathe. A stubborn lump sat at the edge of my throat and stubborn, salty tears sprang up. I had never felt such excitement until that moment. Never, I should say, except for my first kiss with Jerry, at the edge of age nineteen when the excitement was stronger than I could have imagined, when my body and mind were swept into somewhere in outer space.

The king-size bed swallowed me up. I slept with huge whirlpools swirling in my head like nameless galaxies. But I also had a rational mindset. I was glad I was in New York City. Nobody knew me here. No one would ever know about all this. But it aroused me. I rose to a new life, with hope for a new horizon. This night was a restorative remedy for me.

When I got out of bed, the following question struck me: *What am I going to tell my friends? None of them will believe me.* I wanted so much to share the experience and be reassured that I had done well. Or maybe I had actually committed a sin? Then I was shocked by myself, by the thoughts going through my head after the movie I'd starred in the previous night. What would I tell my friends? I grabbed a hold of myself. *Is that what really matters? And what will I tell myself in front of the mirror? And what shall I say to my two sons who guard me like a fortified castle? And what do I say to Jerry when he stands in one of the corners of the room and looks at me with unvoiced questions reserved only for the dead?*

Towards noon I went down to the fine dining room of The Mark, hoping that there was still something left of breakfast and that I could have a coffee. I never imagined that once I sat down there, I would become a predatory animal. After the third omelet sandwich, the waiter gently asked me: *Would madam like anything else?*

I sat there for another hour or so, my whole body burning, hunger still gnawing at me. I felt cramps in muscles I didn't know I had, my right leg fell asleep, a slight burning in my neck, pelvic tenderness. I looked in the mirror and discovered traces that I had to cover quickly. Luckily, I had in my bag the beautiful silk scarf that I had purchased in Mexico.

I didn't know what I was supposed to think, what I was supposed to feel. Was there anything wrong or immoral about this night? Was I supposed to be ashamed of it? On the other hand, I began to say to myself, like a mantra: *Wait a minute! Why are you talking such rubbish? You only live once. You've been privileged to enjoy something that you'd already forgotten existed.* And then I realized it. I thought back to the conversation with Reggie in Mexico, the book she gave me and the thoughts that had been trapped in me for so long and which I could not form into words or sentences. Seemingly, I had an answer to every question. But it wasn't that simple. Jerry was always there in the back of my mind. He didn't speak, he didn't reprimand, he wasn't angry. He was just present, looking at me.

Within me, one question grew to monstrous proportions: *What will I do when I return to normal life in Tel Aviv? What will I tell or not tell when I meet my two sons who are my whole world? And what will I tell Yaffit?* I was definitely a novice, green like a young leaf when it came to such matters, trapped amid hundreds, thousands of thoughts. *You owe it to yourself,* I told myself almost out loud. Then I entered into my habitual bargaining with myself.

In the meantime, it was time for lunch. Once again, I devoured everything that was placed on the table — and asked for more. Tony, maître d' of The Mark's dining room, was watching me; it was unclear whether he was amused or concerned. He stood at a distance that gave me privacy, but also gave me comfort that someone was looking out for me.

The clock moved quickly forward, and then my cell phone again vibrated stubbornly from the bag. It was a WhatsApp from Ben. A concise, cute and funny message. This was followed by a short conversation in which he sounded sincere, but also on-point and straightforward. I mostly muted my embarrassment, and he mostly initiated and suggested that we meet again in three hours.

Where, I asked?

In your room, of course, he answered matter-of-factly and said goodbye to me with: *See you, my love.*

Ben's words resounded in my ears like the music of a magical harp. A subtle excitement overwhelmed every single cell of my body. I felt a stupid smile stretching across my cheeks. I felt light-hearted, beautiful, desirable. The age gap between us had been finally erased. My anxieties about his reaction when I removed my clothes had dissipated as if they had never existed.

I think I may have floated the short distance from the dining room to the elevator, buoyant over the marble tiles. The conversation provided me with intoxicating moments but, when I looked at my cell phone, the blow landed me with a thud back to the floor. A dozen WhatsApp messages from Lavi. Just like last night, terse phrases and alarmed punctuation. Question marks, exclamation points. I skimmed over them quickly. The term cyber was repeated several times. The last text message repeated, word-for-word, the one I'd received in the park.

The man with a thousand faces...

Ellipses? What happened, Lavi? I wondered to myself. *It's really not your style.*

Ben arrived at the hotel about two hours later. He went up to the room and went directly to the armchair in the far corner. A non-threatening location that he chose deliberately. He didn't pounce. He wanted to talk.

Sally, what we had last night was the best sex of my life. I already wrote to you, he said. His speech was quiet, calm, contemplative.

I'm sure you say that to a million women, I replied defiantly.

Ben looked at me for a long time. *Not at all, Sally. We are perfectly matched for each other. I'm afraid to stand up and get close to you.*

Matched? What are you talking about? I asked with genuine sincerity, unfamiliar with the world of dating sites.

You'll see, Ben replied and looked at me with soft eyes.

A minute later we were no longer engaged in an intellectual conversation about the compatibility between men and women, but in a virtuoso performance on the armchair. This time I was the one who closed the distance between standing at the end of the room and the chair. This time I was the one who took the initiative.

59

23:50 hrs.
On the carpet of Room 422, between
business and passion

Ben's skills shocked me. He didn't look like Mr. Universe. His muscles were not defined, but he had impressive physical strength and the ability to give infinite pleasure. Until that day, I had only heard about this prowess in the movies, or in the girl-talk of the Pastel Parliament; but I always thought it was a cocktail of exaggerations and fantasies that never came true. At some point, after many hours on the armchair, on the carpet and in the depths of the sumptuous bed, we found ourselves lying face-to-face, looking into each other's eyes.

Listen, we can't meet anymore in this hotel, or in this room. I had a wonderful time. I'm in heaven, but it's important that we return to work mode. I said the words, I heard them, but I didn't even believe myself. I didn't mean it at all, but I felt that these were the right things that needed to be said. The mind triumphed over the heart and the soul.

Ben listened to me with a serious look, grabbed my head and pressed two soft, long kisses to my forehead. Then he tilted his head and buried it in the hollow between my neck and my shoulder. His lips fluttered ever so gently against my skin. He tightened his embrace, then tightened it more. I felt that he was thirsty for this warmth, for this hug, and he did murmur quietly: *I feel so protected, Sally. I feel so safe here*, he said. I could hear a hint of tears in his voice. I closed my eyes and barraged myself with a multitude of questions. Ben slowly broke away from me. I felt as if every body part began to pulse with pain as soon as he removed his touch.

He stepped into the shower, leaving me lying on my side, hugging the air which had rushed in to take his place.

Ben came out of the shower flushed by the boiling water. *You're right, Sally. It was one of the most special experiences of my life, but I'm not built for a lasting relationship either. I don't want to lead you on.*

You're not misleading anyone, Ben. It won't happen again. It was great, but that's enough for me. I have to sleep tonight. I'm exhausted and have a complicated task to do. What, you forgot about the real estate deal in London?

Ben smiled awkwardly. He'd broken his own ironclad rules. He'd mixed business with his personal, intimate affairs, pushed aside his tasks for the running the company, lost precious time in the deal with the British trio. He stood in front of the mirror, tucked his shirt into his pants, tightened his blue tie and cinched the brown leather belt that hugged his waist. *Sally, I'm going to walk from here straight to the door. I mustn't kiss you goodbye. It will end in disaster,* he said in a serious tone, crossed the room with great strides and went outside.

I dropped the arm hugging the air in front of me and rolled onto my back. My mind exploded. My cell phone kept bouncing on the dresser and wouldn't stop. *I don't have any strength now for Lavi's text messages,* I thought and then immediately attacked myself. *What is this stupidity, Sally? You know that Lavi doesn't play games. He never exaggerates and never warns of idle threats. If he keeps sending messages, it's just irresponsible to ignore them.*

I placed both palms over my eyes, shielding myself from the bright light that penetrated the window. I didn't have the mental strength to pull myself together and roll out of bed. Then the cell phone went from a series of vibrations to the continuous, stubborn rumble of an incoming call. *Good lord, what does he want from me?* I asked myself out loud and reached for my cell phone with my eyes still closed.

What's up, Yaakov? I asked.

There was silence on the line, then a worried voice: *Mom, are you*

OK? It was Michael, calling from his home in western Switzerland. I remained silent for a moment, asking myself what I was supposed to say after the two turbulent days I'd had. Michael then pressed on with all his might. *Mom, you're driving us insane. Roy and I are crazy with worry. What's going on with you?* His tone was vigorous, assertive, scolding.

Michael, everything is fine. I'm just very tired, that's all. Gotta get some sleep.

It's four o'clock in the afternoon there, Mom. Why would you go to bed now? Is everything OK? What's going on? Speak to me, Mom. What's going on?

The next few minutes were full of confusion and embarrassment. Michael wanted to know if I was alone. Then he asked me to start a video call and show him the room around me. Then he asked again if I was sure I was alone in the room. Then he asked if I hadn't found myself in any danger. Then he asked again if I wasn't hiding something from him. *Send me a picture of the room,* he demanded again, and the worry made his voice go up into a virtual scream.

Roy and Michael have always been entwined in my life and I in theirs. But after the death of their father, they became the responsible adults. Two sturdy cliffs to my right and left, sheltering me in Jerry's absence. I loved it. I was proud of their concern, of their maturity, which had now soared to new heights, of the astonishing responsibility they'd taken upon themselves. And yet, in those moments, there was something new in the gap between us. Someone they did not know about and had never seen before. A partner for intimate moments that infiltrated our family network and created a new, unfamiliar situation, both to me and my two bodyguards; perhaps even irreversible.

Ok, ok, Mom, I've gotta call Roy to calm him down, Michael said and hung up, but his tone of reproach still echoed in my ears. I quickly got organized and went down to the dining room. Alone again after the madness of the senses and a body that still whispered within me. Tony was there again, looking at me from afar in his caring way.

After years in this dining room, nothing was hidden from his eyes. He had situational awareness and a keen eye to interpret looks and body language, knowing the plight of every diner he served.

Again I devoured dishes without order, without logic. More food. More energy to restore after a second marathon of sensory madness. Tony shot me a half — maybe a quarter — of a thoughtful look, and smiled.

As I readied for the third course, I noticed a large shadow that obscured the light next to me. It was Simon, the hotel manager. *Sally, how are you enjoying your time with us. Is everything OK? Is there anything I can help with? You are a dear and favored guest.*

I smiled at him. *Everything is great, Simon. Everything is just great,* I said, and I asked myself what made him approach me while I was eating? Had he noticed something? Had Tony told him anything? Was there anything different about me? Was it possible that Roy and Michael called the hotel to find out why I wasn't answering?

I finished eating. By the number of plates cleared from the table, I realized that I had gone overboard again. Tony motioned, with a nod of the head, to the waiter who was quick to place a pot of coffee and a cup in front of me.

A sharp pain gripped my temples. An extreme migraine blossomed in the center of my forehead. My head reeled as various stormfronts converged and clashed: the crazy sex, the challenging mission I'd accepted, Lavi's stubborn warnings, the scolding call from Michael, the man who suddenly burst into our intimate family circle without my two sons' knowledge, my body that was sore and muscled that ached, silent validations from the dating app, notifications that were still pouring in by the bucketful. That I looked good. That young men desired me. That I was still alive despite Jerry's death. That I could start a new chapter in life.

I took a long sip of my coffee and Reggie was once again buzzing in my ears. Short, pointed, clever sentences that suddenly hit home. With her words as my companion, I went to buy some things on the avenue of shops close to the hotel. I called some friends, just simple

Hi and *Bye* check-ins. Idle conversations in which I didn't say anything significant.

I sat down in the room in front of my slender MacBook, but I couldn't concentrate. I was totally discombobulated. I forgot my schedule. I had to find out when and where I was supposed to lecture about my book.

Alternatively, I felt as if I were flying among the clouds. Happiness and relief came to me in a jumble. Every issue which, just two days ago, had a big and frightening question mark hanging over it had now vanished without a trace.

Reggie was right. She's one smart cookie. Reggie had predicted what would happen to me. The thoughts constantly flashed through my mind, gnawing at me. *You have to call her,* I told myself.

I had always thought of myself as a grandmaster, but she showed me a different way to move across the board. She had given me the courage to advance to this square. I came to enjoy the persistent sequence of these thoughts. To deal with the personal, the intimate, the emotional, the philosophical. However, as long as I followed those patterns, it detracted me from planning the plodding moves of operational activity; I didn't need to keep both feet on the ground, and Lavi's piercing warnings were blunted.

Still, time wasn't waiting for me. Every minute that passed brought me one step closer to the moment when I would have to leap headlong into the misadventures and perils waiting for me in the south of France.

60

6:15 hrs., Israel time
Talking to Yaffit about great sex
on the first date

I went to the minibar and gulped down two cans of an energy drink in a row. Something I'd never done before. Then I went back to my MacBook and decided to make a Skype call to my friend Yaffit. It was relatively early in the morning in Israel, but I knew she'd been awake for a while.

A jumble of thoughts swirled through my head. *What's going on with you Sally? It hasn't been even two months since Jerry died. What were you thinking? Hot sex on a first date? And why was it a date all, Sally? It was supposed to be a work meeting.*

On the contrary, you're entitled to have fun! Lord knows you deserve it. Jerry has passed, but life is not over. You deserve to experience these feelings, and shouldn't care what others think. No matter who it is.

While Skype was inching towards Yaffit's house in Tel Aviv, I had another thought. *Even if Jerry saw me, even if it hurt him, he'd want me to be happy. I treated him the best and fairest possible way all his life, and now I deserve this.*

None of these ideas were expressed during the short Skype conversation with Yaffit. As soon as I saw her face on the screen, my brain switched gears. *You're such a coward, Sally*, I thought. Aloud I said to the screen: *How are you, Yaffiti? I missed you. I just wanted to hear your voice.*

Yaffit sounded surprised. *You don't have anything to tell me, Sally? I don't believe you*, she said.

We parted with air kisses. Everything I had planned to say was shelved.

Immediately afterwards, calls and messages from Ben's secretary arrived in succession. One message and text after another, bringing me back to earth. She forwarded emails and WhatsApp messages with additional pieces of information concerning the transaction in France, the sellers, and further details about the owners. I skimmed through the texts and documents, and my eyes searched only for the man with a thousand faces, as Lavi called him. I didn't know much about him, and I was frightened.

Reality put me back into working mode but, as time went on, I realized that I was still floating. I wasn't the same Sally I'd been three days earlier. These feelings also accompanied me to an appointment with Linda Fillmore, the brash and playful real estate entrepreneur who'd visited me in Switzerland with her ten-year-younger companion. This time she came to a discreet and unassuming meeting with her radiant husband, Martin, by her side. Martin, the former senior CIA official who was a soulmate of Jerry's and a partner in missions straight out of the movies but had taken place in real life. He was known for having exceptional operational abilities, a chess player like Jerry, an intellectual with a rare ability to discern. And yet, he had no idea what red lines Linda crossed.

We were joined by Diana and Josh who came all the way from DC. Not quite as old friends as Martin and Linda. I had to dispel the thick cloud of emotions, doubts and self-consciousness that went with me wherever I went. I realized that I could tell Linda and Diana things at a six-course dinner that I would not dare tell anyone in the radius of the Pastel Parliament. Certainly not now.

We ate at the chef's table at The Mark, and the elongated configuration allowed us to settle into two focus groups — the men on one end and women on the other. Martin and Josh immersed themselves in in-depth conversations about their roles in managing the world and the universe. They talked and talked and were shrouded in self-importance.

A triangular women's conversation developed, a kind of continuous whisper. Within minutes, I became the only speaker at the female pole of the table.

It was an out-of-body experience for me, perched somewhere on the ceiling, looking down on myself and my friends. I saw the stunned Sally there, trying to adjust to the new status quo that had become her life, taking a miraculous step. She shared with her two friends what she'd gone through. Without identifying details about the man who is the protagonist of the story, without admitting that he is a client. Without revealing that Martin, at the other end of the table, was the one who sent the mystery man to her. Sally told her friends about the passionate romantic experience. For the first time in her life, she offered vivid details. Salacious descriptions she never conceived of letting form on her tongue – and certainly not in the first person.

I needed this pseudo-distancing from myself in order to get through my 'first time,' in both senses of the term. There were long intervals between get-togethers with Linda and Diana due to the limitations of geography. Perhaps this was precisely why I saw them as candidates for the inaugural erotic confession of my life. I asked them: *Is it normal, what I've been going through? Is it even feasible that I suddenly feel like a thirty-year-old?*

My friends looked at me with a smile and said: *Welcome, Sally. Welcome. We are happy that this is happening for you, too. Your life is just beginning, and it's your prerogative — go for it. You look great, you're doing great. Have fun. You need to control things; don't let them control you.*

They were two good friends who were taking care of their comrade, supporting and encouraging her. On the other hand, they weren't just my good acquaintances from the Pastel Parliament. Both had been close friends of Jerry, too. Both had been confidantes about the state of his health. Linda had flown in specifically to be with me in the last weeks of his life. They had both attended the funeral and the *shiva*.

I was surprised by their reaction. They didn't judge me for my actions so soon after Jerry's death. They didn't pry. They didn't show any signs of criticism. Our roles in the conversation were clear: Sally talks, unloads, is swept away; Linda and Diana absorb, nod, and send a caressing hand to her shoulder.

As I was talking and packing my emotions, I remembered my thoughts, my feelings when I had been faced with my friends' epic tales of their parallel experiences. I had always asked myself: *What's in this for them? Why are they exposing their private affairs? Why are they shaking off their partners in such a way? Why is it such a performance, like a stand-up comedy set, for the delectation of the members of the Pastel Parliament?* I could understand a discreet tête-à-tête, like the one I had with Racheli, when lewd descriptions were passed from one set of lips to one set of ears. But I couldn't understand this phenomenon of simultaneously sharing one's innermost feelings with ten or even fifteen women at once.

You're allowed to have fun, Linda said after an hour of spilling and sharing, unknowingly echoing Reggie's words. I gave her a look of gratitude.

You should enjoy it, Sally. Don't ask anyone, don't pay attention to anything they tell you — and of course don't share this with them, Diana said and nodded subtly towards Martin and Josh, sitting just a few feet away, but light-years away mentally. *You know how much they loved Jerry and, basically, they have no idea what's going on with us.*

I knew Linda was naughty. It was a piece of information I'd suppressed, until it became a crystal clear — even embarrassing — reality in Switzerland, especially when Jerry was around. However, it was a bit shocking to find that Diana agreed. From our limited acquaintance, I recalled a solid woman with a repertoire of affectionate gestures toward her loving husband, not even one of which seemed to me exaggerated.

My depiction of the marathons with Ben was worded in the past tense, with repeated hints of 'that's it.' Intense, brief and a done deal.

That illusion crushed by nine o'clock that night.

Ben called. His intentions were clear. *I'm on my way,* he texted. And suddenly I realized what joy I felt, as potent as a narcotic, leaving no chance that I would stammer some reservation. I was keenly aware of the ripples of happiness passing all through my body. Four short words that made me tingle, an ant parade walking under my skin.

And time suddenly seemed to move slowly. All the words spoken at five o'clock that morning about it being the last meeting, all the insinuations to Linda and Diana that evening about it being a done deal, were shoved aside. I wanted more. Beyond the immense pleasure and the expectation that preyed on me, I now also had legitimacy from two smart, experienced, worldly friends. But most of all, I was happy that I was desirable. That a handsome young man lusted after a woman over the age of sixty.

Ben arrived at the hotel and went directly up to my room. The lobby protocols had become superfluous. In a split second we were replaying our greatest hits, which managed to amaze me once more. After all, I was no longer supposed to be surprised by anything.

Still, I was surprised, to be honest, both by Ben and by myself. Despite all the energy and eroticism, like sex on steroids, Ben remained a mensch the whole time. Thoughtful, sensitive, generous. Even when he was at the peak of ecstasy, even when we were both about to lose consciousness. Yes, he was a cynical American CEO. A corporate raider. However, in intimate moments, at least when he was with me, something completely different emerged.

At a certain point, panting as my heart missed a beat and, in that brief instance just before falling asleep, I found a crack in time to think about myself, to marvel, to tell myself that I didn't know I could be like that. That I am inexhaustible. That under no circumstances would my desire for more ever abate.

Then, the morning after the third marathon, another surprise came. *I don't have any morning meetings. I'm going down to breakfast with you,* said Ben.

I was an enthusiastic novice. I couldn't internalize his words. I wasn't listening to the chorus of clanging alarms. The sex was over — and the busiest CEO in Manhattan was joining me for breakfast.

I was happy to go down to dine with a handsome, young man. It did my ego good. I loved the breakfasts at The Mark. I felt at home there but, this time, a new spice was added to it, unexpected and exciting. The plates were emptied quickly. We both consumed copious quantities, gobbling at a rate I'd never known, refilling our near-empty tanks, accumulating calories and energy for what was to come.

The amazing relationship had lasted about a week, and then came the shocker to top them all. Whereas yesterday he had been telling me about the virtues of friends with benefits, there were now new intonations. *Maybe you'll stay with me in New York... I feel really good and calm with you... I feel safe... When will you fly back to Israel... I think I'd like to come with you... I can work from anywhere in the world... I don't want us to part...*

For a few moments it sounded as if he were talking to himself, innocently musing, answering his own questions. While he was mumbling and not waiting for my response, my WhatsApp came to life. Another vibration, courtesy of Lavi.

Sally, I'm worried...!!!

Three dots and three exclamation points from Lavi. Definitely not a trivial matter. I grabbed my cell phone and shoved it deep under my thigh, letting it vibrate in silence, trapped between my leg and the fine upholstery.

After a third round of breakfast dishes and after a fourth coffee, Ben glanced at his watch for the first time. *Sally, I made us dinner reservations at an excellent Japanese restaurant not far from here. You'll absolutely love it... We'll go enjoy the food — and we won't talk about investigations in France or deals halfway round the world.*

It was 11:30 AM, and I thought I'd go stir-crazy by the evening. I never imagined that I'd collapse as soon as I entered the room, dead to the world, without removing any clothing, not even my shoes. No demanding phone calls from Roy and Michael. No plaintive messages or warnings from Yaakov Lavi. No visits from Linda and Diana wanting to hear the latest trinkets about me and my mysterious partner.

Towards 6:00 PM, I could hear through the cloud of fog in my head knocking on the door of the room. Someone was striking it vigorously with an open palm. I crossed the room with faltering steps.

Through the peephole, I recognized Henry, one of the senior concierges, holding two envelopes in his hand. I opened the door a notch and stammered an apology. Henry said a cynical good morning and shoved the two identical envelopes through the slit. *A message from your son Roy and another from some man named Yuval,* said Henry, leaving the pair of envelopes in my hand and turning around to depart.

I opened the door wide and shouted down the hallway: *Thank you, Henry, thank you so much. I really appreciate it.*

Henry was already halfway to the elevator. He turned back, smiled gently, winked, waved his arm and offered me a thumbs up.

The first envelope contained a single page, written with a fountain pen. A message dictated by someone on the phone. *Mom, Michael and I are very worried! We can't get in touch with you. We called the hotel and asked someone to come to the room, to check what was going on with you.*

The second envelope was from Yuval, Yaakov Lavi's codename for emergency situations. In it was a small note, torn out of a notepad, with the words: *Call me as soon as possible, Yuval.*

I looked at both messages, but they didn't make me feel any guilt or regret or think I was doing something wrong. This time I wasn't open to criticism from my two sons, my own flesh and blood. *I will not be subject to any statement that puts limitations on me,* I told myself. I heard myself speaking to my two sons, saying something like: *Listen, my beloved children, nothing is changing. I'm not leaving you or marrying anyone. But it is important that you come to terms with this. Even if I choose to bring home a chimpanzee from Africa, you will accept it because it is my choice! You know who your mother is. You know I deserve to live my life now. After your father, anything goes. I want to be pampered and wrapped in warmth now. I deserve it.*

And there was the note from Lavi, the latest entry in the never-ending chain of WhatsApp messages from him. He was great. A true friend. One who cared and thought about me and my well-being. But I had suddenly become indifferent, a bit ungrateful and mostly careless. All the iron-clad rules that Jerry tried to instill in me, all the sensory detectors that I developed in those days of Islamabad and Doha, all that was drummed into me during training —it all dissipated, disappeared, as if it had never been.

All I wanted in those moments was just a hug and love.

61

9:30 hrs.
In the dining room of The Mark,
one bridge too far

After two weeks of sensory loss and disorientation, I began to feel suffocated. I realized that this relationship was not love. It was an outburst of the passion that had stored up inside me. A physical need that slowly accumulated in all the cells of my body and waited for a suitable moment. Then the warning bells were no longer muted and the red flags were no longer transparent, all thanks to one sentence that Ben said on the way from the elevator to the breakfast room.

I'm starting to think about relocation.

Relocation...? This word managed to do everything that the stubborn text messages and urgent warnings failed to do. I continued to walk in silence towards breakfast, mixing the lettuce, tomatoes and brie cheese with obvious reluctance and the silence persevered.

Ben was smart enough to connect the word he used to the quiet tension in the air. In preparation for the coffee, I put the knife down, lifted my head and looked directly into his eyes.

Ben, darling, listen... Some urgent matters have popped up. I have to fly tonight — and I have to fly alone.

Ben kept looking at me. Two sets of eyes, expressing a multitude of statements, explanations, reasons, insights, pleas, apologies and regrets that flew across the table, reaching their destination at the speed of light.

Ben's silence made me appreciate him even more. It didn't make it easier for me to stay sharp, determined and disciplined, but it was clear to both of us that mentioning the word 'relocation' was a bridge too far. Then Ben got up from his chair, bent over, grabbed my head with both hands in his delicate grip and pressed a soft, warm and long kiss to my forehead. It was as if he tried to cram into it everything that had gone unsaid during the meal, everything that should have been said at the end of our short-term acquaintance.

I'll call, he said, turned around and walked with brisk steps. I could still feel the warmth and softness of his palms on my forehead and temples but, as soon as his figure disappeared, I grabbed my cell phone and rang Michael.

The conversation was short and sweet. I let him know that I would be flying back to Israel in a few hours. Michael didn't pose any difficult questions. *Love you, Mom. I'll update Roy,* he said and hung up.

My connection with the children is my strength, I have always understood that. At that moment, I felt it even more strongly. We had a rare bond, which I wish for every mother.

The next phone call was to Yaakov Lavi and included all the apologies I knew how to formulate. *You are my angel, Yaakov. A true friend. When I know you're worrying about me, I don't need to. I feel protected.*

Lavi listened in silence. He didn't try to reprimand or seek any apology, explanation or justification. *Sally, if anything ever happens to you because of your lack of discipline — I'll kill you,* he finally said and hung up.

That's Lavi's brand of humor, only to be expected from someone who'd actually lived out every scene from nail-biting spy thrillers; but he loved me unconditionally. He left the phone call free of operational matters. It was only meant for clearing the air between us. He wanted to make sure that I had returned to professional, careful and prudent conduct, as required.

However, a few minutes later, a new opera began. My cell phone trembled beneath the weight of Lavi's aggressive emails and messages which had accumulated over the past three days. The notifications provided preliminary data for planning our investigation on the Riviera, as per Ben's request.

One of the first notifications was about the deposit into our firm's account: a transfer of four hundred thousand dollars from a bank in New York. There was a notation that this was the first payment of two.

I reflected: *I see we are on the autostrada to the nightmares of Monaco...*

62

After two phone calls and one tête-à-tête in the lobby of The Norman Boutique Hotel in Tel Aviv, it became clear that what Ben had presented as a simple task was nothing but trouble — just as Lavi had predicted.

Raanan, Lavi's closest and most loyal assistant, arrived for the latter. He told me: *We have to meet. These aren't topics we can talk about or tap out on a cell phone.*

He chose a corner far from all the other tables, sitting with his back to the wall, examining every movement that occurred in the restaurant beyond my back. For me, it was an opportunity to examine him closely without operational chaos in the background. He had a boxy face and a jaw that was too wide. His palms were huge, his fingers fat and round. He was a perfect match for Lavi, hiding behind semi-dark lenses. His body looked fit even through his oversized shirt: professional, sharp, businesslike, effective. But Raanan was also a professional assassin, veteran of a Mossad unit tasked with dealing with people who had been marked as enemies.

You still have to find out why the client from New York asked you to open an investigation that shares so many similarities with the case Jerry began and you took over, Raanan opened. *Lavi is losing his mind. He won't calm down unless you prove that this is a coincidence. He wants to make sure that there is no substantial connection between the two investigations.*

I reconstructed the sequence of the actions I had taken since the meeting in the lobby of the Mark Hotel and the array of warnings from Lavi. In my mind's eye, I ran through the headshots and some of the follow-up photographs on Ben's laptop screen. I reconstructed the map of our previous case in Monaco. Then, in the blink of an eye, I realized I'd gotten into trouble. My pulse accelerated. I pressed two fingers to my carotid artery and, after three seconds I stopped counting.

The handsome, dreamy man with the professional and innocent demeanor with whom I'd met in the lobby of The Mark Hotel brought me back into the jaws of Dmitri — slipping into another of his thousand faces and re-entering my life but, this time, with a new name.

I don't understand, I told Raanan. Dmitri and his troops left the south of France after he was almost eliminated. There was a world war between the gangs — and they lost. How is he still in the picture? I don't feel like dealing with his type anymore. I want to feel love, I want to run away with my senses, I want to embrace passion.

Raanan smiled and said: *Dmitri is how you encountered him in the previous investigation, but he's constantly changing names and identities. He operates throughout Western Europe and the east coast of the US under twenty other names. For each identity, he has a perfect passport and all the accompanying paperwork. Dima or David or Dmitri or any other name, but he never goes away, Sally. One of his characters is tucked away — and, a short time later, another appears. We already know six of his identities, and we suspect four more who have committed the most daring robberies that have ever been committed in Europe. He is Interpol's number-one most wanted, but he's always got a new identity ready to go when he needs it. We think he's an admirer of Berl Leib Farkash, the jewel thief with a thousand faces who was active all over the world in the 1950s. I personally believe he's trying to break Berl's record.*

OK, fine, Raanan. Got it. He is sophisticated, he is a bastard, he is cruel, he has masses of foot soldiers, he has hundreds of faces, he is constantly changing. I understand, but I'm convinced that he also has his weak spots. It is precisely you, Raanan, martial arts champion, who ought to know that even the scariest bully can be toppled by one blow to his Achilles' heel.

Raanan listened as his eyes continued to wander behind my back. He felt that our meeting had reached its natural end, and he tried to catch the eye of the server.

Just a moment, Raanan! I objected. Why are you in such a hurry? There's something that's pecking at my brain about Dmitri.

You mean Dima, Raanan smiled.

Enough, enough, let's agree on Dmitri. In the previous investigation, I listened to several dozen hours of recordings that we obtained thanks to our three computer and cellular whizzes: Bar, Eliot and Oded. If I remember correctly, we suspected that he had a child who lived in Israel with an affluent family in Herzliya Pituach. Is there a chance that Dmitri is Jewish? Raanan could not hide the astonishment that came to his face. He reached for the cell phone lying on the table. I placed my hand on his outstretched arm. *Just a moment, Raanan. If memory serves, and if there is a chance that Dmitri is Jewish, this is a very sensitive matter. I wouldn't want you to talk about it on the phone, just face-to-face with Lavi, and with him alone. This could potentially allow us to finish the whole investigation in almost no time, and then I can get my life back on track at top speed. That's all I want now.* The continuation of the sentence remained hanging in the air between us. It wasn't the kind of thing I could say to someone like Raanan. that I want to devour life... that I want another experience like the one I had with Ben in NYC. I deserve it. I deserve it...

I'm flying to France tomorrow on a private jet and I'll be staying at the Riviera Marriott, on the border with Monaco. Lavi is staying in the same hotel, and I'll update him. Instead of flying a week from now, you must join this flight. There are still four free seats on board.

I would love to, Raanan, but I would like to talk to Lavi once we have completed all the required homework and effectively utilized all the recorded material and digital surveillance from the previous investigation.

Completed? Utilized? Raanan asked and stared at me. I couldn't tell if his look was puzzled or mocking.

Yes, we will divide the recorded material between us. I have it all on two flash drives. Let's decide who's listening to what and see if I'm right. If he is Jewish, and if he has a ten-year-old child in some villa in Herzliya Pituach, we may be able to crack this case for Ben and his partners, and quickly. Much faster than we could have imagined.

The wrinkles on Raanan's face shifted from cynicism to deep thought. *Tell me more, Sally. What was the topic of conversation when Dmitri may have referred to this child living in Herzliya?*

I placed my palms behind my neck, stretched back and closed my eyes. I was assuming Jerry's posture for concentration and deep thinking.

I know this move. It usually yields brilliant results, said Raanan. *I was by Jerry's side for a few operations, which he probably never told you about. That was always his eureka pose. Close your eyes, stretch, forget what time it is — and suddenly he'd leap up with inspiration. We admired him for that ability. Is that what you're doing now, Sally?*

Raanan, I would love to sit next to you with my eyes closed and find my eureka moment. But that's only after we dive into the recordings together and find the relevant section. In the previous investigation, it seemed to all of us that this whole thing was clearly unimportant. How dumb, how stupid, I said out loud and smacked myself on the head with an open palm.

63

8:20 hrs.
In Florentine, the Hydra rears its head again

The next morning, after more than ten hours listening to the old recordings, I got into a taxi. The driver was Victor, whom I trusted implicitly.

I asked him to take me to 8 Shabazi St. in the Florentine neighborhood, but then I fell asleep. Victor shook me gently when we arrived.

Wait for me here, Victor, I said when I woke up. *It won't take long,* I added and entered the yard through a gap in the fence. There I came upon three wooden doors covered in geological layers of blue oil paint which was peeling off. Only one of them had a peephole. I knocked on it a few times and moved aside, beyond the view of the occupant.

I heard footsteps approaching the door, but it didn't open. I extended my arm and knocked again. This time the door opened.

Eliot came out on the crumbling concrete porch. He was dressed in a ragged bathrobe, bent over and hugging himself tightly, searching around in wonder, trying to figure out who was looking for him.

Look over here, Eliot! I said aloud.

Eliot practically leapt out of his skin from fright. He turned his head and looked shocked. *Sally? How did you find me? Nobody knows I live here.*

No one but me, you blockhead. Don't you remember our conversations in the office on Ibn Gabirol? You told us that you had a one-room apartment that used to belong to your grandmother. You may have forgotten, but I remembered — I even remembered the address, 8 Shabazi St.

His face was pale, as he hadn't been out in the sun for a while.

His mesmerizing eyes had lost their glow and were slightly sunken, surrounded by the shadow of dark circles. I could see the peach fuzz on his cheeks, reminding me that he was still so young, so delicate.

We went inside. Eliot apologized again and again, trying to move some of the hundreds of objects that were strewn in utter chaos across a wooden table; atop a wooden chest of drawers about to collapse; over the tiny marble countertop in the kitchen which smelled of mold and burnt oil; on the cracked tiles of the floors. The whole room was shrouded in a heavy, sickly sweet odor.

Eliot sat down on an old-fashioned fold-out sofa that creaked under his weight. He stared at the filthy floor and looked embarrassed and ashamed.

Listen Eliot, you are a prodigy. I have no idea why a whiz in programming and cybertechnology should live in such a filthy dump! Why aren't you hanging out with your genius friends? It's the middle of the day, and you're still wearing a ratty bathrobe? Why is your hair a mess? Why haven't you shaved in days — or weeks? Why haven't you cleaned up your place? Why haven't you done something about the awful smell in here? Eliot remained silent, his gaze swallowed up by the cracks in the tiles. *I'm gonna pass out any second! Look, it's none of my business, but hear me out: if you can get going, take a shower, clear your head of this nonsense, you can join me on a case that's tailormade for you! Can you find your way out of this pigsty and bring Bar and Oded with you? It's not the State of Israel asking you. It's me, Sally. Remember?*

I was profoundly grateful at that moment for my God-given gift: my ability to communicate with people; to instill a sense of security, succeeding to persuade them to do the impossible. Or, as Ohr put it: *Like water wearing away a stone, you can penetrate anything.*

Eliot pawed at the hair hanging in front of his face and remained silent. Then he raised his head and looked at me for a while. There was a battered and bruised look in his eyes, so different from anything I'd ever associated with him before. *Where did you come from, Sally? You've swooped down like a guardian angel. When we were working on the case in France, I was in the clouds. King of the world. Then Bar,*

Oded and I returned to Israel, and within three months we completed the development of Hydra to seamlessly infiltrate cell phones.

Hydra? Why Hydra? What kind of name is that? And you finished developing it in three months? I asked. I couldn't hide my skepticism. In France, Eliot had told me that he and his friends were developing a super-program for remotely taking over cell phones. I listened with half an ear, maybe a quarter. I didn't understand half of his words and, anyway, it sounded like a fantasy without a chance in hell. I only remembered saying to him then: *If such a thing really existed, we could have completed this investigation within two days.*

Yes, Sally, we finished the development three months after the investigation on the Riviera, but we worked on it a whole year before France – and even then we didn't start from scratch. We had an extraordinary knowledge base. For five years in the army and three years in the Mossad, we played with the most advanced equipment in the world. We also had the best teachers in the world. Two levels above the Americans and the Chinese, and four levels above the Russians. But we always felt that it could be done better and more efficiently. Oded freaked us out. He had this question he'd ask over and over again, until it became a mantra: Can't you see that it's at the tip of your fingers? Let's get this done and we'll be billionaires. He repeated it so many times that we got tired of it. He just freaked us out. And why Hydra, you ask? Very simple. The Hydra in Greek legend was a monster with many heads, like our Hydra. Each time Hercules cut off one of her heads, two more would pop up. Just like our Hydra. You can't get rid of it.

My skeptical gaze remained fixed on him. I waited for the continuation.

Don't look at me like that, Sally. We created a monster, but by accident. We are the first in the world to come up with such an efficient tool, a real speed-demon, undetectable and irremovable, with all its equipment fitting into two rolling suitcases. Venture capital funds and heavy-duty investors began sniffing around us. We did several presentations in Israel and California. People who saw our concept held their heads in their hands. For those who scoffed at us, we did a live demonstration.

We took over the cell phones of two entrepreneurs, the richest of the rich on the West Coast. They began to sweat. One of them, a multi-billion-aire, hysterically snatched his phone up and left the presentation. He just ran away. The numbers they offered were beyond imagination. I'd never heard of that much money for one product. At the height of my euphoria, I planned to propose to my girlfriend Irit, my mesmerizing beloved since the age of seventeen. She's the most beautiful woman you'll ever see in your life. But then, that day, she dumped me, abandoned me and went to live with my best friend. And she did it on WhatsApp, Sally, can you even imagine? The love of my life summed up everything we had in a short text message with one heart emoji and one thank-you emoji. Then I broke down. I just broke down. I felt that the whole world had collapsed under my feet. I debated whether I should leave Israel, or even life itself. I disconnected from Bar and Oded, abandoned all my BEO tasks and just sank into depression.

Bar...? Did your girlfriend go live with Bar? I asked, and my voice went up in pitch to a scream.

No, not Bar, and not Oded, Eliot smiled wearily. *Bar has a girlfriend who's crazy about him. He lives a quarter-mile from here and has no idea where I am. Oded also lives in the neighborhood, but he has a large house and a basement; the same basement where we developed Hydra and some other software that we started working on.*

Eliot finished speaking, lying on his side on the couch whose up-holstery had crumbled, pulling his knees to his chest and hugging them tightly with his arms. His body was trembling. His eyes were closed. He cried deeply, loudly, sobbing. I sat down on the filthy, greasy couch and stroked his head. He needed some human touch, a caress, a dose of empathy. He was thirsty for a maternal hand that would give him some warmth. I remembered his terrible life story and how he was abandoned by both his parents. After a few min-utes, he began to relax and breathe deeply, still folded in half.

I'm taking you out of here, Eliot. There is no room for arguments, I said in a soft but determined voice. *You're exactly the age of my son, Michael... and what I say, goes...*

I waited anxiously for his answer, which did not arrive. He bent his head, pressed his chin to his chest, and his crying resumed. I reached for his unruly mane and combed it with my open fingers. This delicate touch seemed to do it. The tears slowly subsided until they stopped completely, replaced by desperate gasps.

I asked Eliot for his sizes in shirts, pants, sneakers and socks. I went out to Victor and asked him to pop into the nearest mall and purchase five sets of Eliot's sizes, as well as towels, shaving paraphernalia and toiletries. I went back to the room and booked a taxi from Florentine station.

Come on Eliot, we're going to a hotel three blocks from here. You'll shower, shave, and wait for the clothes that Victor will bring you. I'm getting you out of this garbage dump, and I've got a mission that's tailor-made for you. A complex operation where you'll be a superstar. It's time for you to go back to being king of the world.

As I was talking, I grabbed his hands, pulled them out of his self-embrace and placed two thumbs on the protruding arteries at his wrists.

Think it through before you answer, Eliot. I'm checking you out. Have you been using hard drugs during these awful months? Shooting up? Snorting coke?

No, Sally, absolutely not. I don't touch that poison. I have a weed guy, and he comes here every Sunday to deliver food and set me up for the week.

I sat here, among the piles of junk and filth, and smoked my brains out. But I don't mess with that shit, he stressed. *He pulled his hands from my grip and turned them around in front of me. Look. Clean, unblemished skin. I don't stick anything in my body. I'm afraid of that, Sally. My father was an addict and he ruined my mother's life, himself, me and my two younger sisters. And then he took off. We never saw him again. I know what hard drugs do to a person. I'm not crazy enough to get involved with that shit. I'm afraid of it, scared to death.*

Two days later, after a four-hour flight in GS222 and after another hour's flight at low altitude from Nice to the Monaco border, I knocked on the door of Lavi's suite at the Riviera Marriott. He opened the door and his jaw dropped when he saw me standing in front of him with the purple rolling suitcase.

You're surprised to see me, but we're just getting started. Look who else is here. I grabbed his hand and pulled him around the corner. The sturdy Raanan filled up the hall; he had kept our plans secret from his direct superior.

Next to him stood Bar, Oded and Eliot, all cleaned up nicely and dressed in new clothes, even if the pants still needed to be hemmed.

Alongside them, on the wall-to-wall carpet, sat two extra-large black rolling suitcases. Lavi ran towards them, muttering almost inaudible curses. *Maniacs! bastards! ghouls! — for two months I've been looking for you, and you wouldn't respond. Now Sally shows up in France, and you're here, too!*

He briefly embraced Raanan and patted his back forcefully. Then he went over to Eliot, hugged him at length, moved to Oded and hugged him, too.

Finally, it was Bar's turn for a long hug.

You have more luck than brains, Sally. I don't know how you do it, but you keep hitting the jackpot. What is it, the third time, the fourth time in a row? I'm not counting anymore. I heard that this trio had headed off to the private sector, and I was frantically looking for them. There were rumors about this crazy surveillance software they developed, but I could find neither hide nor hair of them. I used all my connections, but nothing. Not a hint, not a whisper. Their cell phones were disabled, their credit cards went unused, their bank accounts were untouched — not even utilities. I went crazy. All kinds of horror stories were running through my head. And here you come and dredge them up like it's nothing, then drag them all the way back with you to the south of France.

I just hope you're not complaining, I told Lavi, smiling with satisfaction.

God forbid, Sally, God forbid. If these three guys are with us, we have a winning team — and a chance of succeeding, Lavi replied and blew me a kiss.

64

7:30 hrs.
A monster in a suitcase on the French Riviera

Lavi's euphoria was soon a distant memory and the French Riviera turned into a nightmare. The azure beaches, usually associated with carefree rest and recreation, were the backdrop for a three-week roller coaster ride of operational, business, and emotional entanglements. It left me reeling and dizzy and more than a little nauseous. Emotion, anxiety and terror as we were constantly straddling the brink between life and death.

The first night evaporated into uneasy sleep. Raanan, Eliot, Bar, Oded and I gave into our exhaustion — each in his room, each in his own bed.

The next day we stormed the mountains of recordings from the previous Monaco investigation. We divvied up the tasks and set to listening to recordings of the live versions we'd already heard in real-time. *Bar, Eliot, you know the material from listening in on the interviews. You have a greater chance of pinpointing the significant segments. Oded, you I need to operate Hydra, but it has to be done from somewhere else. Raanan will take you to our hideout in Monaco. I have no idea where it is and I don't want to know. Get organized and be ready for the moment when we give you the phone numbers.*

What's the mission? Oded asked, one hand grasping each handle of the rolling suitcases.

We need every crumb of information from Dmitri's cell phone implying his Jewishness and any hint about his son who lives in Israel. Does this thing of yours know how to scoop up images as well?

Oded chuckled. *Wake up, Sally. We can get deep in the guts of Dmitri's cell phone and extract everything that's there. Text messages, photos deleted two years ago — hell, we can turn on the camera when he's in the bathroom or having sex. But we need to know the model of the device and its number and, keep in mind that the collection work takes several days. Maybe even a week.*

Sounds good. A week for such a task sounds like a dream. But the problem is that it's illegal. If you're caught, you're done. If we're caught, we're done. Oded, you get it, right? We had a Greek wiretapping and cybertechnology expert who didn't give a damn about anyone, including Interpol. But once he realized that the investigation was about someone associated with the 'Solntsevskaya' gang, he hauled ass without saying a word, just bolted. And that's a problem, because we don't engage in illegal activity. He was supposed to have been the just contractor, only bringing us raw information.

Oded annoyed me when he began to chuckle once again. He made me feel ancient and old-fashioned. *Sally, from the moment I have a number, I worm my way in there, and I slurp everything up within minutes. Then I can start listening and seeing everything that happens, as it happens. Calls, WhatsApp messages, new photos, emails, Outlook meetings. And no one's the wiser.*

And your mythological monster knows how to do all this without touching the subject's cell phone? Without inserting a USB into his computer? Without dealing with servers?

Your Russian won't have the slightest inkling that he's being observed, Oded responded with a chuckle.

I don't care for that confidence, I said, a scolding tone creeping into my voice. *Even the slightest inkling? What do you mean by that? Disrespect for the enemy and arrogance are very bad tactics. Don't be complacent. We are talking about sophisticated and devilishly cruel people, with programming abilities and ample knowledge of cybertechnology. They are not suckers, Oded. They have experts in every single field. They may very well suss out the Hydra infiltration — and there's a chance they'll know how to get to you, too.*

Ok, Sally, I hear you. And let's say you're right. Let's assume that his experts trace Hydra. Dmitri — or God knows what he's called — will dispatch his gorillas to a ramshackle house in the suburbs of Nice. They'll find a worthless transmitter there, a lot of dust and some rats. Come and see our baby, he said and began to open the zippers of one of the rolling suitcases.

I don't want to see it, Oded, I objected, reaching out to stop him. *I don't know and don't want to know what equipment you lugged here from Israel. As far as I'm concerned, your suitcase is filled with underwear, tank tops and socks.*

While the words were still on my tongue, the door of the room opened and Lavi entered.

Fine, listen. Dmitri — AKA Stas AKA Ilia AKA Vitaly AKA who-the-hell-knows — is now going by Piotr Volkov. Sally has already encountered this identity in the States. Please note, Volkov is a wolf... in our case, a predatory wolf. This is our main target, but of course that's a nom de guerre. So that we don't go crazy and confuse all the names, he'll stay Dmitri for our purposes. He came here two months ago with a real passport under the name of Piotr Volkov, a finely crafted false identity as a real-estate dealer. This time, for a change, he didn't steal diamonds or threaten extortion. This go-round, he established a partnership with two fellow real-estate brokers, one British and one French, who are convinced that he is no less than the archangel Gabriel himself. He needed them to develop his facade, very far from the image of a Soviet organized crime gangster. The two were dazzled by him and by his tales of the billions in great assets he has in Geneva, Vienna, Nice, and Monaco.

Lavi paused and then continued: *Since then he has been working around the clock claiming victims, one after another. Your clients, Sally. Ben Mitchell and his partners are part of this conveyor belt of real estate scams. There are three high-rises in the neighborhood close to this hotel, and there's also a palace on the hillside opposite Monaco. They've already sold them four times and received fat advances from all the buyers. His partners are on cloud nine. They took the bait and brought along some assets, which will also fall into the mouth of the hungry wolf...*

These sound like long-term deals to me, I said and looked questioningly at Lavi.

Not at all, Sally, they're not ripping off billions. They'll get down pay-ments on transactions for fifty or a hundred million euros and then – poof – they're gone. Some of the previous rounds were completed in less than a month. If we don't move quickly, the scammer with a thousand faces will disappear again — until the next time.

And what do we know about his current activities?

A good source of mine in the Intelligence Division of the Nice Police says that he has already started knocking people off. There is a whole army of professional assassins around him, monkeys who perform the dirty jobs for him, hand-to-hand combat experts, cyberwarfare profes-sionals. No question he has some cybertech whizzes on the payroll as well.

And what sort of personal security does he have? I asked.

He has only one guard, who doesn't act like a bodyguard so as not to arouse attention. After all, in this incarnation, Dmitri is Mr. Piotr Volkov, a legitimate businessman who came to the region to conduct le-gitimate business. Such a person does not need a squad of bodyguards. Please note, Sally. Our client has gained a lot of weight. He wears a wig that gives him a smooth mane of brown hair. Most of the time he wears black horn-rimmed glasses with semi-dark lenses. The deep wrinkles on his forehead have disappeared; some sort of plastic surgery straightened his nose. His chin is now adorned with a Lenin-style goatee. The two tat-toos that covered the back of his hands are also gone.

Lavi also had more details. *The thousand-faced man spends most of his time in presidential suite number two, on the top floor of the Hôtel de Paris Monte-Carlo. He plays tennis every day there. He goes up to shower, naps for an hour, then heads to the main casino.*

I remember him back when he was Dmitri. Even then, he was a heavy gambler. You can change your beard, you can put on a wig, but you can't shake the roulette habit, I said.

That's right, Sally. Mostly roulette, but quite a bit of blackjack too. He also disappears into the backrooms for hours to play high-stakes poker. He's got the one bodyguard, who's nearby but not too obvious. Another, the size of a refrigerator, wears a tailored suit and is stationed at the en-trance to the floor.

Good job Lavi, as always. But there are other details I need to know. What time does he head back to his suite? Where does he eat? Where does he work out? Where does he meet business associates? Where does he park his car? Does he have a wife, a girlfriend, a companion?

A notch of concern appeared between Lavi's eyebrows. *Sally, I hope you're not going crazy. What exactly are you planning?*

He locked eyes with me and wouldn't let up.

65

11:30 hrs.
At the Riviera Marriot, a determined
suitor with a private jet

Lavi's transparent concern was not misplaced. I did go crazy and I did plan a move straight out of a Bond movie, but suddenly there came a temporary drop in tension. It would take seven unbearable days waiting for Hydra to mature in the cell phones of Dmitri, his bodyguards, his assistants and his gang members, until it could collect the vital information and send it to the computers of our three young musketeers.

It was then that Steve landed into my life.

When Bar, Eliot and Oded said their preliminary investigation would last up to a week, I nodded my head casually. I didn't really understand what seven days with zero action meant, especially now that Jerry was gone, Ben was out of the picture and the in-depth conversations with Reggie had changed my worldview.

I sat in the lobby and played with my cell phone. An endless cycle of clicks: global and financial news, Facebook, Instagram. Everything seemed mundane, bland and unnecessary to me, until an unfamiliar rectangle occupied the screen in front of me, accompanied by an evocative chime. It took me two or three seconds to remember that it was the Match.com dating app that Reggie had introduced me to. Suddenly an image of a handsome man popped up: tanned face, smooth and full hair pulled back, big eyes, piercing look. He seemed atypical for the app. His date of birth appeared: February 19, 1961. *I saw your photo and I'm intrigued. Yours, Steve,* he wrote in Hebrew.

Beautiful, I thought. An Israeli man connects to an American dating app and sends messages to an Israeli woman in the south of France.

His words could have been interpreted as a clumsy and banal attempt to ask me out, but the combination of his handsome face and the message ignited my imagination.

In the next message bubble, he wrote: *I'm a traditional, Sabbath-observant Jew, but I don't wear a kippah.*

I didn't know how to explain it, but I liked him and decided to give it a chance.

That's very nice, I wrote. *I see your date of birth, but at what time? You left that out.* I thought he would be frightened or offended and disappear but, without skipping a beat, the time of the birth appeared on the screen.

Exactly 3:10 PM.

Then I teased him. *If only you were at the Riviera Marriott in Monaco, you could be having a cup of coffee with me right now,* I quickly typed, a smile of triumph on my lips. I felt safe when he was in his apartment in Tel Aviv and I was in the lobby of a hotel by the Monaco border. *With God's help, anything is possible,* Steve responded, adding a praying hands emoji and another heart emoji. And that was that.

I knew I had to consult Ohr now that I had the pertinent astrological information. *Look what I found!*

He replied immediately: *Wow! Pisces, aggressive, opinionated. I'll write you more tomorrow.*

Steve was faster than Ohr. The next morning, as I was having coffee in the lobby before breakfast, my cell phone sprang to life.

My message from yesterday: *If only you were at the Riviera Marriott in Monaco you could be having a cup of coffee with me right now.*

Steve's reply: '*Challenge accepted,*' next to a double heart emoji. I quickly lifted my head and surveyed the lobby, which was almost empty. A few tables away from me I saw the silhouette of a man bathed in rays of sunlight emanating from the window. I narrowed my eyes trying to see who it was, but then I saw him raise his hand and wave to me.

Score one for Steve, I thought as I waved back.

Half a minute later he was already sitting in front of me, smiling, satisfied with himself. Elegant sportswear, black polo shirt, the latest Nike footwear. His full head of hair, swept back with gel, looked better in reality than in his photo. His tan was indeed perfect. He looked at least a decade younger than his age.

Well-played, I said. *Is that a private jet in your pocket?*

I wish, replied Steve. *I caught a ride with a friend who happened to be flying here. One stroke of luck, then another — and here I am.* He spoke quietly, his voice agreeable. His scent was pleasant too, the latest Signature.

I was impressed. I loved the humility. He wasn't trying to impress me. Instead, he let his journey from Tel Aviv to Monaco speak for itself, though I didn't buy his story.

I was very intrigued, he added before I could say another word. *I tried to do my homework on you — and Google unleashed a torrent. Brava on your bestseller...*

Bravo on your resourcefulness and determination, I said and felt my cell phone dancing once more. It was a very long text message from Ohr.

Steve, pardon me for a minute. I have an urgent work message, I said and sank into the lines that came from Ohr's home in Tel Aviv.

Pisces, you already know. He's made of the same stuff as generals and men of war. Arik Sharon, your Jerry, Yitzhak Rabin, Amnon Lipkin-Shahak. Very determined to achieve his goals. It is important for him to conquer, to succeed, to make money. He is opinionated, trying to understand reality intellectually.

I took a breath and scrolled the screen to the rest of the text message, which suddenly filled with exclamation points. *He has no true collective values! In Chinese astrology, it is called three fat horses. He has a lot of mental health problems! There is rage in him! He's living with anger about his childhood! He projects bad feelings on others!*

Sorry, I had to get that message, I said.

Steve was relaxed and patient. *I understand life didn't stop when I entered the lobby. Everything is fine,* he said. Then he looked around at the gloom of the lobby and asked, with the shadow of a smile: *Are your bodyguards around us right now?*

I looked at him and smiled. At the same time, I was slightly excited, in a way I didn't know how to explain. I weighted in my head the totality of Ohr's analyses. Then I considered the man before me. He was handsome. According to him, he was Sabbath-observant but with no *kippah*. He spoke well, his handshake was firm, his scent pleasant. He had made his way from Israel to France as if it were nothing. Maybe to impress me, maybe to be with me. I found the composite interesting, evocative, intriguing... even a bit of a turn-on. I decided right then and there to give him a chance.

Then Steve surprised me again. *I'm not crazy about hotel lobbies. You want to take a stroll? In an upscale area like this, there are some nice places to eat, if you don't mind standing.*

I liked the idea and agreed immediately. We made a circuit around the hotel, and I got the impression that Steve knew the area very well, even the road towards the marina. He intrigued me more and more following a single phone call he answered after apologizing to me. From the little he said, I gathered that he was a man of the world. He had a house in Kfar Shmaryahu and an apartment on the West Coast. It became apparent that he hadn't hitched a ride to Monaco.

The conversation was pleasant. Steve turned out to be a wealthy and successful man. Very knowledgeable, but not full of himself. A good listener. Genuinely curious about some of what I say.

Ohr's warnings, exclamation points and fat horses galloped away as he nonchalantly took my hand and helped me skip over a broken branch that blocked our way along the path leading down to the marina. After skipping, our hands remained together. His grip was somewhat strong. I felt for a moment like a fifteen-year-old walking down the street with her first boyfriend.

Halfway to the Port de Cap d'Ail pier, I remembered that I had to stay just minutes distance from the hotel. I grabbed his hand tightly and turned him back. *Sorry, I have to go back towards the hotel,* I said.

I increased the pace of my step, but my hand was still in his. Steve stopped in his tracks and, with a subtle movement, pulled me toward him, pinned me to him, and kissed me on my lips. It was a precise, evocative and more than a snappy buss. These moments on the cobblestone path between the hotel and the marina felt like a beautiful dance to me. The turn, the hug, the kiss, seemed natural, carefree. His fleshy lips were pleasant, the aromas coming from his face and shirt only adding to the ambiance. I felt a slight heat rise to my cheeks. When we parted, he raised his hand towards a strand of hair that had fallen in my eyes and moved it gently, in a gesture of concern.

Then it hit me. That small little urge which grows into a storm of passion, reminiscent of the electrical currents I felt in the nape of my neck, my earlobes and pit of my stomach, and rendered me helpless in my room at The Mark, when Ben Mitchell grabbed me from behind and pressed his lips to my neck. I wanted all this to continue.

A few minutes later, Steve and I were already in my hotel room. There was not a single crack left open to thoughts, considerations or dilemmas. Everything happened at the speed of desire. Madness of the senses.

Still, one thought managed to creep into the almost-indiscernible distance between me and Steve. *Here is another man, younger than me, who desires me. Here I am, neither too old nor too set in my ways nor too widowed. Here is my new life, which has passion and lust and supreme happiness.* The words of Reggie, Diana and Linda hummed gently in the background and mingled with each other. And no, Jerry didn't look at me from the corner of the room.

This went on for a long time. It was powerful. Even more than with Ben. I gasped. A big, unrelenting smile stretched across my face. *That was amazing, awesome...* I told Steve in a quiet voice.

A minute after the door closed and I was left alone, breathless, spent, I stared at the ceiling and asked myself what exactly had happened there. What sort of energies had been released between us? Was it an expression of sexual intimacy, tenderness, emotion, the initial stirrings of falling in love? Or was it just a raging outburst of wild passion?

My quiet indecision was resolved quickly and easily. The facts were clear and simple. I wanted to prove to myself that Ben Mitchell was not a one-off, not an isolated incident. I wanted to conquer Steve. I wanted to recreate the turbulent highs I'd experienced a month before without thinking about the future, about love, about relationships. Passion, nothing more and nothing less. It was unfathomable that this would be the first and last time.

We arranged to meet again in the evening, after four hours of deep sleep with a huge smile plastered on my face.

Steve called the waiter over to talk about the wine list, and which vintages were conspicuously absent. I got the impression that he was not only familiar with the lay of the land, but also often frequented the Riviera Marriott, becoming well-acquainted with the hotel's sommelier and the more expensive selections. Even as our conversation glided on the wings of three — four? — full glasses of Cabernet, he remained the same Steve: romantic, considerate, trying hard not to make a mistake.

Still, I slowly recognized some of Ohr's astrological exclamation points. From the few phone calls took, always after apologizing, I realized that he was a calculating man, counting every cent, insistent upon every dollar.

Then he really blew me away by suggesting that we take a romantic cruise together. Ten days on a luxury ship. I thought he had to be teasing me, but he was sincere. I asked myself why he was making such an offer after only two days. What need did it serve? Did he want to escape from somewhere, from something, from someone? But then he began to reckon the price of the cruise, meals, round-trip flights, related expenses. His nickel-and-diming every-thing made me uncomfortable. I didn't understand why it was im-portant to get that granular in an ostensibly light and intimate con-versation.

I rang Yaffit and then Racheli. They both thought it was strange, even a little suspicious. *What is it, did you find some nutjob?* Yaffit asked.

Steve was in a hurry. The alcohol and accountancy did not lead us back to the bedroom. He had to hastily leave for what he de-scribed as an unplanned meeting. Still, I felt that he really wanted us to meet again, and indeed he suggested that we meet the next day for lunch at the upscale restaurant Le Lamparo, next door to the hotel and overlooking the bay.

The meeting outside the restaurant began with a fleshy, warm kiss on the lips. Something pleasant. Longer than a hello. Steve com-bined it with a daring hug that was also nice. He whispered in my ear: *Missed you already.*

I asked myself if the warm welcome and the intensity of the kiss hinted that at the end of the meal we would return to pounce on each other in some room, either at my place or at his, but Steve had other plans.

The food was delicious, but it interested me less. I wanted to un-derstand what sort of man would fly specially from Israel to France just to meet me, open his checkbook for a cruise I hadn't yet agreed to, and say goodbye to me last night without showing any sign that he wanted to recreate the hours of immense pleasure we'd expe-rienced together in my room. After about an hour of enjoying the food and the expensive wines Steve selected — and he did know how to choose his wines — we returned to the main course, as it were: the subject of the cruise. I thought for a moment that he'd gotten off that subject, but no. He dived into the discussion of the Caribbean cruise with full vigor — but again with the bookkeeping.

It made me itch. I expressed polite interest in his plan. I felt that a total rejection would hurt his feelings and torpedo the option of after-dinner entertainment, but then came another surprise.

I get the impression that our relationship could become serious. You're not the sort of woman one goes out with just once or twice. We have great chemistry. He raised his glass and indicated to me to do the same. They clinked together with a pleasant crystal sound. He looked into my eyes. Now there was supposed to come a romantic statement or an offer that we retire to his room or mine. But Steve continued to astonish.

Sally, darling, our relationship fascinates and excites me. It doesn't feel like just another one-night stand. We can spend a week here and then some time in Israel, and then two weeks on the cruise. That's why I think we need to address any elephants in the room, anything that might become an obstacle in the future. We can resolve any issues that may pose a serious problem. Sabbath observance, a shared expense account, place of residence. Apart from this, it is important that we make a financial agreement between us...

His words mingled with the cloud of background music that drifted over from the speakers and the breeze that arose from the bay. I thought I was mishearing him. *An agreement about what...?* I asked and my voice rose a bit. I was expecting a wink, the satisfied smile of someone pulling a prank, a profuse apology, a stammering explanation. Any of those would have made sense, but Steve offered none of them. It took me a full two minutes to digest that he meant exactly what he had said. His fixed expression showed not a single hint of embarrassment. In fact, could see that he hadn't the slightest idea that his offer was strange, not to mention bizarre.

The conversation ended shortly thereafter. When my cell phone vibrated in my bag once again with the arrival of yet another text message, I used the opportunity to announce that the meeting I'd been waiting for over three days had finally arrived. I glanced at my watch, slipped the light-weight white jacket on over my yellow t-shirt, and stood up.

Are you running away? We still haven't talked about when we're meeting again. He remained seated, trying to hold on to my hand.

Steve, darling, this is something urgent and important, and I have to run right now. I don't have a second to spare, I replied. I politely and lightly touched his hand, then started walking quickly toward the exit.

That's it, Sally. It's over. It's unlike any of the Pastel Parliament stories you've heard, I told myself and a bitter smile tugged at the corners of my lips. I felt my disappointment grow exponentially. I thirsted for love and a quality connection, but here came sadness and frustration, along with a little hurt that crept into the depths of my consciousness.

The handsome and impressive figure of Steve collapsed in one fell swoop.

66

Lavi was not the type to say in front of others: *I promised Jerry I'd take care of you, to keep you safe from others and even from yourself.* But he didn't have to say it. He was concerned for me. Period.

After four days of operational time-out thanks to Steve, we had a working breakfast where I reminded them of the questions I'd raised about Dmitri.

What time does he go to his room? Where does he eat and work out? Where does he hold business meetings? Where does he park? Is there a woman in his life? Four days have passed, and I still need answers.

Four days have passed and you're still sticking to your crazy schemes, Lavi replied to me — as I deserved. *I asked what exactly you were planning, and you wouldn't answer.*

I don't know what you're referring to, I answered. *But there's no way I'm heading back to Tel Aviv without wrapping up the case for Ben and his partners. It has to be done, but I can't stay here too long. And, in any case, whatever we can't do in two or three weeks, we can't do in two years.*

Lavi sank into his laptop, texted a few quick messages, then shook his head repeatedly, muttered to himself, and dialed. *Raanan, come to the room at once!*

Lavi, many of the security officers in the hotels in the area are your personal friends, right? Or am I wrong? I asked, not hiding my defiance.

Yes, I have some friends here. Some of them I know from the days when both they and I were serving, Lavi replied.

And the security officer of the Hôtel de Paris Monte-Carlo is one of them?

Lavi raised his head and skewered me with a look. I made myself busy with my slim MacBook. I typed a casual sentence, picked up my cell phone from the table, started texting a message and walked towards the balcony. *Sally...*

I felt weird. A little ashamed of myself. Suddenly, I was interested only in a different kind of manhunt. Find a worthy partner and find a new lover. I wanted love so much. I felt I was ready. That I had something to offer. I wasn't interested in any other mission, just the mission to develop a relationship, which I so longed for. But I knew very well that I could not abandon ship while it was in motion. I had to go on if only because it was an operation Jerry was recommended for. It was an unbearable obligation.

Lavi looked at me and tried to read my mind. He thought of saying something more about the cruelty of the Russian mafia, but thought better of it.

The next day, several newcomers graced the Hôtel de Paris Monte-Carlo. Colette and Christine, two shapely, blonde, tanned and experienced chambermaids, were assigned to special duty in the suites. They spoke excellent French. Colette also spoke Russian.

Stefan, a blue-eyed young man who spoke broken French, was the new valet. He was quite handsome and very polite. His job was to ferry the VIP cars from the entrance of the hotel to the parking lot.

Emil, a tennis instructor who spoke basic French and perfect English, was assigned to shifts in the VIP complex adjacent to the hotel. Emil asked the players for their phone numbers and helped sign up couples for games.

A blonde and energetic businesswoman arrived as well, asking for the most luxurious suite in the hotel. *I am interested in a suite overlooking the marina.* Claude, fifty years old and a senior member of the hotel's VIP team, led the blonde to suite number eight, on the top floor of the circular wing.

She examined the suite and asked about internet connectivity. She made it clear that she would be hosting work meetings in the

suite. She inspected the balcony facing the sea and complimented Claude and the suite. *It's a dreamy room*, she said in English and
slipped a hundred-euro bill between Claude's fingers. The concierge had vast experience with the generosity of the idle rich, but
even he perked up at such a sum.

At the end of the tour, the new guest asked to book the suite for
ten days. Then she inquired about the hours at the gym and the spa,
reserving some playing time on the tennis court as well.

Madame, would like to know the price of the suite for the duration?

The blonde woman giggled and kept walking towards the elevator. *Claude, I'm sure you excel at your job. I trust you to arrange a fair
price for me.*

She was gone before he could say anything else.

I'm insanely worried, everything is going too smoothly, Lavi told me
five days after landing in Nice and the day after I settled into suite
number eight. We were meeting at a remote gas station, halfway
between the makeshift operations room at the Riviera Marriott and
the presidential suite at the Hôtel de Paris Monte-Carlo. We chatted
in a backroom over two bottles of mineral water. Lavi entered the
room where there was a dense cloud of sweat and fuel, pulled out
a black sock from his jacket pocket, went to the corner of the room,
rose on his toes and put the sock over a semi-circular red light. At
least the visible security cam had been disabled. Then he bent over
towards me and, in a hushed voice, updated me about the new staff
members at the hotel. He estimated that, within two days, surveillance would be in place to eavesdrop on Dmitri's car and suite, as
well as the vehicle of one of his assistants.

*All well and good, but we need his phone number. The three kids are
ensconced in the hideout. Oded has an excellent command of English
and French. Bar's fluent in French and Russian, Eliot in four languages.
Their equipment is assembled. Oded ran a few tests and it works great
but, without the number, we are wasting our time.*

I updated him on my settling into the suite, four doors from Dmitri's, as well as the excellent relationship I'd developed with Claude and the hotel staff. I had signed up for several tennis matches in the coming week. Three of my slots put me right next to Dmitri. I didn't yet have a game with him, but I would. Emil would see to it. Dmitri was an extremely powerful player. I had watched two of his games; he'd be a real challenge.

Once I'd reported, Lavi did something he had never done before. He moved the two bottles of water from the center of the shabby Formica table between us, wiped the dust off his sleeves and lifted his half-tinted glasses to his forehead. He then grabbed both my hands, pulled them with surprising force towards his chest and asked me to look into his eyes. His grip lifted me straight out of my seat, until I was mostly floating in the air.

Sally I've been holding back for a long time, but I need you give me a full minute of your attention now, with an open heart and a willing mind.

I looked at him closely, running through scenarios in my head. Why had he put me in this position? What would happen next? I couldn't stay indifferent or cold. But Lavi was Lavi. Sharp, focused, no fantasies, no romance.

Sally, I implore you to take caution. Think twice. Count to 1,001 before each move you make. You're a big girl. There are stories about what you did or didn't do last year. You realize that I know what you need to know and what's better not to know. But I'm telling you here and now: we're not in Greece or Pakistan or Iran or Qatar... He stopped for a split second, then continued: *Our opponents are a world-class prodigy professor of mathematics and a chess grandmaster. Both are psychopaths who, in the last decade, have become multibillionaire predators. They are cruel and sophisticated, to an unimaginable degree.*

Lavi fell silent for a moment, still holding my hands tightly, forcing me to bend slightly over the table until our faces were inches away. Our eyes were close to each other, close enough for me to recognize in them an agitation that was highly unusual for Yaakov Lavi. And, in them, I discerned a slight, almost invisible moisture that grew as the conversation progressed.

Something bothered me about that look, as my eyes peered into his. A few more moments passed as I tried to concentrate on the important things he was saying as well as what I was seeing. And then I realized it. Around the orbs of his green-brown pupils curled yellowish conjunctiva.

When I thought back over the past two years, Lavi's always made sure to wear glasses with semi-dark lenses. Even in shady rooms or the gloom of dusk. I had spent sleepless nights diving into the depths of the Internet in search of answers to Jerry's illness. I practically had a medical degree from Google University, and learned that yellow conjunctiva implied a cancerous tumor in the pancreas. When this realization hit me, my eyes also began to burn and then blur; the tears began to flow, and Lavi knew that I knew.

I'm telling you this for the first time and I'll never repeat it, Sally. Jerry caught me for a very long conversation two months before the last hospitalization. Apologies for hiding it from you, but that's what he insisted on. He came to my messy apartment, using all the tactics of evasion and discretion he was a master of, and told me he was going to die. He knew it already, Sally, one hundred percent. Don't know what he told you. I know what he told me.

I was holding Lavi's strong hands, my eyes close to his, my face inches from his, as I burst into tears. It was a minute that seemed to last much longer. I wanted to dive deep into it. To recognize the great soul of this man; to understand how much he cared for me, to realize how important I was to him. To acknowledge that, even as he fought for his own life, he thought of mine first.

I understood from Jerry that you are a real heroine, he said after the silence, slowly loosening the grip that lifted me up and pinned me to him — but he still held me, strong as steel. *He spoke with admiration about what you did during the month in which you went under the radar for all of us. But you know Jerry. He was the world champion in figuring out a thousand-piece puzzle with only a few dozen pieces. He had a rare ability to give the other side the feeling that he was telling the whole story. He did not disclose locations, details, operational activ-*

ity. I only heard general information from him, and that was enough for me. He was proud of you to a degree I don't know even how to put into words, Sally. When he talked about you and your activities, his face beamed. A glowing aura shone from him.

Suddenly, he wasn't the Lavi I knew. A poetic description of the aura that shone from Jerry's face? His eyes sparkled. His gaze held mine. His grip was so strong it hurt my hands, my body, my soul. A thought struck me to my core: I realized that Jerry and Lavi hadn't just been talking about operations and about me. They confided in each other about their diseases, about scleroderma and pancreatic cancer, about fate, about the likelihood that both their lives were rapidly moving towards the inevitable end. I could imagine the way Jerry formulated it — when he told Lavi that his friend would out-live him and asked him to take care of me.

I was supposed to pull my hand back, free myself from the steel grip and revert to leaning back in the chair. But inside I knew that Lavi, in his way, was trying to shake me, to force me to listen to him. To ingrain into my brain the warnings that emerged from his mouth, but actually came from Jerry, who suddenly came back to life to keep me safe.

And there was also a hidden whirlwind of hidden emotions and secrets, repressed and silenced. Something that was forbidden to turn from a fragment of thought in the depths of consciousness into words, into open understanding, into a living emotion. Yaakov Lavi and I were like brother and sister or like two close cousins. A great love that would never come to light.

My dear Lavi, I understand exactly what you are saying, I finally said in a quiet voice and with great deliberation. *But you know me. I'm al-ready here, off to the races, and the mission has to be accomplished. There are no half-measures in my repertoire, just like there weren't in Jerry's. If he can somehow hear us right now, he knows that he cannot impose on me what he himself has never done. Jerry would never scrub a mission before completing the work.*

But at what price, Sally? At any cost? Do you realize how monstrous these guys can be?

I looked at him for a long time and didn't answer. The conversation had exhausted itself. I knew that Lavi was right in everything he said, but I pushed aside everything I understood about the dangers. I could have predicted with maximum precision what else he would tell me, but I no longer wanted to hear.

Lavi let go of my hand and left the room.

Five minutes later, I also departed and walked towards the dark blue Renault Talisman waiting patiently for me. When I opened the door, I caught the faithful observer out of the corner of my eye. Lavi sat in a large sports utility vehicle at the exit from the gas station and watched my car, making sure that no one would pounce on or threaten me. Making sure I wouldn't be followed.

The Renault Talisman had been carefully selected. Not too flashy, but a premium ride that provided stability and an excellent driver experience, accelerating at a surprising rate and maneuvering smoothly between lanes. I needed it. Lavi simply gestured, and that sufficed for me: I performed two consecutive evasive maneuvers on the road heading north from Monaco. It took twenty minutes in total. At the precise same time, Lavi was carrying out similar exercises to shake anyone who might be tailing him.

We don't take any risks, Sally, he echoed, and everything else was already clear.

67

12:00 hrs.
Decrypting deleted text messages
in the Monaco hideout

The next day began with a kick in the head and deep into the heart. Confusion. Horrible anxieties. Complications in the operation. Disturbing news alongside a dramatic breakthrough on the way to the destination. Terrifying announcements alongside successes.

The day actually began with great news. Amnon, under the name Emil, was Lavi's plant on the tennis court. He had managed to get Piotr Volkov to give his phone number to coordinate tennis matches. Among other things, he set up a match with the blonde newcomer from suite number eight. He also verified the device's model number. Both the model and cell number were immediately transferred to Lavi and, from there, to the trio of kids in the hideout.

Colette, Lavi's planted chambermaid, managed to obtain the exact schedule of suite number two, as well as the name and phone number of Yevgeny, the bodyguard. She smiled at him, captured his heart and ignited his imagination, offering to meet him that night in the hotel bar. Yevgeny replied that he was only free after eleven, when his boss returned — after four hours in the casino and five glasses of whiskey — to then collapse on the huge bed in the suite. *Tonight my shift lasts until after midnight, but tomorrow I'll call you. I'd love to have a drink with you,* said Colette and asked Yevgeny for his phone number. She marveled at his cell phone, asking him what model he had, then said goodbye with a meaningful wink.

That was enough for Oded, Bar and Eliot. They divided the work among themselves and, a few hours later, they'd uncovered every possible detail about Dmitri and Yevgeny. They also discovered some information about Oleg, the bruiser who oversaw the entrances and exits of the floor. Within fifteen minutes, they knew all the essentials about Oleg and his sexual orientation.

Whatever... Either Lavi or Sally may be needed to lure him away from his post, said Oded.

As they dove into the depths of the devices, an image of Vladislav, Dmitri's only son in Herzliya, playing soccer with his classmates, leapt out of one of the folders. Soon they had the child's phone number, too. Bar dug around and soon revealed the heartbreaking correspondence from the boy who missed his father and blamed Dmitri for abandoning his son in a distant land.

Meanwhile, the whiz kids discovered an endless series of text messages and images systematically deleted from Dmitri's cell phone. A young, fit, sexy woman. Further clarification revealed her name too: Yvonne Laurent. The name rang familiar to Eliot. He dove into Google and discovered the secret. Yvonne Laurent had been a journalist covering the French Riviera in print and online. She had disappeared a year ago. After months of searching, her body was found in a state of advanced decay in the forest along the A500 highway from Monaco.

She vanished a year ago, they found her seven months ago! Search by date, search by date! Eliot screamed, both excited and thoughtful. His mind came up with all kinds of scenarios.

The tension in the room increased. Bar and Oded charged through the images accumulated during the months in question, and they found an entire folder. Some of the images showed her in intimate situations with a young man. It was obvious that she had been recorded surreptitiously. The rest showed her hanging out in clubs and restaurants.

Keep looking. There is something huge here, I tell you, something huge, Oded maintained. He had the finest senses and the most acute intuition. Another search showed news items about Yvonne's disappearance, also systematically deleted from Dmitri's phone. *Find*

more. In the meantime, I'm going over the articles this poor woman pub-
lished. Google had dozens, and I can see that some are about organized
crime infiltrating Monaco. There are names and headshots, too. I want to
see if there's an article about Dmitri as well.

After a few minutes, Eliot slapped his head. *Forget about Google!*
Take a look at this deleted image, he said excitedly and turned his laptop screen towards his friends. *Here's an article by Mrs. Laurent —*
and see who's starring in it. A little thinner, maybe, not quite the same
look. He doesn't have that crazy beard, but I'm telling you: it's Dmitri.
Bingo! The caption says something else, but what'd you expect?

Oded seemed riled up. *Our monster stalks the countryside. It's alive!*
Without Hydra, Sally and Lavi could run around in circles here for an-
other two years and not discover a thing, he shouted, grabbing Eliot by
the shoulder and shaking him hard. *Do you get it, Eliot? We have a*
hydrogen bomb in our hands. Don't you see? Don't you understand? And
you ditched us in the middle of development!

We must report this to Sally, said Bar.

Oded responded instinctively and smacked Bar's hand as he
reached for his phone. *Don't call anyone! Have you forgotten our pro-*
tocol? Do you want to alert the masses? No phones, Bar. Do you under-
stand? We will print everything and pass it on to Lavi by hand! By hand!

At this point, the color printer in the hideout was called into service. Every deleted photo, every deleted text message, every deleted article was printed on high-quality paper, maximum resolution,
three copies each.

Slowly, three identical binders were created that catalogued the
secrets Dmitri had tried his best to conceal, the damning clues connecting him to the disappearance and death of Yvonne Laurent, as
well as the heartbreaking text messages from little Vladislav, abandoned in a gilded cage in Herzliya.

In the midst of all the drama in the hiding place, I stood in the
center of the spacious suite number eight and spoke to myself, as
was my custom when in tense moments, just before I was about

to fall apart. Nervous, angry, frustrated, overwhelmed with anxiety, I paced frantically, barefoot on the soft carpet, back and forth. I reviewed Lavi's warnings, connected them to Jerry's exhortations and added to them the insane degree of risk that fell on Bar, Eliot and Oded. *Hacking into cell phones on the soil of a foreign country... They could go to jail for ten years,* still talking to myself.

But I directed most of the rage at one person: Martin Fillmore, senior spook, cuckolded husband of my friend Linda, Jerry's best friend and the person who sent Ben to me with this shocking case. I bent my arm to bring the cell phone close to my face. I started dialing, then cancelled. I began and aborted again. I remembered Martin's number by heart. I also recalled that it was stored under the code name Billy. Finally, I forced myself to dial. I addressed Martin by name and let loose.

I heard him take a deep breath and restrain himself, despite the four thousand miles separating DC from Monte Carlo. He was clearly debating how to respond to the fact that I had called him, the time I had chosen, the use of his name, the fiery rebuke for referring Ben to me and landing me in a hellscape. A senior CIA official ought not to be involved in private investigations. I knew all this very well, but I was angry. Martin was the reason why I was just about to challenge a super-predator face-to-face, one of the most dangerous mafiosos from Moscow, one of the worst in Europe. A mobster that left behind him a swath of horror, of mutilated bodies and mass assassinations. An individual well known to the ROC (Russian Organized Crime) unit.

That's OK, Martin. Don't say anything. Just listen. I'll say what I need to say. We are here at a deadly juncture. We have to deal with a criminal with a thousand faces. I'll give you all the names we were able to find out about. It is critical that you find everything possible. Use the ROC unit. Don't ask me how, but I know he's had partners in Little Odessa, in the Brighton Beach neighborhood of Brooklyn for several years.

Martin took a deep breath and remained silent. I could imagine him standing with his cell phone in his hand and about to explode.

I know for a fact that there was a meeting of the godfathers in Puerto Rico three years ago, and he was there. There were at least thirty dons there. I wouldn't want to think that this happened under your nose without your knowledge. I know for a fact that during the month this monster was in Brooklyn, the five biggest restaurants in Brighton Beach went up in flames. At least eight people died. You don't want me to be found in pieces in Toulon Forest, right? Any information or document you find about this psycho can make the difference and allow us to settle the matter without casualties. I'm counting on you, Martin. I trust you and am asking you, very sincerely, to give my warm regards to Linda. Goodbye, Martin.

My farewell was a poisoned arrow, a big, fat hint that if he failed to help me, he'd be in hot water with his wife.

I thought I would feel better after the conversation, but the opposite happened. A heavy burden fell on me. The requests I made of Martin were very simple — a few mouse clicks and a few searches within the infinite databases at his disposal. On the other hand, his involvement with the Dmitri case might result in some hard questions from inside the agency — perhaps even a full-blown internal investigation.

68

9:40 hrs.
At Port de Cap d'Ail, a magnificent yacht
goes up in flames

Nightmares consumed me that night. The fresh information that arrived in the evening from the hideout was superb, but it included such disturbing images: the rotting corpse of the French journalist, several other mutilated bodies discovered in the forests adjacent to the Provence region. I couldn't shake my anxiety about a face-to-face encounter with Dmitri. On top of the waking nightmare of meeting him, came wave after wave of worry about having brought Bar, Eliot and Oded into this mess, and misgivings that I had also implicated Martin.

The wretched night left me exhausted. I knew I had to be at my best on the coming day, but I hadn't managed to sleep for even one consecutive hour. My early morning stupor was cut to ribbons by a cacophony of police sirens. I could speculate, by the sounds echoing along Avenue D'Ostende, that they were rushing towards the hotel. I forced myself to get up. I had barely dragged myself to the balcony of the suite when an explosion lit up the sky, right in front of my eyes. One of the largest yachts in the Monaco Yacht Club Marina went up in flames.

Transfixed by the frightful scene, my fears exacerbated when I witnessed several people diving from the stern into the water, their clothing on fire. I instinctively dialed Claude, who was indeed an efficient and professional hotel staff member, but also a hopeless gossip. He was supposed to know everything and update his esteemed guests, as quickly as possible. *That's part of the service,* he would say with a smile. As far as I was concerned, it was a catastrophe: the yacht that caught fire was the magnificent superyacht, *Princess Anne* — and arson was suspected. *It belongs to two real estate investors, one of ours and one British. They formed a partnership with some Russian who lives here,* elaborated Claude who, for a moment, sounded like a newsreader on the local radio.

These are Dmitri's partners, I thought to myself. *Someone put them in the crosshairs. Things were getting hot, in every sense of the word.*

As I was thinking about what the cause of the fire might be, a god-awful racket filled the common area shared by the presidential suites. I thought about going to the door, but the loud banging and the chime of the doorbell preceded me. I glanced into the peephole. It was Lavi.

He entered the room panting. *I don't need to tell you about the burning yacht. You saw it live under your nose.* He gulped two glasses of water in quick succession. *I am troubled by the fact that the yacht belongs to both of Dmitri's partners. After all, we don't believe in coincidences. But it is very possible that this terrible firestorm has nothing to do with Dmitri. They have been conducting real estate transactions in this area for many years, long before they entered into a partnership with him. They have many enemies, God help us. There are also disgruntled customers. It could be someone who lost money on the property they bought from them. Or maybe it's just the furious ex-wife of the Frenchman.*

I don't think you came this far just for a concoction of rumor and gossip.

Lavi raised his head and smiled tiredly. *We have a much more serious problem,* he said, and fell silent.

Speak, Lavi! I'm gonna freak out in a second! I said too loudly, in a scolding tone. My nerves were raw.

Emil, my plant on the tennis courts, hasn't answered me since last night. I wasn't that worried initially, but I was told they spotted him last night. He left the hotel grounds walking towards the marina with a young woman. I see your look, and the answer is yes, Sally. I asked. No one could say who the girl was, but they were definitely seen embarking on the Princess Anne, which I guess they'll have to rename Princess Ash.

Lavi's speech was dry and technical. There was not a single shred of stress, tension, or distress. He maintained an air of confidence, which annoyed me.

And what will we tell his parents, Lavi? What story will we tell them? The simple truth that we've gotten him entangled with the Russian mafia? Or will we just lie?

Lavi was silent. He bit his nails, his leg twitched nervously; he was engrossed in his cell phone, praying and willing for some sign of life to pop up on the screen.

The next few hours got worse and worse. Exhaustion made me feel like a washed-up dishrag. Lavi continued to update every hour that there was still no trace of Emil. In one of the updates he messaged me that my neighbor from suite number two came out of the hotel with two escorts and a light suitcase. Our plan of action was going completely awry. If Dmitri left, I wouldn't be able to have the little tête-à-tête I had planned for that evening.

I lay on my back in the huge bed and looked at the ceiling. I was angry with myself. I tried to recreate every step we'd taken so far. I struggled to pinpoint what mistake had caused this chain of disruptions. The arson on the yacht, the disappearance of Emil, the departure of Dmitri.

I finally succumbed to fatigue and let myself collapse. In that space of time, between my body becoming limp and dozing off, I managed to tell myself: *You've had a hard day, Sally. Tomorrow will be better. This is the way of the world. When you wake up, everything will have changed for the better.*

I was startled awake by the incessant vibration of my cell phone as well as the blanket I'd fallen asleep on. An unfamiliar number was trying to contact me via WhatsApp. Eight consecutive messages. Greetings and apologies and question marks, from a good friend in Washington.

Sorry, sorry, sorry, I'm available now. Please call me, I typed quickly. A split-second later, a long message appeared. Something obviously prepared in advance. *Your friend asked me to inform you that he found treasures in the Odessa region. He is very busy today but asked me to take his place. I am at your disposal. I'm looking for a way to deliver you a thick envelope. I can't forward anything by email or cell phone.*

After this announcement, a flood of good messages came in. Great messages, actually.

Emil returned with a big, stupid grin on his face, having spent time with a girl he met yesterday. He's fine. Went a little wild. Drank a little. He didn't even notice that his cell phone battery died.

Claude called from the lobby and told me that someone wanted to deliver an envelope to me, but insisted on handing it over in person.

Lavi knocked on the door, closed it behind him and passed on more information from the hideout. All the new information dealt with Dmitri's son, his social awkwardness, his depression. The Hydra artists discovered that Dmitri and his son also occasionally spoke a few sentences in Hebrew.

A moment before he left, Lavi said, *We're back to normal here on the floor, too. Your neighbor has returned to his suite...*

69

19:15 hrs.
Face-to-face with the Russian mafioso
in the suite

At about seven o'clock, Dmitri was observed walking into his suite
after several matches on the tennis court. About ten minutes after
the heavy door of suite number two closed, I left suite number eight
wearing fashionable tennis attire, holding a racket and a ball. From
my left shoulder dangled a thin but heavy white cloth bag.

I walked confidently towards the door of suite number two and
smacked it with an open hand. Behind me, ten feet away, was Colette, the new VIP chambermaid for the suites. She was ready with a
cart loaded with crystal bowls of cut fruit. It took several long moments before the bruiser on the other side of the door opened it a
crack. I gave him a huge smile. *Hello, Mr. Yevgeny Podolski,* I said in
English and looked at his broad shoulders, which his ironed polo
shirt was straining to contain. *I'm here to see Mr. Volkov. I'm supposed
to play him tomorrow morning, but I need to change the time.*

Yevgeny looked bemused. I knew his first name and his surname.
This managed to confuse him for a moment. The chambermaids
planted on the floor had done an excellent job. Thanks to them, I
knew that Dmitri was soaking in his steam bath at the time. I also
how long it would be until he came out, wrapped in a colorful robe,
with a big towel on his head.

Sorry, Dmitri is in the shower, Yevgeny answered assertively, putting on a stern face. He began to close the door, but something in his
professional veneer cracked when I gave him a surprise message.

*Regards from Colette, Mr. Podolski. She's my niece, you know. You'll
see her soon,* I winked.

His eyes opened, a tiny smile split his cheeks and he stared at me curiously. *Really? Is she your niece? Wonderful girl,* he said, and the door gap widened again.

A second later, she appeared in the middle of the corridor, pushing the cart of sliced fruit. She called Yevgeny by his name, waved at him vigorously and motioned him with her hand to come towards her.

Yes, Colette is a fine girl, one-of-a-kind. Go ahead, I said and patted his inflated shoulder. He came out of the doorway. In that second, I went through the open slot, pointed my buttocks at the heavy wooden door, gave it a light nudge — and it shut with a whisper. Yevgeny was left outside, beyond a heavy door that could not be opened from the outside. Colette did her job and gave me two more minutes of quiet to continue with the program.

I turned the key in the lock and pulled it out, sealed the door chain in place and hurried into the sitting room of the suite. The first thing was to open the large glass door separating the living room from the rounded balcony. Then I sat down in the armchair close to an oval glass table facing the bathroom door — just as I had practiced in my identical suite. Then I took out a few dozen documents and photographs from the white cloth bag next to me and placed them in four piles.

A minute later, Dmitri came out of the bathroom with a cloud of steam rising behind him and a huge towel wrapped around his head. He was wearing a colorful Hawaiian-style silk robe. *Hello, Mr. Piotr Volkov. I'm here!* I called to him in English.

He was in shock. He turned his body sharply, noticed me on the armchair and screamed for Yevgeny. There was no response. His bodyguard was otherwise engaged. He began to approach me and launched a barrage of curses in Russian. *Suka, kak ty suda popala? Kto tebja vpustil? Zhit tebe nadoelo?! (How did you get here, bitch? Who let you in? Are you tired of living?!)*

I suggest you don't shout, Mr. Volkov. Sit down and we'll talk quietly, I said, I casually placed my hand on the pile of papers and turned

390

over the top photo. In front of Dmitri's face, a fresh photograph of Vladislav, his only son, was revealed. A colorful, vivid, A4-sized photograph of his son playing soccer at school in Herzliya.

Shalava! (Whore!) was his one-word response, but this time it was a bit softer. Turning to the picture, his eyes went wide and turned bloodshot. The torrent of curses stopped. On the table were three more piles of documents. He looked at them and went back to swearing, but this time in a muffled voice, as if he were speaking to himself. He looked defeated. He stepped back a pace or two, peered again at the door of the suite and finally realized that he was alone. Just the two of us in a space that, until now, had been safe for him.

Then, in some burst of courage, or perhaps despair, he again began to walk towards me with his hateful gaze. *Suka, suka, suka,* he said again and again. I continued to sit there confidently, showing no fear, and pointed towards the balcony of the suite. A translucent white curtain fluttered in the breeze, but the suite was open to the outside world. Beyond the balcony railing, a tiny drone buzzed and positioned itself, facing the seating area. Attached to it was a camera panning right and left in a subtle, smooth motion. Lavi had flown Haggai and Amit to France, two more brilliant young men he'd recruited. They served in the IDF in an experimental unit for the operation of miniature drones launched from suitcases or handheld devices. Before the flight to France, Lavi and the young men practiced flying drones with cameras manufactured by Orion. Their training ground was in front of the balconies of some of his friends in the opulent Yoo Towers in Tel Aviv. However, this mission at the Hôtel de Paris Monte-Carlo was the first active operation abroad.

We're filming you live, Mr. Volkov, I said. Dmitri looked at the drone and his body froze. He tried to walk towards the balcony window to draw the curtains, but his legs couldn't carry him and he landed heavily in the armchair. His face was pale. Cold sweat broke out on his forehead. I toyed with the idea that he might have had a heart attack, but the mobster's instincts compelled him to quickly straighten up from the armchair in another attempt to get closer to me. After the second step, I picked up the another pile of documents and stuck it in front of his face. It was a package of articles about and photographs of Yvonne Laurent, whose body had been found in Toulon Forest. Dmitri looked at the photograph at the top of the pile and stopped, as if an armored glass panel had slammed down between us. He had systematically erased every trace of her from his smartphone's memory, and now her images were fluttering in front of him. He was sure that all these pictures had already evaporated into the ether, that they would never come back to threaten him.

I also have this for you, Mr. Volkov, I said and presented him with a binder of documents messengered over by Martin Fillmore. It was as if a cluster bomb exploded in his gut. The front page displayed four insignia: the seal of the United States, the emblem of the federal judiciary, the logo of the FBI and the eight-pointed star of the ROC unit. Each 'picture' was worth a thousand words. Three names appeared, one after another: Dmitri Ilyich, his alias from his stay in Little Odessa; Vitaly Odeski, his nom de guerre from the conference of godfathers in Puerto Rico; and Masha Gorohovski, the one and only name of his wife. It indicated that she was Jewish too, and provided the real surname of the mafioso with a thousand faces. He reviewed the documents, recognizing locations and dates. Brighton Beach, June 22, 2016; Puerto Rico, June 3, 2016.

Dmitri looked at the names I ought not to have known, in locations I shouldn't have been able to trace and dates, presumed to be secret, cried out to him from the paper. He looked more and more weary. Then he extended a hesitant hand towards the Yvonne Laurent stack, touched it with well-groomed fingernails, tried to pick up the first photograph and discovered that it was not the only one. Beneath it were about fifteen others, some of them compromising. The common denominator of all of them was the embrace, anything but innocent, between him and the nosy journalist, thirty years younger — and the fact that he had deleted them all from his cell phone when it came out that she had disappeared. *Bljad tvoju mat,* he mumbled with pronounced frustration. Out of helplessness. Impugning my mother's character would get him nowhere.

Now it was time for the fourth package. I turned it around with a quick motion, feeling like a stage magician revealing their card to a stunned audience member. Dmitri immediately recognized the statement from his secret Swiss bank account. At the top of the page was a different name, Stas Sidorov. Another facade. Another of the hundreds of identities he had chosen for himself.

Dmitri cringed, his broad shoulders slumping. His face, already ruddy from his steam bath, had now turned blood-red. He approached the bar in the corner of the room and poured himself a Balvenie from a cognac bottle into the crystal glass, filling it up to the top. He raised his chin and downed it all in one swallow. I watched the movement of his throat as he imbibed the burning waterfall. It seemed to contain the fires of hell. He grimaced slightly and poured more Balvenie into the crystal glass, again to its rim. He gulped down half of it, then turned around and walked back and forth in the space between the bar and the armchair in front of me. *Those two glasses of Balvenie are a month's salary for a minimum-wage worker,* I thought to myself.

The storm in Dmitri's head intensified. A category five hurricane. His eyes darted to and fro while he ran through his full repertoire of Russian curses inaudibly. From time to time, he squinted at the four stacks of documents on the glass table and the drone that kept buzzing about and guarding me.

Sit, Mr. Volkov, I said in a quiet voice that had a hint of command. *Please sit down. We're just talking. A friendly conversation, Mr. Volkov.*

Dmitri returned to swearing under his breath. He looked beaten, tired, desperate, powerless. He approached the armchair and perched on it again, in all his glory. The armchair groaned under his weight. The remainder of the Balvenie in his glass sloshed over and stained his robe.

You have a lovely boy, Mr. Volkov, I said. I reached for the furthest pile of photographs and presented him with a picture of his son skillfully dribbling. *I've seen him at school in Herzliya. My nephew goes there, too. If you wish, I can help you with him while you are in Europe...*

The cloud on his face thickened. He didn't look at me. His chin sank to his chest. After a few seconds, he returned to the bar and fixed himself another round. Another full glass of Balvenie tossed off in one gulp; then another glass, half of which he guzzled immediately and half of which he kept in his hand. I could hear the gears of his brain working overtime. We could both hear Yevgeny's hysterical knocking on the door and his shouts, muffled by the heavy mahogany.

He took another light sip of the Balvenie, looked up at me and asked, *What did you say your name was, Mrs. ...?*

I didn't say my name, Mr. Volkov, but I'll tell you now. My name is Rachel. I came here on a flight from New York. I met three partners there who gave you a down payment of twenty-six million dollars. It seems like a raw deal, neither in their nor your best interest. I suggest that you cancel the transaction and return their money. It's simple. No one gets hurt, and everyone leaves happy.

Dmitri placed the Balvenie glass on the table with such a loud smack, I thought it would shatter. He mumbled again one of those curses he had already rehearsed before, then held his head in his hands. *Simple? It's anything but simple, Mrs. Rachel,* he said in a tired voice and reached for his glass again. *Not one cent can be returned to them without the approval of the boss in Vienna. You know that very well. Very well!* he repeated in a voice that suddenly rose in exasperation.

You are a big boy, Piotr Volkov, I said sarcastically. *But I think you shouldn't mess with those guys from New York. Look at these documents. I don't understand how they got them. Most of the documents here are classified. But they claim that they have boxes more, and that it is not good for you. In fact, it's really, really bad, Mr. Volkov. I know that they have been following you for a long time. I also am aware that they have several recordings of your phone calls to Masha, your wife, when she was at that conference in Puerto Rico with all your friends. I also know that they've visited Herzliya. The photos of Stanislav came from them.*

They chose to mess with the wrong people, Dmitri muttered.

I think you should be careful, Mr. Volkov. Ben Mitchell and his two partners have friends in high places, the highest echelons of the FBI and the CIA. They wield tremendous power. Even in the West Wing. That's quite scary...

Mrs. Rachel, do not insult my intelligence. I'm quick on the uptake. Tell me what you want, we'll save everyone time and go out to calm Yevgeny down.

From that moment on, the conversation was very businesslike. Efficient. Swift.

I got up from my seat and headed for the bar to make Dmitri a cup of coffee. *Drink something other than alcohol,* I ordered. My expression brooked no dissent. We had to move forward. *You are to transfer twenty-six million dollars to this account, plus another three million for interest, mental anguish, expenses and wasted time,* I said and put a note on the table. It had Ben's account information on it. Clean, no identifying mark. Dmitri took the note, looked at it for some time and swore again. *As soon as the money is transferred, Mr. Volkov, I'll destroy all the documents here on the table. I suggest that you call your bank right now and have them transfer it right away.*

Stupid bitch, don't you understand that I can't do that? he objected, and his voice rose into a scream.

Mr. Volkov, now I must be the one to tell you not to insult my intelligence, I answered with impeccable etiquette. *You most certainly can do it. Here is your bank account in Switzerland. It's yours alone. We would not want the redheaded Boris from Vienna to know that you have such an account. So please, Mr. Volkov, there's more than fifty million dollars in that account,* I said and handed him the white paper with dense text on it. It was his secret bank account statement. Eliot had marked his current balance with a yellow marker and circled the balance line in black.

Dmitri looked at his watch, picked up the cell phone wearily and dialed. Then he answered an ongoing series of identification questions, passwords and ten-digit code numbers, repeated a few sentences he was asked to say to activate voice recognition, then pointed the cell phone camera at himself and recorded a video of himself speaking and reeling off another password.

Ask them to send you confirmation of the transfer immediately upon deposit.

I knew that the very moment the receipt was sent to Dmitri's cell phone, it was simultaneously printing out in the hideout's printer.

Before I leave, it is important that we talk about another topic, Mr. Volkov.

Enough already with Mr. Volkov. Enough! I'm Piotr, OK, Mrs. Rachel? Piotr!

I smiled. *Now you are Piotr, in America you were Vitaly and in Russia you are Dima — but these are just names. We know that, deep in your heart, you are David. This is the name they gave you when you were circumcised. You are a proud Jew. You are David, like King David, and your son is a prince, the son of a king.* I gave him the long answer all in Hebrew.

Dmitri raised his head and stared at me, stunned. Some of the conversations between him and his son took place in broken Hebrew, which he had learned as a child, reciting it at the secret birthday celebration his parents held underground under the terror of Soviet rule. I had waited until that moment to work Hebrew into the conversation; that was my checkmate.

It was essential to ensure my well-being and the safety of Ben and his partners but, in the midst of the dramatic scene in suite number two, I had a brainstorm. Dmitri could become a great source for Jerry's men. He was in close contact with the ginger boss from Vienna. He had the mobile phone numbers of all his senior capos, some of whom were engaged in the arms trade and the prohibited parts of the nuclear industry. He could gather information on how Boris used his old monstrous Antonov An-124. He could also assist in investigations into the smuggling of spare parts for nuclear bombs, which trickled through the mafia, from Russia and Ukraine towards the Middle East.

This was all above my paygrade. I was supposed to make sure money was transferred from the bank in Zurich to Ben's in Manhattan, where it would vanish at the speed of light. I also knew that Lavi's mind had to be consumed by the sight of the heavy wooden door, closed long after it should have been opened again. In addition, I knew that Yevgeny might call for reinforcements.

Nevertheless, I felt I had to recruit Dmitri. I knew I had a trump card in my hand. A Jew who grew up in a traditional Jewish home. A senior mobster whose secrets had suddenly been exposed. His secret bank account in Switzerland; the murder of a journalist, information that could complicate his life and deprive him of his freedom; the beloved son who grew up and was educated in the State of Israel. Beyond the fanciful opening conditions, I thought I could help the guys from the Mossad cultivate an asset straight out of the land of fairy tales. One who could provide golden information without endangering any of our good guys.

As I thought about the moves required to recruit Dmitri, I looked up to where the ceiling met the decorative cornice on the wall. Jerry was there, looking at me and beaming.

Jerry is proud of you Sally, so proud of you, I told myself and smiled back at him.

70

18:00 hrs.
On Cliff Beach, a scar from stem to stern

Emanuel was the man who taught me humility. From the beginning of our relationship until he mysteriously disappeared, he showered me with one surprise after another, all the while smashing the remnants of my ruminations about men which had been on autopilot for too long. He revealed how superficial my supposedly bottomless knowledge of the subject really was, which was purported to provide me protection from disappointment.

It started with a name which sounded a bit old-fashioned. *Emanuel? Do you mean Emmanuelle, the sexy character portrayed by Sylvia Kristel?* But the man was lightyears away from that. Not that you'd know it from the blurry profile photo he chose to post on Facebook. I knew he was divorced, but little else.

The first glimpse I caught of him in real life just intensified the mystery. It was less than a week after GS222 brought Lavi, Raanan, the Hydra team and me home. We were in the parking lot at Cliff Beach, the northernmost beach in Tel Aviv, close to Herzliya.

You never have a second chance to make a first impression, I reflected. He drove up in an AIL Storm, a sports-utility vehicle that was thoroughly battered and spattered with mud. The only part of it clean and intact seemed to be the windshield.

That's how it is in the Arava, he murmured and approached me briskly. His oversized clothing revealed nothing, and the strappy sandals on his feet were caked with multiple layers of Arava dust too.

What am I doing here? I asked myself with every step he took towards me. *Why are you associating with this mystery man who doesn't even have a clear photo for his Facebook profile? Who doesn't share any information aside from his marital status and hometown? How does a Mossad agent with a classified operational record show up alone, at dusk, based on text messages? What hope could there possibly be for the future, when this relationship seems doomed from the start?*

The connection with Emanuel surfaced sometime before I met Ben, after *shiva* for Jerry ended but before I had the conversation with Reggie that threw me for a loop, breathing new life into me as I struggled with the death of my beloved, sending me into new orbits.

In those twilight days, at the edge of the abyss that threatened to envelop me, when the ink had not yet dried on Jerry's death certificate, inquiries began to come in from Mossad officials past and present, some well-known. I was shocked at how quickly all this happened. I debated whether it was in poor taste or perhaps an attempt to offer me a firm shoulder, a sympathetic ear. And then, out of nowhere — only in retrospect and far later than I should have, did I come to understand the timing — an enchanting message caught my attention. His writing was direct, rough, effective, but it also had the melancholy melody of secret poetry.

Greetings, Sally. I've been following your page for some time. I understand what you're going through. I can't take my eyes off of you. I'm drowning in the green of your eyes — Emanuel.

Brief, to the point. He didn't use any tired references, nor did he address me with *Dear* or sign off with *Yours*. No transparent attempt to seduce me into virtual dating. Completely different. In fact, the opposite of everything I had heard of from my friends in the Pastel Parliament. They'd complained of messages pressuring them with blunt, chauvinistic, suppliant terminology, replete with idle compliments. None of that from Emanuel.

Then came more via Messenger. Shorter. Pithy. Not pestering, not annoying.

I saw your new photo. It left me speechless — Emanuel.

I took a picture for you, too — Emanuel, he wrote, attaching a mesmerizing image of sunrise in the Arava.

Then he sent a short, technical message.

If my messages are a burden, write me and I'll shut up — Emanuel.

However, all of this, as mentioned, was in the black hole era, after Jerry's death when, out of nowhere, strange attempts at courtship came from some of the Mossad members who knew me, who knew Jerry and our relationship.

I put aside all the messages, including Emanuel's, and continued to move forward on the path that mourning had prescribed for me. The trip to the resort in Mexico, including the earthshaking conversation with Reggie. The unimaginable celebration of passion with Ben. The terrifying, suspenseful and alarming investigation in France.

Then I went home, literally. I went into Jerry's study. The bookshelves lining the walls seemed to embrace me with their long arms. I sat down in his armchair and submerged myself in it, enveloped on all sides. My palms hovered over the armrests, which had been caressed for decades by Jerry's strong, gentle hands. I scanned the rows of books, one shelf after another. The covers were a veritable rainbow. The titles were mostly in English, some embossed, some gilt. Some had yellow notes sticking out from their pages. Not a single volume was there for aesthetic reasons. Jerry had read each and every one of the weighty tomes, and I mean that literally. They enhanced his wisdom, his boundless knowledge. I remembered his favorite reading position on the armchair, with the room darkened and only a single lamp directly illuminating the book he was delving into.

Suddenly, a wave of dull pain hit my body, a pain that washed over me from the top of my skull to my feet. I realized that it was a deep, demanding, agonizing longing. I wanted to feel Jerry, all his weight on my body, his strong weightlifting arms around me, his wise gaze riveted to my face. Then, in this cloud of longing, Messenger came to life and flashed a short message.

Are you feeling spontaneous? I'd be happy to meet you — Emanuel, Raanana. I already knew the last part from the personal information section on Facebook. Raanana. I wondered whether that was a kind of hint; many Mossad veterans lived in that town in the Sharon region.

His patience was also noteworthy. He was deliberate, determined, but tactful. Three months had passed since the previous laconic notification. And the timing was interesting. His message interrupted my wandering among the bookshelves, pulled me out of the depths of the armchair and sent my fingers to express a vague answer, void of any logic.

Something pushed me to pick up the gauntlet without thinking too much. Two hours later, I was speeding into the parking lot at Cliff Beach in my Lexus SUV. I saw a couple of empty spaces next to each other and pulled in. Even as I turned off the engine, I caught a glimpse of the dusty AIL Storm out of the corner of my eye, gliding with perfect precision and timing into the space to my right.

No doubt about it. Emanuel was wary of me. He had clearly waited by the entrance to the parking lot, watched me and my car, and crossed the gravel lot only after making sure I had come alone.

The driver's door opened and he stepped out. As he came closer, I took careful note of the mystery man's attire. A sweatshirt, a white hoodie in fact, covered almost his entire face. His shirt was so big and shapeless, almost dripping from his shoulders, that his actual body shape remained an enigma. His sharwal pants were shockingly white too, with a strip of red-green embroidery running down the side. They were ironed and spotless, in stark contrast to the heavy dust that covered the Storm and his Shoresh sandals.

He approached me with a vigorous step and mumbled an apology as he held a straw basket covered in — what else, a white cloth. *I grew these myself. You can take them home with you, but you ought to taste one right now.* He handed me the basket with his right hand as he threw off the hood with his left. The retracted fabric released into the air a volcanic eruption of large, round, soft and bouncy curls, brunette and blond. One of them coiled playfully on his forehead. I was fascinated by the sunburned bouquet that came out of the white hood. Then I turned to examine the face as well. Emanuel's eyes were huge. At their center, a pair of large, inquisitive green irises. Around them grew extra-long eyelashes.

From the first minute of the first date, he stayed very close to me. I could almost count the bristles on his face, look deep into the strange little scar that adorned his left cheek, and carefully examine a similar scar that bisected his right eyebrow. Despite the subtle beard he had cultivated, I also discovered a third scar, which rested in the fold of the smile that stretched over his cheek.

I placed the straw basket on the hood of my Lexus and lifted the white cloth. Beneath it, five red peppers leapt at me like flames. Curvaceous, symmetrical, flawless, enticing.

Just one bite, and you'll capitulate, said Emanuel in a pleasant, quiet, subdued voice, with a shadow of a smile in it. I bit into the blood-red flesh, and it positively popped with a spectacular sound, spraying divine juice on my cheeks and releasing its striking flavor.

Emanuel turned around to his SUV, slung a large canvas bag over his shoulder and motioned to me to follow him. It was evident that Emanuel knew the place very well. He skipped lightly over the rope delineating the gravel path and began to descend towards the shoreline through a narrow trail, which cut through a wall of lavender bushes bursting in purple.

After a few steps we reached a waist-high stone wall. I stopped. I asked myself how I was supposed to skip over this barrier with brand-named leather shoes. Emanuel nonchalantly leapt over, as if he were just taking another step, then turned around to me with a sharp motion, grabbed me by my hips, lifted me up and delivered me safely to the lower level of the stone terrace.

I was surprised. I'm not a heavyweight, but I'm no skinny ballerina either. Emanuel's hoisting maneuver was pleasant and seemed to come naturally, effortlessly. *Do you work out a lot?* I asked, a question that might have been construed as sarcastic, or just awkward. But Emanuel had already moved another three paces along the hidden trail. He stood and faced west, peering at me in silence. I caught up to him. The view was jaw-dropping.

Emanuel and I stood on a sort of natural stage of wild grass above the coastline. The lavender bushes parted and presented the strip of sea that stretched before us in all its glory. Emanuel's journey of shortcuts and scrambles justified itself without words. The sun was already dipping towards the sea and it lit up our path in gold, what seemed like a straight path from our feet all the way to the water. I felt for a moment that if we just stretched our legs, we could step on the gilded road and walk into the horizon.

Emanuel put the large canvas bag on the wild grass and began to pull out surprises. More and more surprises.

First, he took out a surprisingly large red-green floral sheet and spread it on the grass. Then he pulled out a bottle of red wine and two thin-stemmed goblets out of a cardboard container. Finally, he pulled out a corkscrew and a plastic bowl full of dates. For a moment it seemed to me that I was in the midst of Adelbert von Chamisso's wonderful 'shadow' scene. What else would the mystery man pull out of his bag? Then Emanuel just lay down on the full length of the floral sheet, put both palms on his forehead and closed his eyes.

I sat down and looked him over: the sunburnt curls, the palms of his heavy hands, the grains of earth under his nails, the torso still hidden under the huge sweatshirt, the white sharwal pants. A cloud of question marks lingered around him like a kaleidoscope of butterflies swarming.

Seems like you come here a lot, I said quietly.

Yes, Sally, I come here quite a bit. This is the only place where I don't hear the screaming, he reflected softly, stripping off the sweatshirt with a deft move and leaning back down with his eyes closed.

His quiet speech and skillful movement attacked me from two fronts, leaving me breathless. His words hit me like a huge steel sledgehammer. He had mentioned screaming. Now I could see his powerful, finely muscled body with curly, tangled hair. My gaze focused on his firm chest, which looked like two halves of a pomelo.

He displayed a classic six-pack, protruding biceps and a well-defined inverted triangle. From the valley between the two halves of the pomelo, a deep scar trickled downwards, to the navel. It was healed, but its depths remained reddish and shiny. On both sides I saw too many short, well-healed, almost invisible scars.

I couldn't breathe. A round, stinging lump had been shoved into my throat, threatening to strangle me. I had chills down to the bottom of my feet and my temples pounded wildly.

The sea beyond Emanuel's legs disappeared and, in its place, I found myself within the blue-painted walls of the tennis complex in Tehran's Espinas Persian Gulf Hotel, the face of Colonel Reza Moslehi staring me down.

71

19:30 hrs.
An electrifying touch in the desert

I sent a hesitant finger to the upper pole of the long, deep scar and touched it lightly, afraid to cause any pain. *What is that, a heart transplant?* I asked. My voice shook. A lump of pain in my throat gradually descended and formed in my sternum, pressing on my diaphragm with violent intensity.

Emanuel was silent for a moment; then he responded: *No, Sally, not a heart transplant.*

Maybe a heart-lung transplant, I tried again and my voice betrayed me again.

Emanuel was silent for a while, then replied, *No, Sally, not even a heart-lung transplant.* Then in a somewhat halting voice he added: *It was an attempt to tear out my very soul, Sally. They tried and failed.* A single tear glistened in the corner of his eye closest to me.

At that moment, I stopped holding back. Streams of tears flowed over my cheeks. I didn't try to stop them anymore. I bent over carefully and kissed each of the scars, to the right and left of the long and ferocious mark. I kissed and counted. Twenty-three small cuts made with calculated cruelty, absorbing the caustic, salty ice water of the Angel of Death and his companions. Twenty-three diabolical tears in the immaculate velvet of Emanuel's skin. Colonel Reza Moslehi had managed to slice and electrocute, but he had completely failed in his monstrous mission to destroy his will.

I kissed his body as I wondered: *Am I responsible?* It was cruel, too cruel a thought. I felt as if I were losing my mind. I asked myself if I could absorb the remnants of the pain scored into Emanuel's flesh by Tehran's great hero, the man festooned with medals who grinned as the torso was sliced before his eyes, who reveled in the horrific screams elicited by the ice bath — who I had discovered to be nothing more than a fake Islamic ideologue who first took care to satisfy his greed.

Sunset progressed a little further and a light gloom enveloped us. The singing of crickets began to rise from the thicket of lavender. The smell of the sea overwhelmed us, borne on a gentle breeze.

Sally, this is no time for tears, said Emanuel, touching my eyes, protesting the tears rolling from them, brushing them away with the light, gentle strokes of his silky soft fingers, the tenderness in stark contrast with their strength.

This short, obscure sentence was enough to confirm what was already squalling inside me, surging into a tidal wave of epiphany. Emanuel knew everything about me. He knew a great deal about Jerry as well. He may have also shared moments of terror with him, walking together into the brink, into the unknown. He knew Jerry had passed away; he also knew when. He knew that I had heard, in real-time description, of the hell that he had gone through in the colonel's torture chamber. Unanswered questions hovered in the air. How he survived the monstrous scene of the Iranian interrogation, how he escaped from there, how he got to the pepper greenhouses, how he was now lying here in my arms — and how I was lying here too.

I lifted my head from his chest and lay down on the floral sheet with both arms extended at my sides. The graying blue swirled above. The anxiety that overcame me during the dreadful conversation in the tennis complex flew all the way from Tehran to Tel Aviv's northernmost beach.

I feel safe by your side, said Emanuel. His speech was soft, quiet, warm. A second later, I felt his left pinky crawling and landing on my right pinky. A tiny touch that managed to electrify me, to stir every cell in my body, to calm me down from the anxiety that was out of place on Cliff Beach. *Only here can I manage to close my eyes, Sally. Close my eyes and silence the wails. Here, facing the water, facing the sunset, some kind of magic abounds that silences the sounds and keeps me sane.* I bent my pinky and held Emanuel's tightly. The delicate touch turned into a steel grip. I turned around on my side and pulled the pinky with me, which pulled the palm of his hand, which pulled the whole large, heavy, solid body of Emanuel, who turned around and clung to me from behind. I felt his entire length against my body. He embraced me with his subtle intensity, like someone seeking redemption. He hugged more and more and wouldn't let go. Beyond the lavender wall the traffic increased, people making their way down to or up from the shore. Couples in love, shrill young groups, lone men, lone women. They were about three or four yards away from us, some of their heads higher than the lavender.

It was as if Emanuel and I shared one body, bathed in the soft light of the sunset. None of those walking along the path noticed our little love nest on the floral sheet, which was heating up. Our intensifying, burning embrace had become invisible. Emanuel pulled his hand back a bit and brushed my hair away. His warm lips clung to my neck but didn't move. All of him was warm, like an internal combustion engine, waves of heat washing over me. Even as the light faded, the energy of his body remained. Such a wonder.

I dug my elbows into the grass and turned around. I was still clinging to Emanuel's powerful velvety arms, but now our faces were touching. The huge green spotlights of his eyes were now fixed on mine. It was a powerful collision which, in a matter of seconds, turned into an intense storm. It was a miraculous act of love that erupted under the open sky, away from the prying eyes of passersby on the nearby path, beneath the silently watching stars, subject to the gaze of the Creator. What wonderful harmony! We were coordinated like a pair of gears in a delicate Swiss watch. Lips touched lips with precision timing. Heartbeat stirred heartbeat. Hidden fears mingled with trepidation. Hands reached out to the sources of passion. I grabbed the drawstring that fastened the sharwal to Emanuel's waist and pulled it with a swing. The drawstring unraveled from his pants and remained between my fingers. I sent my hand once more across the white silk cloth, and my pupils widened.

Emanuel noticed how awestruck I was. *Let's be gentle, Sally. We must be gentle with each other,* he whispered in my ear, complemented with a series of butterfly kisses descending like a cascade of drops from outer ear to lobe, to the top of the neck, to the soft hollow above the clavicle, to the chest. I grabbed his head with both hands, pulled him up and covered his eyelids with a waterfall of my own kisses. Another and another, until he approached me with the subtlest of motions. Small, minute movements that transported me tens of thousands of light-years to another planet.

72

17:30 hrs.
At the Hilton Tel Aviv, attraction at
an incomprehensible level

Emanuel's disappearance threw me for a loop. It shocked me and I was fraught with anger and uncontrollable anxiety.

We only met twice more. Once at his home in Raanana, and once in a quiet corner of the Hilton Tel Aviv lobby. Then he took off and it was as if he never existed.

In each of our rendezvous, I sensed a quiet, unspoken under-standing in the air that there are things stronger than both of us. That our relationship was about to end with a sharp blow and not by choice. And there was further evidence that reinforced that as-sumption.

The day after the magical meeting at Cliff Beach, I made an emer-gency appointment with Ohr. I had to. I felt that I would not be able to continue without his words of wisdom, without the laser-sharp analysis that he knew to express, based on the date and time of birth.

This time as well, as had been true for the last two decades, nothing escaped Ohr's discernment. He saw Emanuel in his mind's eye, he saw the trauma and the suffering and the nightmares.

However, towards the end, he made another observation. *There's something strange here,* he said. *It seems as if this man's clear and sharp lifeline has been interrupted and becomes very vague. As if there was a dark gray cloud around it. I don't see that his lifeline and your lifeline connect, Sally. And that's not all.* Ohr looked at the computer screen for a long time, confused, then sank back into some of the apps and remained silent. Unlike most of the times I sat in front of him, he looked and stared and mumbled to himself, but didn't raise his head or speak.

Straight from the encounter with Ohr, I went to Raanana. Emanuel's house was relatively far, a fact that turned out to be essential.

A second after the door slammed, we charged at each other with an intensity I had never experienced before. So were the animalistic sounds produced by the dynamic collision of body and body, mind and mind. We cried and shouted and reveled until I felt my heart couldn't stand it anymore.

I've been waiting for you, he said during one of the few time-outs. A simple statement expressing the powerful, rare, incomprehensible bond that formed between us in no time. *Our tryst at Cliff Beach was my first since I traveled beyond the mountains of darkness and returned*, he added with a whisper in my ear that made its way toOo the center of my brain, to the cerebral cortex.

The next day, I scheduled two mandatory appointments for myself. One to meet Racheli to vent and unload; the other with Ohr, to consult my star man.

I felt a pressing need to share my encounter with Emanuel with Racheli. It was divine, intense, rare, but simultaneously so tender. The excitement just wouldn't abate. I felt that if I didn't unload the affect Emanuel had on me, I might shatter to pieces. I also needed another clarifying conversation with Ohr, to try and decipher the unmistakable interpersonal attraction between Emanuel and me. It was incomprehensible, and yet, I was consumed by heretical thoughts. *I'm not going to Raanana anymore*, I thought. *I won't go visit him in the pepper greenhouses in the south either. This intensity has a dangerous core, born of terror and turpitude.*

I felt I needed Ohr's subtle wisdom, his uncommon insights into my mystery man, the meteor that fell from the sky and into my life — or, more precisely, back into my life, as I'd never known about the connection between us.

As it turned out, both Racheli and Ohr were busy. They asked to postpone the meetings for a day. I agreed, but I never imagined what kind of torture awaited me. I wanted Emanuel so much again, utterly overwhelming me, teaching me about depths I never imagined I had, hugging me with soft intensity, lifting me to heights with almost imperceptible pelvic thrusts, believing in me, trusting me. But, at the same time, I wanted to escape — from Emanuel, from the disturbing memories that arose from the contact between our sweaty bodies. I had to rid myself of this powerful bond forged in the realms of evil. Because suddenly I realized — every cell in my body realized — how close I was myself to the hell that Emanuel had gone through. The scar running down the center of his torso, the nearly two dozen to the right and left, the four on his face — they were twenty-eight witnesses to the fact that the colonel was not overplaying his special treatment of traitors. My horrific conversation with him in the lobby of the tennis complex was based in fact, true-to-life. When he finished playing with me, he nonchalantly walked away in his white sportswear, headed from there to the hidden torture chamber somewhere in Tehran, and observed the progress of the interrogation, with Emanuel's screams rending the heavens.

My third and final meeting with Emanuel was at the Tel Aviv Hilton one afternoon. We set ourselves up in the lobby, a table far from the entrance and in front of the magnificent picture window facing the beach. I chose the location and the time. I wanted to see him up close, near the sea and in the setting sun; but I also needed to guarantee we wouldn't be overwhelmed by passion.

Emanuel arrived again in blinding white, from his sharwal pants to his hoodie sweatshirt, both gleaming. The large, bouncy curls gave him a handsome, beatific appearance. Like a Greek god. The green spotlights of his eyes also shone in the relative gloom of the lobby, in the imminent gloaming. I looked at him and felt that I was tearing up with excitement.

This time he brought only a small basket overflowing with dates. I *grow these, too*, he said, and put the sweet package on the table between us.

I felt I had to ask him difficult, poignant, intrusive questions — the kinds which had been out of place in our hidden love nest on Cliff Beach or amid the cyclonic passions which tore through his bedroom in Raanana. What had been his assignment? What had he been charged with doing in Tehran? Had there been a connection between his mission and mine? How had he endured the torture? Had he been implicated by my actions in Doha and Tehran? Had he known about my existence? Had my name come up in the interrogation? How did he escape with his life? How had he gotten back to Israel? How had he known to approach me at the end of the mourning period after Jerry's death? Why had he had such absolute confidence that I would agree to meet with him?

All my plans, all my questions, all my speculations collapsed in a heap the moment Emanuel sat down in front of me.

I looked into the depths of his eyes and understood what was more than obvious. He was not allowed to answer any questions, just as I was not allowed to reveal anything of my own activities. We knew so much about each other and couldn't say a word about it.

We sat there for about three hours, the round glass table separating us. We had two tumblers of water and a basket of Medjool dates, which were quickly devoured. When the sun finished slipping below the waterline and into the soft dimness of the lobby, I suddenly felt his left pinky gently climb onto my right pinky which was resting on the table. Again, that tiny touch which managed to electrify me, to stir every cell in my being.

I pulled my hand away as if it had been seared with a white rod. Emanuel also bent his elbow in a slow motion and his hand returned to his white sweatshirt pocket. We knew that the contact of the pinky would lead to forbidden worlds.

We looked at each other and transmitted tens of thousands of messages to each other without words. It was clear to me, as if a prophetic vision materialized in the air between us, that the time of this conversation would eventually arrive and the time would also come for the facts to be clarified.

But I never imagined that Emanuel would suddenly disappear, and I couldn't imagine when, and under what circumstances, the green in our eyes would meet again.

73

18:15 hrs.
A futile attempt to recreate the
magic on Cliff Beach

The conversation with Ohr was strange and charged. The classic maps of celestial alignment and in-depth insights of Chinese astrology could not help him decipher the riddle of Emanuel but did allow Ohr to perceive the sea of pain and his image fading from my life. I desperately needed Ohr's soothing voice. He had a unique ability to explain things that I couldn't get out of the roller coaster of correspondence with Emanuel, the things we did, and all that was left unsaid.

However, Ohr then volunteered something I hadn't asked for. He saw the lifeline of a man. Another. A new love.

But isn't that Emanuel? I asked quietly, in a defeated voice.

Ohr looked at me for a long time and shook his head right and left. A big no.

It was one of those few times when an appointment with Ohr left me with more questions in my heart and mind than I'd come in with.

I got into my Lexus and drove toward Cliff Beach, as if I were drugged.

Maybe I'll meet Emanuel there and rush him, I thought, as the vehicle moved west on autopilot. *Maybe I'll sit alone on the wild patch of grass facing the water and get answers to the questions buzzing in my mind like a swarm of bees.*

I stopped at the same spot in the parking lot where I had parked ten days earlier. I skipped over the rope that closed off the trail going down to the water and looked for the narrow passage in the wall of lavender bushes. In vain. There was no trace of the slim gap we had threaded ourselves through. The purple blossoms lined up and formed an impenetrable barrier. I walked back and forth along the neatly trimmed bushes and couldn't locate the opening that Emanuel had strolled through so deftly. I couldn't see the path beyond the wall. I couldn't locate the stone terrace. I couldn't spot the wild grassy spot facing the water.

Desperate, I went back towards the SUV, trying to reconstruct in my mind the path I was led down following the white hoodie sweatshirt and the mane of curls. In vain.

An hour later, I was already sitting at the far end of the lobby at the Hilton. Again in the same place, at the same table, facing the same sea. Racheli was supposed to arrive at five o'clock, but I got there an hour earlier, trying to organize my thoughts, to escape the bad feelings that had overcome me.

I wanted to pour out before Racheli my version of our tempestuous trysts in front of the expansive seascape, the excitement, the wonders of the passionate rendezvous with Emanuel. I asked myself if the disappearing passage through the lavender wall was an admissible item for such a conversation. I wondered if it was right and if it was permissible to tell her the story of the scars on his body.

Racheli arrived at five on the dot. Such punctuality! We hugged for a long time. The London events had created a temporary disconnect and resentment, but her relationship with Daniel Geffen became oppressive. She understood that I was right when I talked about his carelessness. She realized that the arrogant and careless Geffen had also endangered her career and her life.

The conversation went on and on. When I told her about the events on Cliff Beach, she teared up. She listened very attentively, did not hide her surprise, and then got up from her place and held me for a long time.

I'm so happy that you experienced something similar to my epiphany at Stella Maris, she said. *It's hard to fathom that things like exist unless they actually happen to you, especially at this stage of our lives. I have no way of expressing how happy I am for you, Sally. I thank God for giving us both this miraculous gift.*

I said goodbye to Racheli but didn't know what was waiting for me in the next few days...

74

At Akirov Towers, a lover not built for romance

My prognosticative reputation suffered another minor blow when Sol emerged, completely by surprise. It didn't take long — not long at all — for him to introduce me to the concept of Chapter Two. This pair of words ascended, rising up from the depths of my consciousness and turning from a vague idea into actuality. Prayers whispered on the lips which manifest into reality.

However, the upheaval began with another affair with another man. Probably somewhere between the stars and the heavens, or in the skies of Chinese astrology, it was determined that this was the correct order of things.

It was Amit. Amit, the devastating stud, the charmer with a tanned face and perfect posture, the successful businessman who captivated me with supernatural timing. I was confused, exhausted, frustrated and stifled after the roller coaster that pulled me along at a terrifying speed, accelerating from zero to one hundred in a snap of the fingers, picking me up and slamming me down in freefall. From the activities in Qatar and Tehran to Jerry's passing, from the battle of the minds against the Monégasque aristocracy to the storm of passion with Ben, from the face-to-face confrontation with the Russian crime godfather in Monte Carlo to the upheaval in heart and soul propagated by Emanuel .

Amit lived on one of the upper floors of Akirov Towers, walking distance from my house. Already in the first moments of the first date, I felt that something exciting was about to happen here. It was precisely for this reason that I surprised him with a direct question. Not wanting to waste time, I asked about his date of birth and the time he was born. And was with Steve, Amit didn't panic, didn't stare at me strangely, didn't burst out laughing.

He smiled gently, fixed his green eyes deep into mine, gave his birthdate and shot me a questioning look. I whispered a creative excuse, noted it on my cell phone and, at the next pause between a hug and light kiss and the placing of our dishes on the table, I sent the details to Ohr.

Urgent, urgent, urgent, Amit, August 9th, 2 AM.

This is important to me. Very important.

I sent the message and forgot about it, but Ohr provided the answer at the speed of light. *Strong astrological map. Goal-oriented, driven by infinite diligence, energies efficiently channeled. He's not built for romance. He has sexual needs, but he is afraid of intimacy. The intimate sector of his life is limited. There is no spontaneous desire, probably due to quite a few disappointments. He has no understanding of what women want and need. If he is looking for a relationship, it would be one that comes from the head, not the heart.*

I read the long text message from Ohr and it frustrated me. I felt that Ohr wasn't on point this time. It would take another two months for me to realize that, of course, he was right — every single word.

Amit portrayed himself as a perfect lover. We sat down for dinner at Turquoise. The entrées were divine. The wine was the finest. Amit, like Steve, fancied himself a sommelier, and he did choose the best of the best. I relished the 2016 vintage Flam Noble that he insisted on. It was a deep and dark red, with a light and pleasant acidity, fruit flavors and subtle hints of wood; it paired beautifully with oven-roasted lamb shank that I polished off with pleasure. There was something sexy, instinctive, about the combinations of flavors, savoring the food and drink.

Amit and I looked into each other's eyes as if we were twenty. Less than an hour later we were already at his place, at the top of Akirov Towers. The apartment surprised me with its tasteful style, its unique design, the meticulous preservation of the balance between luxury and wealth on the one hand and subtlety and restraint on the other. It wasn't eye-popping. It didn't shout: Look at me, I'm rich and successful.

The sound system was magnificent, the twanging of violins emanating from the hidden speakers throughout the vast space of the penthouse. An intermezzo caressed the air — there was Vangelis creeping back into my life, again under the most romantic circumstances. I loved the sophisticated interior design, the sublime music, the genteel Amit himself. And then...

We quickly went from sitting in his leather armchairs to waltzing horizontally on the soft carpet, which blanketed his living room wall-to-wall. The dance was graceful as well. It began when Amit glided slowly onto the carpet, leaning his back on the armchair as he reached out to me. He didn't attack, didn't demand, didn't even speak. He just reached out from his reclining position. I also reached out, sliding down as I mimicked his motion, then approached him. I was curious. Amit put his head on my left shoulder, extended his right arm to subtly embrace my neck, played with my hair and was silent. Perfect lover, zero intimacy. Whenever it was time for intimacy, he found a way to slip away. First, he had to get up and change the music. Then his mouth was dry and he needed a drink of water. Next, something else rips him away from me.

Taking a bird's-eye view, I couldn't fathom what happened to his epic stories of courting women and romantic quests. From his appearance, some homework on Google, and our limited conversation, I knew that he had no dearth of opportunities for explosive, passionate sex. Women simply fell at his feet.

But the more time passed, the stronger my impression became that there was something strange and problematic here. Amit did not initiate sex, nor did he make a move towards me. He just kissed and hugged. And then... nothing.

I was all afire. My body and mind were looking forward to a direct continuation of the experience: the mood-setting music, the gesture of sliding onto the carpet, hugs, kisses. But Amit just got up from his place once more, this time to check something in the kitchen. Our joint dance on the carpet lifted me up to the sky and, just as quickly, slammed me down hard to the ground. This handsome and tanned man, this successful, esteemed and energetic CEO, wouldn't go the distance, leaving me hot and bothered.

A Leo who fears ongoing intimacy... that resonated with Ohr Barkan's reading. The explicit verdict he had pronounced, which I had rejected with disbelief.

Instead, Amit led our relationship elsewhere. Fancy trips around the country, a visit to boutique wineries I'd never heard of, short outings to historical sites he knew a lot about.

I kept hoping that circumstances would lead us back to that turbulent waltz, sinking into the carpet in the Akirov Towers penthouse.

Initially it was nice. *A classy relationship,* I thought to myself. His knowledge was impressive but, over time, it became oppressive. I wanted so badly to go back to the instinctual spontaneity of our first dates and have fun, but the yawning gap between our magic carpet flights and the didactic encounters became strange, and more and more frustrating.

I consulted my friends. Racheli raised an eyebrow via Skype. So did Linda. Yaffit also expressed her reservations when we discussed the issue while walking in the park. They were all asking questions I didn't know how to answer. From time to time, I would refer back to the thorough and unambiguous list that Ohr Barkan had formulated for Amit and, again, I came across the firm assertion that the man was simply afraid of intimacy. And, of course, any consistent, committed, continuous expression of physical attraction.

Apparently he has a problem, my girlfriends concluded. As did Ohr. As did I.

75

16:30 hrs.
Suspicious vehicle on the way to
the pharmacy in Tzameret Park

I waited impatiently for another two weeks, but nothing changed. My friends sealed Amit's fate. He, for his part, carried on with the hugs and kisses in the car, yet another fascinating destination, yet another bottle of fine wine, yet another informative topic.

But in his penthouse, on the carpet, with the whole city spread out before us, there was no spark, not even a twinkle. Just the malfunctioning Amit. *We have different needs,* I told him, starting to cook up a farewell. But either Amit didn't understand or he didn't want to understand. I had become important to him. He continued to offer intriguing excursions and the most extravagant romantic gestures. He repeatedly expounded, at length, that we were a perfect match and that he aspired to a serious relationship.

Then, as I was exploring the right way to say goodbye to him, The One appeared.

It was a random meeting at Super-Pharm, the drugstore chain, which turned into a hot romance reflecting true love, with a real chance of achieving the distinguished title of Chapter Two. On my way to the pharmacy in Tzameret Park, a four-minute walk from my castle, I noticed a vehicle sitting in the red-and-white striped no parking zone. A black Audi with tinted windows. The angle of the sun's rays allowed me to see into the driver's seat. A real bruiser wearing sunglasses? He didn't seem to belong in the neighborhood. Still, I wouldn't have suspected anything if he hadn't looked away sharply the second I met his gaze. He made a show of staring at his cell phone. I peeked at the license plate and memorized the number. A series of seven digits which I turned into a mnemonic. An old habit of mine, inspired by Jerry.

I continued to walk nonchalantly on the sidewalk. I approached the main square of Shikun Park Tzameret, beyond the metal pillars lining the sidewalk. When I got to the far crosswalk, I crossed the road quickly and slipped into the mall. Ostensibly, I needed to relax. But something in the face of the driver of the black car disturbed me. *I know that face*, I told myself again and again as I walked from the mall's entrance to Super-Pharm. *I know that face.*

After walking through the shelves of the pharmacy, and as I made my way towards the cash register, I recognized Amnon, an old acquaintance from the neighborhood, a jumbo-jet pilot, who was chatting with another man. I approached Amnon with a smile, interested in how he was doing. A somewhat liberating and entertaining conversation developed. We remembered a chance encounter of ours in the terminal lounge in Rome a few years earlier. The friend standing next to him listened quietly and did not interrupt.

However, about an hour after bumping into him, a message from an unknown number came in. *Hello, my name is Sol. I was with Amnon when you ran into him at Super-Pharm. I'd love to get to know you.* The text message was accompanied by a photograph. He looked handsome, his full silver hair pulled back; yet I hadn't noticed him at all at Super-Pharm.

Bad timing, Sol, bad timing, I thought to myself, After all, Amit was still in the picture. I was fed up with dating. From the relationship with Steve, who had unexpectedly suggested a prenup, to the strange relationship with Amit, who went from lover to tour guide. I wanted to give up on trying to meet someone, reluctant to begin yet another romantic relationship. But, for some reason, I didn't turn him down.

We arranged to meet by his car for only ten minutes. My heart wasn't in it, and I showed up for the date with an obvious lack of enthusiasm.

However, my not-so-secret admirer turned out to be a sixty-year-old Virgo, energetic, slim, athletic, a walking aficionado, a lover of the sea, six-foot-one-inch of style. At first glance, he seemed European, not Israeli. Full silver hair. Well-preserved body. He had a pleasant speaking voice, radiating intelligence and self-confidence.

Quite surprisingly, it turned out to be a fun outing. The conversation flowed. We gathered the prerequisite data. He intrigued me. I felt that he was also intrigued by me. Alas, Sol was also the one who brought up the fact that the 10 minute time limit we had set had passed and that the date was over.

I was astonished. In preparation for the next date and the one after, I learned that, beyond the pleasant smile, there was also a degree of firmness and assertiveness that I liked. I also found out that Sol grew up in a house with a traditional religious background.

Our relationship began slowly, but it was nice. Only after the fourth meeting did I feel that something interesting was developing between us. I discovered that Sol was an alpha male. He knew what he wanted, but he was affectionate, sensible, warm, and generous with his praise. He had a high emotional intelligence. He was well-versed in courtship and romance.

Then a surprising statement came out of his mouth.

Sally, I'm not looking for a fling or friendship. I'm looking for a relationship. I want us to be a couple, with everything that entails. I am a one-woman man.

I looked at his face for some time, trying to read it, trying to understand how serious he was. It was the kind of thing that men recite from a relationship instruction manual, but somehow I believed Sol.

Maybe it's the chemistry of two Virgos, I thought and waited for Ohr's answer. The reply was thorough and included many details that I had already gleaned. *A Virgo. Available in trying times, stable, balanced. He upholds values, embraces nostalgia, respects tradition, religion and family life. He is a gentleman. A mensch. He loves the good life and sports. He appears to be a man who understands the needs of a woman, knows how to compromise, knows his own limits, thinks before he acts. He seems to be a man who will bring flowers to the woman he loves and will make sure to open the door for her,* Ohr emphasized.

I smiled. Ohr was precise. He put his finger on what I already felt to be true. Somewhere in the back of my mind, I began to feel that I had reached the place I wanted to be. I felt like I was home again.

I still did not dare say that phrase aloud, but it buzzed within me with increasing intensity, until it was joined by another insight: *We have fun together. I want to spend as much time with him as possible. I'm not interested in finding any other suitor.*

The more we met, the tighter the bond became. We had discovered what we had in common, more and more topics on which we were on the same wavelength. As we were spending more and more time together, spiritual insights started creeping into my mind — beliefs I had always held, that there is a higher power that drives the course of our lives. At the same time, I realized that it was my resolve that brought about the events, proving that there is continuity in life, in relationships, in love.

There is always something to aspire to.

We continued to date regularly. It began to feel natural; it went without saying that we would be spending almost every day together.

We were about to meet for lunch at Yulia on the boardwalk of the Tel Aviv port.

On my way there, I got a call from Yaakov Lavi.

Sally, I've got good news and less good news, he commenced matter-of-factly. *Where should I begin?*

Always lead with the good news, Yaakov. Let's start on the right foot, I replied with a smile on my lips.

Fine, let's do that. The good news is that the entire sum, including the compensation you asked for, has been deposited in the account belonging to Ben Mitchell and his associates.

Great. Wonderful. Glad to hear it, I said, but I couldn't hide that I was impatient.

The less good news, Lavi continued, *is that we checked on the guy in the black Audi driving around your neighborhood. He's suspicious. Very suspicious. A Russian national. According to facial recognition, he belongs to Dmitri's gang. Don't let down your guard, Sally. These guys don't play games. They're serious, and they're dangerous. For our part, we'll keep tailing him. If necessary, we'll ask him to come for a cup of coffee...*

The conversation was over in under a minute and I returned to Sol with Lavi's words ringing in my ears.

It's not over, Sally, I told myself. *It's not over.* I wanted to wrap myself in Sol's arms for a benign hug, but suddenly I felt a strange stiffness in his body, his arms, his expression.

Sally, I feel like you're hiding something from me. Some of the things you said just don't add up. There are pieces of the puzzle missing. When I ask you about them, you say you don't remember. Even when I asked your age, you couldn't give me a straight answer. You can't explain what you were doing out of the country all those years. You haven't told me where you were when your late husband was working abroad. I'd like you to be more open with me... about everything...

I said nothing. Sol was quiet too.

The thick silence felt heavy, then oppressive.

We sat down on one of the sofas facing the edge of the wooden deck. Sol softened a bit, stroked my hair and gently kissed me on the cheeks. We were silent as we watched the sun go down, and then he began to open up and share with me the process of his separation from his wife. He seemed sincere. He did not try to cut corners, hide, or disguise his feelings. I liked it because, in the same conversation, he exposed his vulnerabilities — his struggles, the distress following his divorce, which was not by his own volition. It was clear to me that I had to answer honestly, even though there were secrets I could never tell.

Sol gently pulled me into a tighter hug. It was pleasant, but also somewhat stressful. I had not officially ended it with Amit. All I needed now was for him to suddenly pop into Yulia and discover

425

me in another man's arms. At that moment, I was angry at myself for not being determined enough to say a proper goodbye to Amit.

Sol saw the small cloud hovering over my head, the tiny wrinkles of worry that creased my chin below my pursed lips. He hugged me gently. His gaze rested on me in a way that moved me. He understood me better than any other man I'd met since Jerry passed away.

Then, in the middle of my date with Sol, my cell phone came to life. It was a message from Lavi. I read the text message with half a glance. *We have a problem. Talk to me as soon as possible about the visitor in your neighborhood. I'm worried!!!*

Lavi's message was meant to put me on alert, but I decided to shut off the screen and put my cell phone back in my bag.

The bond with Sol was growing stronger. I was afraid that the magic would slowly fade away but, in reality, we felt a special connection. Eventually, I felt it was right to invite him to a Shabbat dinner at my son Roy's house.

He was only the second man invited for Friday night dinner with my family. The tension in the air broke as soon as I looked into my two sons' eyes and knew that Roy and Michael had accepted Sol into the family.

Fin.

But not the end...

Printed in Great Britain
by Amazon